A Heart Divided
By
Iris Bolling

Siri Enterprises
Publishing Division
Richmond, Virginia

Siri Enterprises
Publishing Division
Richmond, Virginia

A Heart Divided

ISBN-13: 978-0-9801066-3-3
ISBN-10:   0-9801066-3-X

Library of Congress Control Number: 2010902844

Cover and page design by: Judith Wansley

The Heart Series
By Iris Bolling

Once You've Touched The Heart
The Heart of Him
Look Into My Heart
A Heart Divided

www.irisbolling.net
www.sirient.com

Acknowledgements

Thank you my heavenly father. Raymond, Chris and Champaine, thank you for your love, support and patience. Judith Wansley, thank you for the ability to "draw a little bit."
Linda Gordon, Kathy Six, Monica *"Helesi"* Simmons, and Cathy Atchison, thank you for your time, knowledge and encouragement. Roz Terry, LaFonde Harris, and Gemma Mejias: the roots to my tree, thanks for always answering the telephone. Valarie Johnson and Tanya Thompson, thank you for keeping it real.

Wiley "Devin" Franklin, thank you for sharing your knowledge. To the beautiful people, Monica Jackson, Sakeitha Horton, Justin Wansley, Jason Wansley and Stephen Howell, may God's blessings always be with you.

To Beverly Jenkins and Gwyneth Bolton, thank you for sharing your knowledge and experience.

To my mom, Evelyn Lucas, my sister Helen McCant and brother Albert "Turkey" Doles, family is the strength that binds us forever and always.

To all of my readers, your wait is over. Enjoy book four of The Heart Series as the saga of JD and Tracy's journey towards the White House continues. The pieces of the puzzle to JD and Tracy's lives are about to unfold.

Dedication

This book is dedicated to, Monica Jackson; thank you for always being ready to ride. Love you.

Prologue
Ten Years Ago

Walking along the bank of the James River, checking the abandoned buildings, a shiver traveled down the back of Officer James Harrison's neck. Normally he would credit the cool air to being close to the waterfront—but tonight he knew better. For the last three blocks of his beat, he was being followed. Two men trailed, one a building down, across the street on the right and the other directly behind him. They seem to know the beat he normally walked--building by building. Taking a few steps off his normal path, he looked into the window of an abandoned building he knew was being used by the homeless as sleeping quarters on warm nights, he called out. "Charlie, are you in there?"

"Hey Mr. H," the man dressed in a dirty white tee shirt, ripped shorts and a pair of sneakers that were clearly at least one size to small answered. "What you still doing out here? You should be home with that pretty wife of yours."

"Charlie, I want you to do something for me."

"What you need?" the man eagerly asked.

James smiled at the man he had come to consider a friend. "I want you to hold on to this." He pulled off his wedding band and put it in Charlie's hand through the broken window. "I want you to take this to my house and give it to my wife."

A concerned look covered Charlie's unshaven face as he looked down at his hand. He looked up into the eyes of the man that had tried several times to get him cleaned up and off the street. "What's going on James? You in some kind of trouble?"

"Things going to get a little heavy around here and I don't have time to explain. When I reach the corner, I want you to haul ass out the back. Don't stop to look around, just keep going."

"Man, you need me to call back up or something?"

James thought about that, but his back up was the very man, plotting his death. "I just need you to get out of the area. Now go."

James waited before turning. He wanted to make sure Charlie was out of range of danger. The people following him would not want any witnesses. Walking down the street, he wondered if he should have done anything differently. Should he have forsaken the blue code of silence, to tell what he knew? It was too late to think about that now. The one thing he knew for sure was that he was not ready to die. If they were going to take him out tonight, he was going down fighting.

Using his radio was out of the question, the person pursuing him would be listening to the same channel. He was trapped. Releasing the clip that secured his weapon to his belt, he slowly pulled the weapon out and held it down at his side. At the sound of wheels, screeching around the corner, he raised his weapon and froze as he looked into the eyes of a young boy. It was a second later that he recognized what the child was holding. The first blast hit his left shoulder. He got off a few rounds, but his revolver was no match for the semi-automatic weapon the boy had. The second shot hit his chest--those that followed were a blur.

He was a God-fearing family man, who loved his wife, son, and precious daughter. Closing his eyes for a moment, he prayed, *Lord if I have sinned against any person please--forgive me.* His wife crossed his mind. *Please give my wife the support she will need. Make sure she knows each day how much I love her. Watch over my children. Lord, have mercy on my soul.*

Opening his eyes, he saw his partner standing over his now numb body. "The law is not always black and white, James--there are gray areas. You never understood that."

Barely audible, even to the man standing over him, "I understood the blue code," he choked out. "Revenge shall be mine, saith the lord." The last thought to enter his mind was of his son.

J.D. Harrison had fallen asleep, lying across his bed in his apartment near campus, studying. He was two weeks away from graduating from law school and one month from taking the bar examination. His father entered his dreams. "Take care of your family, Son. Always—take care of your family," his father was saying as he had so many times before.

"I will Dad, don't worry," he replied. Only this time his father did not say, if anything happens to me. When JD turned to remind him of the words he missed, a sound jarred him from his sleep.

Groggy and dazed, JD reached for the telephone on the nightstand next to his bed. "Hello."

"JD, this is John Roth. Son you need to come home."

Chapter 1
Present Day

Jeffrey "JD" Harrison, the Attorney General of Virginia, sat in his office on the tenth floor of the state office building in downtown Richmond. Standing beside him behind the desk was his friend and Chief of Staff, Calvin Johnson. Brian Thompson, another friend and head of his security team, sat in a chair facing the desk, as the sitting Governor, Gavin W. Roberts stood at the far end of the office with his back to them looking out the window. As the men talked JD's attention wandered to the door of his office just as his wife Tracy appeared at the opening. A pleasing smile creased his lips as he stood to walk over to her with his arms stretched wide as the anticipation of holding her began to build within him. Just then, Al "Turk" Day, his imprisoned brother-in-law appeared behind her. His heart rate began to increase as a frown formed on his forehead. Before he could ascertain why Al was there in his office and not in federal prison, a shadow crept over the two standing in the doorway and a sense of danger grabbed his heart. He raced to gather Tracy into his arms just as an explosion went off.

JD sprung up in his bed at a sound, bewildered. He ran his hand down his face as remnants of the dream held him captured. The fact that the dream mirrored his life left him a bit disoriented. Looking around at the furniture in the room, it took him a moment to realize he was in his own bed, in his own bedroom, and in his own home. Lying back against the pillow he sighed loudly as he touched his chest to ensure that his heart was still intact and found that his skin was moist. He closed his eyes and exhaled a sound of release as he realized it was just a dream, again. But this time the people in the room had faces and he recognized all except one of the players—the shadowy figure. One of them was Tracy and she was in danger. He reached over for her and found her side of the bed empty. He sat up and looked at the clock on the nightstand beside the bed. It was four-fifteen in the morning. Listening to the quietness to determine where she might be, he glanced at the baby monitors sitting on the night stand on her side of the bed. No sounds were coming from his son JC's nor from his daughter Jasmine's bedrooms. That really didn't mean anything, for Tracy had been known to fall asleep in one of the children's bedrooms regularly, especially lately. Throwing the comforter and sheets aside, he slide into his slippers and went in search of his wife to put her back where she belonged—in bed beside him.

He cracked open the door across the hallway and smiled at his two year old son Jon-Christopher, "JC", sleeping with his thumb in his mouth and the caboose to the train set he'd received for Christmas, in the other hand, hanging off the bed. As quietly as he could, JD walked over, put the caboose on the floor and gently pulled the thumb out of his son's mouth. He pulled the covers up to his shoulders and lovingly rubbed the back of his head that was neatly braided. Closing the door behind him, he looked towards the room next to the master bedroom, where he found his six-week-old daughter, Jasmine sound asleep on her stomach inside of her crib. It was apparent that she had recently been fed. On a stand next to the crib were an empty bottle and a cotton diaper folded neatly across the arm of the rocking chair. Unable to resist he walked over and kissed the child that look so much like her mother, he fell in love all over again the moment she entered the world. But there was still no sign of Tracy.

Closing that door he walked forward into the upstairs open foyer and listened. He thought he heard a sound downstairs, and was about to descend the steps to investigate when he noticed a light in Tracy's office. Retracing the two steps he had taken, he walked to the other side of the open foyer and stood in the archway of the room. Tracy was curled up on the sofa with a book. Papers were on the top of the desk as the screensaver on the computer ran a collage of pictures of him, JC and Jasmine across the screen. Moving the mouse to shutdown the system he noticed a document from Next Level Consulting on the monitor marked urgent. Next Level Consulting was a company Tracy and his sister Ashley had started when they were in college. The multi-million dollar grossing company was Tracy's brain-storm and she loved it as if it were one of her children. Not one to question her affairs, he clicked the save button then the shutdown button and waited for the system to close down. He then turned to his sleeping wife and smiled.

It was clear that he was highly favored by God. His wife of a little over four years was as beautiful today as she was the first time he'd met her. Nothing or no one but God could have prepared him for the impact that smile, he'd witnessed across the breakfast bar in his condominium five years ago, would have on his life. The once carefree bachelor with everything within his grasp was now the Attorney General for the Commonwealth of

Virginia with a wife and two children, on their way to twelve. A wife that he had taken a bullet for, a wife he'd almost lost to a brutal beating and a wife whose eyes were void of that special gleam they once had whenever she looked at him.

Before they married, he withheld information from her regarding the identity of her biological father from her. Nine months ago, the vengeful Carolyn Roth-Roberts, daughter of the powerful state Senator John Roth, revealed the truth to Tracy. Since that time, Tracy had grown more and more withdrawn. When she told him she was pregnant with their second child, JD was so elated. This was the second chance he needed to show her how much he loved her. For a while things were getting better, but then his job began taking him away from home. To complicate things more, his brother-in-law and campaign manager, James Brooks, was pressing him to run for Governor in the next election.

For months, it seemed his heart was divided between protecting and serving the citizens of the state of Virginia and keeping his wife happy. Desperately, he wanted the shine and unwavering trust back in her eyes. But more than anything, he wanted to see her smile reach her eyes again. Tracy, even with the discord in their marriage, made his days warm as sunshine just knowing she would be waiting to greet him and his nights hot with her unyielding passion and love.

His mistake came in wanting to protect her from harm. But it was apparent that his over-protectiveness caused her more harm than good. Now he had to find a way to gain her trust back, for he still loved her beyond reason. If there were any way he could turn back time, he would have handled things differently. With all the power he had within his hands, he could not change the past. Only God and time could heal the wounds he had caused her. For now all he could do was make sure she knows how much he loves her and their children. Without her, he could not and did not want to survive, for she was the core, the soul, and the heart of him.

Just watching her sleep had his heart racing and stirred his body's lower regions into action. He walked over and noticed she had been reading a book. That, in itself, was not surprising; he believed Tracy had read every book in every library within a hundred mile radius. Gently sliding the book from her grasp he read the cover, then he turned it over to read the back and realized it was a romance novel. *Why is she reading a romance novel?* He wondered which of her friends it had come from, his sister Ashley, or could it have been Rosaline. No, more than likely, it was her friend Cynthia trying to corrupt his baby's mind. "She doesn't need that." He placed the book on the table next to the sofa. Bending down he picked her up into his arms and kissed her forehead.

She sighed as her arms circled his neck, she kissed his throat, "Hi babe."

"Hi yourself," he replied as he carried her to the bedroom and quietly closed the door with his foot. Placing his half sleeping wife in the spot he had awakened from a few moments before, he began to unbutton the top of his pajamas that covered her body. Once that task was complete, he marveled at the smooth, flat, paper bag color skin that was before him. It was hard to believe that only six weeks ago his daughter had been there. Unable to resist, he kissed her navel honoring the stomach that had carried his two children and was the future home of more. The feel of her skin beneath his lips caused his manhood to throb with the sensation of needing to touch his wife. Her leg moved beneath him as if knowing he needed access. Sliding his pajama bottom to the floor, he joined her on the bed and began planting kisses on the inside of her thigh, just above her knees, creating a trail up her thigh with his tongue. Her inner scent mixed with the vanilla body gel she used, called out to him to taste her, but he resisted, he want to savor the precious minutes he would have her to himself. Leaving the right thigh he then followed the same path on her left thigh with his tongue until he reached the very core of her. The moment his lips touched her he felt her body awakening, and he could not help but smile at her response. It never failed, whenever, however he touched her, her body would respond as if it was waiting just for him. That simple knowledge always moved him to the core and prompted him to give her all he had to give. Her hand lovingly rubbed the back of his head as her hips moved up bringing the center of her snuggly to his lips. Holding her waist securely, he pulled her body to the edge of the bed to him, planting kisses up her stomach, to the curve of her breast, finally reaching her lips just as the tip of his manhood slid easily inside her. The sound of her moan always surged through him like a rocket, straight down south to where his love for her swelled and cried out for relief.

Beginning with a slow rhythm that warmed the love he needed to release, he then steadily increased the pace until they were both soaring to the boiling point that neither ever tired of. Running his hands down her thighs, she instinctively complied with what he wanted by bringing her legs around his waist and clamping them tightly in place. Her inner walls enclosed around him securing the knowledge that the release he was seeking was only seconds away and he was eager to feel the love that only she could give. Kissing her throat as he bestowed her with the love he knew no other woman would ever experience, he cried out her name. The moment her hands pulled his back closer, her hips higher and her legs tighter, the explosion they both sought hit. His body jerked several times before he could think clearly or speak coherently. He rolled over pulling her on top of his chest, never breaking the intimate connection and simply held her as their juices flowed between them. She cuddled closer bringing the top of her head just below his chin. Kissing the top of her head, he leisurely caressed her back.

"Why do you always make a mess on my side of the bed?" she asked sleepily.

"It's my way of getting you right where you are, closer to me." He felt her smile against his chest as her lips barely kissed his nipple. Moments later he felt her shallow breathing and knew she had fallen asleep again. Only then did the memories of his dream fade away as a distant thought. Tightening his hold on her, he soon joined her in a slumberous state.

The minimum security federal prison located in Petersburg, Virginia was locked down for the night. Bed count was completed and all inmates were accounted for. The night shift guards had settled at their posts, two deep at each station. The administrative staff had vacated hours earlier, with the secure feeling of another good day without any infractions from the inmates. He had a good staff, Warden Emilio Escobar thought as he locked the door to his office and bid good night to the guards on his way out. The gates sprung open as he waved at the guards in the tower. Driving through, he slowed and watched through his rear view window, as he did every night, until the gates closed. Flashing his lights, he pulled off in the direction of his home.

Standing in the hallway of the administration, building looking out of a window, a guard watched as the warden's car drove out of sight. As with each night for the last month, the guard pulled a key from his pocket, opened the door to the warden's office and turned on the computer sitting on the desk. It was almost as easy to get the password to the computer, as it was to get a copy of the key to the warden's office. It only took him a few hours to determine the wife's' maiden name and year of birth was the password to the computer. How ironic, the pictures on the desk and the use of the wife's name was clear evidence he loved her, yet, it was a woman in a hotel room that was able to keep him occupied long enough to have a copy of the office key made. Go figure. But for the man sitting at the desk, his only interest was in locating the inmate that was there under an assumed name. Once he determined which of the five hundred and sixty-two inmates it could be, this hellish job would be history and he would be richer. So far, he'd eliminated three hundred and thirteen. Tonight he planed to view another fifty records. It shouldn't take much longer.

An hour later, after reviewing photographs, birthdays, relatives and other information on each inmate, he finally came across a strong candidate. There was information as with every file he viewed, but this one had no photograph and the history was only ten years deep. He switched over to the internet and did a search on the name – Huntley A. Doles. On the surface, the search did not reveal much—a few fraud related stories and an embezzlement charge. However, unbeknownst to him the search sent a signal to another computer.

The knock on his door startled Donovan Tucker and he instinctively reached for his revolver. "Who is it?"

"Tuck, you are needed in the Situation Room."

Tucker looked at the clock on the night stand next to his bed—four-fifteen in the morning. He fell back on the pillow—it was only two-thirty when he got into bed. This was really getting old. Shaking himself awake, he threw back the comforter, stood and put on his robe. "This better not be another one of Monique's antics," he mumbled. Monique was his boss' daughter, whom he had asked Tucker to watch over while he was incarcerated. The six-teen year old was nothing but trouble. He opened the door and walked down the hallway to the next room. The bedroom had been converted into one of the most sophisticated, technically advanced communication centers available to a man of his means. The occupants of the tact room at the FBI headquarters would be impressed. "What do we have, gentlemen?" Tucker inquired to the three men in the room as he slumped into one of the chairs in front of the three flat screen monitors hanging on the wall.

"A signal went off from the warden's computer. Someone just did an inquiry on our man."

"When?" Tucker stood, concerned with the information on the monitor.

"At 4:05."

Tucker looked at the clock; it was now four-twenty. "Get one of our people from the administration building on the phone." Once the call was placed, Tucker gave instructions.

Convinced he had found the right inmate; the guard took a stroll over to the Ponderosa building to the location of the inmate in question. The Ponderosa was one of two buildings in the federal pen complex located in Petersburg. The other was called the South Fork Ranch. The occupants were usually your higher class white collar criminals that were given a few luxuries. "Hey, Wally, I'm going to do a quick walk through. You want to come along?" He asked, not really expecting the other guard to join him.

"I'll pass. Enjoy your stroll."

He chuckled, "All right man, I should be back through in ten." The guard walked down the corridor and up a flight of steps. He reached what some referred to as the pent-house, because the cell was on the corner end of the corridor and had a clear view of the entire cell block. He stopped and casually looked around to see if there were any wandering eyes. Thinking all was clear, he looked inside the cell. To his surprise, the inmate was awake and standing as if he was expecting him. The sight threw him off balance for a moment, but he soon recovered. "Everything okay man?" he asked as if he was concerned.

"I'm good," the inmate replied glaring back at him.

"Get you some shut eye, man," the guard said, and then walked away.

The encounter sent a shiver down his spine, but he shook it off. Tomorrow, he would have enough money to leave the job and never look back.

When he returned to his station, the guard sat back in the chair at the desk, pulled out his cell phone, and placed a telephone call. Finally, he was on his way to the finer things in life. "Chief, sorry to call this time of morning, but I think you will be pleased with my news. I believed I have just located one, Al "Turk" Day. The question is can you meet my price?"

Chief Wilbert T. Munford walked into the kitchen of his multi-level six bedroom home happy as a jay-bird. He finally had a handle on an itch he had been dying to scratch—Al "Turk" Day. By this time tonight, if all went well, his nemesis would be dead. As he did each morning at six he turned on the television to catch the morning news. The news caster was talking about an accident on Interstate 95.

> "The lone passenger in the vehicle was
> identified as Franklin Stafford.
> According to the police report, he was a prison
> guard here in Petersburg.
> The cause of the accident is unknown at this
> time. We will report more as the scene continues
> to unfold.
> This is Victoria Murillo reporting live."

The coffee cup Munford had just picked up dropped from his hand as he stared intently at the television monitor. A shiver went up his spine as he turned and surveyed the room. The very man he knew to be incarcerated had previously invaded his home. After hearing the news of the guard's death, Munford knew it was only a matter of time before Al Day made another appearance. There was no time to start the process again. Al Day had to be eliminated soon or his plans for reigning over the city of Richmond would be ruined. Options were running out, he was down to one--J.D. Harrison, the states Attorney General.

Like it or not, it was time to use every weapon at his disposal into reach his goal, to become the first elected Mayor for the city of Richmond. Munford picked up the telephone and dialed. "It's time to speed things up. I need that information from Harrison or his wife and I don't care how you get it."

Tracy turned over without opening her eyes and reached for the remote. When she pushed the button, she heard the television monitor retracting into its cabinet.   Subconsciously she knew the voices she continued to hear were not coming from the television. She heard a child's giggle and knew it was the voice of her son coming through the monitor. It seemed he was telling his father that his mother should be up with them. She listened as his father explained, "Mommy was up late taking care of daddy and needs a little extra time to sleep. I need you to be a big boy and help daddy with Jasmine."

"Jazz," as he called his baby sister, "hungry?" he asked his father.

"Yes, I think she is," JD replied. "Get her bottle for me."

"No daddy--do your shirt."   Tracy frowned until it dawned on her what JC was trying to tell his father. Smiling, she threw the comforter to the side and stretched as she heard the conversation between father and son continued.

"Shirt up daddy,"

Tracy walked into the nursery just in time to save JD who now had a serious frown on his face. "Daddy's can't do that JC only mommies can."

"Mommy," JC screamed and ran to grab her legs as JD watched.

Picking her son up, she hugged him, "Hello my precious." JD stood with Jasmine on his shoulder and she marveled at how handsome her husband was. His six-two frame towered over her five-six inches and filled the room with his undeniable presence. A smile that was reserved just for him appeared on her face. It was useless to try to hide the blush she revealed each time he looked at her. "Good morning to you, again."

He reached around her waist, pulled her to him, and kissed her with an urgency that left her weak at the knees. As soon as he pulled away JC clapped his hands as his mother held him on her hip. "Daddy kiss," he held out his hands to his father, who immediately placed a kiss on his son's lips. JC then turned to his mother, cupped her face between his small hands, and kissed her on the lips.

"I'm jealous. Good morning beautiful. I was about to feed this one, when JC informed me I wasn't doing it right."

"So I heard," she replied as she placed JC on the floor and reached for Jasmine. "Let me take her before she messes up your shirt."

JD was dressed in his shirt and tie, but his suit jacket was hanging on the knob of the door. "No, she's good. I'll feed her and keep JC busy while you dress."

"You sure? It's late you know."

"Yeah, I called Calvin earlier; he reset our morning briefing for ten, so I have a little time."

"Okay, I'll take you up on that offer then." Just as she turned, to walk out the room, his cell phone rang.

"Harrison," he answered.

She closed her eyes and sighed inwardly, the moment was over. Opening her eyes and smiling she turned to her husband and reached for Jasmine.

JC watched his father's retreating back and then looked up at his mother with sad eyes and said, "Daddy work now?"

"Yes baby, Daddy has to work now."

Tucker stood in the visitor's room of the Federal penitentiary, waiting for his boss to appear. The area was empty with the exception of the guards located near the entrance. When the doors in the back opened, he turned to see Turk walk through. He smiled and gave his boss a pound. "Hey man. You look good."

Turk returned the sentiment and took a seat, Tuck did the same. "What do you know?"

"He was one of Munford's people."

The two sat forward resting their elbows on their legs. "Did he pass any information on?"

"No, but now Munford is desperate. The referendum to make the Mayor for the city of Richmond an elected position is on the ballot in November. He has to eliminate you soon, therefore he has to locate you. The quickest way to do that is through Harrison."

"Has he put anything in motion?"

"Not that I know of, but Harrison has."

"What?"

"Harrison launched an investigation on Munford and he may have enough to take him down."

Turk smiled, "Anyway to help him along?"

"Yeah, we can tell them what we know."

"I don't know if Harrison can handle that yet. He's still emotionally wound tight. I don't want to have a negative impact on his future. How is Tracy handling the situation with the Senator?"

"There hasn't been a lot of contact. A few appearances here and there with Harrison and Roth at the same place, but that's it. Harrison is catching hell at home."

"She's holding JD to the wire." He smiled, "I'm proud of her. She got him sweating. That's good. Let him know he has to work to keep her."

"You need to stop. They are good together. It's good to see real black love and that's what they have." He became serious, "I don't want to see them torn apart by this."

"You getting soft man," Turk laughed.

"No, but just like you, I was there from the beginning. What they have is real."

"Then nothing will tear them apart. In the mean time keep an eye on Munford. Monique still giving you trouble?"

Tuck sat up and literally rolled his eyes. "Turk, I'll move heaven and earth for you, but your daughter has me on the verge of committing murder—premeditated murder and you know I don't roll like that."

Turk laughed, "I know man, she is just like her mother. But you got my support, do what you have to to keep her in line—whatever you have to do."

Chapter 2

The briefing was more detailed than JD expected. It seemed the information he had received from an informant a few years ago, has resulted in a year-long investigation, with the Chief of Police of the city of Richmond, at the very core. Turning to his life-long friend and chief of staff at the AG office, he asked, "Calvin how sure are we about this information? Is there any chance we could be wrong?"

"Mr. Harrison, because of the names involved, for the last three months we double checked all the information we received," Rossie Brown a rookie assistant attorney general in the office, eagerly explained.

Samantha Sullivan, a left over from the previous administration chimed in to support Rossie's statement. "Actually JD, we triple checked the information and it all leads back to Munford. This man has made a small fortune using young gangs to do his dirty work. It's as if he was pimping the gangs out to the highest bidder."

"If someone needs to be eliminated, he uses one of the gangs to handle the hit. In some instances he uses a new recruit to handle the job as an initiation. That pisses me off." Rossie stated angrily and then nervously added, "Mr. AG."

JD smiled at the young man, who he had come to respect. Rossie Brown was just out of law school and was intent on clearing a way for young men and women to follow in his footsteps. He simply wanted to show them, there is another way, then turning to the street. Not that he was old, but Rossie reminded JD of himself not long ago. He still had that same urge to stop the senseless loss of life to gang violence. "Call me JD, Rossie. What do you need to bring this case to court?"

Rossie sat up with a little more buoyancy as he took a quick look at Samantha for encouragement. A slight nod of her head indicated he should continue. "If we are going after the Chief we better have our ducks in a row. An undercover operation is the only way we would get irrefutable evidence against him."

Looking to his most trusted advisor and friend Calvin, JD hesitated then stood. Calvin understood the concern he saw in JD's eyes. "Going after Munford is going to cause issues," he stated in his normally composed manner.

Placing his hands in his pocket, JD looked to the floor. After a few minutes of thinking he yelled, "Son-of-a- bitch!. All kinds of doors will open if we indict him. Every criminal he ever arrested will have a means for an appeal."

Rossie held his breath and thought, *here we go, another man that put politics before justice. He's going to shut down the investigation.*

"Calvin, get a group together to begin reviewing all of Munford's case files. Let's catch as many on the front end as we can. Get with Brian to arrange for a person to get on the inside of Munford's inner circle. Samantha and Rossie, start doing your legwork. Make sure you have him. Don't discuss this case with anyone, not even

me. Years ago my father was once Munford's partner on
the beat. Keep Mr. Johnson informed daily. Don't put
any indictments in place until you know without question
you have this man. Good work you two."

Samantha patted Rossie on the back, "You got your
go ahead."

Rossie, who sat a little shocked at JD's reaction,
released a chuckle as he shook his head. "You never
cease to amaze me Mr. AG, never." He followed
Samantha out the door.

JD waited until he and Calvin were alone before he
continued. "This is going to get ugly."

"There's no way around it. If Munford is into half of
what they have uncovered there will be a lot of dirt
thrown." Calvin looked up at his friend whom he had
known since elementary school. Even back then, it
seemed JD Harrison carried the weight of the world on
his shoulders with ease. All through high school, he'd
handled with the poise of the debate team on stage and
the rugged hits of the football team on the field. And he
handled all with strength, determination and grace. Now
that he was into the political realm, he could see his
friend was destined for more. "This situation with
Munford could have an adverse affect on your
campaign." Calvin advised.

"I haven't decided to run," JD replied as he walked
over to his desk.

Calvin grunted, "You save that for Tracy, I know you.
You don't leave anything half done. The people of this
state needs and frankly deserve a good man like you in
the Governor's seat. Surprisingly, with all that's
happening in his personal life, Gavin has done well.
Now, you have to carry the ball to the finish line. We still
have work to do. So, when are you going to tell Tracy?"

JD looked at his friend, "I'm not sure which way to go
on this. If I run, it is certain the information about

Senator Roth and Tracy will surface. I don't want to see my wife hurt again."

"See, that's how you got into this trouble in the first place. Tracy is not a child who needs you to make decisions for her. She is your wife. You should share your concerns with her and the two of you decide how things should be handled together. I know you love Tracy. And I know you want to protect her, but just incase you missed it—your wife is a strong woman. She has to be to deal with you every day. Stop short changing her with your macho man tactics. Let her grow into the wife you are going to need when you reach the White House."

JD frowned at his friend. "You don't understand. Tracy is so naive to the cruelty of the world."

"You are joking, right?" Calvin raised his voice. "She grew up with Lena Washington as a mother. Tell me again that she doesn't know about cruelty. It's you and her brother Al Day that refuse to see just how strong a woman she is. Yes, Tracy is naive to some things, but my God, man, look at what she has dealt with since you came into her life. Give your wife some credit. Go home, talk to her like she is your equal and not one of your children. Then let me know when we can start campaigning."

Watching his friend placing items inside his briefcase, JD stood. "There was a time that I actually liked you as a friend. I'm beginning to question my own judgment." He smiled. "And what in the hell do you mean my macho man tactics?"

They both laughed, "I don't know man. It's something Brian said one night," Calvin replied. "Speaking of Brian, where is he?"

"He's at the house with Tracy."

Calvin stopped and looked at his friend. "Stop doing that."

20

"Doing what?" JD asked as he picked up his briefcase and opened the door for them to leave.

"Stop sending Brian to your wife."

"Calvin, I trust Brian with my life. I can certainly trust him with my wife and children."

Calvin walked out of the office door shaking his head, "I be damned if I trust Brian around my wife. The man works out every day and it shows, walking around looking like LL Cool J with those damn muscles."

"You're jealous." JD joked.

"You're damn right." Calvin laughed.

Before going home, JD stopped by to see his brother-in-law, James Brooks. A decision still had to be made regarding the Governor's race. Unlike the daily decisions he made as Attorney General of Virginia, this one was difficult. As AG the choice was always between right and wrong. There was never a conflict for him; he simply followed the law. But there was no law book or case reference he could review to assist with this decision. It was difficult to make a choice between serving the citizens of Virginia and making his wife happy. This decision would have a tremendous impact on her and their children.

"Clearly you're torn," James uttered as he sat in the leather chair behind his desk at the campaign headquarters office, watching JD stand at the window with his hands in his pockets. When he looked down at the floor and began pacing, he knew JD was in deep thought. Looking down at the floor with his hands in his pockets was his thinking stance, James always thought. Sometimes he wondered if JD believed the answer to his dilemma would jump into his mind from the floor.

James understood the magnitude of the decision before his friend. "You and I know, this decision is not just about the Governor seat. When you win, Covington, as the head of the National Democratic Committee, would be obligated to encourage you to run for President in four years. You have to understand that fact from the beginning. Neither race is going to be a breeze like the previous. Republicans did not have an issue voting for you as AG, however, the top position in the state will be a different matter. You best believe the wolves are circling their prey, which happens to be you. They know you are an undeniable threat to them. Hell, Dan said the conservative right was holding prayer meetings, asking God to keep you out of the race." JD never raised his head, but smiled at James' comment. "Yeah, I laughed too, but I believe him."

A knock on the door interrupted the conversation. "Mr. Attorney General, you have a call on line one," James' secretary announced.

Looking up, JD replied, "Thank you," as he picked up the telephone receiver on James desk and pushed a button. "JD Harrison," he announced into the telephone. "Hey Calvin, what's up?" He listened intently to the information Calvin relayed. Wondering why he did not call his cell, he pulled out his blackberry and realized it was turned off. Turning the telephone back on, he noticed the missed calls from his sister Ashley, his mother and Calvin, but nothing from Tracy. "I'll return to the office before I go home." He hung up the telephone and stared at the screen on his blackberry that held a picture of Tracy and his children. Smiling, he shook his head. "Jasmine looks so much like Tracy it's frightening."

James stood abruptly, walked from behind the desk and looked at JD's phone. Yes, pictures of children excited two of the most powerful men in Virginia politics. "Hey, we don't have that picture. Is it new?" he asked.

JD possessively took the phone back, "Yes, it is, but it is exclusively mine." James looked offended. "Every time I get a good picture of my wife and children either Ashley or momma takes it. I'm keeping this one for myself." He hit the off button and placed the phone back into his pocket.

"Alright, you want to be like that, fine. I guess I'll keep the pictures of the twins Ashley told me to give you." James declared as he walked back to his chair and retook his seat.

"Keep your picture; I'm sure Ashley gave Tracy one anyway. You're lucky I convinced my sister to marry you in the first place." His face saddened, "I never have enough time to spend with them." With hands in pocket and head down, JD walked back over to the window. "I miss spending time with Tracy. I vowed to make her happy every day of her life and she's not. She would never say it, but I see it, I feel it in my gut. Lord knows she has kept her end of the bargain. I have two beautiful children and a home any man would be proud to walk in. I'm just having a difficult time keeping my end up."

James stood and walked over to the man he now considered a brother as well as a friend. "It's difficult to live the life you want when you have committed yourself to public service. It takes a special couple to survive. I believe you and Tracy have the kind of love that can endure it all. Those are my thoughts; you have to decide if Virginia is worth the sacrifice. Talk to Tracy; Covington can wait another day or two."

He looked at James and then turned back to the window. "Tracy will support anything I do. But I don't want to settle for that. I need to know she is there with me, every step of the way. I can't do it without her. Hell I don't want to do it without her." He exhaled, "The situation with Senator Roth has put a strain on us—she's become distant. She hasn't really talked about it much, but I can feel she doesn't trust me. When I make it home at a decent time she is coming down the stairs with Jasmine in her arms and JC running beside her to greet me as if all is well. Then what little time we have is spent with the kids, until my cell rings and I'm called away for one reason or another, then she shuts down on me. By the time I return home, she's usually asleep. We wake up the next morning and begin the routine again."

He turned to look at James. "I want the Governor's seat. There are so many things I want to do to make life a little easier for the citizens here." He thought a minute longer. "Maybe I'll take Tracy away for a few days, so we can seriously talk about this without interruptions." His cell phone rang, this time it was Brian Thompson, his friend and the head of his protection detail. "This is Brian, I have to take this. Tell Covington I will have a decision for him in a few days." He shook James' hand and left the office.

James sat at his desk for a minute as he watched JD leave. It took a lot to impress James and his brother-in-law was at the top of his list of good people. He knew that once he put his hat in the race for Governor, there would be no limit as to how far he could go. What worried James was the effect the political world would have on JD's personal life—especially his marriage. The bomb shell that exploded privately last year was going to come out. It was only a matter of time before the public would learn that Tracy Harrison is the illegitimate daughter of US Senator John Roth. When the media got a hold of that, there would be hell to pay and Tracy would be the one paying the price. There was no doubt in his mind that JD and Tracy could weather the storm, but what would be the cost?

For now James had his own price to pay. Tracy might not be holding JD to the fire for keeping the information a secret, but his wife, Ashley Renee Harrison-Brooks was not holding her tongue on the matter. It's been a year and he was still getting hit with it every now and then. But, he could take it as long as he had Ashley at his side. He picked up the telephone and dialed home, "Hello sweetheart."

Tracy heard the door open downstairs and turned to look at the clock on her desk, it was nine thirty. Jeffrey was home early. She ran down the steps and walked into the kitchen. The smile faded as she looked in the eyes of Brian. "Hey," he said.

"Hey Brian," she replied as she walked further into the room "Where's Jeffrey?"

"He was called back to the office. Did you need something?"

"No," she smiled. She exhaled and walked over to him, kissed him on the cheek and asked, "Have you had dinner?"

"Not yet," he smiled as she walked over to the refrigerator and began to pull out items to prepare him a plate. "I'll go wash my hands," Brian said as he rubbed his hands together.

"You know having you at my dinner table is becoming a habit." She placed the plate in the microwave and turned it on as Brian came out of the bathroom.

"I'll take a hot meal over fast food any day." He sat and waited for the plate.

Tracy took it out of the microwave and placed it in front of him with a drink, napkin, and silverware. She then sat down in front of him. "How was your day today?"

"Pretty good," he smiled, ate, and told her about his day. "How about you? Did you get the information for the new business?"

"Yes I did," she replied excitedly. "It's going to be a breeze to get it started. I even have a possible list of clients targeted. I'm so excited. I can't wait to tell Jeffrey about it."

"Well, he shouldn't be too late. Have you figured out how you are going to get his approval?"

"I'm not asking his permission or anything, I just need to let him know what my plans are."

Brian stared at one of the most intelligent women he knew, with an inner beauty that shined through. Which was saying something, her best friends were Ashley, JD's sister who could be a centerfold in somebody's magazine, Roz Marable, who was an exotic beauty and there was Cynthia Lassiter, who could be on the front cover of every glamour magazine there is. "Ha," he laughed, "you and I both know JD is not going to like this."

"Yes he will, you wait and see." She pouted. "You could help me convince him—you know."

Shaking his head while taking his plate to the sink, he laughed. "No, you are on your own."

"Chicken!"

"Damn right," he said, kissed her on the cheek, and walked out the patio door.

Tracy fell asleep waiting for JD to come home. After Brian left, she put JC to bed, fed Jasmine and put her down an hour later. Sitting up at her computer, she worked on the investment portfolio for Next Level Consulting, the company she and her best friend and now sister in law Ashley had started while in college. For six years that was her baby. She gave her all and it paid off handsomely. It was now a multi-million dollar company that had clientele across the state of Virginia. Recently they opened another office in Arlington, Virginia and were securing clients from the D.C./Maryland area.

The business was flourishing under the hands of her Chief Operation Officer, Monica Jackson, but she missed it. After having JC and Ashley giving birth to twins, Jayda and Jayden, they both left the company. Ashley was okay with being a full time mom, but Tracy wasn't as secure. The business had been her security blanket since college. If anything were to happen between her and Jeffery, what would she have to turn too? Until last year, the thought of having a backup plan was never a major concern. But after learning Jeffrey had kept the fact that Senator Roth was her father a secret for several years, the insecurities that she had prior to their marriage began to resurface. It was hard to imagine Jeffrey Daniel Harrison, the prominent District Attorney, would actually fall in love with a girl with no experience and from the wrong side of the tracks, but he did. And for the last four years she had allowed herself to believe in the fantasy. With all that was revealed last year at her friend's wedding, it was imperative that she make sure her future was secured, not just for herself, but for her children as well.

Jeffery was against her going back to work. And to be honest, Monica was doing such a great job; there was no reason for her to return to Next Level. So she had been playing around with opening a non-profit company that would assist people who wanted to start small businesses and call it J&J Enterprises, after her two children. Jeffrey's argument was simple, two small children less than two years apart, it would be best that she stayed at home. In his position as AG, he was called into the office and meetings at any given time. The children needed at least one of their parents at home with them. The logic was sound, but Tracy felt lost. Jeffrey had his career to fill his creative needs she had nothing. She loved her children and fully expected to have more, but for now she needed to feel a part of something that she could call hers. To tell the truth, she needed something more to fill her time and keep her mind off of Carolyn Roth-Roberts, and the issues she had been having since finding out they were half-sisters. Tracy could not understand the drama, nothing had changed for her. Senator Roth was still just—Senator Roth, her mother's husband. She had lived this long without a father figure, and she had turned out okay, right?

Then there were the different news articles with pictures of him and the new political advisor. She had not shared her concerns about the number of pictures hitting the print media to anyone. Besides, Jeffery was coming home to her every night and was making love to her just as passionately and often as before, so there was no need for her to be concerned with other women, their marriage was okay, right? Getting over the fact that Jeffrey, her mother and Lord only knows who else, kept secrets from her was easy—just ignore all and move on with your life, right?

Now, that JC was about to turn two and Jasmine was almost six weeks, Tracy thought it would be a good time to start the small company. The thought of returning to work world filled her with so much excitement; it was difficult to wait to talk to Jeffrey, but she made it a habit not to disturb him at work. She understood that his full concentration was needed to deal with the issues of the state. So, she took the initiative to put all the pieces in place before, talking to Jeffrey. She placed a call to Olivia Gordon, who was his nurse when he was hospitalized after being shot in the court-room by gang members a few years ago. Since Mrs. Gordon retired, she was the perfect person to help with the children. Besides, there was no way Jeffrey would argue about having Mrs. Gordon to care for the children. When she called her, Mrs. Gordon was thrilled to become the caretaker for the Harrison household and their children. In fact, she stated she would be by in the morning to see the house and meet the children.

With that in place, Tracy was determined to wait up to talk with Jeffrey. She curled up in the chaise lounge in her office with a cup of hot tea and her new romance novel to read about the romantic things she and Jeffrey use to do together. With a coverlet over her legs, she relaxed and continued with the story.

The house was quiet as JD entered the kitchen through the garage door. As he placed his keys on the holder, he noticed a note on the refrigerator door. Pulling the note down, he opened the door and took out the plate of food he knew would be waiting for him and two Heinekens. He placed the plate in the microwave, pushed the reheat button and sat the beers on the breakfast bar.

The note read: *Jeffrey if I'm asleep, wake me when you get in. Luv Tracy.* Just as he finished reading, the microwave sounded and the French patio doors opened.

"You pulled a long day. What's up?" Brian asked as he picked up the beer his friend sat there for him. Brian Thompson, Calvin Johnson, Douglas Hylton, and JD had gone to high school together. JD and Calvin went on to law school while Brian joined the FBI. Douglas opened a promotional business and now owned one of the premier nightclubs in the city. While JD was a prosecutor for the City of Richmond, a number of cases against gang members had generated threats against him.

At the time, Brian was then assigned by the bureau as head of his security detail. The red tape of the agency prevented Brian from protecting JD and Tracy the way it was needed. Subsequently JD was shot in the courtroom and Tracy was brutally beaten. James Brooks decided to assist Brian in starting a security agency with his primary client being the Harrison family. Brian now owned Thompson Security Agency; his number one priority was keeping JD and his family safe.

JD sat the plate on the bar, bowed his head and blessed the food. "The information we received from Al Day a few years ago has turned out to be significant in more ways than we previously thought."

"What did they find?"

"It seems our friendly Chief Munford is a very busy man." JD yawned, as he put his fork down, not able to eat at the late hour. "I'm staying far away from this one. Calvin is heading up the investigation. I'm sure he'll call you tomorrow with an assignment for your team. Have you eaten?"

Brian nodded, "Tracy and I ate earlier."

JD pushed his plate aside as he took a swallow of his beer. "You ate with Tracy and the kids tonight?"

Brian nodded his head, "Tracy—the kids were in bed."

"Anything happening here on the home front I need to know about?"

"No, it was pretty quiet today. The contractors finished the secure exit from the basement and the camera monitors were installed." Brian stated, "I'll test them throughout the night to make sure the lens angles are what we need before they are activated. I see you got Tracy's note."

JD picked the note up and glanced at it again, then looked at his watch. "It's late. I'm not going to wake her up. You know what it's about?"

"Possibly, but I was occupied while she was writing it."

The manner in which Brian made the comment intrigued him. "Occupied—with what or should I say with who?" Brian grinned and took a drink from his beer bottle. JD knew exactly what or who was keeping Brian busy these days. "You know if Samuel Lassiter finds out what you are doing with his little sister, there is going to be hell to pay."

"You plan on telling him?"

"No, but you know what happens in the dark will eventually come to light."

"We are two consenting adults."

"Yeah. Tell that to the Lassiter brothers."

"I don't think that I will." The two laughed. He finished off his beer. "Tomorrow, Magna will check the connection at the police station. By the way, now that we have a good size staff I'll be rotating agents through here."

JD knew he was working hard to recruit only the best to join his staff. That he was grateful for. His staff would be guarding him and his family, if he decided to run for Governor or more. "Congrats man, James mentioned you have two new agents in addition to Samuel."

"Yeah, Donnell Williams and his sister Ryan. Now she is a looker and tough as nails.

"Man, what is it with you and people's sisters?"

Brian looked shocked, "Hey, I'm a free man, the only one of the crew that's left, I can look. Hell, I can do more than look. Besides, the sisters need me."

"You forgot about Douglas, he's not married."

"His nose is wide open man."

JD sat up, "Really—who?"

"Karen Holt."

The shocked expression on JD's face said it all, then he shook his head. "Well, she's not a bad looking sister. But her ex-husband is crazy as hell. "

"You and I know that, but apparently Doug don't give a damn." Brian stated as he headed out the same door he'd entered. "I'll catch you in the morning."

"Alright man." Loosening his tie, JD finished his beer and placed the bottle in the trash.

He locked the door, put the alarm on, turned off the lights and began removing his suit blazer as he climbed the staircase. The first stop was JC's room. The night light was on and he could see the model helicopter, motorcycle and corvette hanging from the ceiling. The cover was hanging off the bed and the caboose was clutched in his hand. JD placed the cover over his son's shoulders, removed the thumb from his mouth and kissed his head that was covered with braids. There was never a time, even in sleep mode, that his children were not tidy. Closing the door quietly, he then ventured into the nursery to see Jasmine. She was sleeping soundly in her crib, but he could not resist picking her up. The small bundle opened her eyes, the eyes that looked just like her mother's and smiled. JD kissed the little hand she held up as she stretched. "Hello Jazzy. How's my beautiful baby girl tonight? You are as pretty as your mommy, you know that?" She presented him with a wide toothless smile. JD sat in the rocker with his daughter and watched as she settled in and reclosed her eyes. He sat there holding her for a good twenty minutes, thinking of ways he would ensure that she and her brother remained safe and secure.

Placing Jasmine on her stomach, he pulled the cover over her shoulders and left the room. As he entered the master bedroom, he placed his suit jacket and tie across the chair then jumped into the shower. He pulled out the bottom to his pajamas, pulled them on and walked out of the dressing room. As he approached the bed he saw Tracy was not there. He sighed with a smile, stepped

into his slippers and walked down the hallway in search
of his wife.

The pool house had been converted into a security
house. Electronic tracking and surveillance equipment
had been installed as well as a safe room. For now the
security system handled things at night, but tonight Brian
needed to test the newly installed equipment. His mind
wondered to the staff he now had working with him.
Magna Rivera, who was a gang activity specialist out of
Washington, DC was holding down administrative duties
and handling a few lower priority cases for now.
Eventually he had to hire office staff before Magna really
lost her patience and shot him. Donald Williams, who
was an ex-police officer with the City of Richmond, was
handling in-house investigations and background checks,
leaving him and Samuel Lassiter, an ex-Navy Seal to
rotate covering JD. The new trainee Ryan Williams,
Donald's baby sister, would be handling surveillance on
low priority cases, but would eventually be covering
Tracy and the children when the time came. The agency
was growing with the addition of more cases and they
needed more people, but this would have to do for now.
The ringing of his cell phone interrupted his thoughts.
Anyone calling this time of night should be a booty call,
but as he checked the number, he knew it wasn't.
"Thompson."

"Tucker here."

"Oh hell man, every time you call, my life gets
complicated."

"Hey, I'm not feeling the love here," he joked.

The two men were on different sides of the law, but
over the years a trust had developed between them.

Brian knew when Donovan Tucker calls—you listen. "What's up man?"

"Intercepted an inquiry on the bogus name used for my man. Thought your man should know. I'm out."

Brian disconnected the call and exhaled, "Oh hell." He sat back in the chair and thought, then he pulled up to the computer and keyed in the local news website. Second story on the page was what he was looking for. A prison guard from the Federal penitentiary was killed in an automobile accident this morning. He had glanced at the story earlier today, but at the time had no reason to be concerned. Now, his gut told him the two incidents were related. Not one to take chances, he placed a call to Samuel Lassiter.

"Hello," Samuel's wife' Cynthia answered.

"Hey pain," Brian smiled as he spoke to the woman he thought of as a little sister. "How's the whale coming along?"

"You know, if I didn't love you like a brother, I would curse you out. What do you want this time of night?"

"Your husband."

"Switching sides?"

"That's not remotely funny. Put the man on the phone."

Hearing Cynthia's laughter was a wonderful sound. She and Samuel married almost a year ago and are now expecting their first child. "Hey,"

"We may have an issue. Can you contact your brother?"

Chapter 3

Fried apples? No, bacon. Fried apples, bacon, biscuits and coffee. Hmm, he must still be dreaming. The smells were the same as from his childhood on Sunday mornings before going to Sunday school and church with his parents. He sniffed before opening his eyes. It wasn't a dream, the scents were real. The realization prompted him to not just open his eyes but to sit up. Looking around he noticed Tracy was not in bed. He threw the covers back in a huff and wondered who was in his kitchen cooking. He loved Tracy more than life itself, but he knew there was no way the scents coming from downstairs were from her.

As he descended the stairs he wondered if his mother was supposed to come over this morning and he forgot. Oh, Ashley, his sister must be over. She cooked just like their mom. Thinking it must be family; JD didn't bother to put on a top to his pajamas before going downstairs. The heavenly smell was so strong at the bottom of the staircase he rubbed his stomach, anticipating the feast that was awaiting him. As he turned the corner, JC's laughter could be heard over Tracy's voice. "Daddy," his son called out.

"Hey big man," he said as he reached around his wife's waist and pulled her backside to him. "Good morning beautiful," he said before his lips captured hers in a sensuous kiss. He broke away quickly and moved towards the stove. "Where's momma?"

"At home I guess," Tracy replied as she continued cleaning up behind JC.

"Where's Ashley?" JD asked as he continued to pile his plate.

Tracy stopped and looked at him with a bit of confusion. "With her husband, I would think. Why?"

JD knew he was treading on dangerous grounds here, but he was an honest man and did not know a way around his next question. He bit into the biscuit, which literally melted in his mouth. Closing his eyes, he savored the wonderful flavor that assaulted his taste buds. "Mum, this taste better than you babe." He said without thinking. When he opened his eyes his wife was standing with her hands on her hips and a not so great look on her face.

"Well, let them sleep beside you tonight."

"Too crumby," he replied with a smile. "Who cooked?"

"I beg your pardon," Tracy questioned with a raised eyebrow.

"Babe, I love you, but you did not cook these biscuits." He put a fork of apples in his mouth and the flavor was rewarded with a groan. "Nor these apples mum mum."

"I'm glad you are enjoying them," Mrs. Gordon laughed as she came out of the laundry room with Jasmine on her shoulder. Shocked to see her, JD immediately put the dishtowel over his naked shoulder and looked to Tracy. "Oh boy please, don't' act shy around me. I've seen all you got to offer and some when you were in the hospital. Ain't nothing for you to be ashamed of."

Tracy tried to hide her laughter, but couldn't. "Jeffrey, you remember Mrs. Gordon from the hospital."

"Of course I do. Hello Mrs. Gordon. Would you excuse me for a moment?" He asked as he rushed upstairs to change clothes. Mrs. Gordon had helped them through a rough time. What he didn't understand was why was she in his house on a Saturday morning, cooking and apparently washing clothes.

After putting on his sweat-shirt and pants he returned to the kitchen to find Mrs. Gordon outside sitting at the table on the patio with JC and Jasmine. Tracy was at the table waiting for him drinking a cup of tea. He retook his seat and continued to eat. "When-ever you are ready I'm listening."

Taking a deep breath, she sat forward and exhaled. "Mrs. Gordon has agreed to work for us to help out with the house, cooking and the children. Now when we have to go out for one of your many functions or work we don't have to worry about who will be home with the children."

"We're back to that again."

"Jeffrey, I miss working, meeting with clients, developing reconstruction plans and most of all I miss Ashley."

"Ashley is not there anymore, Tracy. She's home with her children. If that's enough for her why can't it be for you?" He stood, walked over to the sink and rinsed his plate before putting it into the dishwasher. He turned, leaned back against the counter top and folded his arms across his chest. Looking at her he could see the disappointment in her eyes. That light that was there earlier was now gone. He did not understand why she didn't see that he was trying to protect her. Didn't she remember? The thought of her being harmed nearly killed him before. He could not take a chance on anything happening to her or his children. Telling her that would cause her to be frightened and he didn't want that. Sighing, he knelt down in front of her. "Tracy," he took her hands and she looked away. "Tracy, look at me." She did and it hurt him to see the sadness there, but not enough for him to take a chance on her life. "I love you. I would do anything in the world for you, but, I don't want a stranger raising our children." Tears were building in her eyes, but she held them back. "I tell you what. What if we let Mrs. Gordon stay? That way you could work from home part-time."

"Jeffrey, it's not the same as going into an office and being around people."

"Tracy with the caseload at the office and the campaign about to began, we will be busier than ever. Eventually, you would have to stop working again anyway. Besides your company according to Black Enterprise Magazine, is one of the top in your field and is doing quite well. It's practically running itself. You don't have to be there."

"When did you decide to run for office again Jeffrey?" she asked perplexed. "Did you consider talking with me about that, before you committed yourself to another cause?" She pulled away and stood at the window watching JC talking happily to Mrs. Gordon. He stood and put his arms around her waist, "I haven't talked to anyone about my decision yet. I told James to tell Covington to give me a few days before I decided."

"It sounds like you've decided to me."

He turned her around to him and placed his hands on both sides of her hips. "That depends on you. If you tell me not to do this I won't. When this term is up I can walk away. Calvin and I can start a law firm and defend people that break the law."

She frowned at him. That was the last thing he would ever do. She knew it and he did too. "Who knows, I might be good at it," he smiled.

"You would be good at anything," she replied to the smile that warmed her insides. She sighed, "Is this what you want to do, run for Governor?"

"Yes I do."

That determined look, she knew very well entered his eyes. If he ran, he would win and their life would never be the same. As he accomplished his dreams, she would be letting hers go. "Have you considered the impact this decision will have on our family, life will never be the same."

"I thought about that. It's one of the reasons you need to be home, Tracy. Our twelve children will need someone to guide them and keep them grounded," he grinned.

"I'm not having twelve children. That I will not compromise on. You get five and no more."

He kissed her on the side of her mouth. "Well, since Mrs. Gordon is here, we can go upstairs and start working on number three." He captured her lips with his and slowly felt her disappointment slip away. Just as he began plunging deeper into the recesses of her mouth, the telephone rang. Reluctantly, he pulled away and answered it, holding her close to him. "Time got by me man, I didn't know it was this late. I'll meet you there." He hung up the telephone.

"You have a nine o'clock court time with the boys," she said as she pulled out of his grasp.

"I can cancel Tracy and stay here with you."

"No. You go ahead. You would just keep me from doing what I need to do around here." The time alone was needed to get over the two blows he had dealt her in a matter of minutes. Not only was she not going to have the opportunity to go back to work, but she also was going to have to endure another campaign. That meant dealing with her step-sister, Carolyn Roth-Roberts, and the likes of her.

JD stepped outside and spoke to Mrs. Gordon. When he returned, he took her hand and pulled her up stairs with him. "What are you doing Jeffrey?"

We are going to spend the day together. That will give Mrs. Gordon a chance to get to know the children a little better and you and I sometime out of the house, together.   He turned towards her while walking backwards up the steps. "I need time to beg your forgiveness." He waited until she stepped up to him and he took her in his arms. "I love you Tracy and I realize it seems like I'm being selfish, but I know, I can't and don't want to do this without you. Please baby, just listen to my thoughts on the election and if you can't handle it, I will call Covington and tell him today, I can't do it."

"Oh, you want to say my wife said no," she said in jest.

"No I will tell him the love of my life will not allow me to serve at this time." He touched her lips with a very delicate kiss. "Let's get dressed before we end up spending our free day in bed."

The two spent the day at one of Tracy's favorite places, The Renaissance Club, shooting pool, having lunch, and enjoying having her husband to herself. This was something she had not experienced since he decided to run for office a few years ago. As long as she could have moments like this, she could support him in anything. However, her experience with his previous campaign had left a lot to be desired. For Tracy, the campaign had been intimidating. The crowds were huge and everyone seemed to want to touch or talk to JD. With the exception of James and Ashley, Tracy felt completely out of her element around most people. There were political advisors and consultants that seemed to be at odds with Tracy at every turn. One way or the other they considered her to be a hindrance. Some felt she was a distraction for JD. There were times when they wanted or needed his undivided attention on an issue, but his first concern was where was Tracy or how did Tracy feel about a particular issue. At one point an advisor suggested to Tracy "you would serve JD much better if you remain at home." Of course the suggestion was made in private and JD never knew why Tracy was not on the campaign trail with him. There was no point in denying the inevitable; Jeffrey was going to run for Governor and eventually President of the United States. She needed to take steps to be in a position to support him in every way she could. The idea of going back to work really had to end. "What are you thinking about?" He asked on their way home.

"Can we pull over for a minute?"

Checking the traffic to his right, he put his signal on and pulled over into the first parking space he reached and turned to her curiously. "What is it Tracy?"

She took his hand and looked into his eyes. "Jeffrey, this decision is not just about the Governor's race. Once you become Governor then the DNC is going to ask you to run for President. This is a major life change you are asking us to make. There will be an impact on our children as well as our marriage. Their safety and welfare is my number one concern. I don't want their lives interrupted by anything you or I chose to do with our lives."

"I don't want that either. We will have to decide how we can make sure they are not dragged into this political circle. What about you Tracy, will you be a part of this?"

"I will be your biggest supporter, from here to the White House."

Staring at her, he wondered what he'd done to deserve her unconditional love and support. Whatever it was, he thanked God for brining her into his life. "I guess we need to talk with James, Ashley and Momma."

"She is going to be so proud of you. I don't know how we are going to keep her from exploding with pride."

"Yeah I know. Well at least she can take out the "my son for President" buttons she has stored away."

Tracy smiled then looked out of the window. Now they had to touch on a subject that had been avoided for a year. They had to talk about Senator Roth. "Jeffrey, how are we going to handle the situation with Senator Roth? The press is going to have a field day if this isn't handled right. I know Carolyn does not want anyone to know about this. Just speaking from my experience, it's better to put the truth out there, before it blows up in our faces."

JD knew she was referring to the way he handled the situation and there was nothing he could do to change the past. He used his finger to bring her eyes up to him. "I am so sorry things happened they way they did. Please know I did all I could to keep you from being hurt."

She stared at him with an intensity that he had not experienced from her before. "You did everything except tell me who my father really was. It was the same when you found my mother. In fact, it was around that time that you and James knew, but you didn't bother to share that information with me. It's the same with Turk. To this day, I don't know where he is incarcerated. But just like with the other things, you believe you know what is best for me. For some reason you believe I'm too gullible to think for myself. In some things you may be right, but there comes a point when everyone has to take off the rose colored glasses and face life as it truly is. My time has come harshly, but it's here." She turned away and

JD's heart slumped along with her smile. "I'm not willing to allow another person to be hurt by deceitful acts. We should meet with Gavin, Carolyn, Senator Roth and my mother to determine the best course of action."

"Tracy," JD spoke softly, "I did not deceive you. I simply did not tell you for fear of Carolyn's retaliation."

She never looked up, "Whatever the reason, a number of people were hurt, Carolyn being the main victim. We have to find a way to handle this that will not hurt her any deeper."

"What about our children Tracy? We have to consider their part in this." The look she gave him warned him to tread lightly. "Babe, technically, Senator Roth is their grandfather. Are you going to willfully deny them the chance to get to know him as such? Other then when he comes by with your mother? You haven't spent any time with him to allow him to explain his reasons for wanting to keep this a secret. It seems you are holding him responsible for what happened and he is as much a victim as you are."

She snapped, "I have no reason to spend time with him. And why are you saying he is a victim here, Jeffrey?"

JD exhaled, "Yes babe you do have a reason. He is your father and the children's grandfather. And remember, he just found out about you a few years ago. He didn't know he was your father."

"You need to make up your mind. First you didn't want me to know the man is my father, now you want to force me to accept him as such. You can't have it both ways Jeffrey." He could hear the hurt, anger and confusion in her voice and knew there wasn't anything he could do about it, except to listen. "This isn't even about Senator Roth, Jeffrey, and you know that."

"Then what is it about Tracy?"

"You're an intelligent man, Jeffrey. I don't have to tell you this is about a man keeping something important from his wife. How do I know you aren't keeping other things from me?"

That cut was deeper then she could have imagined. This woman, who he would give his life for, had lost trust in him. "What do I have to do to gain your forgiveness? Tell me Tracy and I will do it. I don't ever want you to doubt me. How can I expect the public to trust me if my own wife doesn't?"

"That's just it; you seem to have this strong sense of integrity when it comes to everyone except me." She sighed and shook her head frustrated. "I'm sorry Jeffrey. This isn't what we were supposed to be discussing. Let's just go home, okay." Tears welled up in her eyes and tore at his heart. A feeling of doom seemed to enter the interior of the vehicle just as a flash from a camera caught his attention. He started to get out of the car and take the camera from the reporter, but Tracy's hand on his arm stopped him. "Please Jeffery, let's just go."

He turned the key in the ignition and pulled off. "This conversation is a year late Tracy. We should have talked about this when it first happened. I should have told you about the DNA testing when that first happened, I know that now. I can't change the past. The call on how to handle this from now on will be yours and only yours. I refuse to allow this to continue to grow between us. I love you too much to lose you over a mistake that was made years ago."

When JD pulled into the garage, neither had spoken a word since the reporter showed up. As they got out of the car Tracy stood by her door and waited until JD came around. She immediately went into his arms, "I'm sorry."

He held her tightly against his chest. "I'm sorry too. But it's apparent you haven't forgiven me yet. Things aren't going to be right between us until we deal with this."

"I just need some time."

He kissed the top of her head. "Take all the time you need. Just don't shut me out." She looked up at him and he kissed her lips. "Let's go see if Mrs. Gordon survived the kids."

They walked in through the kitchen door to find Mrs. Gordon cooking. "Well how was your day out?" she asked while wiping her hands on a towel.

"It was time needed. Did our children run you crazy?" JD asked as he checked out the pan on the stove.

"No, they are angels, both of them. Jazzy is asleep in the basinet and JC went down for his nap about an hour ago." She looked at JD whose attention was now in the oven, then turned to Tracy, who was clearly upset about something. "You alright baby?"

"Yes. I'm fine. I see you cooked dinner."

She checked out the two and knew something was amiss, but she had just started this job and it was not her place to speak on the goings on between husband and wife. "Yes I did. You had a fully stocked refrigerator so I put some of it to use. If it's all right with you, I'm going to take my leave now."

"Do you think you'll be able to work for us?" JD asked as he watched Tracy. "Tracy wants to start a new business and will need the time away from the children to get it going."

Tracy looked up at him and smiled, "Actually," she sighed, "Jeffrey has decided to run for Governor, and there will be times when both of us will have to be out of the house." She turned to Mrs. Gordon. "I will feel so much better if I knew they were with you and not being dragged between Ashley and Mrs. Harrison's house."

It was apparent the two were trying to work out something here. "Well, I'm a woman of my word. You got me as long as you need me. Now that my daughter and her children have moved to Atlanta, I have plenty of time on my hands. So how is Monday through Fridays – six to six and you call me when you need me on the weekends. Now I'm going to have to charge you extra for overnight stays. You know I do have a social life."

JD and Tracy both smiled at the woman. "Name your price."

"All right now, ya'll children take care and I'll see you bright and early Monday morning."

When the door closed behind Mrs. Gordon, JD looked at Tracy, "I love you."

"I love you more," she replied. As she took a step to walk into his arms, his cell phone chimed. She turned to walk away, but he grabbed her hand, pulled her close, and kissed her as if he had all the time in the world. Breaking the kiss, she looked up at him, "Take your call." She smiled and walked up the steps.

Samuel sat on the sofa, with his wife in his lap asleep. Life was certainly full of surprises. No one could have told him The Wizard of Oz was going to become one of his favorite movies. Yet, now it was.

"I can't believe a grown man is watching this—much less my big brother."

"How long have you been here?" Samuel asked his brother that had an uncanny knack of appearing out of thin air. Occupational habit, he supposed, since he worked for the CIA, he had to be invisible more times than not.

"Since the damn witch was melting," Joshua Lassiter said as he took a seat across from where his brother sat with his sleeping wife. He smiled at the scene, "You look happy man."

Samuel returned the smile as he rubbed his wife's protruding stomach. "I can't begin to explain it, but I would kill the first man that calls me back into service if it meant leaving my wife."

"Ha. That's funny coming from you. You realize if you are called it will be from the President, a man you swore to protect with your life."

"Now, that would be a damn shame, because I like the brother."

Joshua laughed then sat forward. The man was always impeccably dressed. Tonight it was an Armani suit, tie, shirt, and shoes. At six-four, the man could be a walking billboard for the Tall, Dark and Handsome Weekly magazine. "I did a little research on Franklin Stafford, the prison guard that was killed in the traffic accident. He was on Munford's payroll. You need to take precautions with your man." He put a piece of paper on the table next to him. "This person needs to be watched 24/7. The Harrison's are at risk."

"We have them covered."

"No you don't. He was out earlier today with his wife and there was no coverage. Neither the man nor his wife should be anywhere without a body on them." He stood, "I'll be around for a minute if you need anything more."

Samuel looked down at his wife, who looked like an angel, then looked back up to see his brother had disappeared as quietly as he had arrived. Leaving his wife when she was so close to her due date was not a pleasant thought, but he had a job to do. JD Harrison was the future for this country and he had taken an oath to

protect him and his wife with his life. Picking up his cell
phone, his first call went to his mother. One of his eleven
brothers or sisters was going to need to move into his
house until this threat was over or Cynthia gave birth.
The second call went to his boss, Brian.

Brian sat in a booth at Maxie's social club waiting for
Donovan Tucker to arrive. Meeting with Tucker meant
things were about to heat up. The first time was because
a contract had been put on Tracy's life. The last time, it
was because of Cynthia. The information from Tucker
was appreciated, but damn if he wanted to be there. A
look of amazement appeared on Brian's face when
Tucker walked through the door. The man was
impeccably dressed, in a tailor made suit, French cuffed
shirt and Italian leather shoes. "Damn man. What in the
hell has come over you?" Brian grinned.

"Well, you know, a brother has to clean up his life
sooner or later," Tucker replied as he ran his hand over
his neatly groomed beard.

"You look like a high priced lawyer coming through
the door," Brian teased.

Tucker frowned, "Man, you ain't going to the other
side are you?"

Brian frowned, that's the second time today someone
had asked him that question. "Hell no. There are too
many women out here that need a hard working brother
like me," they both laughed.

"I know that's right. I'm trying to get my life right. So,
man—what's up?" Tucker asked as the waiter arrived with
the drinks Brian had ordered.

"The breach at the prison last night was Munford's
doing. The guard was one of his men and so is this man.

We need him covered, but it can't be any of us. He's a detective and will recognize my people."

Tucker looked at the information and nodded. "We'll cover him." The two finished their drinks, wished each other well, and left the bar.

The unmarked vehicle Samuel had been following for the last few hours came to a stop a block away from JD's house. The upscale neighborhood did not have many cars parked on the street, because most of the homes had at least a two car garage. Each block had approximately six homes on each side of the street, giving each home an acre or more between them. Having one parked vehicle on the street might have been inconspicuous, but two would not have been. Samuel decided to park on a side street and walk through the back where the security house sat on the property. Fortunately, the property was in the middle of the block with other homes on both sides making it easy for him to go unnoticed. Since it was late on a Saturday evening, he did not expect anyone to be on guard. When he unlocked the door to the security house, he noticed the computer was up, a cup of coffee was on the desk, and monitors were positioned on the unmarked vehicle he had been following. Whoever was in the office had observed the vehicle and was curious. "That was good," he said while taking a seat. The chair was low and had to be adjusted to fit his height, before he could get comfortable. Reaching over he adjusted one camera to scan wider around the vehicle until he noticed a figure standing off to the right. "Ryan, my girl," he smiled. The two met while he was on protection detail for the woman who was now his wife, Cynthia. Ryan was watching over Cynthia the same as he, just for another purpose. The two began working unofficially together.

Once the case ended, Samuel convinced the woman to come over to his side of the law. Now she was in training to become a part of the Thompson Protection Agency. Her instincts in Cynthia's case were on point then and seemed to be intact now. The zoom on the camera did not reach the inside of the vehicle, but it did make out the license plate number. He pushed a button and captured the still picture. The record button was still capturing the live feed.

A vehicle pulled around the corner and the figure in the vehicle slouched down in an effort not to be seen. He saw Ryan duck back between the houses as Tracy's vehicle turned into the driveway and stopped. She was about to get out of the vehicle when the garage door opened and Ryan stepped out. Samuel smiled, at the woman in her signature jeans and spiked boots. Her actions let the figure in the unmarked vehicle know someone was at the house. Samuel let the camera continue to record while he walked into the main house.

"Hello Tracy," he said then picked up JC. "lil man," he joked.

"Hi, Samuel. How is Cynthia?"

"She is glowing. Where's Ryan?" he asked looking around the house.

"She took Jasmine upstairs to the nursery.

"I'll take JC. All right lil man, you want to walk or do you want a shoulder ride."

"Ride," JC beamed up at the man who was bigger than his daddy.

"Ride it is," Samuel picked the child up giving another two feet to his six-six frame.

"Watch his head," he heard Tracy say as he was walking up the steps. He saw Ryan standing at the window in the upstairs foyer. "Is he still there?"

Ryan never turned around, but answered. "Yep. Do you know who he is?"

"Not, sure, but Brian wants eyes on him 24/7. Your people will be handling that end for us."

She turned and glared at him. "That's an unmarked police car. Munford's at it again?'

"Looks that way. I'm going back to the security house to keep an eye on him. You stay in the house with Tracy and the children."

"Potty Uncle Sammy, potty," JC cried out and began to squirm.

"I'll take him," Ryan offered.

"I'll take care of him. You keep an eye on that car."

Tracy walked up the steps to find Ryan leaning against the wall by the window in the foyer. The archway to the alcove she'd made into her home office was near the area where she was standing. "What are you looking at Ryan," she asked as she stepped into the hallway.

Ryan looked over her shoulder and sighed, "Just looking out the window." Tracy extended her a glass of wine and carried a cup of tea for herself. "Thank you." Ryan smiled and took a sip. "Hmm, that's good. I don't know if I've said this, but you have a lovely home."

Accepting the compliment, Tracy smiled. "Thank you. It's still a work in progress," she stated as she took a seat at the desk in her office.

"I would have never thought of putting an office there. The openness would keep me from working. I'm easily distracted."

"I doubt that Ryan. You're having a conversation with me, but your eyes are on whatever is happening out that window. Is there something I should be concerned about?"

Ryan liked Tracy from the first time she met her. If she had to come over to this side of the law, she was glad it was to protect someone worthwhile. When the time came, Tracy was going to be her protectee and that pleased her. The woman was reserved, welcoming, and a

lot wiser than people gave her credit for. Not one to
sugarcoat anything, Ryan shrugged her shoulders. "We
have a suspicious vehicle parked out front."

"Is he a threat to us?"

"I don't know. But I'm keeping my eye on him until
we know for certain."

Tracy tilted her head to the side and displayed that
signature smile. "I'm sure you will," she almost laughed
as she sipped her tea. "Ryan is an unusual name for a
girl."

"My father wanted another boy, as if five wasn't
enough." She rolled her eyes heavenward. "My mother
said when the doctor told them it was a girl; my father
told him to put me back and bring the boy out."

She smiled, but Tracy got the feeling there was a little
contempt in the statement. "Is that why you chose this
profession, to prove to your father you are just as good as
your brothers?"

"You don't pull any punches, do you?" She laughed
then became thoughtful. "I guess you could say that. But,
this job, sort of fell in my lap when your friend was in
trouble."

"That's right. Brian said you helped Samuel protect
Cynthia. Thank you for that." Tracy sat back in her chair
and crossed her legs. "Are you now here to protect me?"

"To some extent."

"Why?"

"It's not so much for now, as it is for later. Your
husband is an important man for a number of reasons.
Especially since so many people see him as the future for
our country. Some people are uncomfortable with his
stance on a number of issues and the fact that he can't be
bought. So they have to find a way to control him or they
will have to eliminate him. Brian and Samuel's job is to
keep him from being eliminated and my job is to keep
him from being controlled. Anyone that knows JD,

understand the role you have in his life. You are not a trophy wife. You are the woman he loves and those children are his life. If someone got a hold of you or them, they have control over him."

"Jeffrey does love his children," she smiled and turned to her computer.

Something in the way Tracy replied made Ryan wonder if the woman did not know just how much her husband loves her. Anyone with eyes could see it whenever the two were in the same room together. Sensing the discussion was over Ryan retook her vigil over the vehicle parked out front. Moments later, she heard the sound of the computer coming on. Observing the vehicle, she heard the subtle gasp from the office. She glanced over for a second, "You okay?"

The hesitant weak reply came. "Yes,"

Accepting, but not believing the response, Ryan turned her attention back to the window. A few minutes later, Tracy walked out of the office and into the master bedroom down the hallway. The view of her face was only a split second, but Ryan was sure she saw tears in her eyes. When she heard a door close, Ryan walked over to the computer and moved the mouse around to clear the screensaver. On the screen was a story on the internet with a picture of JD and a woman. Examining the image, it looked as if the two were sharing a private moment. Ryan learned long ago to look pass the surface and concentrate on the content. A closer examination of the picture showed the woman was smiling up at him; he was looking at something over her shoulder. If you did not know what to look for, it could appear that something was going on between the two. "Hmm. Someone is trying to cause problems." Ryan stepped away and resumed her place at the window. Her job was to protect Tracy from harm. The woman in the pictures intent was to cause her harm. To her way of thinking, it was her job to keep that woman on her radar.

Tracy washed her face and composed herself the best she could. The constant barrage of pictures hitting the media with this woman and JD was getting to her. Although she and JD had spent the day together and she really believed he loved her, there was always that little doubt that crept into her mind. She understood the woman worked for the campaign, but did she have to be around Jeffrey all the time? There was something about the woman that bothered her even though they had never met. Tonight when Jeffery got home, she was going to talk to him about it. With that decision made, her heart began to beat rapidly. She closed her eyes and prayed she was not about to lose her husband.

Chapter 4

Governor Gavin W. Roberts had it all. He was prosperous, had a beautiful wife and a promising political career. His next move was to run for the State Senate seat his father-in-law, US Senator John Roth, was vacating. The future was looking auspicious until a year ago. All the occupants of hell had descended on his life all at once. First, the partner he had as a rookie on the police force, threatened to kill his friend, JD Harrison if he did not publicly support his bid to become Mayor of the City of Richmond. As a rookie, he'd backed the man by falsifying a police report and from that point on, it had been one cover up after another. It was small things at first, but once Gavin graduated from law school and joined the District Attorney's office the power shift changed. The ex-partner would give him tips on criminal activity, which increased his conviction rate and moved him further up the ladder in the DA's office. The higher his ex-partner moved up the ranks and the more power Gavin gained in the political arena, the more the man demanded. After a few years Gavin felt he was in too deep to pull out.

Then he met a young district attorney that had a zest for doing what's right regardless of the consequences. JD Harrison had a way of making you want to do the right thing, even when he was fresh out of law school. Gavin was elected District Attorney and JD began his career fresh out of law school as one of his assistants, but he would be the first to tell you the young man inspired him and continues to do so, even now. The outside looked at him as JD's mentor, but in all honesty, it was the other way around. He is the Governor now, but he knew JD was going to surpass him in the political arena. There was no doubt in his mind that Jeffrey Daniel Harrison would be President of the United States one day even if JD didn't believe it himself—yet. That was the reason he had to finally stand up to his ex-partner. There was no way he would allow Wilbert Munford to harm the man he believed would be President one day. As long as the man kept his distance from JD he would have had no problems out of Gavin. But once he threatened him and confessed that he had JD's father, James Harrison, shot down in the streets, the line was crossed. Gavin had to take a stand.

He didn't know James Harrison. The man was Munford's partner before Gavin joined the force. But he'd heard a lot about the man. In fact, no one at the station had a bad thing to say about Harrison. They all seemed to have respected the man, except for Munford. According to the rumor mill, Harrison believed in right and wrong. There was no grey area like the one that existed for Munford. What Munford did not understand was that back in the day; Harrison was also a strong believer in the blue-code. Police officers had each other's back, no matter what. As hard as Munford tried to get Harrison on the payroll of local dealers, he'd never turned. The code on the street was honest people can't be trusted and that's the code Munford followed. The deeper he became immersed into the street life, the more of a threat Harrison became. One spring night in May, Munford ordered the drive by shooting of James Harrison leaving behind a widow and two children.

Now, the son of the man whose life he'd snuffed out was his nemesis. His plan was to use Gavin to control JD, but it hadn't worked. Gavin refused to betray the young man he'd come to admire and turned his back on Munford instead. In retaliation, Munford attempted to kill a woman Gavin cared deeply for and almost succeeded, until, as rumor had it, Al "Turk" Day appeared.

Gavin wasn't sure what Day had on Munford. Whatever it was stopped Munford in his tracks and kept him quiet for the last year. But that short period of time, when Munford was wreaking havoc on the city, affected his life considerably. His political life could have been destroyed, but his wife Carolyn, and her unmatched political mind, stepped in and saved his career. But then her life was turned upside down and now it was his turn to help her through a rough time. During her quest to protect him, she discovered that her father had another child. For most families this would be an easy adjustment, but not for Carolyn. The politically savvy, dangerously conniving, extremely beautiful socialite Carolyn Roth-Roberts, first lady of Virginia had turned into a closet drunk. As much as Gavin loved her, he had not been able to penetrate the hurt the discovery rendered. Gavin's future was not so certain now, but he still had to finish out his last year as Governor.

The telephone call from JD and Brian interrupted a quiet afternoon with Carolyn. One that was long overdue and desperately needed. If it had been anyone else, he would have refused the call, but he knew just like him, if JD had a choice, he would be home with his wife, Tracy.

"Governor, Attorney General Harrison, and Mr. Thompson are here. Shall I show them in?" the housekeeper asked.

"Yes, thank you." Carolyn, who sat leisurely by the window looking like the quintessential wife, sat her drink on the table and stood to leave. "You don't have to go. Stay here with me. This shouldn't take long."

"I don't want to deal with JD's condescending looks today. His precious Tracy may object to him being in the same room with me."

Walking over to her from behind the desk where he read his reports, he took her hand. "Let's not go there today. Please."

Carolyn looked up at her husband, whom with each passing day she loved more and smiled. He was the only bright light in her life. "I'll be in the bedroom when you finish. Maybe you should join me," she smiled, slowly stepped away holding on to his hand until the distance was too great to touch.

"I will," he smiled as she opened the side door leading into the back foyer and closed the door behind her.

"Gavin," JD extended his hand as he walked through the door from the opposite side of the room.

"Hello JD. Brian."

"Gavin," Brian replied.

"We have a situation." JD said as he took a seat. Gavin moved behind his desk and sat while Brian remained standing near the door. "A number of unrelated incidents have taken place in the last 48 hours that have prompted me to believe it may be time to initiate an indictment on Munford. The reason I'm coming to you prior to taking any action is the potential impact taking a police chief may have on previous cases."

"What type of incidents are we talking about?"

JD and Brian looked at each other, and then turned back to Gavin. "Al Day was placed in the system under an assumed name. His file was breached last night. The guard that breached the file is the same man that died in the single car accident this morning. Our investigations have found a connection between the guard and Munford. We also found another officer involved with Munford's undercover operations."

"I thought we crippled his operation last year with the situation surrounding Cynthia."

"That's just it Gavin, we don't know how many officers Munford has working with him. This investigation is identifying more officers than we originally thought. The US Attorney General will have to be contacted. The number of cases that could be over turned because of Munford's illegal activities is substantial and some are federal."

"Who handled the investigation?"

"Calvin."

"Good man for this type of case. How many cases to date?"

JD shook his head, "Two fifty-seven at last count."

Gavin looked flabbergasted at his response, he sighed. "Have you placed the call to the Attorney General?"

"No. We have the officer we think may be Munford's head man now under surveillance. Before we take action, we need more on Munford."

Gavin exhaled and shook his head. "Who's handling surveillance?"

"My people," Brian spoke. The two men stared each other down. There was no love lost between them. Neither liked the other. Gavin had a certain level of respect for the job Brian did while he was on his protection detail. But Brian did not and probably never would like Gavin, mainly because of the way he'd treated Cynthia.

Gavin turned back to JD. "Tell me what you have thus far."

Carolyn stood in the hallway long enough to hear JD enter the room. She then closed her eyes exhaled and walked up the back staircase leading to their bedroom. Inside she walked into her closet, pushed the button to activate the rotating shoe shelf, pushed the button to stop it at her selection of red pumps, pulled out the bottle of bourbon she kept hidden and walked back into the bedroom. Taking a glass from the bathroom, she sat on the chaise lounge, poured a drink, closed her eyes and waited for the effect of the smooth liquor to ease the pain. She filled the glass again, downed it, then a third time. Ahhh, there it was, the numbing of the pain inside her chest. Every time she thought about having to share her father, the pain grew sharp. When she thought about sharing him with Tracy Harrison, the pain became unbearable. Why her, of all the fatherless children in this world, why did she have to share with Tracy. The woman had stripped her of everything. The man she wanted, the dream she had and now her father. A boulder the size of Mount Rushmore could have fallen on her head and the impact would not have been as crucial as the day her daddy acknowledged he was Tracy's biological father. She took another drink, and sat back. She hadn't spoken to her father since. When they appeared at social events, she was cordial, but had nothing to say. Gavin tried on numerous occasions to get the two together, but Carolyn just couldn't do it. Her father was the one person in the world whose love she knew was unconditional. She was his baby girl. The papers she found in his safe, changed that in every since of the meaning. Tracy was technically his baby girl. Her children were his grandchildren. That woman and her ghetto-fabulous mother had taken her father from her, now she had nothing. At this point, the only thing that made her feel good now was when Tracy hurt. Yes, she displayed a snake like smile. Hell, if she had to be miserable, she might as well have company.

JD entered his house from the garage, walked through the kitchen and went straight to his office located on the first floor near the front door. Tracy came down the stairs that ended near the front door. She could see when she reached the bottom stairs that Jeffrey was on the telephone. Walking slowly towards his office, she waited in the foyer until he was finished with his call. JD turned on the computer on his desk.

"Jeffrey."

He looked over near the door and smiled. Looking at his wife in her cotton lounge pants and tee-shirt top, she had to be the sexiest woman alive. Her hair was in a ponytail, showing her makeup free face, which gave her such a fresh look. To him, her five-foot four-inch body with curves in just the right places was beyond perfect. But it was her eyes—those doe like eyes, especially when she smiled, that was the sunshine of his life. Standing, he walked over to her. "Hey babe," he kissed her and pulled her into an embrace. "Why are you up so late?"

"I need to talk to you about something."

Holding on to her, he kissed the top of her head. Standing in her slippers, she barely reached his chin. He exhaled at the pleasure of having her in his arms. "It's going to have to be quick babe. I'm expecting a call from Washington."

She looked up at him concerned. "Is there a problem?"

Looking down at her, he wanted to take her upstairs and make love for what was left of the night, but knew he couldn't. He nodded, "There's a situation. But I can't go into it now."

"What did you want to talk about?" He asked as he rubbed her arms.

Before she could answer, Brian came in through the patio door. "JD," he called out.

"In the office," JD replied.

"I just met with Samuel. We have another situation." He stopped when he walked into the office to find, Tracy and JD in an embrace. "Sorry about that man. Hey Tracy."

"Hey Brian." She stepped away from JD. "I'll get out of your way."

JD held onto her. "Brian, could you give us a minute?"

"No, that's okay. We'll talk later," she smiled up at her husband. When he held her, there were no doubts in her mind of his love for her.

"You sure?"

"Yes, I'm sure. You two do whatever you do. I'll be upstairs. Good night Brian."

"Night Tracy," Brian said as he watched her walk out the door. "You are a lucky man."

JD smiled, "I know."

Brian sighed, "The man Samuel followed tonight was parked in front of your house until an hour ago."

"What?" JD all but yelled. "Where in the hell is he now and what do we know about this man?"

Attempting to ease JD's concern, he put his hand up. "We have it under control. I have someone on him. We will know his every move.

A worried JD sat behind his desk. "What in the hell was he doing outside my home with Tracy and the children here?"

"We don't know."

"I don't want Tracy out of this house alone. I don't want the children out of our sight. Mrs. Gordon will be coming in on Monday to work. When she takes the children out, I want someone on them at all times. Who's covering Tracy?"

"Ryan."

"No. I want you and Samuel on Tracy at all times."

"JD let me do my job. Samuel or I will be on you. Ryan, and if need be Magna can handle Tracy and the children."

JD sat forward in his chair and looked at his friend. "I didn't mean it that way. You pledged your life to protect me. And man, I do appreciate it. But my life ends if anything happens to Tracy. I need to know you are protecting my wife"

Brian knew how much his friend loved his wife. It damn near killed him when she was attacked a few years ago. He vowed then never to let anything happen to her again. So far, that vow had put a strain on their marriage. In JD's effort to protect her, he was suffocating her. Each day Brian could see the life draining out of her. If it were up to JD, he wouldn't let Tracy out of his sight. But as the owner of a multi-million dollar company, there were times when she had to take care of her business. After all the couple had been through, Brian understood, this was JD's way of keeping her safe. "All right man. I'll cover Tracy, but Samuel is with you 24/7 and I'm not compromising on that."

After the call from the US Attorney General, JD climbed the steps to the bed-room. He stopped in to see JC and Jasmine, then he continued to his bedroom. Tracy was in the bed asleep on top of the comforter. The sight of her stirred his body to attention, as it always did. But tonight he sat in the chair by the door and just watched her sleep. The news from Brian tonight shattered him more than he let on. Earlier he received a call from the warden at the federal prison where her brother, Al "Turk" Day, was housed. Someone had infiltrated his filing system. The assumed name for Turk was compromised. Now it had to be determined, if the information was shared with anyone. The perpetrator was killed in a vehicle accident, when leaving the prison. Was it just a coincidence, JD didn't think so. The question was, did the person who hired him take him out once the information was received or did one of Turk's people take the man out. Then to be told, a man was parked outside his home, turned JD's world upside down. There was one common denominator in the two incidents—Chief of Police Munford.

Feeling helpless did not work well with JD. Thanks to his father, he had been an expert marksman from the age of ten. They would go to the range at least once a month to practice, it was their time together. Now, he needed that skill to protect his family. He knew Brian would do everything in his power to keep Tracy safe, but he was her husband and if Munford was coming after her to get to Turk, he would have to go through JD first. Sitting forward he rested his elbows on his knees and smiled at the woman hugging his pillow in her sleep. The day he first saw her in his condo, his heart dropped. She was so young and naïve, he knew it was best he keep his distance from her. Years later when a case reconnected them, he knew she was going to be his wife. She caught him off guard and it took him a moment to accept the inevitable, but once he did, she had him hook, line and sinker. The other women in his life couldn't believe he was letting them go for her, but when he looked at Tracy, he saw a person as rare and precious as an African diamond. He saw his life, his future, his world reflected in her eyes. There were times when he wondered if she knew just how much he loved and worshipped the very ground she walked on. One thing was for certain, he would die before he allowed anyone to harm her or their children. With that final thought he went into his walk-in closet and opened the safe that was on the top shelf behind his shoe boxes. Putting the combination in, he pulled out his 9mm and clip. He placed them in the drawer of the night stand and locked it. Afterwards he took his shower, got into bed, and gathered his wife into his arms. The clock showed it was three-fifteen, in four hours he would be up and on his way to another day away from her. He fell asleep wondering if being in this political world was worth it all.

Why can't he ever come home to a clean house, Officer Jonas Gary angrily pushed the chair that was a fraction of an inch off centered. All he asked of her was to keep his house clean, cook a hot meal for him each day and have sex with him every once in a while. Was that too much to ask for? He took a seat and tried to calm down. The chance to finally make it out of the hell he was living was too important to risk over the damn woman he called his wife. All they had to do was clear the weapons through Richmond and he would be a very rich man but, just in case, he had recordings of every conversation and every order, he ever received from Chief Munford. That was his "get out of jail free" card. The thought of working with the gangs ate at him, but if this was what had to be done to get his payday, so be it. His concern was bigger now, Munford assigned him to tail JD Harrison's wife. Why, he did not know. What he did know was that Harrison was not a man to play with. Shaking his head and getting more and more agitated, he walked into the kitchen, opened the oven and his dinner was not there. He slammed the door shut. Why couldn't she do the simple things? He stomped through the house until he reached the bedroom. He reached over snatched his wife's sleeping body from the bed by her hair and dragged her into the kitchen. After working all day he deserved a hot meal. Julianna Gary looked at the man through frightened eyes as she opened the microwave and pulled out the dinner she had wrapped in aluminum foil and placed in a plastic container to keep it warm until he got home. He back handed her for making him search for his food.

Samuel sat outside the house located in a neighborhood he knew to be controlled by two factions; the Eagles and Day gangs. If he was going to be here, he needed to let Tucker know. After making the call to Brian, advising him of his location, Samuel waited until Tucker showed up. No words were exchanged, in fact neither got out of their vehicles. To the average person it was just one car parking and another pulling off.

Tucker placed a call back to Brian, "Eyes are in place. Ears will be up by the morning."

Chapter 5

Mrs. Gordon was in the pantry taking stock of what was there. The shelves were arranged so neatly, with the cereals in alphabetical order, the can vegetables the same and according to height, the condiments neatly stacked and every imaginable juice or soft drink aligned at the lowest level. "That child had too much time on her hands," she chuckled to herself.

"Mrs. Gordon," Tracy called.

"In the pantry. Child, it looks like you are feeding an army up in here. I don't think I'll have to purchase groceries for a year."

"We never know when company is going to stop by and I don't like to be without." Tracy replied with Jasmine on her shoulder and JC standing behind her. "My sister-in-law Ashley is coming by for a visit. She has twins that are just beginning to walk and they seem to be all over the place. I wanted to make sure that was okay with you."

Mrs. Gordon turned and looked at her as if she had lost her mind. "Mrs. Harrison, this is your house. I work for you. You don't have to clear anything with me."

"This is your first day and I didn't want you to get too overwhelmed."

Mrs. Gordon gave her the most incredulous look. "Mrs. Harrison, give me that baby." She took Jasmine from her and then reached down for JC. "You enjoy your company. When Mrs. Brooks gets here give me a holler. I'll come get the babies so you can have a nice visit. Child, I've been taking care of babies all my life. It's the only real enjoyment in the world." Tracy wasn't sure what else she said as the woman took her children and began walking up the stairs. She wasn't sure, but she thought she was being chastised. The doorbell chimed. Tracy opened the door smiling at James and Ashley, each holding one of the wiggling twins.

Ashley put Jayden on the floor and he took off up the steps following Mrs. Gordon. Shaking her head, she laughed, "It's like, let me go—let me go—my little feet can take me places. He doesn't ever want to sit down."

"Any where he goes Jayda has to follow." James added in his rich baritone voice, as he put Jayda down. Sure enough, the little girl followed her brother up the stairs as they watched.

Tracy closed the door behind them. "You know when babies start walking early; they are just getting out of the way for the next one."

"Ha-ha, very funny," Ashley scowled.

James looked offended. "I could use a few more."

"Okay, if you carry them for nine months."

"You two are too funny. Come on back and have a seat." Tracy turned and walked towards the sun-room with the couple following her. "James did you take off from work today?"

"No. I'm actually here on business."

Ashley sat in her favorite chaise lounge chair near the fire-place, while James sat in the Queen Anne chair near the floor to ceiling windows that overlooked the garden and pool house.

Tracy sat on the love seat facing the windows. "Really," the excitement was clear in her voice. "What do you need?" The idea of something to keep her occupied was enticing.

"Campaign business," he clarified. "Sorry about that. I know it's not what you want to hear. But it's that time again."

The deflated look was quite noticeable. "Arrgh!"

James couldn't help but smile, he knew how much she hated campaigning. "I hate putting you through all of this, but if I thought there was a better man to be governor, I would go out and find him, just so you wouldn't have to go through it. Unfortunately, you and I both know, that person is JD."

Tracy sat back and smiled demurely, "I know."

"I also wish I could say this campaign will be easier, but the truth is it will be more difficult and more intrusive than before." He hesitated and looked at Ashley, whose smile encouraged him to continue. "The situation with Senator Roth is bound to come out. We believe it would be better to put the information out early, rather than wait for it to explode in our faces."

"Did Jeffrey ask you to speak to me about this?"

"No, in fact I was hoping you would talk to him. JD is not going to do anything he thinks will make you uncomfortable. We have to get him to see that an inquiry into this would be far more devastating than you and Carolyn answering a few questions."

"Devastating to the campaign, you mean. I can't imagine it being more devastating to Carolyn."

"Tracy," he sympathized, "Everything JD did during that time was out of his concern for you. He had a few choice words for both Senator Roth and I the night we told him. Never once did he waiver on how this would affect you, when the Senator decided to keep this information a secret. You forgave Senator Roth and me. At some point you will have to find a way to forgive JD and move past this."

Tracy responded pensively, "What make you think I haven't forgiven him?"

"The fact that you can't look me in the eyes at this moment. Coupled with the conversation JD had with me last week. You two are so in tuned with each other, yet you walk around on eggshells afraid to hurt each other's feelings. I know this is difficult, but it's my job to make sure that things like this do not interfere with the campaign."

Ashley cleared her throat, "Tracy, more importantly we hate to see you hurting, and when you hurt, so does JD. It seemed the only happy moment you two have shared in the last year was the birth of Jasmine. There was a time when you were a little angry about that."

"I was never angry about Jasmine—never." Tracy stood as she exclaimed. "Jeffrey wasn't there when she was born. He was in some meeting, that he deemed more important than seeing his daughter come into this world. That's what I was angry about." She folded her arms across her chest and stood at the window looking out. She exhaled. "I don't want to cause any problems for Jeffrey during the campaign." She turned back to James. "What he is trying to do is important. Just tell me what you need from me." She replied sounding dejected.

"Tracy," Ashley stood to walk over to her.

Tracy put up her hand dismissing Ashley's protest. "Whatever you need from me, I'll do," she repeated to James. "You need me to travel, or speak to people just put me down."

James stood and looked between the two women, who had been thicker than thieves, since he met them. Neither he nor JD could ever get either one of them to budge when it came to their bond. Now, there seemed to be a wedge coming between them. He knew Ashley had tried on several occasions to get Tracy to open up about the situation concerning her father, but so far, she had not been successful. In fact, JD and Ashley each have mentioned Tracy was becoming more withdrawn. When people were around, that wonderful smile of hers would be in place, but it hadn't reached her eyes in a very long time. He hoped Ashley would be able to get her to open up soon. "I'll keep that in mind." He smiled at his wife, "I have to go. You two have a good visit." He kissed Ashley and hugged Tracy before he took his leave.

As soon as Tracy returned from walking James to the door, Ashley unloaded. "Enough already. I refuse to allow another day to go by with you walking around like a lost puppy. What is going on? There is more to this, than Senator Roth being your father. The only thing that puts you in a stupor is JD. So what did my brother do this time?"

Tracy walked over to the window, then turned back to the woman she loved like a sister and smiled. "Nothing, Jeffrey is fine." Which really wasn't a lie, her husband was fine. Even with the tension in their lives, there was one thing for certain; she loved Jeffrey Daniel Harrison. As disappointed, as she was, there was no mistaking the unconditional love she still had for him.

"Bull!" Ashley literally yelled. "You can give that line to Momma, but I know better. I know you. Hell I lived with you for eight years. Was there when you gave up the booty for the first time and was there when you caught JD and Vanessa. So don't stand there like your world is all rosy. Open up--share."

Tracy rolled her eyes and turned away, but the truth was she needed to talk. It was just difficult to talk to Ashley concerning Jeffrey; after all, he was her brother. With the campaign looming, it would be even worse if the press ever got wind of the discontentment in their home, they would feed on it like a pack of rats attacking a piece of cheese. Talking, even to Ashley was difficult. "Who are you supposed to be Oprah or Dr. Phil?" Tracy teased as she flung herself down onto the sofa and grabbed a pillow.

"At the moment I will be whoever you need me to be. Oh, wait a minute, I take that back, neither of them look as good as me." She thought for a moment, "I got it. I'll be Tyra. She is tall, curvaceous and almost looks as good as me."

Shaking her head with a light chuckle, "And you call Jeffrey conceited," Tracy replied.

"Well, in my case it's true. But it made you smile." Ashley became serious. She sat down on the sofa next to Tracy and took her hands that were lying on top of the pillow. Rubbing her hands together was a nervous action for Tracy. Ashley knew the signs very well.

"Look at me Tracy." She could see the unshed tears brimming at the edge of her eyelids. "There are only a few things I know for certain. As conceited, chauvinistic, selfish, and big headed as my brother is—he loves you. The thing is he knows you love him too, and in knowing that he takes you for granted. That much I know. Now, you tell me the rest."

Tracy squeezed her friend's hand as a teardrop fell. Shaking her head and swallowing back the lump that was building in her throat. "I don't know where to start."

"The beginning is usually a good place." The uncertainty was so clear on her friend's face and all Ashley wanted to do was wipe away the hurt and fear. She raised her hand and wiped the tear that trickled down Tracy's face. "It's me Tracy. You can tell me anything and I will do all I can to help. You know I love you and JD. Please let me help."

The children could be heard running around in the play room upstairs giggling. Tracy had missed the joys of being a child, carefree and loving life. Her childhood was anything but joyous, but she was determined to make sure her children enjoyed theirs. That meant putting her feelings aside and keeping them in a loving environment. But it was getting more and more difficult. The last year had been devastating on her marriage and as a result, she simply did not believe her husband loved her anymore. She knew he cared, but love—was something altogether different.

"Come with me." Tracy and Ashley walked up the stairs to her office. She sat at the computer and turned it on. Ashley pulled up a chair beside her and watched as Tracy opened a file marked private. Tracy sat back and allowed Ashley to review the file. She heard the gasp from Ashley and saw her body tense as she moved from picture to picture.

"Have you talked to JD about these pictures?"

"No."

"Why the hell not?" she yelled.

Tracy looked forlornly at her friend. The reality of her life being sucked out of her materialized. She no longer had any idea who she was or what role she played other than giving birth to Jeffrey Harrison's children. In fact, she was certain some people would have been better off if she had never existed. Knowing how that must sound she kept those thoughts to herself. But it was difficult not to think, her brother Turk, would not be incarcerated if he had not felt the need to protect her. The man she once knew as her father would still be alive. Her mother definitely would have lived a happier life. And Jeffrey would not have to deal with the negative publicity of her being his wife as he put in his bid for Governor.

Ashley took her hand, "Tracy, why haven't you asked JD about the pictures?" she demanded. Tracy turned to her with the biggest crocodile tears Ashley had ever seen.

"I don't want to lose my husband. This is the only life I know is mine. I would be lost without Jeffrey and the children."

"He's in pictures with another woman and you are worried about losing him. Do I have this right?" Tracy nodded, but before the motion was completed, Ashley jumped up with so much force the chair sailed backwards. "Where did the pictures come from and who in the hell is she?"

"I don't know," Tracy pensively replied.

"It's time you found out and when was the last time you went to Jeffrey's office for a visit? These pictures were taken in his office."

"I've never gone to Jeffrey's office. I don't like to interfere when he's working."

"You don't...." Ashley was so outdone she couldn't finish her statement. She took a breath. "You haven't made your presence known to those heifers in his office?"

"Ashley, they're not heifers," Tracy shook her head.

"You're right, they're not, they're worse. They are barracudas and you are giving your husband to them on a platter." Ashley grabbed Tracy by the hand, pulled her into the bedroom, and did not stop until she reached the closet. "You sit your ass down until I find the right outfit." Tracy started to walk away, but Ashley gave her a look that dared her to move. Satisfied Tracy was not going to make her become violent; Ashley began searching the closet and fussing at the same time. "It ain't JD that needs to make a change—it's you. Walking around here as if you belong in the shadows while the vultures are circling. Vultures—I tell you—Vultures. And they will eat you and your husband alive if you let them.

But, I got something for them." She pulled out a red dress and smiled. She gave the dress to Tracy, "Go put this on."

"Ashley..." Tracy began to say something but was stopped.

"You say you don't want to lose your husband. Well, it's time for you to let the women in his office know, they got competition at home."

"What is Jeffrey going to think when I just show up at his office?"

"If you work it right, he will not have a mind to think. His concentration will be on you. The next word out of his mouth once he sees you in this dress should be "cancel all of my appointments for the rest of the day." Now go get dressed. And take your hair out of that damn ponytail."

JD sat in his office listening to Calvin give the update on the Munford investigation. Rossie was gaining more of his respect each day. The young man was relentless with gathering facts. With each witness he interrogated, he was compiling more information without giving any indication why he was asking questions. Listening intently to Calvin explain the strategic steps Rossie had taken, he never noticed that Madison Gresham, his political advisor had taken a seat on the edge of his desk and crossed her legs. The short skirt that clung to her body displayed a good portion of her upper thigh. But JD's mind was on the information being presented.

"We have to connect Munford to The Eagles if we want this case to stick," Calvin interjected from a seat at the conference table.

"Once we make that connection we will turn the information over to Homeland Security."

"That could be politically dangerous JD," Madison stated as she touched his arm.

"Politically dangerous or not, it's going to be done." He turned towards her in his chair as he replied and saw Tracy standing in the doorway in the most provocative dress he had ever seen and damn if she didn't look good. His mind went completely void of the conversation and was now zoomed in on his wife.

She smiled at his response, for it was exactly what she needed. However, it was difficult to dismiss the woman, who she recognized from the photographs, sitting on her husband's desk with her crotch practically in his face. The Tracy of old wouldn't say anything—but things were about to change. "There are several chairs in this room. I would think you would be more comfortable in one of them." She said to the woman. As JD walked towards her, he looked back to see what she was referring to.

"Oh no, I'm comfortable here," The woman replied with a smile.

"Are you—well I'm not. Please remove your behind from my husband's desk."

Calvin raised an eyebrow, surprised, but proud of Tracy's demand.

The woman looked from Tracy to JD, who was staring at his wife not paying one iota of attention to the conversation taking place. "I apologize I meant no disrespect. We're a little informal around here."

JD turned to see Madison glaring at Tracy. Whatever was said between the two wasn't good. However, at the moment, his wife had his attention and he could care less what pissed Madison off. He kissed Tracy. "Hey babe, what are you doing here?"

She looked up to see the look of desire in his eyes. That look saved him and the woman that was sitting on his desk. "I thought I would finally come to see where you work and entice you into taking me to lunch."

That sexy "vote getting" smile appeared, "I have no idea what is on my calendar, but for you I'll clear it."

"We have a lunch meeting planned JD," Madison intervened.

"Cancel it. I'm having lunch with my wife." The two stared at each other dismissing the fact that other people were in the room. Neither caught the daggers being sent in Tracy's direction. But Calvin did.

JD turned to Madison, "Babe, this is Madison Gresham. She is a political advisor from the campaign."

The mask was back in place on Madison face. "Please call me Mattie," she extended her hand.

Tracy was reluctant, but took it. "Ms. Gresham, Why are you here if you are a part of the campaign? Why aren't you at campaign headquarters with James?"

"I've been wondering the same thing," Calvin said as he stood and hugged Tracy. "How have you been?" She returned his smile. "Aw, you are killing me with that smile. If you ever want to divorce him, I'm yours."

"You're married fool," JD reminded him laughing.

"Oh yeah, that's right."

"How are Jackie and little Calvin?" Tracy asked.

"Jackie is as beautiful as ever and the boy is taking over the house. I'm going to take Mattie out of your hair. We can discuss any issues this case may have on your political campaign."

"That's really something JD and I would need to discuss," Madison countered.

"You can discuss that with Calvin. Whatever he says goes." If JD had looked a little closer, he would have noticed the condescending look.

"All right," Madison reluctantly conceded and followed Calvin out of the room.

Tracy looked up at her husband, "So, are there more of her involved in the campaign."

"I'm sure there are."

"Should I be concerned?"

JD found himself laughing. "The way you are wearing that dress, I'm the one that should be concerned. How many heads turned when you walked in?" He asked as he pulled her into his arms.

"Since my eyes were only looking for you I didn't notice."

This was the first time Tracy had come to his office. He knew without a doubt that word of a woman with her body being in the building was spreading like wildfire. When they walked out of the office, he anticipated there would be an unusual number of employees near the elevator to see who she was. He beamed with pride, after just giving birth six weeks ago his wife could still turn heads. Suddenly his thoughts grew serious, "I'm glad you came. I don't like the tension between us. I accept full responsibility for it. But I need your love to keep me strong. It kills me inside knowing that I've hurt you."

"I share in the blame; I'm not handling the situation too well. It's time for me to meet with Carolyn and Senator Roth. A decision has to be made on how we are going to handle this. We can't allow this to affect your campaign. It's time for me to take charge of my life. And my first priority is to take you home and show you just how much I love you."

"Really," he smiled. "I have a better idea." For the first time in a long time, he saw a flicker of a twinkle in her eyes. "I could simply lock the door and demonstrate all the things flowing through my mind that I'd like to do to your body right here. Just you," he kissed her eyelids "and me," he kissed the tip of her nose, "and this dress."

"That would certainly give your office something to talk about." She grew serious as she stared into his eyes. "I love you Jeffrey. But there are some things you and I need to talk about beginning with you and I making decisions regarding our life together, Mr. Macho-man."

JD laughed as they turned to walk out the office door, "Baby you are wearing the wrong dress for a discussion, but I will do my best to keep my hands off you while we talk." She smiled up at him as they walked arm in arm to the elevator.

"Mrs. Langston, I'm gone for the day."

"Yes, Mr. Attorney General," she replied with a knowing smile.

JD looked around. There were four groups of men at least three deep in conversation as they reached the elevator. He beamed proudly as Rossie approached him.

"That's you Mr. H?"

"ADA Rossie Brown—my wife Tracy."

They shook hands, "It's an honor to meet you," Rossie stated then turned to JD, and gave him a pound. "I ain't mad at you man, I ain't mad at you at all."

"Thank you Rossie. Now get your eyes off my wife."

"No disrespect Mrs. H, but you got it. Whatever it is— you got it."

Tracy returned the young man's infectious smile. "Thank you," she replied as the elevator arrived. The two climbed aboard and the doors closed. JD could hear the cheers as the elevator descended. "You know the males on my staff will not get any work done for the remainder of the day because of you."

Tracy stood in front of him and began to remove his tie. "Neither will their boss," she replied as she pulled his lips to hers.

"I'm out of here," Madison said as soon as they reached the hallway after leaving JD's office. She turned to walk towards the elevator, but Calvin took her elbow to stop her progress. "No. I think you and I need to have a conversation." He turned to Mrs. Langston, who'd been with JD since he joined the district attorney's office ten years ago. "Mrs. Langston is anyone in the conference room?"

"No, it's clear. May I join this conversation?"

"I wouldn't have it any other way," Calvin replied.

"Both of you will be talking to yourself, because I'm not going anywhere with you." Madison attempted to pull away, but Calvin's grip tightened.

"Oh yes you are," he said and pulled her through the doors. Mrs. Langston closed the double doors behind them. Calvin released her as soon as they reached the room. He slammed the files he was holding on the table. "Whatever game you are playing, find someone else. JD is married and as you can see happily married. I'm sure he will be the first to tell you how much he loves his wife, in fact, I've heard him say that very thing in your presence several times. Now, JD is a gentleman and he ignores the little flirtatious moves you make on him, but I don't."

"And neither do I," Mrs. Langston added in her quiet, "I mean business" demeanor. "Allow me to add this, from this moment on, anytime you wish to see Mr. Harrison in this office, you are to clear it through me in advance. There will be no more just showing up whenever." She took a step closer to the young woman. "If I ever witness you disrespecting Tracy again, you will think Attila the Hun sat on your ass. Do I make myself clear?"

Madison gave them a contemptuous smile, "Neither of you has what it takes to get JD to the governor's office. If you did I would not be here. It's clear—very clear to me that he is an ambitious man and will do whatever it takes to make it to the top. I plan to assist him in any—any way that I can. I don't care if either of you or his wife likes it. Now the next time either of you attempt to try and stop me, you will pay dearly" She stepped closer to

Mrs. Langston, "Do I make myself clear." She smirked and walked out of the room.

Calvin and Mrs. Langston stared at each other. "I must be missing something," Mrs. Langston commented.

"That makes two of us. But I don't want her in this building alone with JD under any circumstances. In the mean-time, I'll have a talk with James to find out exactly who she is connected to and who placed her on this campaign."

Chapter 6

Campaign headquarters was located inside prime real estate in downtown Richmond. James, who named it after his wife, The Ashley, owned the building. While most of the offices within the ultra plus ten-story building were leased out, the second floor housed Thompson Security Agency, Brian's business. The third floor housed Brooks Realtors, which was owned by James sister, Nicole Brooks. The first floor consisted of the local campaign suite of offices, a 1200 capacity ballroom, a restaurant, a few conference rooms and a spa, all owned by James. There is a private parking and entrance located at the back of the building, which offered valet parking.

James sat in the conference room at the round cherry wood table listening intently to Calvin, Douglas, Senator Roth, and Brian as they waited for JD and Samuel to arrive. The men were personal advisors to JD and he trusted all of them completely. This group of men were the inner realm. No decisions were made without each of them having a voice at the table. Tonight was the beginning of many meetings that would take place over the coming months as they prepared for the Governor's campaign.

"This campaign will have to concentrate heavily in the southwest. That's an area of weakness for him," Senator John Roth stated as they reviewed the large map of Virginia on the 50 inch monitor on the wall. From the computer console at the back of the room, James circled the area the Senator was referencing, and highlighted it in yellow on the screen.

"Hmm, maybe not. A few years ago JD handled a case in Roanoke that brought a lot of attention," Calvin commented. "If I remember correctly, he brought home the bodies of a number of children to parents in that region. They will certainly recognize the name. I think an area of concern maybe the beach front; the republicans seem to have a strong hold there,"

"Is there a way we could remind the people in Roanoke of the case?" Douglas asked.

James shook his head. "JD would see it as trying to benefit some way from the children's deaths and that could back fire. We need to find another way to get name recognition there."

"As for the beach front area, I say put JD on the beach in swimming trunks. It'll drive the women crazy. The women love those dimples and his smile," Calvin laughed.

"Then put Tracy on the beach in a thong bikini." Brian added with a smirk, "That will certainly capture the male vote, democrat, and republican." The men around the table laughed in agreement.

"You need to get your mind off women—at least the ones connected to this campaign, including Pearl." James stated, "You're lucky Samuel hasn't found out about you and his sister."

"What?" Brian asked with a guilty look. "We had a mutually satisfying friendship with benefits."

"Tell the Lassiter brothers and see what they think of you, their sister and that friendship with benefits," Douglas laughed.

"Hey somebody has to satisfy the single women. All of ya'll are connected at the hip," Brian explained. Calvin and Jackie, James and Ashley, JD and Tracy and you and Karen," he said to Douglas.

James looked over at Douglas with a surprised expression. "Karen Holt?" he asked.

Douglas looked at Brian as if he could have cut out his tongue. Karen was previously James deputy when he worked at Special Services. When he resigned to take over JD's campaign for Attorney General, Karen became the director. It was Douglas that helped her get over an abusive marriage and now he was hoping to become a permanent part of her life. But all of that was supposed to be kept under wraps. "Karen and I are friends, no benefits involved," Douglas added for Karen's sake.

James smiled, "That's nice man. She could use a good man in her life. Now, if we could get back to the business at hand. Daniel could help with the southwest and Gavin could assist with the Virginia Beach area. If they would line up a rally or two and get a crowded together, JD can get them to listen."

"Who am I getting to listen?" JD asked as he walked into the room with Samuel behind him.

Everyone stood and shook his hand then retook their seats. Samuel closed the door and took a seat in an empty chair near the door. JD turned to him, "You need to be at the table," he then turned back to the group. "What are we working on?" Samuel looked at Brian, who nodded his confirmation that he should be in on the decisions. He was now a part of the inner realm.

"Daniel's working southwest on behalf of the campaign and Gavin's helping with the Virginia Beach area," James answered.

"I spoke with Daniel," JD stated. "He has decided to make another run at Lt. Governor. As for Gavin, he's dealing with a lot at home. I'm not sure what his intentions are at this time."

"He's making a run for my seat," Senator Roth announced.

"You are definitely stepping down?" James asked shaking his head. "It will be difficult imagining Virginia politics without you."

"It's time." John Roth stated as he sat forward at the table and clasped his hands together. All the men sat forward to hear what the man and, in some cases, their mentor had to say. "The last thirty years of my life have been devoted to public service. Until this year, I have never regretted any moment. This year, things changed." He looked at JD and James. "The decision I made concerning my daughters was wrong. Now, my fear is that the decision has damaged my relationship with both, Carolyn and Lena. I don't know what to say about Tracy." He looked away. "In addition, it could have an impact on this campaign. In a month or two, I will be announcing my retirement from public service. But know I will be in the background all the way until you take the White House." He smiled at JD. "You are a natural son. The concept is overwhelming, I know. But it's destiny and it's time for you to accept it." Addressing the entire table, he continued. "This campaign we are putting together is not about the Governor's race. It's about the next level, the White House. I've claimed this election on your behalf," the men at the table laughed. "The directive now is to make the connections needed across the country with those you will need in six years to do the job of running this country. Our mission now is twofold. Stack the House and Senate with strong people to carry out the agenda put in place for the country and then, elect Jeffrey Daniel Harrison as President of the United

States of America. If there is anyone at this table that doesn't see the vision for the future, now is the time to step away." No one made a motion to move. "Very well," the Senator nodded his head and smiled. "It's time to make a change."

"The first step," James chimed in, "is to win Virginia."

JD listened and hoped the fear he was feeling inside did not show on his face. It was humbling to think the men at the table believed in him enough to want to send him to the White House. How arrogant could they all be to think such a thing could happen? The thought caused a smile to crease his face as he looked around. The men at the table had large enough egos, that if it could be packaged, it would feed every hungry family around the world. Calvin Johnson was one of the most intelligent men in the country with academic records to back it up. Douglas Hylton had an international network of promoters and entertainers to help with spreading the word across the country. Then there is Brian Thompson, the protector of them all. With him and his FBI connections, JD never had to worry about his or the family's safety. Samuel Lassiter brought the international security into play, with his connections to other countries and Homeland Security. The man already had clearance levels JD was probably unaware existed. James Brooks had a family history of making powerful men throughout history. With unlimited wealth, intelligence, and commitment, the man was a power broker with finances. Then there is Senator John Roth. The man had been a fixture in his life for as long as JD could remember. As a young boy, there were only a few Sundays that Senator Roth and his father wouldn't be at the dinner table discussing politics and world affairs. Once Senator Roth told him, his father had always kept him on the straight and narrow. Since his father's death, the man had been a mentor and father figure to JD and now, he was actually his father-in-law.

JD stood and walked over to the windows that lined one entire wall from the floor to the ceiling. Placing his hands in his pockets, he looked out over the City. His father loved the City of Richmond. It was rich with history, good, and bad. It was once the capitol of the Confederacy, standing against freedom of slaves. Now it was a mixing pot, welcoming all races and nationalities. It was the first state to elect a Black Governor, Douglas L. Wilder.

JD's father dedicated his life to this City. Now, he was being asked to do the same thing, but on a much larger scale. Was he ready for the challenge? He looked down at the floor, then turned to the men staring expectantly at him. "The first thing we are going to do is have a press conference announcing publicly Senator John Roth is Tracy's father. I want Carolyn and Tracy together. I also want you," he looked up at the Senator, "to make the announcement. Then, I'm going to become Governor of Virginia." Before he could say anything more; the men turned to each other and began discussing strategy. JD's confirmation was all they needed to spring into action. Senator Roth walked over to JD and shook his hand. "I'm proud of you son. Now, it's time to get to work."

Tracy had the presence of mind to call ahead before arriving to visit Carolyn. Now, if she could get her nerves to cooperate things would be fine. The history between the two women had been volatile to say the least. It was time to put that behind them and move forward. "Whew, I pray this goes well." Tracy said as she pulled into the private entrance to the governor's mansion.

"There is no reason it shouldn't. You're just going to talk to the woman," Ryan stated as she gave the guard at the gate her credentials.

"If only it were that simple," Tracy murmured.

"You've been cleared," the guard announced. "Just pull around to the back. Someone will meet you there."

"Thank you," Tracy smiled. "One hurdle down—twenty more to go."

She parked the car and walked up to the door with Ryan behind her. "No matter what you hear, don't come in."

"The boss isn't going to be happy if something happens to you in there."

"It's the mansion, what could happen?"

"Two women fighting over the same man has led to murder on a number of occasions."

Tracy frowned at the young woman just as the door opened. "Mrs. Amelia. What are you doing here?" she asked, surprised to see the woman.

Amelia stepped aside to let the women in. "I came over to help Ms. Carolyn a few months back. Let me take your coats." Tracy complied.

"I'll hold on to mine," Ryan said as she surveyed the foyer.

Amelia looked at the woman dressed in a leather jacket, jeans, spiked heel boots with the short hair cut, then looked at Tracy dressed in a light grey cashmere sweater, and dark grey dress slacks with her hair down around her shoulders and a strand of pearls. What a contrast between the two women. "I was happy to receive the message that you were coming over. What took you so long?"

Tracy looked confused as they followed Amelia through the foyer. "I'm sorry."

Amelia gave the coat to the butler and turned back to Tracy. "I expected you to come sooner and so did your father."

Tracy turned, "Ryan would you mind giving us a minute?"

"No," Ryan replied as she continued to survey the rooms. "Is it okay if I walk through? I've never been to the governor's mansion before."

Amelia smiled at the eagerness of the unexpected request. "Not at all. Mr. Helms will give you a tour. She nodded at the butler and he put his arm out and waited for Ryan to take it.

Ryan looked over her shoulder at Tracy. "You're sure you will be okay here?"

Smiling, Tracy replied, "I'm sure." As the two walked off, she turned to Amelia.

"The Senator told me about the situation. He knew that it would be you that extended the olive branch. So he told me to expect you. I wish it had been sooner."

"You seem concerned, is there a problem?"

Amelia exhaled, "Come with me." They walked over to the wrought iron staircase leading to the second floor. "Governor Roberts is very good with Carolyn and when he's home, she does well. However, when he is away, like now, things get a little ugly."

"What things Amelia?"

"This has been a rough morning. I'll let you see for yourself. You are a caring woman Ms. Tracy. You are stronger than Carolyn and I expect you to help your sister through this."

Tracy stopped when they reached the landing of the second floor. Amelia had taken a few steps ahead of her before she realized Tracy wasn't next to her. "Is Carolyn still drinking?"

"Yes."

"How much?"

"A few bottles a day when the Governor isn't home. He's been in Washington for a few days now." Amelia walked back to Tracy. "She has no one to turn to. Her mother hasn't given a damn about her since she was a child. The only person she had was the Senator. Now she has to share him with you. I know some of the things she has done to you in the past. But now—you two are going to need each other more than you will ever know. Helping her is helping yourself."

The hesitation wasn't that she did not want to help. The hesitation was dealing with her demons from the past. Her father—the man she thought was her father would drink and become violent. The day he disappeared was one of the worst in her life and she just wasn't sure if she had the strength to help anyone out of this situation. "I don't know if I can help," she reluctantly replied.

"See, that's where you are wrong. You are the only one that can."

Tracy looked at the woman with questioning eyes. She didn't know what she could do. "I'll try," she finally said.

Amelia smiled. "Come on child. It's going to be a long day. We might as well get started." She opened the double doors at the end of the hallway then stepped back. When Tracy walked inside, she closed the door.

The room was lovely. It appeared to be a sitting room, with several white antique high back chairs, a sofa with Victoria backing and a table, all surrounding a fireplace. On the opposite wall were pictures of Gavin and Carolyn at different functions. Tracy had to smile at them. The two had such a rocky start, but it seemed they have finally become a couple. Bringing her attention back to the present, Tracy walked through the opening that led into another room. "Carolyn?" she called out.

"What in the hell are you doing in my house?"

Tracy turned to the door where the voice came from and could not believe her eyes. The shell of a woman standing before her could not be Carolyn Roth-Roberts. "Carolyn?"

"And I ask again what in the hell are you doing in my house?"

"I came to see you," Tracy calmly replied.

"Well I don't want to see you. Get out." Carolyn walked by her and stumbled over her own foot. Tracy reached out to keep her from falling on the floor, but Carolyn pushed her hand away. "I don't need your help!" she snapped.

"Carolyn," Tracy started almost at a loss for words. "What's—what's going on with you?"

"Nothing another drink won't cure," she snarled then walked into the other room to a cabinet next to the bed. She took a bottle of brown liquor from the cabinet and began to pour a drink.

Tracy didn't know a lot about alcoholics, but she did know that the last thing Carolyn needed was another drink. And from the looks of things, this was not going to be easy. She took a deep breath, stepped out of her heels and walked over to the woman that clearly needed some intervention. She took the bottle from Carolyn's hand, some of it spilled on the carpet. "You don't need this."

Tracy turned to walk away but Carolyn grabbed the back of her hair and pulled her backwards. "Bitch if you don't give me my bottle I'm going to whip your ass."

A shocked Tracy pulled away and turned back to Carolyn. She was sure she saw daggers coming from Carolyn's eyes. "I'm not giving you this bottle." Then she reached out and snatched the glass from her. "And you don't need this either."

Before Tracy could take a step, Carolyn tackled her to the floor grabbing for the bottle. It took Tracy a minute to take in what had happened. When Carolyn got off her and crawled on the floor on her hands and knees to the bottle of liquid that was spilling out of the bottle and began trying to lick it up Tracy knew things were just as bad as Amelia said. Tracy got up off the floor, walked over to the door, opened it, and yelled. "Amelia!"

"Yes."

"Get Ryan up here. Call the Governor and let him know his wife will be staying with me until his return. Then call my house and tell my housekeeper to prepare the guest room." Tracy turned to go back into battle, but stopped abruptly. "Oh, tell her to take all the alcohol out of the house and put it in the pool house."

"Yes ma'am," Amelia smiled knowingly.

"I wouldn't smile if I were you. While you are packing a bag for Carolyn, pack one for yourself. You're staying at my house until Gavin comes home."

"But...."

"But nothing, I have two children at home. I don't have the time or patience to deal with three. Now you have a choice. Accept my help the way I'm willing to give it or refuse it and I can go on with my life." Tracy stared at the woman.

"I'll pack a bag."

"That's what I thought," Tracy replied and closed the door.

Looking at Carolyn sitting in the corner turning the bottle up to her lips, took her to another level of angry. This woman has it all. A loving husband, beauty, wealth, everything at her disposal and she is drowning her sorrows in a bottle. All because she found out that, her father has another child. Tracy pushed the sleeves of her sweater up her arms. "Bath time Carolyn."

"Go to hell Tracy," Carolyn replied and took another drink.

Tracy walked over, grabbed her hair, and pulled her out of the chair. "You first." She said as she dragged the woman kicking and screaming across the room to the bathroom.

Ryan ran through the door with her gun drawn and began to laugh at the sight. "What in the hell are you doing?"

"Trying to get her into the shower. Grab her feet."

Ryan holstered her weapon and did as she was told. "This is the first lady, I take it."

"It is," Tracy replied as she took another hit from Carolyn's swinging arms. "Knock her out!" Tracy yelled.

"What?" Ryan asked, shocked at the request.

"I said knock her out. You can do that—can't you?" Ryan dropped Carolyn's feet, drew back, and punched the woman. Tracy looked incredulously at Ryan. "I didn't mean like that. I meant like Mr. Spock does on TV with the arms and neck thing."

"Oh—sorry," Ryan shrugged her shoulders. "Well she's out."

Tracy was so out done. They both laughed. "That she is. Let's get her undressed and in the shower."

With each passing visit, Tracy's respect for Ryan was building. Not only did she help her with the guards at the mansion when they questioned why the first lady was in the backseat, she also carried Carolyn in the house and helped put her to bed. Now, Tracy has the chore of convincing her friends to help put an intervention together for a woman she knew none of them liked. But there was something that made her want to try. At this point, she hadn't given any thought as to how she was going to explain any of this to Jeffrey. Walking into the kitchen, Mrs. Gordon looked at her and laughed. "I don't believe you child. You got another woman under the same roof with your husband. Not just any woman, a

woman you know had a thing for your husband. How do
you think he is going to feel?"

The woman must be reading my mind. "Jeffery is
going to support my efforts."

"Ha. Like hell."

The doorbell rang as Tracy opened her mouth to
respond. She looked at the door then back at Mrs.
Gordon. "It would help if you were a little more
supportive." She turned and opened the door.

"Hey, you said it was an emergency, so I picked up
Roz and Cynthia on the way." Ashley said as she rushed
through the door. "Did you see more pictures or what?"

"No, nothing like that. But I do need you guys—all of
you." Roz walked through the door and held it open for
a very pregnant Cynthia.

"Okay, this better be good. I think I have a middle
line backer in here."

Tracy smiled brightly at her friend. Of all of them,
seeing Cynthia pregnant and happy was one of her
greatest joys. "You are radiant." She hugged her.

"What's going on Tracy? You sounded so serious."
Roz asked.

"We have a situation and I need your help. Especially
yours Cynthia."

"Okay, you got it. What do you need?"

"Well, it's not so simple. I need you to put Carolyn
back together again."

Cynthia's brow raised and she gave her friend an
incredulous look. "What?"

The other women echoed the same sentiment.
"Come with me. I'll show you what I'm talking about."
Tracy ran up the steps and her friends followed. Cynthia
took a little longer than the others did, but she eventually
made it up the steps to where the women stopped in
front of one of Tracy's guest rooms. "Now, I'm going to
warn you, this may shock you a little." Tracy inhaled and

opened the door. "Amelia, would you give us a minute." Amelia looked at the women and shook her head, then left the room.

Ryan sat at the table in the corner working on her laptop and looked up as the women walked in. "Well, well, well. The Calvary is here. This ought to be interesting."

Tracy frowned at Ryan, who only raised an eye-brow at her. "You're not helping."

"Mrs. H. you're going to need more than my help when Mr. H. finds out what you are up to."

"What in the hell happened to Carolyn?" Roz asked looking at Tracy.

"Ryan accidently hit her."

Cynthia began to laugh, as did Ashley. "Accidently?" Ashley asked.

"Well, she was struggling while I was trying to get her to take a shower and I asked Ryan to knock her out. But I didn't mean for her to do it with her fist." Cynthia was still laughing. Tracy looked at her and frowned. "Stop laughing before you wake her up."

Ashley was trying not to laugh, but she asked with a chuckle, "So—you what, brought her here to take a shower?"

"Well, let's step outside," Tracy whispered. After closing the door, she explained all that took place.

"So you kidnapped the first lady?" Ashley asked still trying to stifle her laugher.

Cynthia was beside herself, bending over holding her stomach laughing uncontrollably. Tracy put her hands on her hips and whispered a shout, "Will you stop that?"

"Tracy," Roz exhaled, "Why did you bring her here?"

"I want to help but I'm not sure how. She has been drinking very heavily and I'm afraid she's going to hurt herself if we don't intervene."

Ashley sobered and stared at Tracy. "You have got to be joking."

Tracy looked at her with unshed tears in her eyes. "Have you really gotten a good look at her? We have to clean her up."

"We who?" Cynthia asked, finally calming now. "I don't believe you." She put her hands on her hips, "You call me over here to help that heifer. You have lost your mind."

"Ignore her," Roz raised her hand. "What's wrong with Carolyn? Why is she drinking?"

Tracy exhaled. "Last year Carolyn and I found out we are sisters." Cynthia was walking towards the staircase but stopped and turned back to Tracy in shock. Roz's mouth was wide open. Tracy took a seat and continued. "During the time Jeffrey decided to run for Attorney General, they ran a background check on me. James and Jeffrey uncovered the fact that Senator Roth is my biological father. They decided to keep the information to themselves, but somehow Carolyn found out. Needless to say, she was not happy and she began drinking."

"Who told you this?" Cynthia asked still not believing.

"Carolyn did—at your wedding," Ashley replied.

"My wedding! Carolyn wasn't at my wedding."

"Yes, she was. Not only was she there, she caused a scene like you would not believe."

"Where was I?" Cynthia asked.

"In happily ever after land," Roz answered then looked at Tracy. "How do you feel about this?"

"It doesn't bother me. But see, Carolyn has been the only child all her life. Now she feels like she has to share her father with me—of all people."

"Tell me you are not feeling sorry for her," Cynthia rolled her eyes.

"I don't feel sorry for her, but I do understand. And whether I want to accept it or not, she is my sister."

"Half-sister," Cynthia clarified.

"All right, half-sister." Tracy sighed. "But she still needs our help."

"I'll help you kick her behind and move on, if that's what you need," Cynthia offered.

"I would prefer you help me get her hair back into shape and her dressing back on point. Roz, she will not eat, do you think you could help with that? And Ashley I need you to set her straight. Of all of us, you are the one that she fears the most."

"Not, anymore." Ashley looked at Cynthia remembering the fight between the two women and laughed. "I think Floyd Mayweather Jr. over there," she point to Cynthia, "has taken the rights to that title."

Roz had to laugh, "I have to agree. In fact, I think Cynthia is the one person who could pull Carolyn out of this funk."

Cynthia looked at her as if she had lost her mind. Then she looked at the expressions on Tracy and Ashley's faces and shook her head. "All of you have lost your minds if you think for one minute I would expend any energy to help Carolyn Roth-Roberts. Have you all forgotten how she's treated us in the last four years?"

"No, I haven't forgotten, but I have forgiven her and you should do the same." Tracy stated. "In fact I agree with Roz. I think you should be thankful to her."

"What in the hell for?"

"Well," Ashley chimed in, "If it wasn't for Carolyn you wouldn't be with Samuel today. You would probably still be hung up on Gavin."

"How do you figure that?"

"If Carolyn had not married Gavin, you may have." Roz said as she folded her arms across her chest. "Now, from what I know about Samuel, I don't think he would mess around with a married woman."

"I know he wouldn't," Ashley sneered. "If you had married Gavin would you have ever experienced your world standing still when Samuel looks at you?"

Cynthia looked around at her friends, "None of what you've said convinces me that I should be willing to help Carolyn."

"Then do it for Jeffrey. He is going to announce his candidacy for Governor soon and we have decided to have a press conference to tell the public about my parentage. If we don't do it, the opposition will. We need Carolyn to do that. Please Cynthia, if for no other reason I need your help." Tracy looked at her almost pleading.

Still not convinced, Cynthia remembered all the hell Carolyn caused JD and Tracy in the past and was not at all thrilled to be helping her.

"It would help Gavin too," Ashley added. "According to James, Gavin maybe running for a US Senate seat. He certainly can't do it if Carolyn is still in this condition."

"I'll do anything for you Tracy and JD and even Gavin. But Carolyn—I don't know, that's asking a lot of a human being."

Ryan opened the door. "Your prisoner is waking up."

"She is not a prisoner!" Tracy stomped her foot.

"Well, whatever she is, she's cursing like a sailor. You want me to knock her out again?"

"No!" Tracy exclaimed.

"I'll handle her," Cynthia walked into the room. "No one else—just me." She slammed the door behind her.

Ryan looked at the women in the hallway with a concerned expression. "Do any of you think we should call Mr. H. and tell him what's about to happen in his house? I mean he is the AG and it's not going to look good if little momma kills the First Lady."

"He's your husband," Ashley said to Tracy as they all looked around at each other.

"And it was your idea to bring her here," Roz added.

Tracy exhaled and put her hands on her hips exasperated, and then she smiled. "You know I think the information would be better coming from Brian. Why don't you call your boss and advise him of our day."

"Tracy did what?" Brian waited for the response. "Have you lost your mind?" Brian yelled into the cell phone. The men in the room turned to him with curious expressions. "Who else is there?" he asked. "How much damage did you do to her?"

A concerned JD walked over to where Brian stood. "What's going on?"

Brian put his hand up signaling for JD to wait. "Has anyone called Gavin?"

This time Senator Roth walked over concerned. "Is something going on with Carolyn? Why does Gavin need to be called?"

JD shook his head, "I don't know."

"Nobody leaves until we get there." He hung up the telephone and looked at JD with the most incredulous look. When he went to speak, he began to laugh, which somewhat relaxed JD. He knew if something were wrong, Brian would be racing out of the room. "Your wife just," he broke out laughing again. He stopped to compose himself, looked up at JD, and began to laugh again, this time he turned away and shook his head. Now he had the undivided attention of all the men in the room. "All right man, here it is." He pointed to JD, "Your wife just kidnapped your daughter," he pointed to Senator Roth. "And your wife," he pointed to James, "and your wife," he pointed to Samuel are holding her prisoner in your house," he pointed at JD.

"What?" JD asked, not sure if he understood or believed what Brian said. "This is why I'm never getting married."

Calvin began to laugh.

"Don't laugh," Brian stated. "I'm sure they are going to call your wife next."

Chapter 7

JD looked from the women sitting together in his kitchen and wondered what in the hell he was going to do with them. With their husbands standing behind him with angry frowns on their faces he asked. "One of you want to tell me what's going on?"

"I know I don't. But somebody needs too." Mrs. Gordon said as she walked out of the room.

"Amelia?" Senator Roth called out.

"All I know is I was told to pack a bag for Mrs. Roberts and myself. That's all I know."

Tracy looked at the woman who insisted she do something to help Carolyn and was now proclaiming innocence.

JD leaned back against the counter top crossed his legs and looked at his wife who was doing all she could not to look up at him. "Tracy?"

The smile on his face was a facade and she knew it. "Jeffrey."

"Yes Tracy."

"Okay, Carolyn is staying with us until Gavin comes home."

"Why?"

"Well, she's having a little problem."

"What problem is that Tracy?"

"Well, you said I need to resolve my feelings about Senator Roth and Carolyn."

"How does kidnapping the First Lady and bringing her into this house help you resolve your feelings?"

"Well, see, she is having a problem and I'm helping her through it. So by helping her, I'm in essence helping myself."

JD chuckled and shook his head then exhaled.

"Where is Carolyn now?" Senator Roth asked impatiently. "And what kind of problem is she having?"

"I don't care what kind of problem she is having, Carolyn cannot stay here." JD said looking over his shoulder at Senator Roth.

"Let's take a moment," James suggested, realizing they were not getting the full story. "Ashley, tell me everything?"

"Well, honey," she hesitated, "I don't know everything. I just know some things."

Brian threw his hands up in the air. "One of you needs to tell us something before the security at the mansion realizes the first lady is missing and call the state police."

"Oh, we took care of that. Ryan told the guard she was staying with friends until the governor returns," Tracy happily explained.

Samuel looked at Cynthia, "How did she get a black eye?"

"I swear I did not do it this time," Cynthia declared.

"Who did?" JD asked looking at Tracy, "and what happened to your face?"

"Well, babe, there was a struggle. And I'm fine, but I sort of got hit a few times."

Calvin could not hold in his laugh any longer. "Roz, please tell us what we need to know."

"Sure, since my husband isn't here to chastise me. I'll be happy to give you the details as I know them." The men turned their attention to Rosaline and waited. "I received a call from Ashley saying Tracy was in trouble. So naturally, Cynthia came along to help in any way that we could."

"Naturally," JD said sarcastically.

"As it turned out, Cynthia was the only person that was needed. Being the good friend that she is to you," she pointed to JD, "and Tracy, Cynthia took control of the situation and I'm happy she did, because now Carolyn has been cleaned up."

JD looked at James, then at Samuel. "Are either of you getting any facts?"

"Not a damn one," Samuel stated.

"I'm going up to see Carolyn," Senator Roth stated and walked towards the steps.

"I don't think that would be a good idea at the moment," Cynthia stated.

"Why is that Cynthia Antoinette?" Samuel smiled at his wife.

"Well, she's not very happy and I think you should wait to see her tomorrow like we planned."

"Yes," Ashley agreed.

"Yes, me too. I think tomorrow will be soon enough for anyone to see her." Tracy said and stood to push her chair under the table as if that ended the conversation. Ashley and Roz did the same, but Cynthia was having a little trouble getting out of the chair. "Okay ladies let's convene to my office upstairs." Roz helped Cynthia up while the men stood there looking at each other.

"Stop," JD yelled. "We are not done."

Tracy walked over and hugged him around the waist. "Babe, it's been a long day and everyone is tired. A good night's sleep will help this situation immensely."

The men looked at each other and knew something was wrong. JD hugged his wife and kissed the top of her head. "Brian, go upstairs and see if Carolyn is still alive." He held Tracy away from him by the shoulder. "Anything you want to tell me while Brian is upstairs?"

"Well," Tracy trailed off and looked back at Ashley.

"She kind of got knocked out again, okay," Cynthia exclaimed and retook her seat. "When I went into the room we had a struggle because she did not want to take a shower. So..." she began to laugh. "I asked Ryan to knock her out again. That's when I bathed her and did her hair. And if I may say so, I did a damn good job of cleaning her up. Now, she looks like her old self, except there may be one or two bruises." Ashley and Roz turned to hide the laugh that was about to emerge.

"Knock her out again?" Samuel asked emphasizing the word again.

"Yes again. Tracy asked her the first time." Then she rushed on to explain, "But the second time Ryan did not punch her, because we did not want to leave any bruises. So she did something to her neck."

"Yeah, and then we were all able to bathe her and do her hair and nails without any more fuss at all." Tracy smiled. "Once she wakes up all will be well with the world."

At that moment, Ryan walked into the room and looked around. "I have to say, you folks are not the boring group I thought you would be. I have truly enjoyed this day."

"Ryan," Samuel began to speak but she raised her hand.

"I know. If you gentlemen would step outside, I will be happy to give the details on today's events."

The women all looked at Ryan as if she had lost her mind. The men stepped outside and Ryan looked back over her shoulder at the women and smiled.

"I think we did a good job of confusing them. Will she mess that up?" Ashley asked.

"No," Cynthia shook her head. "Ryan can handle her own with them. Let's just pray Gavin doesn't get here until the black eye is gone."

"How long did it take for the last one to heal?" Roz asked.

"A few days," Cynthia replied. "But that one was much worse.

"Ladies thank you for helping Mrs. Roberts. I don't condone your methods, but I like the results. Let's hope she appreciates what you have all done. I'm going up stairs to check on her now," Amelia stated as she left the room.

As the men returned to the kitchen one by one each gathered their wife and left the house. "We'll see you early in the morning," James said as Ashley gathered her things.

Samuel came in next. He held his hand out to Cynthia and she took it with a smile. "Let's go home babe," he said as she stood.

"See you tomorrow Tracy," she said.

"No you will not. You're staying home tomorrow."

"Why?" Cynthia asked curtly.

"Because I said so, now let's go. Roz, we'll give you a ride home."

"Thanks, I appreciate that. Tracy, I'll call you."

Senator Roth walked in and went straight upstairs. Tracy sat at the table watching everyone leave and knew JD was the only one that had not returned inside. That wasn't good.

"Mrs. Harrison, I'm leaving now. The children have had their baths and are both in the bed. JC promised he would not go to sleep until you come to kiss him good night."

Tracy smiled and exhaled, "Thank you for everything today Mrs. Gordon."

"You are welcome child. You have a good heart and your husband knows you are trying to do something good here. So don't sit there and fret over what he's thinking."

Tracy only nodded. "Good night Mrs. Gordon," and watched the woman leave. Tracy didn't bother to get up for she knew Jeffrey had some things to say to her. Looking down she closed her eyes and thought about her actions, there wasn't anything she would have done differently, except maybe not asking Ryan to knock Carolyn out, but other than that—nothing.

When she opened her eyes Jeffrey was there looking down at her. "What possessed you to bring Carolyn into this house? Just make me understand why you thought this was okay?"

Not liking the tone he had taken with her Tracy stood and exhaled. "My intent was to open the doors of communication between Carolyn and me. You were the one that stated I had to deal with my family issues."

"And you thought the way to do that was to put Carolyn under the same roof with me? This woman has done nothing but try to come between us. I used to sleep with that woman for god's sake. Did you ever once consider my feelings in this?"

"Did you consider mine when you kept all of this from me in the first place?

"Tracy, I have apologized for that several times. But I'll gladly do it again. I am sorry. I wanted to keep you from harm. Carolyn, will use whatever she can to hurt you. You don't let the enemy inside your home." He said angrily. "I love you and would not deny you anything. But I will not allow anyone—anyone to harm you. And that especially goes for that woman upstairs. She cannot stay here."

"Jeffrey, this is my house too. I want her to stay. Please Jeffrey, just until Gavin comes home."

JD looked down at the woman he loved more than life and wondered what could have propelled her to bring Carolyn into their home. "No."

"Jeffrey didn't you see how bad she looks?"

"No Tracy, because I don't give a damn how she looks. The woman has been nothing but trouble for us. Babe she is Gavin's problem, let him handle it. Send her home."

"I'm sorry Jeffrey I can't do that. She needs help."

JD stared at his wife in disbelief. "Tracy," he said calmly "send her home."

"I can't."

He closed his eyes and exhaled. He walked over to the chair, put on his suit jacket and walked out the door. Tracy watched as he walked out and wasn't sure what to do. She loved Jeffrey, but she couldn't turn her back on a woman in need. She had no idea how long she stood rooted to that spot, but when she finally turned Senator Roth was standing in the doorway.

"You never allow anything to come between you and your husband. I've asked Amelia to gather her and Carolyn things. I'm taking them home with me. Standing up for Carolyn was a good thing. I don't believe she would have done the same for you. The decision not to tell you wasn't JD's to make—it was mine. If the situation were happening today, I would make the same decision. Don't make him pay for something that was not his doing." He walked over and stood in front of her as a tear drop down her cheek. I'll get her the help she needs. As for JD, don't worry he'll be home."

"I have everything Senator," Amelia said from the staircase.

Senator Roth looked at Tracy then went upstairs, retrieved his daughter and walked out the door with her in his arms.

Hearing the beep of the alarm indicating someone was walking in the door caused Martha Harrison to look over at the clock on her night stand. There were only two people that had keys to the house other than her and they were JD and Ashley. She had just finished talking to Ashley, so it could only be her son. It was well after ten at night. If he was there, it only meant there was a problem at home. Throwing the covers back, she placed her feet into her slippers and picked up her robe. Walking down the stairs, she wondered if he was ready to tell her what's been going on with him and Tracy for the last year. Other people did not feel the tension, but she certainly knew there was a strain on her son's marriage. But she made a promise never to interfere in her children's lives. As she reached the bottom of the steps, she looked into the kitchen to see JD sitting at the table with a slice of chocolate cake and his long legs stretched out and crossed at the ankles. *That boy is the spitting image of his father.* The thought made her smile. A memory came to mind of a night when her husband James had come in late from work, sat in that very spot, and looked as if he had the weight of the world on his shoulders just as JD did.

She said the very same thing to JD that she said to her husband. "Whenever you are torn, go with what you know in your heart is right."

JD looked up, just as his father did that night about a week before he died. "Hey momma. I didn't mean to wake you."

Martha walked into the kitchen and kissed her son on the forehead. "I wasn't asleep. Have you eaten dinner?"

"No, I skipped dinner tonight."

She smiled knowingly and walked over to the refrigerator. Pulling out a plate of fried chicken, she talked as she prepared to warm up the food. "You know when I came downstairs I thought of a night about a week before your father died. He sat in that very spot and looked about as tormented as you just did." She smiled, "We made some of the best love of our entire marriage that night."

"TMI Mom," he said shaking his head.

Martha laughed; "How do you think you got here?" she popped him with the dish cloth that was in her hand. Taking the plate out of the microwave, she went back to the refrigerator and pulled out a bowl of potato salad and put some on the plate, then sat it in front of JD.

"I don't think I can eat anything Mom."

Placing a glass of tea on the table next to the plate, she simply said, "Hum hum." She then poured herself a glass, took a seat at the other end of the table, and just waited. JD never lifted his eyes from the cake he was eating. When he finished he pushed the saucer aside and pulled the plate of food in front of him. She just smiled at the man who couldn't eat anything.

"I don't ever remember you and Daddy having an argument or disagreement."

"Ha, boy. Your daddy and I used to fight like cats and dogs. You don't remember because we never did it in front or around you and Ashley. Whatever was happening between your father and I was just that—between us. You children had nothing to do with it and we kept it away from you."

"What sort of things did you fight about?"

"Him taking you to the gun range. We had a few whoppers over that. And when he took Ashley, Lord I just about lost my mind." She shook her head, "But that wasn't our biggest fight. The big one and only time I put him out of my bed was when he came home without his wedding band on. I told him, he was welcomed back in our bed when he had his wedding band back on and not a minute before."

JD stopped eating and looked up at his mother. "When did that happen?"

"You had just started high school and Ashley was still in junior high. I was not sleeping in the bed with any man I wasn't married to. Those wedding bands represented our bond, our pledge to each other. Him misplacing it was an indication to me that he had also misplaced our vows and I was not going to stand for that."

"So what happened?"

"He found that band, that's what happened. He came home from work about three in the afternoon, grinning, holding his hand up with the band on. I made him pull it off to make sure it was the same band. Sure enough, the engraving was there, *Forever, For Always, For Love.*" She smiled remembering that day. "They never found his wedding band."

"What do you mean?"

"When your father died, his wedding band was missing. I spoke with his partner at the time and he said James wasn't wearing it. I know that was a lie. James never took the band off after that first time. Never."

JD saw the faraway look enter in her eyes and knew she was missing his dad. "Tracy and I had an argument," he said as he looked down at the now empty plate. "I left the house without kissing her good-bye. I just left." He pushed the plate away, sat back in the chair, and sighed. "She's having a hard time forgiving me for something I did before we got married. I don't know how to get her to forgive me and trust me again."

"Forgiveness and trust can't be forced. It comes with time and understanding. If you broke her trust, you have to be patient and wait for her to be ready to give it back to you. Whatever you do, don't continue to do the same things that caused her to lose trust in you in the first place.'

JD sat up and wiped his face with his hands, "Momma, it's not that easy. I know things that I can't tell Tracy for her own protection. I've kept things from her in the past for the wrong reasons, I see that now. But at the time, my whole being just did not want to see her hurt. Now, there are things that could get her killed and I won't risk that, even if I have to suffer through her distrust of me. I just will not put her life in danger. I love her too much."

Martha stood up and removed the plate from the table. "Get up son. Go home to your wife. Put your arms around her, tell her how much you love her and don't stop until she believes you."

"I can't. I have to wait for Brian."

Martha noticed he was traveling with more security. "Are you in danger son?"

"It's just a precaution. There are things going on with a case. I can't go into details."

"I understand."

JD hesitated then sighed, "I decided to run for Governor."

"I think that is wonderful, son," she said as she stepped away from the sink. Looking down at him she could see there was more, so she took the seat next to him. "Your father always wanted that for you," she smiled. "He said the only way to make a real difference was from the top down. My son is going to make a difference in this world. I always had to remind him you were my son too, not just his." JD smiled, and then sighed. "How does Tracy feel about that?"

"She's not thrilled, but she is supportive. All the drama today was really about her trying to do what she could to help me."

"If you know that why are you here and not at home thanking her?"

"Because she had Carolyn in my house and I don't want her there!"

"Okay," Martha replied gingerly. "Carolyn Roth?"

"Roberts—yes."

"Why was Carolyn at your house?"

He started at the beginning and told her the whole story.

The house was quiet and dark with the exception of the light streaming from the upstairs hallway as JD entered the kitchen through the patio doors. It was about three in the morning when he and his mother finished talking about Tracy's situation. It did not surprise him when his mother upheld Tracy's resentment of not being told by him. He wondered if the women in his family would ever back him against his wife, shaking his head as he walked towards the stairs, he doubted it. He turned to walk up the steps but saw Tracy on the third step up. She lay there in one of his dress shirts with her hair hanging in her face, her arm supporting her head and her brown legs hanging down the lower steps. Reaching for her, he pushed her hair back, the light cast a low beam over her face, and he could see the tearstains on her cheek. His heart clenched. His touched must have startled her, for she opened her eyes and looked up at him. She sat up just as tears began to flow from her eyes. "I'm...."

Without a word he reached around her waist, gathered her to him, and kissed her so deep and thoroughly she couldn't complete the sentence. He stretched out the full length of his body over her. His intent was to kiss her until every tear washed away memory. "Please don't cry babe." He kissed her throat, then the spot right behind her ear and applied pressure until he heard the moan. Knowing every inch of her body was his greatest joy, for anything that gave her pleasure, pleased him more. She arched her body up to meet his more intimately as one of her legs wrapped around his thigh placing it directly against her center while his manhood grew against her other leg. The desire to have him inside her grew urgently, she needed to be one with him, needed to be filled by him. That was the only way to make the pain of him walking out the door go away.   Reaching down she unzipped his pants, reached in and freed his throbbing member from his briefs. At her touch, Jeffrey returned to her lips as she guided him into her moist hot fold. "Tracy," he whispered against her lips at the feel of her touch. It did not matter how many times they had made love before, each time for him was new. Every time they joined was fresh, hot, and passionate. He pulled her on top of him and held her at the waist as she unbuckled his belt and pushed his pants down between her thighs, but the brief would have to stay, he was not pulling out of her to remove them. Zealously, he eased further into her heat, sitting up with her head back, he heard the release of a soft breath of satisfaction from her, and it was his undoing. He lifted her by the waist until the tip of him was nearly free of her, then began to push his body up while bringing her down on him feverishly. Her fingers dug into his arms as she held tightly, relishing in every powerful thrust. "Again Jeffrey," she cried, "again," and he urgently complied, filling her until her walls began to vibrate against him, squeezing, demanding her release. The fire was raging within her and he could feel it mounting. "Let it go babe, I need to feel it, I need to feel your love shower over me. I need you Trac. She looked down into his eyes and all he could see was the passion ready to explode. She reached down and ripped his shirt from his body as buttons popped everywhere. Running her hands up his chest, she placed a trail of kisses to his nipples, than ran her tongue against one. His thrusts instantly became more powerful, more determined. His grasp on her waist tightened and he plowed into her over and over and over until they, both screamed their release. Tracy collapsed against him, feeling the beat of his heart pounding against his chest. Holding her against him, the realization that they were on the stairs came to him and he had to laugh. With one hand possessively holding her round behind snuggly against him while his manhood continued to throb within her and the other hand rubbing her back, he kissed the top of her head. "Since we have company I think we should take this to the privacy of our bedroom."

Tracy's mindless stroking of his nipple slowed as a tear dropped from her eyes. "I'm so sorry Jeffrey. I will never defy you again."

Without breaking their intimate connection, he pulled her up to look into her eyes. "No, babe, it wasn't that. I will rile against anything I think will hurt you and I believe Carolyn will. But you were right. This is your house too. When you make a decision, agreed or not I should support it, the same way you support me." He took her face into his hands and looked into her eyes. "I'm sorry babe." He gently kissed her lips as her tears continued to flow.

She looked away. "When you walked out the door, I remembered my daddy walking out and never coming back. I was afraid you weren't coming back," she cried.

He fervently kissed her eyes, her nose her cheeks. "Never—babe. Look at me Tracy," when her eyes met his, he continued. "I would never walk out on you

Tracy—never. Believe that babe, please believe that—never," He kissed her deeply as if willing the words to seep into her soul. He was still lodged deeply within her, but it wasn't enough. He reached between them and pulled the shirt she had on apart, sending more buttons down the stairs. Pushing the shirt away, he held her body with no barriers between them, other than his briefs. Hesitantly, he pulled out of her, shoved them down his legs. She whimpered against his shoulder, then sighed at his re-entrance. Bare chest against breast, her legs wrapped securely around his waist he carried his wife up the stairs, to the bedroom and closed the doors behind them. Pressing her body against the now closed doors, his hands roamed her curves, as if it was the first time. Taking her hands, he placed them above her head and held them there with one hand, while taking a breast in the other leading it to his wanting lips. He took the tip of the mount into his mouth as if it was his only lifeline and feasted there until Tracy's body, squirming against him demanded his attention. He switched hands and breast and gave the same honor to the other. "Jeffrey," she called out in a sexy ragged voice as her thighs tightened around his waist. She began to move her body in a slow circular motion and his concentration withered, she had taken control, he released her breast and returned to her lips. "Open your eyes babe; I want to see when you drain me." He whispered against her lips. She opened them and just like before, it shattered him. "Take all of me, it's all yours, only yours." She squeezed her pelvis and another explosion ripped through them. His head fell back and he growled as if the lion had just captured his prey. Tracy purred, still lodged between him and the door, but she was content. His head now resting against her, with sweat streaming down neither wanted to let the other go. "I will never leave you Tracy." Cupping her face in his hands, he pushed her hair from her face. "Tell me you believe me."

"I believe you Jeffrey." He smiled revealing the deep dimples she loved so much. The temptation was too much to resist. Her tongue snaked out and the tip landed right in the middle of one.

His smile widened, "Let's see we ruined two shirts and a pair of underwear. We are probably going to have to re-paint the door and you're still not satisfied."

"Are you?"

His smile faded as he looked into the eyes he loved. "I'll never get enough of you."

"You sure do use that word never a lot," she teased as she tongued the other dimple.

His eyes closed and he groaned. "I'll change it to, never-ever." He placed a sweet kiss on one side of her mouth, then kissed the other side.

Wrapping her arms around his neck, she squealed as his hands now tickled her waist, "Okay."

The voice she used when she said okay always sent his body into a tailspin, and this time was no different. He began to swell within her yet again. "I think we better take a shower before we ruin another wall." He carried her into the bath and set her on her feet. She reached into the shower stall and turned the knobs until all the heads were running. They both stepped in and began bathing and tantalizing each other. Afterwards Jeffrey pulled a towel from the warmer and snuggly wrapped it around her as she stepped out of the shower. Patting her dry in front, he circled to her back, but suddenly stopped. Tracy looked over her shoulder at him to see why. He dropped the towel to the floor, circled her waist with his hands, and pulled her back against his chest. "Look babe," he said nodding towards the door with the full length mirror on the back. "Watch my hand," he whispered into her ear. His fingers spread across her stomach then slowly lowered to her hips. She leaned back against him as his hands traveled slowly up the side of her waist, to the side of her breast then over her nipples. Her eyes closed and a slow moan escaped her throat. "Watch babe." Her eyes opened and met his in the mirror as he used his thumb and forefinger to massage and pluck each nipple until they were hard and in need of his mouth. He bent his knees and braced his back against the wall. "Spread your legs for me babe." She did and could feel his erection between her legs. "Put your hands on mine." She did. His hands began to move slowly down her body. "If you ever wonder why you and no other woman could please me, I want you to remember this night." His hands continued to move down, now reaching her stomach. "Are you wet again?" she nodded but never took her eyes from him. "I know," he said as his hand moved further down to the apex of her thighs. "Know how I know?" She shook her head no. He smiled, "Look at your skin, it's glistening. Your breasts are heaving. Your lips are now parted and your eyes," he licked his lips, "your eyes are mesmerizing." His breathing was becoming ragged as was hers. "Look at us together with no barriers between us, your skin against my skin, your body against my body." His hands were now covering her womanhood as one of his fingers dipped inside her. Her body jerked as did his. "Can you see the desire building within your body, not just feel it, but, can you see it between us? I can, every time you walk into a room. It's the only thing I can see. When you are not there, it's the only thing I can think about." His other hand, with hers on top, moved further back between her legs as he bent her body slightly forward and took his manhood into their hands. He now covered his hands over hers and closed it around his shaft. "Do you feel that Tracy? That's what you do to me." Her hands began to move up and down him, he moaned in response. It was a battle not to close his eyes at her touch, but he couldn't pull away from her eyes in the mirror. Moving their other hands to her stomach, he pulled her back closer. "Take me in Tracy. Take me inside of you. Love me Tracy." Bending her forward a little, more she guided his shaft into her fold and welcomed him with a need so deep she thought she would scream. "Don't close your eyes. Watch." He whispered. And she did, as he bent his knees and braced their stance with his strong thighs. "Our bodies complement each other babe. Can you see that? Can you feel it? I do." The couple in the mirror was so passionate, so sensual, so sexy that neither could continue to watch. Their desire needed to be quenched and they both knew the moment was near. Their breathing was heavier; their hands were moving feverishly together in and out, in and out. His hold had tightened around her waist. And their bodies were on fire. His lips touched her cheek, "Watch our explosion Tracy. Watch what happens to your face when your love flows through me. See what I see." Heaving heavily against her back, "Come with me babe. Explode with me....His words trailed off as they both burst into a thousand pieces with their juices flowing down her inner thighs, his shaft still slick and wet, moving slower, relishing the feel. Holding her securely, they both sagged to the floor. He took the towel, draped it over her body, and held her until their breathing regulated. "You are going to kill me one day, woman." He said as he kissed the back of her head.

"I like that mirror thingy, can we do it again."

Chapter 8

"Mrs. Roth, Mr. and Mrs. Harrison are here to see the Senator." The maid indicated.

Lena sat at the table in the kitchen of the mini mansion she lived in with her husband. They would be celebrating their third year of marriage in six months. However, their recent houseguest was putting that in jeopardy. Her step-daughter Carolyn Roth-Roberts had caused havoc in their marriage from the start. But the last year was the worst. First, it was the revelation that John, her husband, knew he was the father of her child before she did. Sounds crazy, but it's the truth. Over the years, she wondered how different her life and her daughter, Tracy's, lives would have been if she had known that, a one night stand with a young Senator John Roth had resulted in a child. Would she have married Billy Washington, the man she thought was Tracy's father? Would her daughter Joan still be alive, since she technically died at his hands? Would her son Turk have turned to the streets when he could no longer deal with the drama at home? The answers to those questions would never be known, but she was not one to dwell on the past. She lived her life to the fullest and she made no excuses for that. However, she was concerned about the effect all of this was having on Tracy. She hadn't been the best mother in the world and she had her reasons for that. Now, all she only wanted was to help Tracy as much as she could from this point on. "Thank you. Would you show them back here?"

At fifty eight, Lena Roth could easily pass for a forty-five. She was an attractive slim woman that still turned heads when she stepped out. Having to deal with Carolyn in her house might change that.

"Hello mother."

Lena turned to see her daughter and her daughter's husband walking into the kitchen. She and JD might have their differences, but there was one thing for certain, he made Tracy happy. "Hello Tracy. You are absolutely glowing. Hello JD."

If she and her mother had a different type of relationship, she would tell her the glow was the result of several hours of good loving from her husband. However, they were not the normal mother and daughter team. Lena had her life and Tracy had hers. Until a few years ago, Tracy did not have a relationship with her mother. Once Tracy was married, they made more of an effort to build a plausible relationship. Then last year with the revelation that Senator Roth was her father and her mother had not known it, things had become somewhat strained again. "Thank you." She placed her purse on the table.

JD walked up behind her and placed his hand around her waist. "Hello Lena. We're here to see how Carolyn is doing."

Lena never moved from her seat at the table as she replied. "She is upstairs in her old room being catered to by her father. Some things never change." She picked up her cup and sipped her coffee. "How are the babies Tracy?"

"They're fine. Thank you for asking."

She looked past the couple to see Brian, who she knew was security and another woman standing behind them. "Traveling with security?" she questioned.

"There are some things going on," JD stated.

"I see. Is my daughter safe around you?"

"She's safer around me then she ever was with you."

"That's enough you two," Tracy scolded. "Mother this is Ryan Williams my personal security agent. Ryan my mother Lena Washing---- I'm sorry Roth."

"Mrs. Roth," Ryan spoke.

Lena nodded. "Brian I see you are still sniffing around."

"Good to see you too Mrs. Roth."

"This is going to be a family discussion and I don't think anyone will harm them in this house. So you two can leave."

"They're staying." JD responded. "Where's the Senator?"

"Right behind you." John said as he extended his hand. "Hey JD, Tracy. Are you two straight?" he asked referring to the incident of the night before.

The two smiled at each other thinking about the activities of the night before. "We're good." JD replied as he kissed his wife's temple.

"How's Carolyn?" Tracy asked.

"I've seen her better, but she looks good. She'll be down in a few minutes. I called Gavin. He's cutting the trip short and is on his way home. JD he said something about needing a secure area to talk to you. The library is secure." JD nodded as John looked at Tracy. "Thank you for all you did yesterday. It may have been the intervention we needed to get her life back on track."

Tracy wasn't sure where her feelings were with him, so she simply nodded and turned to JD. "We've decided to follow Carolyn's lead on this situation."

"What about you. Are you able to move forward?"

Looking back at the Senator, she replied. "I am. My only question is will Carolyn be ready for a press conference in three days."

"I'll be ready."

Everyone turned and looked at the doorway. Carolyn looked around the room at the people her father had lectured her about the night before. It was the first time in her life her father threatened to disown her completely. *"You are walking around as if some did something to you when in all actuality you have been ridiculing everyone that gets in the way of what you want."* He walked over to the window in her old bedroom and looked out over the gardens below. *"The blame for your behavior to your husband and Tracy is not completely your fault. Lord knows I spoiled you rotten. And until now, I could forgive you anything. But now,"* he turned to face her, *"you have shown me just how much like your mother you are. I didn't like the selfishness and total disregard for her husband she portrayed and I don't like it in you."* He walked over to the door then opened it to walk out. Without turning around he said, *"Gavin is a good man. He loves you. Don't cause his love for you to dissipate like your mother did with me. Tracy did you a huge favor with her little innocent intervention. You could learn a lot from your little sister."*

Looking around the room, the memory of her father's words haunted her. She never wanted to be like her mother. With all that she had accomplished with her life, Carolyn finally understood, she would never earn her mother's love. Hell, Tracy cared more for her in that one day, then her mother had all of her life. Tracy. It seemed all of her woes centered around her non-acceptance of this woman that was now her little sister. She exhaled. Once Gavin told her "you can't continue to live life the same way and expect a different outcome." Maybe a change was due. She pushed her hair back from her face and nervously smoothed down her skirt. It's time to change her life.

Carolyn was not quite her well put together self, but it was a hundred percent better than how she looked yesterday. "Damn, you clean up pretty good." Ryan smirked.

Tracy turned and frowned at her. Ryan raised an eyebrow and shrugged her shoulders. Brian cleared his throat. "We will be doing surveillance on the outside. Let's go Ryan."

"Is that the beast that struck me?"

"That's the person that helped us subdue you, yes," Tracy replied. "But she is right, you do look nice."

Carolyn smirked. "I have you beat even on my worst days."

Tracy smiled, "It's good to have you back Carolyn."

"Why don't we take this to the family room where everyone can take a seat and be comfortable," Lena suggested walking out of the room not waiting for anyone to reply.

As they all gathered, and received refreshments, Lena looked around to see who would get the ball rolling. Since no one started, she did. "I understand there is to be a press conference JD. Who do you want involved and to what extent?"

"Before we start there, I think there are some things that need to be said," Carolyn stood. "Daddy, I owe you an apology for my behavior. I am sorry for the worry I caused you over the last year. I am not sorry for the things I said for it was what I felt. Tracy in my heart I know this was not your doing. You are as much of a victim as I am in all of this, but I'm used to taking my frustrations out on you so that probably will not change. JD, well I'm still pissed at you. Lena, I don't like you and

I probably never will." She stopped and exhaled, "I feel so much better."

"I'm not very fond of you either my dear. However, I do love your father and will make an attempt to put up with you. But don't push your luck."

Tracy ducked her head trying to suppress a laugh, while JD cleared his throat. "Well, Carolyn, I'm not clear at this time why you are pissed with me, however, it's not important. If you stay out of my marriage, we can survive."

"Look, I realize we will never be this one big happy family, but all I'm asking is that we do nothing that could be detrimental to any other person." Senator Roth stated. "If we start there, I think the rest may be a little easier."

"I agree," Gavin said as he walked through the doorway.

"Gavin," Carolyn stood and went directly into her husband's arms.

"What happened to your face?" he asked as he kissed his wife.

"Tracy did it."

Gavin looked over at Tracy and frowned, "Tracy?"

"I did not hit her Gavin, but I did have someone else subdue her."

The question was still very evident on Gavin's face as JD stood and shook his hand, "Welcome home," he joked.

"Thank you, I think," he frowned and looked down at Carolyn. "Anyone wants to tell me what's going on?"

JD and Senator Roth both exclaimed, "Don't ask," and laughed.

The tension in the room seemed to diminish a little. "Here's where we are now," Senator Roth began. "JD has made a decision to run for Governor. We believe it should be our camp that releases the information regarding my relationship to Tracy."

Gavin looked at JD. "I agree with both decisions. You know you have whatever support I can give. When is the press conference?"

"Three days from now," JD replied.

"If Carolyn is okay with that," Tracy added.

Carolyn looked up at the woman she was supposed to despise, but she was slowly creeping up on her. It was hard not to appreciate what Tracy tried to do to help her yesterday. If they had any type of a decent relationship, she would be patting her on the back, laughing at the way Tracy pulled her out of her house, although she did not appreciate the bruise on her face. "There is no way I'm going out in public with my face like this."

"You can hardly see the bruise and in three days it will be nothing. Now that the decision is made we need to move forward," JD asserted.

Tracy touched his arm. "It's really Carolyn's decision if she is comfortable enough to stand in front of the camera. Actually," she looked at JD, "I'm not comfortable with the press, I could use the extra days to prepare."

JD looked at his wife's twinkling eyes and knew what she was up to. He reached out and rubbed her shoulder, "Okay babe we can move out a week if you need. We'll get Pearl to work with you again."

Carolyn, who was sitting wrapped in Gavin's arms in the chair, sat up. Tracy was not going to have the opportunity to outdo her. "I can be ready in three days. Go ahead and schedule it for noon."

"I don't know Carolyn. It may be better if we wait," JD insisted.

"Go ahead and schedule it JD. Carolyn will be ready and she'll do us proud." Gavin smiled down at his wife, then looked up at JD. Lena laughed and shook her head. Tracy won that round.

"All right I have my people working on the speech. I'll make the announcement, but all of you need to be ready for questions from the press. Senator Roth looked at his daughter. "Carolyn there can be nothing negative said even if questions come up regarding your past relationship with JD. JD you are going to be hit with the questions regarding your sleeping with sisters. I hope you are ready."

"I'll handle it. What about you babe? Are you going to be able to handle those questions?"

"It happened prior to us meeting. I didn't know either of you during that time and I certainly did not know Carolyn was my sister. So frankly, I have no thoughts on the matter. However, if it was happening now, I might have a thing or two to say."

"Just know they are going to dig deeper. We are all going to have to monitor our responses." Gavin stated.

"It may be a good idea for Tracy and I to make a statement showing some sort of unity prior to the conference ending. It may eliminate some uncomfortable questions." Carolyn sat up, "In fact, we probably should make it a point to do some appearances together."

JD and Lena looked at Carolyn wondering what she was up to. "I don't know if we should push the issue," Lena stated.

"I don't recall anyone asking you," Carolyn replied.

"No one asked me to whip your ass either but I'll be happy to do it." Lena said as she stood.

"Well, okay. This lasted longer than I thought it would." Gavin stated as he stood. "JD we need to talk. Senator we will leave you with, um... your women." Gavin smiled. JD looked down at Tracy as he stood. She smiled and he walked off with Gavin.

Senator Roth stood in the middle of the room with Carolyn standing on one side of him and Lena on the other. He looked from one to the other, and then looked at Tracy. His plea for help was answered. "Carolyn may I have a moment of your time?" she asked.

Carolyn reluctantly relinquished her stance by her father and followed Tracy into the foyer.

"I wanted a moment just to make sure you forgive me for what happened. It was my intent to try to help."

Carolyn waved her hand as if dismissing the statement. She stood with her back to Tracy then turned back. "You are nothing like your mother."

"I know. She is a beautiful woman. I can only hope I look as good as she does when I get to be her age."

"No you are not beautiful. You are worse—you are radiant. And it generates from within. Every time you smile all the love that is within you shines. That's what caught JD. The love and passion the two of you share is what will keep him. Don't be foolish and allow this family squabble to come between you. So he didn't tell you about Daddy. He did it to protect you from me."

"Do I need to be protected from you Carolyn?" Tracy asked.

"Hell yes! You still do need to be protected from me and others just like me. What you don't get is, in this political environment, we will do anything to get into power. In JD's case, he used this cover up to protect you, not to gain power. He scored on two fronts. He saved you from my wrath and he will gain the respect and admiration from thousands of women voters that are in awe of the man who loves his wife and openly shows it." She looked at the woman who took her dreams away. "Take this as the only sisterly advice you will ever get from me. Give JD a pass on this one--he deserves it. Then take the time to work with Pearl Lassiter to get you ready for this campaign. And whatever you do, don't show any fear. The moment the press senses that you are afraid of them, they will come after you like rabid animals." She hesitated, "Look, you and I will never be sister or friends. So let's acknowledge that up front. With that on the table, there are a few ground rules. Neither of us will do anything that will hamper our husbands campaigns. And no more taking me out of my home against my will."

"Okay," Tracy nodded. "As for you, no more drinking and I mean not even a glass of wine. And no more pictures."

"I'm done with the drinking. I'm too good looking to be a drunk. And don't know anything about any pictures so I can't agree on that."

Tracy narrowed her eyes at Carolyn. "You haven't been sending me pictures of JD and his political advisor?"

Carolyn frowned and shook her head, "No." She watched the look of disbelief and confusion showed on Tracy's face. "How are you getting these pictures?"

"Through my work email."

"That could be a problem if they get into the wrong hands. Have you asked JD about them?"

"No, because I thought they were coming from you and I didn't want to add fuel to the fire."

"Who is his advisor?" Carolyn asked.

"Mattie something or other."

"Madison Gresham?"

"Yes, that's it. Do you know her?"

Carolyn exhaled, "Yes, I know her. Here's a word of caution. Keep an eye on her. JD is a sucker for women in distress. And from what I understand she's going through some things with her brother."

"How is having an affair with my husband going to help with her brother?"

With a wave of her hand, she dismissed Tracy's question. "JD is not going to have an affair with anyone. So let that go. But there are going to be women all over him and you might as well get used to it. He is tall, dark,

and handsome, and has power to boot. Women are
going to come out of the woodworks after him. I know, I
was one of them. The only thing you can do on that front
is to believe and trust in your man."

Tracy smiled at the woman who had been a thorn in
her side longer than she could say. "Don't go getting all
mushy on me. This advice is a onetime thing. After the
campaign, the gloves go back on."

Gavin and JD sat in the library on a conference call
with the US Attorney General's Office. "The President
believes Absolute would be helpful in your investigation
of Munford. Apparently, he has a connection to
Munford and some weapons flowing through Virginia.
He could follow the weapons to ensure they never reach
the intended target. He's in your area and will make
contact," the US Attorney General stated. JD knew
Absolute was a code name for Joshua Lassiter, a CIA
operative and Samuel's brother. Where there was
Absolute, there were dead bodies. "In the meantime,
you have to get the evidence needed to remove Munford
from office, by any means necessary. I've received the
package from your office and this is going to cause issues
with a number of cases. However, that cannot deter us
from the mission. If this man has elevated to moving
weapons, I want him out instantaneously."

"There may be someone that could expedite
Munford's removal, but we may have to make an offer,"
Gavin stated.

"Is it someone we have in custody and what kind of
offer are we talking about?"

Gavin hesitated and looked up at JD who sat in the
chair in front of the desk. "Mr. Attorney General a few

years back I prosecuted a young man and placed him in federal prison under an assumed name."

"Your brother-in-law, Al Day."

"Yes. The reason it was handled that way was because of some information he gave me. The information was what initiated the investigation on Munford. I believe he knows more, but is not the type of person to turn on anyone."

"But he gave you this information?"

"Yes, but at the time he used it for leverage to get protection for his sister, who is now my wife."

"Mr. Attorney General, I believe Day will give this information to JD in his own time." Gavin interrupted, "However, if we could make it worth his while to give it to us now, it would go a long way at getting Munford out of office."

"We are trading one criminal for another. Which is more dangerous to society on a whole?"

"We'll defer to your judgment on that. I'll have JD prepare and send you a proposal to your office. Your decision will be final."

"Fair enough. Harrison, this is going to make your campaign vulnerable. If we take Munford down, it will result in some convictions being over turned and it could be looked at as you're being soft on crime. If we make an offer to get your brother-in-law an early release or pardon, it's going to be looked at as you're being soft on crime. I hope your campaign can take this kind of hit and still win. If not, the President is not going to be happy."

"I'm sure the President wants the public servant that is abusing his position removed regardless of the impact on my campaign."

"Don't sell yourself short. The President is very aware of who you are and what you mean to the future of this party. He will care, so much so that, as soon as I receive your proposal, in the next forty-eight hours, I'm taking it to him for approval before we proceed. If there is nothing else gentlemen, I'll take my leave. Good job, Harrison, Gavin."

When the call was disconnected, the two sat there for a moment taking in all that had transpired. "Can you pull it together in 48 hours?

"I don't have a choice. I'll start on it right away."

"Have someone in your office handle it. You have a press conference, or have you forgotten."

"Not at all, but for once, I'm not the person on the hot seat."

"You didn't mention Al gave you information on me too." Gavin stated as he looked at JD.

"That was irrelevant." The two stared at each other. "You gave Al a way to be released early. Did you do that for me or Tracy?"

"Both." He exhaled, then smiled, "Do you realize, we are brothers-in-law?"

"Interesting, isn't it? How do we help our wives through this?" JD asked.

Shaking his head, Gavin simply said, "I don't know. But, I'm buying a hard hat for protection. And suggest you do the same." The two men laughed.

Brian turned as he heard the door behind him open. Tracy stepped out closing her jacket around her body. The March wind was still a little chilly. He smiled knowing the conversation must have been a trying affair. "Are we one big happy family now?"

Returning his smile, she exhaled, held her head up to the sky and asked, "Why me?"

Brian laughed.

"It's not funny," she pushed him with her elbow then leaned against the car with him.

Ryan, who stood on the other side of the door, shook her head. "Ms. H, you know I have your back. Just give me the word and I'll take her out."

"That won't be necessary Ryan, but thanks for the offer."

The door opened again. JD walked out and put his arms around Tracy. "We ready to go home?"

"Definitely, "she replied as she circled his waist and kissed his cheek. "How was the meeting?"

He would give anything to be free to tell her about the conversation with the AG, but doing so might get her hopes up. So, he smiled and hugged her. "It was a good meeting. I'm going to be busy for the next few days and you may have to handle things for me with the press conference. Can you handle that?" he asked looking down into her eyes.

"I'll call Pearl as soon as we get home."

JD reached around opening the back door to the vehicle and Tracy got in. He looked up at Brian, "Who do we have watching Munford?"

"Williams."

Nodding his head, JD thought for a moment then replied. "We may need Samuel on Munford things are going to get dangerous."

Brian opened the front door of the car, then stopped and looked back at JD. "Absolute coming to town?"

"I'm afraid so," JD replied as he got into the backseat of the car.

"Oh hell. I'll alert the morgues to make sure they order extra body bags."

Chief Munford stood in the center of his office in downtown Richmond pacing nervously, waiting for the telephone to ring. He was expecting two calls that would ensure things were in place for his next move. The five hundred thousand in commission was sitting in an undisclosed location waiting to be moved. Payment was contingent on a timely delivery and there was no way, he would allow anything to interfere with collecting that money. The telephone finally rang. "What in the hell took you so long to get back with me?" he angrily barked into the telephone.

"We could spend time discussing that or I can tell you what I have so far. Which do you prefer?"

He hated smart-ass women. Regardless of what you had on them, they always had a lethal mouth, but he knew the remedy. "It better be good or your brother will face twenty years in jail." The phone line was silent. "I'm waiting."

"In an hour I'll be in the house. I'll take a look around and check out the security layout."

Munford thought for a moment. "Harrison is not going to have anything lying around. You will have to search the house. Start with his office, then check his bedroom."

"How do you propose I do that without getting caught?"

"That's not my problem. I expect a report tonight." He disconnected the call. Finally, he had access to Harrison's home. Things were looking up. The next call did not come until a few hours later, but it was just as rewarding. "Talk to me."

"Delivery arrangements are in place. All we need is your drivers."

"And payment."

"Half will be placed in your off-shore account when the keys are picked up. Once you have authorization of the deposit, the road trip will begin. The balance will be deposited upon delivery."

"Good, good. Make the call."

"The call will be made when I receive confirmation of a fifty thousand deposit into my account."

Munford squirmed. Gary had been heading up his operations for a year now. This was the first time he requested payment up front. "The agreement was you get paid when I do."

"It's insurance for my legal fund. Besides, my next bit of information will make your day."

Now, his interest was piqued. "What do you have?"

"Guess who's' inside the Harrison house?"

"I don't have time for guessing games. Who?"

"Donnell Williams' sister."

"Ryan? What in the hell is she doing there?"

"Good question, but since you are not into guessing, I'll keep my thoughts to myself."

"The fifty thousand will be deposited."

"Good. Here's what I think. I don't see Ryan and Tracy Harrison running in the same social circle. We know Ryan was hanging with Day's people."

"She was their go to person until last year."

"Is it possible they have her watching Day's sister's back?"

"With her background, I don't see Harrison knowingly allowing Ryan in his home." He nodded. "This could be useful information. See if we have anything outstanding on her. If we do, pull her in. Let's see what we can find out."

Munford's mind began to work overtime as he processed the information he received. Ryan Williams had never been arrested for anything and did not have a record. But she had been suspected in several disappearances of gang members. In fact, she was the lead suspect in a shooting that took place last year at Gavin Roberts' mistress' home. He was close to getting what he needed then, but Al Day interfered. That bastard had been a thorn in his side since he was sixteen years old. Munford rubbed his aching knees, remembering the gunshots that caused the injury. "If all goes well, he could eliminate Al Day and Harrison at the same time. Just for the hell of it, he'd throw in Tracy Harrison."

Chapter 9

It was nine o'clock Monday morning and Tracy was already wishing she could go back to the weekend and spend time alone with Jeffrey and the children. Instead, she was in the family room of her home with Press Secretary, Pearl Lassiter, who happened to be one of Samuel's sisters, Ashley and Madison Gresham. Pearl and Ashley were fine—Mattie, as she called herself, was an entirely different story. "What's the problem with the statement, Ms. Gresham?" Tracy asked as tactfully as she could.

"Please, call me Mattie, Tracy. We are going to be spending a lot of time together over the next eighteen months. There is no need for formalities." She sat on the edge of the table and crossed her legs. "The first problem is mentioning JD in any of this. I mean this is your personal problem, to deal with not his. In fact, I'm not too sure he needs to be at this press conference."

Pearl and Ashley looked at each other. Neither was getting a good vibe from this woman. "Where would you be if it were your husband, Ms. Gresham?"

"I can see we are going to have a problem with theses names aren't we."

"Not really." Tracy replied. "Your name is Ms. Gresham. My name is Mrs. Harrison. See it's very clear. Just like what you are sitting on is a table. Right next to the table is a chair. One you sit in, the other you don't."

Mattie stood slowly, then took a seat on the sofa. "I'm just here to help, Mrs. Harrison." She emphasized the name. "It is imperative that all statements made, with or for JD, are free of any type of scandal. Remember, he is running for Governor of the state. He, not you, will have to answer to the public for any shall we say indiscretions on his part. He does not need to add your family issues to a growing laundry list of items the opposition can use against him."

"Their family is one in the same, Mattie," Pearl stated.

"I don't see any incidents regarding the Harrison family coming to the surface." She crossed her legs. "The truth of the matter is Mrs. Harrison's family's growing complications are going to hurt this campaign. As it is we already have to explain, a brother that is a felon, and a missing father or a man that she thought was her father. Now, there's a new father, who happens to be a very popular Senator, and a step-sister, who not only is the First Lady of Virginia, but she used to sleep with your husband. None of you may like what I'm saying, but all of you know enough about politics to know each of these issues are going to be thrown at us and we better have an action plan in place on how we are going to handle each of these situations." She stood. "Now is a good time for me to leave the room so you can rant and rave about my attitude while I'm gone. But be ready to work when I return. Where's your ladies room?" She asked Tracy all in one breath.

It was a minute before Tracy replied. "Around the corner on the right."

Mattie frowned, "Is that one of those little powder rooms with a commode and a sink?
"Yes," Tracy replied.

"No, I need a big bathroom. One that doesn't feel like the room is closing in on me."

Trying hard to be a gracious hostess, Tracy replied. "There is a bathroom upstairs between the children's room. I'll show you."

"You stay here, I'll find it. I'm sure your friends have things to discuss with you."

The women watched as Mattie walked up the stairs. "She's right I don't like what she said, I don't like the way she said it. But she missed the most important one. I don't like her." Ashley declared as she stood and pointed to Tracy. "You better watch her. That woman will do anything including sleep with your husband, if it means winning."

"It's not about JD or the fact that he is damn easy on the eyes," Pearl added, "It could be any man with power including your husband." She looked at Ashley. "Mattie Gresham likes power. Look at the way she came in and took over this meeting. Has anyone else spoken or given an opinion? No. It's power and intimidation that she feeds off of. Tracy she sees you as an inconvenience that has to be dealt with during this campaign. Now is the time for you to establish two things." She waited until Tracy was looking at her then continued. "First and foremost, you are Jeffrey Harrison's wife and you have a say and a place in this campaign that she cannot and will not interfere with. Then you need to make sure your husband understands, if she crosses the line even once, her ass is out."

"I'm not sure I can interfere with Jeffrey's staff in that way. He needs these people to win."

"Well, I can certainly interfere in who works in my husband's office." Ashley stated as she looked towards the stairs. "Why can't you?"

"Do you think she would ever talk to Carolyn Roberts that way?" Pearl asked. "No, she wouldn't. She worked on Gavin's campaign and I will bet money she never crossed Carolyn. We can think whatever we want about Carolyn but she is one of the most powerful women in politics today. She's smart, fearless, and she goes after what she wants or what her husband wants. Once this press conference is over, I suggest you mention Madison Gresham and some of the things she said to you today and I can guarantee she is going to have something to say about it."

Tracy walked over to the picture window and looked out on her quiet residential street. The image of news trucks and reporters played in her mind for she knew that's what the streets would look like a few days from now. It was time for her to ask for help. Pearl was right, Mattie would not talk to Carolyn the way she did with her. "I'll talk with Jeffrey about Ms. Gresham."

"That's another thing. Stop calling her that. Call her Mattie. Continue to insist she refer to you as Mrs. Harrison. Establish here and now your role in this campaign." Pearl stood and walked over to the doorway of JD's office. "I'm going to use the office to call headquarters. I think the statement is fine the way it is, I don't care what Mattie thinks." She stepped into the office and closed the door.

Ashley looked at Tracy. "That woman is after your husband. She did not need to be here for this meeting—why is she here?"

"James indicated Mattie wanted to make sure the statement doesn't have a negative impact on Jeffrey." Tracy replied.

"I'm going to have a talk with her." Ashley stated and began walking up the stairs.

"Ashley, Jeffrey asked me to handle this and I don't want to disappoint him."

"I'm just talking to her. I'm not going to kill her or anything. Go get something to drink and calm your nerves. I'll be right back." Ashley stated and continued up the steps.

When she reached the door to the bathroom Mattie had been directed to she saw that it was empty. She walked down the hallway to the double doors that led to the master bedroom. Mattie was coming out of JD's walk-in-closet. "What in the hell are you doing in here?"

A startled Mattie jumped at the sound of her voice. "This is a beautiful house. I was taking a look around."

"In someone's private bedroom?"

"The master bedroom is the heart of any house." She waved Ashley off and walked towards the door. "But I'm sure you know that. I would love an opportunity to see your house someday."

As Mattie attempted to walk out the door, Ashley's arm blocked her exit. "You will never set foot in my house. If you're ever invited by my husband, I suggest you turn him down. If you don't I will have him retract the invitation and will be glad to tell him why."

"Mrs. Brooks, I'm just doing my job." She acted as if she was offended. "The things I have to tell clients are not always nice and sometimes I'm not as tactful as I should be. But I am very good at what I do."

"I have no doubt that you are. The question I have is what exactly you are up to. Unlike Tracy, I don't see the good in people. I see what is. And I don't like what I see in you. So here's my advice. You better cover your tracks well. If one more picture of you and my brother, in close proximity of each other hits the media or is sent to Tracy, I'm going to kick your ass. Then I will make sure your professional life becomes non-existent." Mattie stared Ashley down, then walked out of the room. "Mattie," Ashley called out. The woman stopped and turned back to her. "I want you to really think about who I am and the power at my disposal before you make another move." She walked up to her. "Do I have the power to do what I said? Yes—I'm a member of one of the wealthiest, most powerful political families in the country. Will I do it? Yes I would do anything to protect my friend. If I do, how far will I take it? " She smiled and began walking down the stairs. "Answers—yes—yes and until life as you know it no longer exists." She looked over her shoulder and said, "Try me—I triple dare you," she then continued down the steps. "I found her. We can finish up now."

Tucker waited for the man to leave and was surprised to see he was watching the home of a police officer. Before he reached his car, a woman came out to give him his hat. He raised his hand to take the hat and the woman ducked. Tucker sat up. He knew that sign. He'd seen it time and time again when he was growing up. The officer took the hat, said something, then got into his car and pulled away. Tucker watched as one of his cars pulled off behind the officer, then turned back to the woman. She was wearing a dress that was too thin for the March weather, he thought as she bent down to pull something from the flower bed near the door, then walked back into the house. He sat there for a moment. Getting a look at the house would be a little difficult with someone inside. But he had to get inside. Getting out of the car, he walked across the street dressed in a business suit and a long black trench coat that hung opened. He knocked on the door and wasn't quite prepared for what he saw. Stunned it took him a moment to speak. The woman couldn't be more than five three or four at the most. If she weighed one hundred and ten pounds, he would be surprised. Her short stylish hair cut was very attractive on her and a face that clearly belonged to an angel, even with the signs of recent abuse.

"May I help you?" She asked in a smooth silky voice that reminded him of Toni Braxton.

It took him a moment to gather his thoughts, which was unusual for the smooth talking confident man. "Hello. I apologize for the interruption. I'm looking for a house for my mother and I noticed there are a few houses on the block for sale. Would you mind answering a few questions about the neighborhood?"

"I'm sorry. I really don't talk to strangers."

He put his hand to his chest. "Please forgive me. I didn't notice anyone else around until I saw you walk in the house." He looked around. "I guess this is a working class neighborhood." He turned back to her. "It's important to me that my mother is safe and comfortable wherever I decided to buy her house. You know with neighbors that will watch over her and visit every now and then."

She smiled at him and placed her hand above her breast. "That is very thoughtful." She looked out the door, then took a step out. "Well, there are a number of seniors that live on this block. Um, there's Mrs. Gray on the corner and she's been here for a while." She pointed to the house in question. "Then there is Mr. and Mrs. Turner directly across the street from her. And of course there is Mrs. Lewis, who will definitely let you know anything that goes on in the neighborhood." She smiled. She wrapped her arms around her body as the wind picked up a little. Tucker took off his coat and put it over her shoulders. "Oh no, I can't take your coat."

"Please Mrs.?"

"Mrs. Gary. Julianna Gary."

"Mrs. Gary. This is so important for me. Where my mother is now, is just not safe. And she doesn't deserve anything but the best life can offer. No woman does." He stated and hoped she was listening.

Julianna pulled the coat around her and relished in the warmth within. Looking around, she didn't see anyone looking. "Why don't you come inside for just a minute and I'll tell you about some of the homes."

"Thank you Mrs. Gary. I would really appreciate that."

Calvin sat in JD's office waiting for him to complete his conversation with Mrs. Langston. Each morning they met to go over case assignments and office issues. "Mrs. Langston please hold all of my and Calvin's calls for the next hour. Also, send Tracy some flowers and on the card write, Forever-For Always-For Love."

Mrs. Langston stood back and looked at him. "Somebody had a good weekend."

JD couldn't help but smile. "All hell broke loose at my house, but all is well now."

"As long as all is well now, that's all that matters. I'll take care of this right away." She smiled and closed the door as she walked out of the office.

"Well, how did the situation with Carolyn turnout?"

"It didn't go too well at first. I even walked out." He saw Calvin frown, "I went to talk to my mother."

"So you ran home to mother."

"Who else? I'm glad I did." He hesitated then looked up. "Calvin is it possible to pull the case file on my father's death?"

"I'm sure we could." Calvin flinched in his seat. He knew more than JD did about James Harrisons' death.

He, Brian and Samuel decided not to divulge what they knew to JD. "Why?" He asked as casually as he could.

"My mother mentioned his wedding ring. She said it was never returned to her. I'd like to find it and give it back to her."

Calvin relaxed. "I'll see what I can do."

"I appreciate that. As for the situation, we all decided to hold a press conference this week. Senator Roth is going to make the announcement in conjunction with his decision to retire from public office. In addition to that, the Attorney General wants a proposal within forty-eight hours on the merit of offering Al Day an early release in return for his assistance with getting Munford off the street."

"That's not a bad trade if you ask me. Day is one criminal. Munford is one plus many others he is allowing to roam the street. Day did not make a commitment to protect the people of this community or to uphold the constitution, Munford did. Day, at the very least had a reason for turning to a life of crime. Munford's reason is greed. Shall I go on?"

JD smiled, "No I get your meaning. How do you think it will play out in the world of public opinion?"

"They are going to say you did all you could to get your wife's brother out of prison. Those on the right will accuse you of abuse of the office, while the brother's on the corner will praise your actions. Then you have the men in the barber shop that will say, *have you seen the body on his wife, I'll let the brother go too, just to keep her happy.* Bottom line, you are not going to please everyone with everything you do. Regardless of the fall-out, you have to do what's right. Or you will not be able to live with yourself."

JD grinned and looked away. He stood and walked over to the window with his hands in his pockets and stared at the floor. Calvin smirked and waited. "Al has always been a man of integrity in his own way. At sixteen he did what he had to, to protect his little sister and has been doing it ever since. How many brothers has he helped start their own businesses in North side? What was it he said, 'Get in, get what you need, and get out.' He encourages all of his people to go legit. What do you think Al would be if he was legit? Tracy says he is twice as smart as she is, can you believe that?" He shook his head, and Calvin remained quiet. He knew JD was thinking through the situation and would arrive at his own decision without any input from him. "For him to run his empire as smoothly as he did—or does, he would have to be a genius. To tell the truth, if he hadn't come forward, we never would have gotten him—not on what we had. I think Al took the opportunity to get out of the business gracefully. When he comes out he will be ready to go legit." With a decision made, JD returned to his chair. "Calvin, get me Al's file. Get what information you can on anyone he helped with starting a business and that may be willing to write an affidavit about it today. Ensure that any person, who comes forward, does so under immunity for any past discretion. After you gather the information, I want it delivered directly to my house. Bring Rossie with you when you come. I want his feedback on what we are about to do and what we write."

"You realize he will be your hardest critic on this."

"That's why I want him," JD replied as he picked up the telephone.

Within an hour of placing the call, Tracy opened the door to find Carolyn there. "Hello Tracy. Pearl called and said you needed me. Here I am." She walked through the door as regally as a queen addressing her court.

Tracy simply shook her head and smiled. "I'm glad you could come on such short notice." Pearl said as they walked into the living room. "I think you know everyone."

"Yes. Mattie, Mattie, Mattie. I'm pretty sure you are the reason I've been summoned."

"Carolyn," Mattie spoke as she stood. "It's good to see you on your feet."

"Tssk Tssk Mattie," Carolyn smirked. "It's un-lady like to be condescending." She looked around. "Hello Ashley."

"Carolyn, you're looking well."

"I know. I'm just remarkable like that."

"She's back," Tracy smiled.

"So I understand we are working on the speech and Mattie has concerns," Carolyn stated as she stared directly at the woman. She looked around the room at a few curious faces and smiled. "Madison you must have said something you had no business saying to upset this very mild mannered woman. Whatever it was, I suggest you get the hell out of my face and go back to the office, before I start naming the men you have used to climb your way to whatever it is you do."

Madison smirked at Carolyn, "Your term as First Lady is coming to end soon. What will you do then?"

"Continue to be a nightmare to you when I become wife of Senator Gavin Roberts."

"Are you sure about that? It seems there are a number of skeleton's in your closet from your brief stint with the bottle. Do you really think the public is ready to forgive and forget?"

Carolyn shrugged her shoulders, "I don't know and don't care. But I can tell you this, Tracy is now family. You screw with her, you screw with me. Whatever is left when Ashley is finished with you, I will devour." She smiled sweetly at the woman, then looked up at Pearl.

"Mattie is one of the brightest minds in politics. If she has an issue, you should listen and make adjustments. But let's make sure everyone is clear. Tracy is the candidate's wife, her wishes come first. If she is not comfortable with the statement, it will not come across as believable to the public. Tracy, you cannot stand idly by and allow Mattie or anyone else to control this situation. You run them, they don't run you. Okay, now that all the cards are on the table, let's get down to work. What is your issue Mattie?"

Sitting in the interrogation room at Richmond Police headquarters was not a regular occurrence for Ryan. Her father, brothers, and uncles were all cops. Whoever, had her brought in, had to have a death wish. When they knocked on her door, she sent a text message to her boss, telling him what was going down just in case she was late. She then called her brother. Taking a glance at her watch, she'd been sitting and waiting for close to an hour. How cool, she thought, they're trying to make me sweat. She reached into her purse pulled out her cell and was about to send a text message when she heard commotion outside the door. Apparently, her brother had arrived. To her surprise, he wasn't alone. She smiled as Donnell, Brian, and Samuel appeared in the doorway. "I guess they waited too long."

"You can't fix stupid," Samuel stated as his six-six frame filled the room. "What are they holding you for slick?"

"No one has bothered to inform me."

"Why the hell not," Donnell yelled as he knocked on the two-way glass on the opposite side of the room.

"Maybe we should call your attorney." Brian stated as he pulled out his blackberry. "I'm sure he can find out why you are being detained."

A few minutes later two detectives walked into the room. The first man through the door was a tall, slim black man, not bad on the eyes, but had an exasperated look. The other was a little shorter white guy with a pleasant disposition. "Let me guess—good cop—bad cop," Ryan pointed to the black detective first then the white one.

"Sorry, I'm the nice one," the black detective smiled. "He's the hard ass."

"Are any of you gentlemen her attorney?" The white cop asked.

"Gary, don't make me whip your ass in your own precinct," Donnell threatened.

Brian touched Donnell's arm, pulling him back. "Is Ms. Williams under arrest?" he asked.

"Since you chose not to provide me with an answer I don't see any reason I should reciprocate." Gary replied.

Samuel and Brian looked at each other and grinned. "Such a big word for such a little man." He put the blackberry on the desk.

"Gentlemen, I don't believe I got your names when you introduced yourselves. Allow me to show you how it's done. My name is Vernon Brooks. I am Ms. Williams' attorney. I'm not there in person, because I'm in a meeting with the US Attorney General. Would either of you gentlemen like an introduction?" Vernon Brooks was one of the top criminal defense attorneys in the country and happened to be James' brother. The two detectives looked at each other they immediately recognized the name. The black detective put his head down and tried to suppress his grin. "The rule of etiquette dictates that when one introduces oneself to unknown persons in the room the gesture is reciprocated Detective Gary."

"Detective Cole," the black officer stated. "And as you know Detective Gary, at your service, counselor."

"Ah, the good cop," Vernon chuckled. "Gentlemen, my time is limited and my client will not converse with you, without me. Prior to my client sharing as much as her name, you will explicate to my satisfaction, the series of events that impelled you to seek out my client. Anyone need a dictionary to understand my vocabulary?"

"I think we understood your question counselor," Detective Gary snidely replied.

"Good. Answer the question," Vernon commanded.

Detective Cole looked up at Detective Gary with a question in his eyes. "Mr. Brooks, what proof do we have that you are who you say you are?"

"You're as big of an ass as your chief." Vernon sighed. "Brian, escort Ms. Williams out of the station. Detective, if they are delayed by as much as a minute tell your chief to expect a law-suit. Do not attempt to approach my client in any fashion without contacting my office first. This meeting is complete."

Ryan stood in her signature stilettos boots, jeans, tee shirt, and leather jacket. "Well gentlemen, it's been real." She picked up her purse and looked at Brian. "I'm impressed boss." She turned to the detectives and smirked. "I'm sorry we didn't get a chance to chat. Next time don't make me wait so long."

Following the group out of the door, Detective Cole touched Donnell on the shoulder. "You have a moment?"

Donnell looked him up and down, and then motioned for Brian and Samuel, "I'll meet you at the car."

"I worked for your father in Hampton. How's he doing?"

Donnell stared at the man at first wondering why he stopped him from leaving. "He's doing well," he answered hesitantly.

"When you talk to him, tell him hello for me."

Detective Gary stood listening intently to the conversation. Once he was comfortable with the conversation being had, he walked away. "I'm going to make a call while you continue your love feast."

"This will only be a minute." Detective Cole stated as he watched the man walk away. "This was a dirty grab." He said but continued to smile as if it was a general conversation. "Your sister was summoned down by the Chief and he is not going to be happy with the outcome. I'm not privy to the questions he wanted answers to, but I will tell you this. He's gotten wind of questions coming from the AG's office." He patted Donnell on the back and shook his hand. "Watch over her." He said as he walked away.

Donnell walked out and got into the SUV waiting outside the building. He read the note that was placed in his hand. It was a phone number. Written underneath it said "disposable"

"What was that about?" Brian asked.

"I don't know. You got a disposable cell phone?" Donnell asked.

"I know where you can get a few untraceable if you need them," Ryan offered. Donnell, Samuel, and Brian all turned to look at her. "What?" she asked.

"Anything we need to know about?" Samuel asked.

"No. I have no idea why they brought me in." she declared.

Donnell, who sat in the back seat with Ryan, looked up at Brian. "According to Cole, Munford ordered her to be picked up."

"Why?" They all looked at Ryan.

"Look I'm getting sick of y'all. Can we leave this place?"

Brian stared a moment longer, then turned around and pulled off.

"There was a glitch—she lawyered up," Officer Gary spoke into the phone.

"I don't give a damn about a lawyer. Question her anyway," Munford stated.

"We had to let her go or risk questions being asked. You're forgetting—Cole is my partner."

"I need access to Harrison's house. The information to Day's location has got to be there. Pull the Williams woman back in and pump her until you get something useful."

"I don't think that's the way to go."

An angry Munford shouted, "I don't give a damn what you think. Get the information and get it now!" The call was disconnected.

Gary exhaled and put the telephone away. "Emotions are the beginning of the end." He said to himself while shaking his head.

"Everything alright man?" Cole asked.

"Yeah. I think I'm going to ride home—grab some lunch. I'll see you in an hour."

Cole watched as Gary walked out of the station door.

Tucker sat in the unmarked SUV across the street from the Gary residence and thought about the woman inside—Julianna Gary was the kind of woman who could make a man go straight. The woman sparked his interest like no other—but she was married. His cell phone chimed as he shook the thoughts of her smile from his mind. Looking at the number that appeared he shook his head and exhaled. It was his boss' daughter. "Yes Monique."

"Uncle Tuck I want to come to Richmond this weekend but Mommy said I can't go."

"Why do you need to come here?" Tuck asked as he watched a car pull into the driveway of the house he'd just left. "I know I told you to stay away from Bear."

The girl smacked her lips. "I ain't thinking about Bear, Uncle Tuck. Me and Kaylen want to go to the mall."

"There are malls in Norfolk," he replied as he saw a neighbor talking to Officer Gary.

"I want to go to the new one in Richmond," the sixteen year old whined.

"No." Tuck replied with his patience running low.

"Look you ain't my daddy. I was just trying to be polite to call you in the first place."

"Keep your ass in Norfolk. Goodbye Monique." Tuck closed his phone. The device he'd placed in the living room, and bedroom of the home should be sufficient for what he needed. He listened and watched as Gary entered the house. His initial fears were realized as he watched the monitor. The impact of the back hand Gary rendered on his wife prompted Tuck to exit the SUV, but he stopped knowing if he interfered, it could affect the case.

"You had a man in my house. I'm working and you had a man in my house." Gary yelled.

Julianna was on the floor in the living room crawling towards the kitchen when he kicked her.

The kick was more than Tuck could take. He started the SUV and pulled up in front of the house. He quickly

got out, walked over to the car, and placed a devise under
the bumper. He then walked up to the door and
knocked. He waited and knocked again. When the door
opened, Tuck had one hand on the butt of his gun that
was secured in the back of his pants. "Hello. There was a
lady here earlier that helped me with the house down the
street. I was wondering if I could speak with her again."

"She's not available," Gary replied and was about to
shut the door when Tuck stuck his foot in. Gary looked
the man up and down as his eyes narrowed.

"You must be her husband, Officer Gary." The man
did not reply, but continued to stare. "I want you to take
a good look at me. Officer Gary." Tuck took a step
closer until they were almost nose to nose. "I think it's a
good idea for you to return to work—now. If you put your
hands on her again, for any reason, you will see me when
you least expect it."

"Who in the hell are you?"

"The man who will take your life if you touch her
again. Tell your wife goodbye and go back to work
Officer Gary." Gary went to push the man out of his
doorway when he suddenly felt the hard cold metal of
steel at his forehead and froze. "Leave now, while you
can."

Gary stepped out of the door-way, "I'm a police
officer."

"You will be a dead officer if you don't leave, now."
Tuck put the weapon down by his side. He stood at the
door as he watched Gary get into his car and pulled way.
Tucker watched until the vehicle was out of site. He
walked back into the house to find Julianna curled up in
a fetal position in a corner of the kitchen. Her face was
red from the hit and her lip was cut. She wrenched when
he reached out for her. "I promise I will not allow him to
hurt you again. Come with me." Tucker took off his coat
and covered her with it. He then picked her up as she

cried out in pain. He placed her on the back seat of the SUV and pulled away. Knowing he'd just caused a whole heap of trouble, he called Brian. "We have a situation," he said as he looked in the rear view mirror at his passenger.

Officer Gary stormed into the precinct and went directly to the computer. He knew the man's face from somewhere. Checking every data base available, he found nothing. He slammed his fist on the desk. "Damn. Who in the hell was he?" Then it hit him. He pulled out the folder he had on JD Harrison. Inside were photos from the crime scene when Tracy Harrison was nearly beaten to death. There he was Donovan Tucker, Al Day's lieutenant standing in the background.

Chapter 10

Brian sat at his desk in the pool house with Donnell trying to figure out why Munford wanted Ryan called in. Nothing they came up with made sense. "Does Munford know Ryan is working for us?" Brian asked as he looked at the computer.

"According to Cole, Gary had been working exclusively for Munford on a number of things. Unfortunately, there are a few others that are under his control. He believes if we could get something on Gary, he would roll on Munford."

Brian's cell phone chimed as he asked Donnell, "What do we know about Gary?"

"Not much, he came after I left the force."

"Thompson," Brian answered his call.

"We have a situation," Tucker stated. "We need to meet now."

Brian stood as he shut his computer down. "Where are you?"

"My place," Tuck stated and gave his address and hung up the telephone.

Brian looked at the phone. Tucker gave him the address to his house. He looked up at Donnell and shook his head. "Something's not right. You ride with me." They both left the office just as Brian's cell phone chimed again. "Thompson."

"Boss, Gary is here at the park sitting on the bench with Mrs. H."

Brian stopped dead in his tracks. "The park by the house?"

"Yeah. You want me to take him out?"

"Where are the children?" Brian asked as he picked up speed walking to the car.

"I have JC—Jasmine is with Tracy."

"Approach. I'm on my way."

Tracy was sitting on the bench waiting for Ryan and JC to return from the restroom when a man approached her. "Mrs. Harrison."

She looked up from feeding Jasmine and smiled. "Yes."

"You have a beautiful smile."

"Thank you. Do I know you?"

"No, I'm sure you don't. I know your brother."

"You know Turk?" she asked excited to meet someone who knew her brother.

"May I have a seat?"

"Of course you may," Tracy said as she slid over as the man took a seat.

"Actually I ran into a friend of your brother's this morning at my house." There was something in the man's tone that caused Tracy to now proceed with caution. She looked around, but did not see Ryan and JC. "He took something that belongs to me."

"I'm sorry, I didn't get your name," Tracy said as she tightened her hold on Jasmine and prayed the panic did not show on her face.

"That's because I did not give it," Officer Gary stated as his smile faded.

Tracy looked around and saw Ryan staring at her talking on the telephone. She stood to place Jasmine in the stroller. "I don't really know any of my brother's friends."

Officer Gary looked up as Ryan approached them." Before he could stand, the bench was surrounded by Brian, Donnell, and Magna. Because there were other families in the vicinity, they did not pull weapons. But their stance indicated they were ready to take him out if they had to. Ryan took Tracy and the children to the running SUV. Secured them inside and pulled off.

"Officer Gary, we meet again," Brian stated.

Gary never moved from his position. "It took me a moment to figure out who Donovan Tucker was. Then I had to wonder why he was watching me. Then I remembered, Donovan Tucker was Al Day's right hand man. If he's watching me that means he thinks I'm a threat to Tracy Harrison."

"Are you?"

"Not yet. However, he crossed the line. My possession was taken and I want it returned."

"I have no idea what you are referring to. If you have an issue with Mr. Tucker, I suggest you take it up with him and stay away from Tracy Harrison or I will have you arrested. I don't give a damn who you work for."

Officer Gary stood. "I'll be granted immunity before you can blink an eye regardless of what I do."

Brian stepped into Gary's face, "The woman you sat next to is very dear to me. If anyone thought of harming a hair on her head, they would be dealing with me directly."

"Be nice Thompson. Your boss may need me soon." Officer Gary stepped around Brian and walked off.

Brian looked at Donnell. "Stay on him. I want to know where he is every minute of the day. Magna, I want you at the house—seal it. No one in—no one out." He then pulled out his cell and dialed. "You want to tell me what in the hell is going on?"

Tucker exhaled. "You'll see when you get here."

Tracy walked into the house clutching Jasmine to her and with JC's hand held tightly at her side. Ryan walked in as Tracy took a seat to check her children over once again. "Mrs. Gordon has anyone been to the house?"

"Yes, a police officer stopped by to see Mrs. Harrison. I told him you were in the park. Did he find you?" She asked Tracy.

"Yes, he found us." Tracy replied as she took the children upstairs.

"Is something wrong," Mrs. Gordon asked Ryan.

Ryan was busy securing the house. "I'm afraid that wasn't a friendly officer."

"Oh my goodness. Did something happen?" Mrs. Gordon asked distraught.

Ryan touched her on the shoulder. "Everything is fine. I think you will need to stay here tonight. Can you do that?"

"Of course I can."

"Good." Ryan continued with what she was doing as Mrs. Gordon went upstairs.

Magna walked through the door. "Everyone okay?"

The adrenaline was still rushing through Ryan as she took a seat. "Yes, everyone is okay."

Magna looked at Ryan. "How did he get that close?"

"I took JC to the restroom."

"You are not here to babysit. You are here to protect."

"I know that."

"Apparently you don't. Tracy and the baby could be dead right now."

"Don't you think I know that? I knew the moment I walked out and saw him on that bench."

"Are you here to replace me?"

"No. But I'm sure coverage is going to double up on everyone."

Ryan exhaled then went upstairs to see Tracy. She found her in the master bedroom with both children curled up in the bed. "Mrs. H."

"Yes Ryan." Tracy replied without looking away from her children.

"I am so sorry. I should have been there with you."

"You were helping me Ryan. It wasn't your fault."

"Yes it was. My job is to protect you, not help you. I may not return after tonight and I wanted to tell you how much I admire you and your husband." Ryan turned and walked out of the room.

Brian made it to Tucker's home in fifteen minutes flat. When he arrived, he had to be buzzed in through a private gate. "I must be in the wrong business." He said as the gate opened. Pulling into the circular driveway and parked. A man stood at the front door to let him in.

"Mr. Thompson," the man held out his hand. "Mr. Tucker is waiting for you in his study."

Brian shook the man's hand and followed him as he looked around. When he entered the room, he stared at Tucker who stood behind a cherry wood desk. "What in the hell do you do?"

Tucker laughed. "I'm an investment broker, if you must know."

Brian shook his head as he looked around. "Why?"

"Why do I work for Al? The man has been good to me. I would not be here if it weren't for him."

"Damn." Brian said as he took a seat. "What in the hell have you taken from Gary?"

"His wife."

Brian's eyebrows rose. "You took the man's wife—why?"

"He was beating the crap out of her and I couldn't sit there and watch it happen."

"Where is she?"

"Upstairs with my private physician."

"You have a private physician that makes house calls?"

Tucker laughed and shook his head. "I tell you the man was beating the crap out of his wife, and all you can ask me is about the doc?"

Brian held his hand up. "Man you are catching me off guard. Okay, Okay, you took the man's wife. He wants' her back."

Tucker shook his head, "Nope, he can't have her back. Any man that puts his hands on or uses his feet to kick a woman deserves a bullet in his head."

"Is she here on her own will?"

"She is under my protection now."

"You didn't answer my question."

"I didn't ask her."

"Are you planning to ask her?"

"No."

Brian looked at Tucker, who seemed very relaxed as he reclined back in his chair behind the desk, to see if he was serious and decided—he was. "All right man, at the very least, you have to let me see her."

Tucker thought for a moment, then stood. "I can do that." Brian followed Tucker out of the room and walked towards the stairs. "No man, this way," Tucker stated. They walked into what Brian at first thought was a closet, but it turned out to be an elevator. While riding to the third floor Brian could only stare at Tucker in amazement. Tucker leaned against the back panel of the elevator and crossed his legs at the ankle. "Don't try to figure me out."

"You are blowing me away here man. All these years you've been playing at being a thug."

"Don't get it twisted. I am a thug through and through. But, even a thug has to know when to move on. Al and I moved on the day he went in. All we do now is act as peace keepers on the street. Neither of us runs anything anymore. We just keep the peace."

The elevator door opened and they stepped out on to the third level of the house. "Why keep up the façade?"

"Because your man still needs us in place." They walked a hallway that resembled the Ritz Carlton in New York, including the plush carpet beneath their feet that felt like you were walking on air. Turning down a corridor, a set of double doors was at the end of the hallway with a man sitting on the outside. "Is the doc still here?" Tucker asked.

"Yes sir," the man stood and opened the door.

Stepping inside there was a sitting area with a fireplace. Walking through to the next room there was a bed, with beautiful silk linens, and what appeared to be a very small woman in the center, lying under them. A man who, Brian assumed, was the doctor came out of the bathroom with a glass of water in his hand. "How's our patient doc?" Tucker asked.

"Badly bruised, but she will be fine." The man replied.

The woman remained on her side looking out of the windows that overlooked the garden and pasture in the distance. Tucker walked over to the other side of the bed and sat down next to her. "Juliana someone is here to see you. His name is Brian Thompson and he is an FBI agent. He needs to make sure you are safe. Will you speak with him?"

Brian was amazed at the softness in Tucker's voice that he would have never associated with the man. Tucker stood and nodded at Brian to come forward. As Tucker walked by, Brian could only stare at the man in amazement. Tucker shook his head and stepped to the side.

Brian looked down at the woman and knew instantly why Tucker had taken her. Even with the bruise on her face, it was clear she was a vision. Brian inhaled then spoke. "Mrs. Gary, I've spoken to your husband. He has asked that Mr. Tucker return you. Do you want to go home?"

"Yes," Juliana replied.

Brian looked at Tucker who had not changed his stance and remained expressionless at her response. Brian turned back to her. "Would you like for me to take you to your husband?"

"He's not my husband."

A frown formed on Brian's face and Tucker took a step closer to the end of the bed. "Jonas Gary is not your husband?" Brian asked for clarification.

"No. He took me from my home on my eighteenth birthday." For the first time her eyes moved from the window to Brian's face. "I want to go home."

"Where is home Juliana?" Tucker asked.

She looked over at him and a faint smile creased her lips. "Your mother isn't moving into the neighborhood, is she?"

Tucker returned the smile and shook his head. "No she isn't."

The two continued to stare at each other. "You were there for Jonas?"

"We think your" he paused, "we think Jonas is into something pretty bad and I was watching your house."

"If you arrest Jonas, where will I go?"

"You can stay here until you are ready to go home."

She turned back to the window. "My parents think I'm dead."

Brian looked at Tucker, then back to Juliana. "How long have you been gone?"

"Ten years this May."

"Where are you from Juliana?"

"My name is Juliana Maria St.Clair from Spokane, Washington. I'm the only child of Julian and Maria St.Clair."

"Would you like for me to contact your parents?" Brian asked.

Tears streamed down the woman's face. "They may not remember me now."

Tucker walked over and sat down on the bed. "Juliana, look at me," he quietly demanded. When the woman complied, he tilted his head and gave her a comforting smile. "Your family will be very happy to know you are alive and well. Trust me."

The woman eyes never left his. "Men keep taking me. First, Jonas and now you."

Tucker jaw clenched. "Do you think I would hurt you like Jonas?"

"I don't know," she replied and looked away.

Tucker stood and looked at Brian. "Juliana, you will be safe here with Tucker until we contact your family. I'll come back as soon as I locate them."

The doctor stepped forward. "It's important that she rest for a while. You can question her more later."

Tucker nodded and as the doctor walked around the bed to give her a pill, they stepped out of the room. "Now we know why he wanted her back." Brian stated. He looked at Tucker. "Can you handle this?"

"I'll find her parents. But I can't promise I'll let her go."

"Gary took her from her home, abused her, and caged her in. Now, I'm no expert, but, I believe if you help her find her way home, then let her go. When she returns, she will always be yours." He shrugged his shoulders, "I'm just saying."

Tucker stared at Brian. "That's deep for a brother that doesn't have a woman."

"Who said I don't have a woman. I have plenty of women."

Tucker frowned at him and began walking back towards the elevator. "You're a little touchy on that subject aren't you?"

The moment he pulled into the driveway and entered the garage, JD knew something was off. The door closed as Samuel parked outside in the driveway. He walked into the side door of the garage with his weapon pulled. "Stay here for a moment." Walking over to the door leading into the kitchen he could see Magna leaning against the counter drinking a cup of coffee and Ryan pacing back and forth. He put the weapon away and motioned for JD to get out of the car. "Hmm, I'm not sure we want to go in right now."

Closing the car door JD walked over, opened the door, and walked in. Everyone stopped and stared up at him. The scene would have been funny if everyone didn't look so serious. "Good evening everyone," he said as he placed his keys on the tray. No one replied. JD looked back at Samuel, who shrugged his shoulders. "Did someone get kidnapped today?" He asked with a chuckle. The smile quickly disappeared as he dropped his briefcase and walked briskly by them. "Where are Tracy and the children?" He asked, not really waiting for an answer.

"They're upstairs Mr. H." Ryan replied.

Taking the steps, two at a time JD reached the hallway to find Tracy wrapped in Brian's arms, crying. The sight of Tracy in another man's arms would have bothered him, if it was anyone but Brian. "What's going on?"

Tracy turned to see Jeffrey on the steps. She pulled away from Brian, ran over to him throwing her arms around his neck, and cried into the crook of his neck. "Shh babe," he said as he kissed her cheek and held her close. Looking over his shoulder at Brian, he silently questioned what was happening.

Brian lowered his head. "We'll talk once you two have a moment." He walked by them and went downstairs. It had been a long trying day and Brian knew the night was going to be even longer as he walked down the stairs into the kitchen. He stood in the doorway with his arms across his chest and just stared at Ryan. Every instinct in his body wanted to shout and fire her on the spot, but he'd just promised Tracy that he wouldn't do that.

"Boss, look," Ryan started.

Brian held up his hand, "Don't." he stated then looked at Samuel. "Where are you tonight?"

"I take it, not at home with my wife."

"No. I need Absolute on Officer Gary like yesterday. If he makes one wrong move, take him out." Samuel stepped back into the garage to make his call.

Magna placed her cup in the sink. "My vote is she stays."

"I don't recall asking," Brian stated as he stared her down.

Picking up her jacket, Magna smiled. "I know you didn't. But I want you to remember she saved Cynthia and Samuel's ass more than once. That coupled with the fact that she can break a piece off in your ass like that."

She snapped her fingers, kissed his cheek, and walked over to Ryan. "Let him have his say. He has to feel like he is in control."

"I'm standing right here," Brian said.

Magna turned, smiled, and said, "I know." She then walked out of the door.

At the sound of the door closing, Ryan looked over at the man that held her fate in his hands. She knew if he told JD that she was staying, that would be that. But if she did not have his support, her short stint on the good side may be over.

Brian was furious that she had allowed someone to get that close to Tracy, but he knew this was a mistake that rookies make. They get too close to their client. Hell, he was too close. Knowing the kind of man he was dealing with now made this situation more dangerous than he had previously thought. Jonas Gary wasn't just a police officer. He was a dirty cop with violent tendencies. Tracy could be dead. Just the thought still brought chills to his spine. When he was upstairs, holding her was as much of a comfort for him as he hoped it was for her. Now he had to ensure that her life was not put in danger again. He spoke quietly, doing all that was in his power not to let his temper explode. "It is not your job to do Tracy's bidding. You do not assist in kidnapping her sister, or help her with the children. Your job is to detect and deter danger. Nothing comes before her life, not her feelings, not her happiness, not her sadness. I know how hard it is to put those things aside with a person like Tracy. But it is imperative that we do to save her life. You are new at this and it is hard to separate the personal from the business, but you have to find a way to put what is best for the client first." He relaxed his stance and put his hands in his pockets. "JD is going to want me to relieve you from Tracy's detail. I won't do that because I believe in you. I believe that you can do this job and be good at it. You have thirty days to prove I'm not wrong. You are dismissed."

Ryan was not an emotional person. Being raised with males taught her to hide her emotions, but this was one time she had to let them show. This man believed in her and she appreciated him telling her so. She walked over, kissed his cheek, and left out the patio door.

He waited until she was gone before he touched his cheek. In his mind, Tucker's words came back to him. He had women. He just held Tracy in his arms, then was kissed by Magna and Ryan. But none of those women were his. The idea of having someone to call his own had played havoc on his mind for a while now. Especially since all his boys were now settled down. At the moment, he had to get this situation under control. Something was about to hop off. He could feel it in his soul. It was his job to make sure, JD and his family came out of it alive. Samuel walked back into the house. "Anything on Absolute?"

"Yeah, but you are not going to like it."

"Gary is already a person of interest with the weapons distribution. He is the one making the arrangements, not Munford. Unless JD has more, we can't get Munford on the weapons."

"Things got a little more complicated today."

"How so?"

"There is an issue with Officer Gary."

"Brian what in the hell happened today," JD yelled. "Is this the same man that was watching my house? And how in the hell did he get that close to Tracy and my children?"

Both men turned to see JD standing near the stairs with a diaper and Jasmine across his shoulder burping her. The anger in his face and the way he was holding his daughter was a direct contrast to each other. But that was the nature of the man, he could be warm, loving, understanding, but then that, temper could explode with no notice. "JD," Brian began, "there were one or two issues today."

"No shit!" JD exclaimed as the door bell sounded.

He turned towards the door as Samuel looked at Brian and smirked, "Saved by the bell."

"Ha, Ha," Brian said exasperated.

"Laugh if you want to, but you are the one about to get your ass chewed out."

"Hey Brian, Samuel," Calvin called from the doorway. "What's up?"

Brian walked over and gave Calvin a pound and shoulder bump. "We need to talk," he whispered.

Calvin nodded, "Alright man."

"Calvin, introduce Rossie and show him around while I put Jazzy to bed," JD stated as he started up the steps. He looked over at Brian, "We are not done."

"I'll be here," Brian stated.

Calvin looked at JD's retreating back then to Brian. "What's up?"

"Let's go in the office."

The men piled into JD's office as Calvin introduced Rossie. Once seated, Brian began to fill Calvin in on the events of the day. JD walked in and took a seat behind his desk as they talked.

"Based on all that was said, it's clear that Jonas Gary is the point man. Can we get him to turn?" JD asked clearly with an edge to his voice.

"Possibly," Brian replied.

"Possibly, what the hell does that mean Brian."

"Just what the hell I said, possibly." He stared pointedly at JD. "There's another piece to this. Tucker took who we thought was Gary's wife. Gary's purpose of contacting Tracy was not for Munford's benefit, but his own. He wanted his wife back."

JD sat up a little calmer. "Can we do an exchange?'

"That would be reasonable except, she's not his wife. Turns out, he kidnapped her ten years ago and to complicate things more, Tucker is refusing to give her back."

"Donovan Tucker? Al's man?" JD asked.

"Yes and no. It seems Tucker and Al both left the business. When Al went in, he cut all ties with the gang. Their only connection is as peace keepers."

JD, Calvin, and Rossie all looked at each other. That information was going to make their task a lot easier to accomplish. "If that's true, making an argument for his release will be easier if he actually has something to take Munford down. That's the piece we don't know Mr. H. We don't know if what Al has will put Munford away. We are only assuming."

"Synopsis Calvin," JD asked.

Calvin shook his head, "Man there are too many pieces going on here. The key is Al. What does he have on Munford? We know we can't take him down on the weapons charge unless Jonas Gary is willing to turn on him. We have a number of cases leading to him on corruption. Without a credible witness, none of them will stick. Munford has a ring of gangs working at his disposal. The only one that has no ties with him is Day's people. Why?"

"Al has got to have something on him." JD stated as he sat back thinking. "Munford likes control. He is not the type to let even an ounce of it get away. How did Al manage it?" He looked around the room. "Brian we have to prepare this proposal for the US Attorney General by Wednesday. Is it possible to check out Tucker's story before then? If Al is really out, he may be willing to turn on Munford. As a back up, get all we can on Officer Gary. If he did kidnap this woman, let's get her back to her family. We could offer him immunity in exchange for what he has on Munford."

"I'll check further into it and let you know," Brian replied.

"You know," Samuel spoke. "Munford has been known to act foolishly when he is cornered. Remember last year at the church." He looked at JD.

Calvin nodded, "That was a stupid move. He had to take a step back and regroup."

"That's right," Samuel agreed. "What do you think he would do if he knew you were coming after him?"

"You mean leak it to him?" JD asked.

"No. I mean make a public statement regarding the investigation."

Calvin sat forward, "That could be dangerous. Besides, we don't have enough to put him away."

"That's true, but we do have enough to show abuse of office," Rossie offered.

"The dangerous part concerns me especially after today's events," JD looked at Brian.

All eyes went to Brian. "We can handle it."

The events of the day were still not clear to JD. The only thing he knew was that a man who was a threat to his wife and children had gotten too close for comfort. However, he believed in Brian and knew he would do all he could to protect his family. "Alright. We will work on the proposal. Afterwards you and I will have a sit down." He said to Brian.

Tracy stretched as the smell of coffee invaded her senses. Reaching over, the area where Jeffrey slept was empty, but still warm. She sat up quickly, hoping he hadn't left yet, to see him sitting by the door dressed in his shirt and tie.

"Good morning beautiful," he smiled.

Returning the smile, but seeing Jeffrey sitting near the door dressed, gave her a sinking feeling; she threw back the comforter to get up.

"Stay there," he said as he walked over to her side of the bed. He stacked the pillows behind her and positioned his arms on the bed on both sides of her. He smiled at her tousled hair and sleepy eyes. "Mrs. Gordon is downstairs with JC. We had breakfast together and I discussed some things with her. When Carolyn told you about your father, I made you a promise that I would not keep anything from you. However, as Attorney General there are things I will not be able to share, even with you."

"What's wrong Jeffrey," Tracy fretted.

He rubbed her arms to ease her concern. "The office is involved in an investigation that may be a little dangerous. The person of interest is someone that is not necessarily fond of your brother or me. I'm afraid they may target you and the children to get information. I'm not sure why he has such an urge to find Turk. As for me, it's my job to bring him down."

"Okay," Tracy mused. "Is that why the man approached me?"

"Yes, and until things calm down, I need you to stay close to home. Brian will be here with you. I explained the situation to Mrs. Gordon and she understands she has to live here until this is over. She said that she has no intention of quitting."

"What about you?"

"I'm not quitting either," he smiled to lighten the conversation.

She touched his cheek with her fingers, "I know you're not. Where are you going to be?"

"I'll be at work and Samuel will be with me." The look of concern clouded her eyes. Pulling her into his arms, he tried to calm her fears, "I will not allow anything to happen to you or the children."

"I know, but I'm worried about you."

He kissed the top of her ear as his hand smoothly caressed her back, "I'll be fine." He pulled back because his body was doing what it always did when he held her, reacting. "There's more. James called this morning. Immediately after the press conference with Senator Roth, he wants to jump into fund raising. The DNC wants to hold a primary fund raiser next weekend. A meeting with you and some of the wives of major contributors is also scheduled for Saturday. I've asked Mattie to be there and help in anyway she can. Only do what you are comfortable with, nothing more. I have all the confidence in the world in you. Remember, for awhile, no going out of the house without protection."

"I'll remember." Tracy lay back on the pillows and sighed. "Running for Governor is going to be different; you know that as well as I. Raising money is going to be a priority. Women play a major role there, you are going to need me, whether I want to or not."

JD smiled at the look on his wife's face. "Tracy, I need you beside me in whatever capacity you are comfortable with."

Sitting back thoughtfully, Tracy considered all Jeffrey had told her. "Who is the person that wants you and Turk and why?" She asked with her eyes looking down at her hands that she was rubbing together.

JD recognized the nervous reaction and covered her hands with his. With his thumb he lifted, her chin until her eyes were looking directly at him. "This is one of those things I can't tell you."

"Is this also why you won't tell me where Turk is?"

"Yes. All of that is my job to worry about, not yours." He kissed her. "I have to go. I'll call you later."

The next twenty-four hours were a blur. JD submitted the proposal to the Attorney General along with the plan on how they wanted to take Munford down. Brian had checked into Tucker's claim to be clean and found it was true. He also acquired Douglas' help with Juliana St. Clair. Tucker allowed Karen Holt, who had been through a similar situation to come and talk with Juliana. They also located the woman's parents, but did not make contact.

The press conference went off without a hitch mainly due to Carolyn and Tracy. The two women answered every question that was hurled at them without hesitation. They had the press eating out of their hands. Now it was a matter of dealing with the backlash of the announcement.

Thursday morning Chief Munford sat in his office enjoying the article in the paper regarding JD Harrison's wife. "I guess his image isn't as squeaky clean as we first thought."

"Don't fool yourself," Jonas said. "Harrison is still and will always be very popular. It is hard to discredit his public image. Even this announcement earned him sympathy, especially with women voters."

Munford looked over the top of the paper. "Aren't you a ray of sunshine this morning? Is everything set for tonight?"

"It's set," Jonas shook his head. "You should put it off."

"For what reason? Something happening I don't know about?"

Jonas did not intend to tell Munford about the situation with his wife. Nor did he plan on going to jail because of Munford's greed. "Just a feeling."

"My decisions are not based on your feelings. You'll feel a lot better once you receive your part of the payment."

"Has it ever crossed your mind that those weapons will be used against us?"

"You're growing a conscience now?" He put the paper down on the desk and glared at Jonas. "These weapons are moving out of the state. Does that ease your mind?"

"The money in my account eases my mind," Jonas replied and stood. "I'm out. The trucks are in place. All they have to do is drive away," he chuckled.

"Good. That money will finance my Mayoral campaign." He looked sideways at Jonas and smiled. "It's getting so close now, I can smell it. The only thing standing in my way is Al Day. Have you gotten a way into Harrison's house?"

"I've been keeping an eye on Ryan Williams. She's working as security at the house. I'll push a little harder. Maybe she will turn."

"You do that. In the mean time I'll work my end."

The fallout from the press conference wasn't devastating, but it stung. Mattie thought as she read the newspaper articles on line. Now she was checking the blogs to see how the news coverage played out on the internet. So far, there was only one reporter that may have to be called in—Chris Piozzi's blog was a little rough. It read;

"Well, it seems our illustrious Attorney General
believes in keeping things in the family.
We all remember a few years ago when
J.D. Harrison and Carolyn Roth were a hot

item around town. That is until the beautiful,
inside and out, Tracy Washington-Harrison came
out of nowhere and snagged the ever so popular
Harrison from the ranks of the free and single.
Well, she didn't appear out of nowhere after all.
Tracy Washington-Harrison is the daughter of
the one and only Senator John Roth.
That's right folks that makes Tracy
Washington-Harrison, our very own First Lady's
half sister.
Now is that a hoot or what?
We saw the interaction between the two earlier
this week.
I wonder if they compared notes.

She exhaled. She wouldn't worry about this one
article, but if he posts another with the same tone, action
would need to be taken. Her cell phone rung and she
answered without checking the number. "I want
information on the layout of Harrison's home now.
What do you have?"

Mattie would give anything not to help this man with
whatever he had in mind for JD. But her brother's future
and freedom were riding on her. How many times had
she told him about getting high? Eventually he was
bound to be caught holding. It was just her luck he was
caught by a dirty cop who knew his connection to her.
Now Munford was using her to get information on JD
Harrison. When she went after this assignment at
Munford's insistence, she was only here to get what she
could to have her brother's record cleared. Now, she
actually liked what JD stood for. She wanted this man to
win, if for no other reason than to get men like Munford
off the streets and locked up like they should be. "I've
only been in the house once. What do you want from
me?"

"See Madeline, it's not what I want from you. It's what your brother needs from you. What do you have?"

"Alright. The master bedroom is on the second floor on the north back side of the house. There is a master closet, but I did not see a safe of any kind. I never had the opportunity to go into the office."

"That wasn't so hard Mattie. Now, you will get into his office."

"There is no valid reason for me to be at his house."

"Find one and do it soon. The DA is pushing for a court date for your brother." The called ended.

Mattie looked at the phone and was about to throw it against the wall when James walked in. "Hey Mattie, you have a minute?"

"Sure," she smiled. "What do you need?"

"Mr. Attorney General, the Governor is on line one," Mrs. Langston stated.

"Thank you," JD replied and picked up the phone. "Hello Gavin."

"JD, the proposal was accepted. You have the okay from the Attorney General to approach Day and take down Munford."

JD exhaled and dropped his head. "This is going to be a bumpy ride. Are you ready?"

"You have my unwavering support. Take him down."

JD hung up the telephone and hesitated, then placed a call to Calvin. "We're on. My place tonight." He then called Brian to gather the best security available. This meeting was to ensure the security of his family. Munford was going to attack anyone close to JD when he went down. They had to be prepared.

Chapter 11

Tucker stood in the visitor's room early in the morning, waiting for Al to appear. This was the first time he was concerned about Al's reaction to a decision he'd made. The last three days with Juliana in his home, made him want more. He wanted her in the worse way. It was clear she had things she needed to work through, but on the second day when he actually heard her laugh, the sound clutched at his heart and he found himself doing anything to hear the sound again.

"Hey man, did you hear me?"

Tuck turned to see Al standing there looking expectantly at him. Extending his hand he laughed. "No man. Did you say something?"

"Nothing important. What's on your mind?" Al asked, wondering what had his right hand man so off point. Tuck would never be caught off guard

The two friends took a seat as they normally did, but this time moments went by and Tuck did not speak, nor did he look at Turk in the eyes. Turk chuckled at the bashful look on Tuck's face and took pity on him. "It must be a woman." Tuck looked up and the two laughed heartily. Tuck shook his head at the thought of how well

Turk knew him. "It had to happen sooner or later," Turk laughed. "So who is she?"

Tuck placed his elbow on his knees and relaxed. "Of all the sister's in the world, it had to be someone with issues. Man, I think she got me."

Turk took the same position as Tuck, but his voice was filled with concern for his friend. "She's in the life?"

"No. Nothing like that." Tuck exhaled, as did Turk, but he didn't say anything. Now was the time for him to listen. "Thompson requested our help watching the house of Munford's new lead man. We needed eyes and ears in the house so I charmed his wife into letting me in." Tucker hung his head, "Man I think I fell in love with the woman the moment she opened the door." He exhaled and continued. "The neighbor must have seen me go in and told her husband. He walked in and backhanded her. I was cool for a minute, but when she was on the floor and he began kicking her, I couldn't let it happen. I went in, told him to leave, and then took her out of the house." He looked up at Turk, "And I'm not giving her back."

Turk sat back stretched out his legs, crossed them at the ankle, and folded his arms across his chest. He leveled a look at Tucker that would have made most grown men run. "Why didn't you kill him?"

Tuck's lips curved slightly at the end. "We don't kill unless someone is trying to kill us."

Turk nodded his head in agreement. "That's right, but you have a situation on your hands. First, you can't keep a woman against her will." Tuck motioned to speak, but Turk held up his hand to stop him. "Second, you pulled a weapon on a police officer. That makes you a target." Turk sat forward, "If that's not enough, you now have a bigger problem." Tucker looked him in the eyes. "I'm in here and can't be your best man."

The two men eased into a knowing smile, and stared at each other with understanding. "You know that can be rectified at any moment," Tucker laughed. He shook his head, "There's more. Turns out, they are not married. The man kidnapped her on her eighteenth birthday. The man made contact with Thompson by approaching Tracy." Turk's eyes narrowed, but Tuck continued. "Now, in exchange for information on Munford, he wants her back. I'm not giving her back."

Turk smiled at his friend. This was a man that watched his mother beaten within an inch of her life by a man. There was no way Tucker would turn the woman back over to an abusive situation. "Did Harrison agree to the exchange?"

"Not as far as I know."

"Does he have what he needs to take Munford down?"

Shaking his head, Tucker exhaled, "I'm not sure man. But I do know there is some serious action going on at his office. A good number of DOJ officers checked into a few hotels downtown and are reporting directly to him. Word on the street is some weapons are running through the city. The Eagles are handling the transportation."

"Munford has lost his damn mind thinking he can run weapons. Is Lassiter in town?"

"The brother?" Tucker asked and Al nodded. "Haven't seen him, but that doesn't mean he's not here. You will only see him, if he wants to be seen."

Turk took a moment and thought. "It must have drove Harrison crazy to know the enemy made contact with Tracy."

"I'm sure it did." He looked at Turk. "Do you think he's ready?"

Turk raised his eyebrows and sighed in resignation, "It may be time. Give me a day to think on it. In the mean time, keep an eye on the weapons. Make sure they leave the state. We've worked too hard to keep our people alive and prosperous, for them to lose their lives over greed. It may be time to end Munford's reign." He stood to end the visit. Reaching out he gave Tucker a pound and shoulder bump. "You've divested everything—you are totally out?"

"Yeah," Tucker replied as they stood toe to toe.

"Good. What's her name?" Turk asked.

"Juliana," Tuck replied with a smile.

"Juliana. Nice name." Hands still gripped tightly together like brothers, Turk held Tucker's gaze. "You have to return Juliana to her family. If you love someone, you have to let them go. It has to be her decision to return. You have to give her a reason to make no other decision but to come back. Do it right, and she will be yours for life." Turk turned and walked out of the room.

Tucker stood and watched as he walked away. The man lived his life helping other people, maybe not in the traditional sense, but certainly in the humane sense. There were families in the Richmond and Norfolk, Virginia area that were living a good life because of Al "Turk" Day. To Tucker's way of thinking, it was time for Al to live that life.

It had been a full week for Carolyn and she had not taken one drink. As she looked in the mirror, she liked what reflected back. Life wasn't back to normal. Her father was still married to the woman of ill repute, so that hadn't changed. Tracy was still her half-sister, so the media kept reminding her, so that hadn't changed. However, the way she was looking at her life had. Gavin walked out of the closet with his tie hanging lose around his neck. He reached out, wrapped his hands around her waist, and pulled her back against his chest. Pushing her hair aside with his chin, he kissed her neck. "Good Morning" he said as he caught her eyes in the mirror. Carolyn starred at the reflection and for the first time in a while, she saw happiness in both of their eyes. "You have put up with so much from me. How do you do it and keep smiling?"

Gavin's eyes never waivered, "With love. You, like this, is all I've ever wanted."

Carolyn held his eyes and knew he was in love with her and she certainly loved him. She just had a hard time showing it. She covered his arms with her hands. "Don't ever give up on me. I'm going to get it right."

"Carolyn," he rolled his eyes upward, "if I haven't given up on you through your fiascos with JD, Holt and now your father, believe me, I'm hopeless. I'm not going anywhere." He kissed her cheek. "What do you have planned for the day?" He asked as he pulled away.

"I'm repairing some damage."

"Oh really," he smiled as he continued to dress. "With who?"

"The ladies of the ton. I'm meeting with the wives of some contributors to open a few doors for Tracy."

Gavin froze in place. "You're doing what?"

Carolyn had walked into her closet on the other side of the room, while they talked. "We have the private fundraiser tomorrow with Stanley Covington's group. Most of those women are not going to accept Tracy into the fold. I'm going to open a few doors." She said as she walked back into the room. Gavin had taken a seat on the bed, watching and listening to his wife. This was the Carolyn he knew she could be. "I think Mattie Grisham is up to something, so I need to make sure she is operating within her boundaries and keeping her hands off JD. You know how she loves a man with power." Carolyn sat on the bed and began to pull on a silk stocking, then hooked it to a garter belt. "I know JD is not looking, but Tracy is and the last thing she needs is to be distracted." Still not noticing her husband, who had now taken off his shirt and tie, she put on the other silk stocking then stood before the mirror in her camisole, boy shorts, garter belt, and stockings. Turning to see the view from the back, she smiled with satisfaction, then walked back into the closet. "She has to be sharp and on point with these women." She walked back into the room with a navy blue power suit in her hand. "Everyone knows, if you get the wives attention, the men will fol....." Gavin reached out, grabbed her by the waist, and was on top of her completely naked before she could finish the sentence. His tongue thrust into her open mouth before the scream could escape from the surprised seizure of her body. The other hand moved the boy shorts to the side giving him open access to her body. With one powerful thrust, his engorged member slid right in. They both moaned at the invasion. The suit fell from her hands onto the floor as she reached around his neck to keep his lips in place and wrapped her legs around his waist to push him further in.

The need to show her just how much love was flowing through his body for her at the moment was ludicrous. A bomb could hit the mansion and he would not have been able to stop. His lips moved from her lips to her neck as he pumped into her with a force so strong it moved the bed. His hands moved down to her thighs. His fingers massaged them and positioned them so that her knees rested on his shoulder. She cried out as he pushed deeper and hit that spot. The one that made her scream his name and beg him not to stop. And he didn't. He filled her time and time again until he felt her begin to contract around him and her voice peaked higher. He whispered in her ear, "I will always love you Carolyn— always," he said just as a million pieces of light exploded behind her eyes. Her inner walls pulled at him and pulled at him, but he didn't want to let go—he didn't want the moment to end. Until he heard her call out his name, "Gavin." Only then did he drive into her one last time and allow all his love to flow freely and relentlessly into her body. The two held each other, neither willing to let go first. Suddenly, a chuckle began to rise from Carolyn's throat. Gavin opened his eyes and looked down at his wife with a smile. Tears fell down her cheeks and he wiped them away with his thumbs. She eased her legs from his shoulder as he adjusted his body over her.

"I could stay like this for the rest of my life and be happy." He said.

Carolyn smiled at her husband. "I wish we could, but we have work to do." She pushed him onto his back without breaking contact, and then straddled him. Gavin placed his hands on her hips and admired the beauty of his wife. She rubbed her hands across his chest. "I have to get you elected to the Senate." Her fingers trailed over his nipples and his member swelled inside of her at the touch. Their eyes met and held. He raised his legs to support her as she laid back and began to move her body in a circular motion as she held her hair high on her head. "But, first, I'm going to give you some babies." She closed her eyes, slid down his shaft, and began to draw the life from him.

It was the day before the fundraiser and Tracy's nerves were getting the best of her. The women she had to hobnob with did not particularly care for her. To make matters worse, Tracy hated talking in front of people. This campaign was much more high profile than the last one, so taking a back seat was not an option. As the wife of a candidate for Governor, she had to take a leading role, especially at fundraising. The last big event she'd done was successful primarily due to the efforts of Ashley's mother-in-law, Gwendolyn Brooks. The contacts that woman had were unbelievable. Even the First Lady had attended the event. This time Tracy wanted to accomplish a victory on her own. She would definitely invite the Brooks, more for emotional support than financial, but she would not ask for any assistance with getting the right people in the room. According to Mattie, Stanley Covington would ensure the right people attended. Madeline Gresham, Tracy sat at her desk and wondered how in the heck she was going to deal with the woman. There was something about the woman that Tracy did not like and definitely did not trust. "So what do you do?" She asked aloud, but was really talking to herself. Picking up the telephone, she called her mother. If there was anyone that knew how to handle a woman like Mattie, it was Lena Washington-Roth.

"Hello mother," Tracy said as she sat back in her chair.

"Hello daughter. Are you talking to me now?" Lena asked as she took a seat in her family room.

"I haven't decided yet. But I need your help?"

"Well at least you're honest. I always liked that about you. What do you need?"

"There seems to be a woman on the campaign that keeps pushing her way next to Jeffrey. How do I stop it?"

Lena thought for a moment. "Hum, Is JD oblivious to her?"

"Completely."

"Men usually are," Lena rolled her eyes. "Well, if it was me I'd tell her little ass off and keep it moving."

"I can't do that mother. She is a valued member of the campaign."

"So are you. You have to establish your position here girl. Stop sitting back as if you work for them. It is the other way around. She works for you. It's time to let her know that if it comes to a choice between you and her, girlfriend would be out of a job. Is she going to be at the fundraiser tomorrow?"

"Of course," Tracy grunted.

"I'll check things out and give you a better answer tomorrow. In the meantime, you make sure you bring your "A" game. You know what I mean?"

"Alright mother."

"Have you talked to your step-sister?" Lena asked putting emphasize on the p.

Tracy had to laugh, "Not since the press conference. Have you?"

"We don't talk honey, we growl at each other. Both of us are still trying to stake our claim to John."

"Hey, I'm staying out of that mess. I have enough going on in my life."

Lena grew serious for a moment. "John mentioned the incident in the park. Tracy, you know JD and I don't see eye to eye on anything. But when it comes to you and the children's safety I agree with him one hundred percent. You need to stay close to the house until this case is resolved. I don't want you or my grandbabies to get hurt. You understand?"

"Are you worried about me?" Tracy asked teasingly.

"Girl, I'm too gorgeous to worry. Worry doesn't do nothing but put wrinkles on your face."

"It's good to know your priorities are in order. I'll talk to you later mother." Tracy smiled as she looked down at the phone.

"Nice to see you smiling for a change," Brian said from the doorway.

"Hey." Tracy stood and hugged him. "What are you doing here? Where's Ryan?"

"We have a few twenty-four hour days coming up and I gave her today off."

"Are you sure that's all there is too it? I want Ryan with me."

He shrugged his shoulder, "She's feeling a little bad about what happened and needs to regroup. She'll be here in the morning." He looked around, "Is Pearl here yet?"

"Oh, so you're here to see Pearl," Tracy gave a knowing smile.

"Man, why is it every time I look you have your hands on my wife?" JD asked as he walked into the kitchen and kissed Tracy. Brian stepped away. "Morning babe."

"You're the one always leaving her in my hands," Brian winked at Tracy.

"For protection only, remember that," JD replied as he poured a cup of coffee. "What's on your agenda today?" He asked Tracy.

"Preparing for tomorrow. Ashley is coming over with outfits for me to try on and Pearl is coming over with questions and conversations for me to practice."

JD sat at the table and watched as Brian continuously piled his plate with food. He and Tracy laughed at the sight. "You have enough B?" JD joked.

Placing his plate on the table, Brian went back to the stove to get another biscuit. "I'm straight now," he said and took a seat.

"Jeffrey, do you think I could take the children over to your mother's house today?"

JD and Brian looked at each other. "We are short on security," Brian hissed.

"It may be better if mommy comes over here," JD added. "I'll give her call later, okay babe."

"Okay," Tracy replied as she watched both men pretend everything was cool. The doorbell sounded. She looked up at the clock; it was barely seven-thirty in the morning. "Who could that be this early?"

"Good morning JD. I am so sorry to bother you at home, but I just could not wait to share this with you." Mattie stated as she walked into the kitchen with Mrs. Gordon behind her with a frown on her face.

"Ms. Gresham to see Mr. Harrison" she hissed out.

Tracy tried not to laugh at the woman's exasperated frown. "Thank you Mrs. Gordon."

"Good morning Mattie," JD said as he stood and wiped his mouth with his napkin.

"I have the results of the poll we took after the press conference and oh my God you are not going to believe this," she screeched out with a perky voice. "They are so good."

"Really?" JD replied as he took the envelope from her hands. "Let's go into the office and take a look at them."

Tracy watched as the two walked out of the kitchen towards Jeffrey's office. Mattie's hand resting on his back a little too comfortably for her liking. It was a moment before Tracy realized Brian had spoken. She turned, "I'm sorry, what did you say?"

"I said, I guess she didn't see anyone else at the table."

"I guess she didn't," Tracy mused. "Would it be disrespectful, if I put her out of the house?"

Brian sat back, "You want some help?"

Tracy smiled at him. "My knight in shining armor. Always there to help."

"Always." Brian emphasized.

"You know, I think Ms. Gresham is one of those things I am going to have to handle on my own."

"You go girl," Brian said and continued to eat.

A few minutes later, JD and Mattie emerged from the office. "Tracy," he called out as he entered the kitchen. "Mattie has offered to stay and help you with your prep work. Isn't that wonderful."

Tracy turned to see Mattie standing at the end of the table next to Jeffrey with a diabolical grin. "Just peachy," Tracy replied as he kissed her goodbye. "Samuel is out front. We'll be riding in together for the next few weeks."

The statement took Tracy's mind from Mattie for a moment as she looked up at her husband. "Be safe Jeffrey."

He held her in his arms for a moment longer. "I will." Then he was gone.

Brian sat at the table looking from one woman to the other.

Feeling an awkward moment, Mattie extended her hand. "Mattie Gresham," she said to Brian.

Brian stood, but did not take her hand. "Oh, I know who you are." He looked over at Tracy. "Handle your business." He nodded and walked out the patio door.

"Well, that was rude of him," Mattie stated looking at his back.

"Mattie, we need to establish some boundaries. If I need your assistance, I will ask for it. It was clear, very clear, that last time we tried to work together it was not a good match."

"You see the polls show something different. And JD feels I could contribute to polishing you up a bit."

Tracy tilted her head, "Really?"

"Yes, Tracy. That's why I'm here. Are we working out of his office? If so, I'll just take a seat in there until you are ready." Mattie turned to walk away.

"Mattie," Tracy called out, then walked toward her, and stopped just in front of Jeffrey's office, which was only a few feet from the front door. "You work on Jeffrey's campaign. You don't belong at his office or in his home."

"JD wants me here."

"But I don't," Tracy raised her eyebrow and held the woman's gaze.

Mattie finally blinked, "Fine, I'll just tell JD you didn't want my help." She turned and walked out of the front door.

"You do that." Tracy said and slammed the door behind her.

Damn, Mattie thought as she sat in her car. "So close." She shook her head. She would just have to find another way to get into JD's office.

The conference room at the AG's office was a buzz. There wasn't an empty seat, or walk way anywhere to be found. The large number of agents, from the Department of Justice, were needed to assist with the order once Munford was relieved. Some were needed to review files on current cases. Then Rossie needed a crew to help with the interrogation of officers. Unfortunately, what JD did not know was just how many officers were involved with illegal activity along with Munford and Gary.

"It is imperative, gentlemen and ladies, that the citizens of Richmond know that justice is at the forefront of our actions and that law and order will prevail. If the mission is not clear to everyone in this room, now is the time to ask questions." JD stood in the conference room that now held approximately fifty Assistant Attorney Generals and twenty agents.

"Mr. Attorney General, have all the precinct commanders been cleared?

"Yes. There are four precincts. None have been linked to illegal activities. However, Munford does have at least one lieutenant in each. Our plan is to take each of them and Detective Jonas Gary, who they report, to out of contact first."

"Won't Munford know we have taken them out?"

"Not if we execute the plan precisely as written. Deputy Attorney General Johnson will break-down phase one of the operation. Calvin."

JD took a seat as Calvin explained the plan. "Timing is of the essence. As we speak, we know each target's location. They will not be aware, but their cell phones will be disabled. Here's why the take down must be swift. If any of them has an untraceable cell and are able to use it, our plan may be in jeopardy. Precisely at six o'clock p.m., our first targets will be taken and brought directly to the basement of this facility. Team one, headed up by Rossie, will handle the interrogation. Simultaneously, the weapons will be seized by Federal officers, along with the suspects who were hired to transport the weapons."

"Phase two, will commence exactly two hours later," JD took over. "Team one, has one hour to extract the information on the number of officers that may be involved. Team two, headed up by Samuel Lassiter, will have one hour to obtain the location of each suspect and take them into custody. Each precinct commander will be escorted to this building, and advised along with the acting Chief of Police, of our actions. Phase three, will be the press conference." JD paused and looked around. "People, we are sworn officers of justice. The public has placed a trust in us. When that trust is broken, the punishment must be swift and uncompromising. It must leave a clear message that we will not tolerate illegal actions from those we have entrusted to serve and protect our citizens. As you all can see by the timetable, there is no room for error. A mistake could be fatal to one of you. I want to shake each of your hands on the other side of this operation. Everyone has their assignment. Take a look at the clock on that wall." All heads turned to the clock. "Synchronize your watches now. Everyone is to contact their lead every hour from now on. If you are five minutes late, we will assume your position has been compromised and act accordingly. Are there any questions?" JD looked over the room at the committed faces. He could feel the adrenaline flowing in the room. "Succeed or fail people, we will be the talk of the town, twenty-four hours from now. Good luck to each of you."

Sitting in her office at campaign headquarters, Mattie suddenly noticed people scurrying around, she looked up to see what was causing the disturbance. To her surprise, it was the Governor and Carolyn. She would address her as the First Lady when she started to act like it again. Mattie stood in her doorway and watched as staffers, got autographs, and pictures with the first couple. The two women's eyes met, as Carolyn turned to respond to the receptionist. She poised for the picture then said something to Gavin. He looked up and waved at Mattie. Waving back, Mattie smiled until Gavin turned to walk into James' office. To her further surprise, Carolyn walked in her direction. She had to admit, Carolyn was impeccably dress in navy blue, looking like her old self again, only there was something more. The closer she got, the more apparent it was that Carolyn had a damn twinkle in her eyes. "Why Carolyn, if I wasn't mistaken, I could swear you were glowing."

"I'll take that in the vain way you meant it. How are you Mattie?"

Mattie was a little thrown. "What no sharp come back. Just a how are you Mattie? You must have conquered something. Do tell."

"Just my own demons Mattie. What about you?"

"Me? I don't have any demons to conquer."

"Don't you?" Carolyn asked. "How's your brother?"

A shocked Mattie glared at Carolyn just as Gavin called her. Carolyn turned, "Be right there darling," she answered then turned back to Mattie. "We all have our demons to conquer. When you need help, call me."

Stunned speechless, Mattie quickly closed her door after Carolyn left. Could she know about her brother? Even worse, could she know about Munford? A knock sounded at Mattie's door. "Come in," she managed to answer.

"Mattie, Mr. Brooks wants you in his office, now." The receptionist said and walked away.

"Oh shit." Mattie began hyperventilating. "Calm the hell down." She took a deep breath then let it out. "There is no way they could know." Standing up straight, she took another calming breath and walked into James office.

"Mattie," James said as she entered the office, "JD is on his way over. Certain events will have an impact on the campaign. He wants all of his advisors in the conference room in fifteen minutes. From the sound of things you may want to cancel any plans you have for this evening."

A relieved Mattie just stared at him for a moment. Then replied, "I don't have any plans."

"Good, it's going to be a long night."

Chapter 12

Tracy fell asleep on the sofa in the family room waiting for Jeffrey to get home. When the telephone rang she assumed it was him calling, but to her surprise it was her sister Valerie. Tracy hadn't seen Valerie since the wedding, but they had managed to talk every now and then. She could hear the distress in Valerie's voice as she talked. "Tracy, I'm sorry to call this late, but I need your help."

"That's okay Val," Tracy said as she sat up and looked at the clock. "What's going on?"
"My daughter Kaylen just called. She is somewhere in Richmond with her cousin, Monique, Turk's daughter. Kaylen is not street smart like Monique and she is afraid. Is there any way you could go to pick her up and I will come to your house to get her?" Valerie explained.

"Did she say where she was?" Tracy asked concerned. "She said she was on Phaup Street in some projects across the street from a school. Do you know where that is?

"No, I haven't heard of it, but I'm sure I can find it. Did Kaylen give you a phone number she was calling from?" Tracy asked as she put her shoes on.

"She called from her cell." Valerie said then gave Tracy the cell phone number.

"Okay, don't worry about it. I'll find her and call you as soon as we are in the house."

Tracy thought for a moment. JD would have a fit if she left the house and angrier if she went to the projects by herself. For an adventure like this Tracy would normally call Ashley, but she had the twins. Then there was Cynthia, but she was too close to giving birth and Roz was out of town with her husband. "Who could she call that would know the projects." She picked up the telephone and called Brian.

Brian's night with his new female friend was just getting started. They had just settled down on her sofa talking when the phone played the theme from Shaft. Brian knew that ring was from JD's home number. The woman watched him intently to see if he was going to answer the call.

Brian grinned, "I know what you are thinking. I did not plan this."

"Sure you didn't," she smiled as she sipped her wine. "It just happened to ring when we were about to talk. Something you have been avoiding since the day we met."

The tune played again, "I have to take it," Brian said then answered the call.

"Yeah," he said.

"Brian hi, it's Tracy."

"Hey, Tracy what's up," Brian frowned. The woman rolled her eyes and sighed. Brian smiled and ignored the look.

"Brian I need your help. My sister's daughter is somewhere in Richmond and I need to pick her up. Could you go with me?"

This was his last night off, before the plan was put into action and it didn't help that this woman had placed her leg across his lap. "I'm a little busy right now Tracy" Brian said as he began to rub the exposed thigh. "Where exactly is she? Maybe I could call Ryan to pick her up."

"She's on Phaup Street. Do you know where that is?"

Brian paused. "What in the hell is she doing there?" He said with intense tone.

"I don't know Brian, but I have to go get her. Her mother is worried. She said Kaylen was afraid. So could you tell me how to get there?"

"You can't go there Tracy. Where's JD?" Brian asked standing up.

"He's in a meeting. Brian I have to go, just tell me how to get there."

"Tracy, you cannot go there by yourself," Brian said almost yelling into the phone.

"Then that means Kaylen should not be there either. Now are you going to tell me how to get there or not? I'm going to get that child with or without you."

"Where on Phaup Street is she, do you have an address?"

"No," Tracy replied.

"So exactly what do you think you are going to do, knock on every door on Phaup Street until you find her?" Brian asked curtly.

"If I have to. You know what Brian forget it, I'll find her myself." Tracy said a little angry and hung up the telephone.

"Tracy, Tracy," Brian called into the phone to no avail. "Shit!" he exclaimed.

When he turned, his friend was standing by the door with his suit jacket in her hand and a smile. Brian exhaled and walked towards her. "You have a reprieve Mr. Thompson, but this evening will be concluded on a later date."

He kissed her goodnight. "I will make this up to you," he promised then he left.

Brian called the house number back. No answer, he called Magna, who was covering the house. He advised her of the situation as she told him Tracy had just pulled off in JD's BMW. His curse grew louder. Hanging up the telephone with her, he called Douglas. He knew the players in the area. "Doug, we have a situation on Phaup Street. Tracy is on her way over there looking for her niece. I need you to meet me over there."

"Tracy?" Douglas asked. "Is she alone?"

"Yeah and she doesn't exactly know where the girl is. All she gave me was the street."

"Let me make some calls. I'll meet you at the high school on Cool Lane."

Brian called Tuck. This was once a part of Al's turf. If they were in Fairfield Court Tuck would know who, when and where. Having Tuck in the area was guaranteed protection. In Fairfield Court, the players in that area did not give a damn who you represented; they would try to take your ass out. Brian shook his head. With everything that was about to go down, he did not need this tonight.

As Brian drove down Cool Lane, he saw Douglas parked in front of the school. He parked and got into Douglas' Navigator. "Have you seen her?" he asked.

"Not yet. What is she driving?" Doug asked.

"JD's BMW, probably for the navigational system. Let's start at the curve then follow up."

Douglas pulled off and made a u-turn then headed towards Phaup Street. As they came around the curve he spotted JD's BMW parked in front of the elementary school. Tracy was standing on the outside of the car and a group of young guys were talking to her.

Brian got out of the Navigator with his weapon drawn and walked up the sidewalk. Douglas drove up the street and parked in front of Tracy, he got out of his vehicle with his weapon at his side. Tracy saw Douglas as he walked towards her. She smiled, relieved to see him. "You seem to show up in the nick of time," she said looking in his direction. The guys standing around her turned in Douglas direction.

"Tracy, what's up?" Douglas asked in the coldest voice while assessing the group of men surrounding her. He could tell from the bulge in the back of their shirts at least two of them had weapons. As he got closer he made sure they could see the weapon in his hand. One of the boys stepped towards him. "We're handling some business here, you might want to turn around and go back to where you came from." The group slowly surrounded Tracy.

"Wrong woman to be handling business with Youngblood. You might want to leave this business to us." Doug said.

"What, damn us; I don't see nobody but you," the boy in the back yelled out.

Brian put his revolver next to the young boy's head. "The us would be me," Brian said coldly. He reached in and pulled Tracy from the circle and put her behind him. "Take it easy gentlemen; we just want the lady and a little info." Douglas said.

"Yeah, well you have the lady we want the car," the self appointed leader of the group said.

"Man you don't want that car," Brian laughed. "Believe me you don't want that car or this woman or the fact that this incident took place to get back to the owner of that car."

The young boy, who Douglas put at about nineteen, looked at him and asked, "What the hell y'all want around here?"

"We are looking for a young girl that came into town today. Any of you know anything about that?" Brian asked.

"Two young girls," Tracy said as she stepped from behind Brian.

Brian never took his eyes off the boys, nor did he lower his weapon. He gently pushed Tracy back behind him with his free hand.

"What's in it for us?" One boy asked as he lit a cigarette, unconcerned with the situation.

Another vehicle pulled up to the scene, which seemed to draw a lot of attention from others that were milling about on the street. It was a familiar vehicle to the neighborhood. No one seemed to be afraid, just in awe. Tuck stepped out of the vehicle and approached the group. When Brian recognized him, he lowered his weapon. Tuck did not say anything to the young boys, but they all seemed to know who he was. He walked over and stood next to Douglas.

"Did they give you what you need?" Tuck asked.

"Not yet," Doug replied. "Youngblood wants to know what's in it for them."

Tuck smiled and walked over to the boys "Where's Bear?"

"Over at T-Bo's place," the boy replied.

"Is Monique with him?"

"Was earlier, with another little honey from Norfolk," another said.

Tuck walked over, pulled a wad of money out of his pocket, and gave half of it to the boy.

"Keep half of this for yourself and split the rest with your boys. I need you to keep an eye on the cars and the lady; understand," Tuck said.

"You got it," the boy said.

Tuck, Brian and Douglas talked for a moment away from Tracy. As they started across the street Tracy followed behind them. Brian turned and stopped her. "You're not going in there, stay here"

"No, Brian I have to go in there to get Kaylen," she said, then looked behind her, "You are not leaving me with them. Besides Kaylen doesn't know you. She will not leave with you."

"Alright, but stay behind me and don't speak."

"Okay," Tracy obeyed.

Douglas went around the back as Tuck and Brian approached the front door. Tuck knocked. "Who is it?" a man's voice came through.

"Tuck."

You could hear moving going on inside the house. Tuck shook his head. "Youngbloods, they will never learn."

When the door opened, Brian kicked it wide. Tuck, Brian and Tracy entered and closed the door behind them. Douglas was walking through the back part of the house with a guy and girl who'd attempted to go out the back door. They made the three guys in the house get on their knees with their hands behind their head. Brian held his weapon on the three. One young girl sitting on the couch appeared to be terrified.

"Kaylen?" Tracy asked.

"Yes," she meekly replied.

"Come with me, baby," Tracy said. The girl looked at Tracy and hesitated. "I'm your Aunt Tracy. Your mother asked me to come get you. It's okay, come with me."

Kaylen walked over to Tracy and hugged her. "Thank you for coming."

"You called her?" The other girl yelled out. "You stupid little bitch, you know her husband is five o." She made a sucking sound with her teeth and rolled her eyes.

Tuck walked over to Monique "Didn't I tell you to stay away from Bear?"

Monique put her hands on her hips and replied, "You ain't my daddy. You don't tell me what to do."

Tuck nodded his head. "You're right. But I tell Bear what to do. Now, I got to take him out." Tuck motioned to Douglas. He pointed to the one caught running out the back and Tuck acknowledged he'd selected the right one. Douglas took the boy who was now pleading with Tuck into another room.

"Uncle Tuck, that's not fair. I love Bear," she began to cry and tried to follow the men into the other room.

Tuck grabbed her by her braids and held her back. "He'll be glad to know you loved him to death."

"Don't do it Uncle Tuck, don't do it. I promise to stay away, I promise."

A few seconds later a gunshot rung out. Tracy and Kaylen both screamed. Monique called out, "Bear!"

Douglas came back into the room with the boy unharmed.

"See how easy that could be," Tuck said to Monique. "I'm not your daddy and I don't give a shit about your feelings. If you don't stay away from him I will take his ass out."

Monique looked at Tuck with tears running down her face. "Okay, Uncle Tuck," she cried.

"Now go with your Aunt Tracy and don't you cause her any trouble, you understand," he looked at the little girl. Tuck had lied, he loved that little girl as if she were his own. But he would never let her know, he wanted Monique to be afraid of him. It was the only way he could keep her in line. If anything happened to her, Turk would not forgive him.

"Wait," Tuck said, "Are you carrying?" he asked.

"No!" Monique replied with a little too much defiance.

"Empty your bag," Tuck said.

"I said I ain't got nothing," Monique insisted with a lot of attitude.

"And I said empty your bag," Tuck replied without raising his voice.

Monique emptied her bag on the table. A bag of marijuana, papers, and condoms appeared.

Tuck looked at her and then Bear. He picked up the bag of marijuana and handed the condoms back to her. "Now you can go."

Tracy was too stunned to move. Kaylen was holding on to her waist so tight she couldn't move.

"Take them to the car Tracy," Brian said. When Tracy didn't move, he turned to her. "Now Tracy, take them to the car now."

Tracy looked up at Brian with pure shock in her eyes. She grabbed the two girls and went out the door.

Tucker stopped her on the porch with pride showing brightly in his eyes. "I've known you since you were a little girl. It's nice to see you face to face."

For whatever reason, Tracy did not fear the man standing before her. She instantly knew he would never do anything to harm her. "Thank you for helping the children."

"It's been my honor." Tucker watched as they got into the car and pulled off.

It was well after one in the morning when Tracy arrived home. She called Valerie and allowed Kaylen to talk to her. Afterwards she convinced Val to let the girls stay overnight. They could pick them up in the morning. Tracy asked Monique if she wanted to call her mom and she said no. Tracy looked at the two girls. They were as different as night and day. Kaylen was a small girl with a shapely body, long brownish hair that was parted on the side and fell just below her shoulders and the prettiest light brown eyes you ever wanted to see. She had on a pair of hip hugging jeans and a white tee shirt that revealed her navel. She appeared to be the very image of a middle class neighborhood girl. Monique was street through and through, from the multicolor braids in her hair, to the fake nails with the fake diamond mounted on them. She was dressed in a jean skirt that barely covered her behind and a white tee shirt that had, "yes, I'm a bitch," written across the front. Tracy looked at the shirt and began to laugh. Monique looked at her as if she was losing her mind. "What you find so funny?' she asked with attitude.

"You," Tracy replied. "You don't have to advertise you're a bitch, it shows. Come on let me show you where you are going to sleep. You can take a shower and I will find you something to sleep in."

"Ain't staying here." Monique grabbed her purse and pulled out her cell phone.

Tracy shrugged her shoulders, "Your choice. Come on Kaylen."

Before they reached the stairs, JD came in through the kitchen. He looked at Tracy then at the girls. Brian called and had filled him in on what went down. JD couldn't believe Tracy would attempt to go anywhere alone after the incident earlier that week. But he would deal with that later. At the moment, he had to deal with Al's daughter and the small portion of the conversation he'd over heard from the garage. "Hang up the phone," he said to Monique.

She looked at him sideways, rolled her eyes, and said. "You don't know me like that and you can't tell me what to do."

JD looked at Tracy, then at Kaylen then back to Monique. He walked over took the phone out of her hand. "Hi, I'm JD, that's Uncle JD to you. You must be Monique. Now you know me." He walked over to Tracy kissed her then said hello to Kaylen. "That was a smart thing you did tonight regardless of what your cousin might say to you."

"Okay," Kaylen replied with a smile.

Tracy took Kaylen upstairs to take a shower and get ready for bed. JD stayed downstairs with Monique. He had a long day. The office was hectic and up in arms concerning a weapon's case that will have national if not international implications. There was the meeting with James Brooks and the staff concerning the potential political backlash of the case and then, of all things, a call from Brian indicating his wife was in the projects trying to save her nieces from what he wasn't certain. But the niece standing in front of him, spitting daggers, was at the center of the mystery. Now, the outcome of the weapons case was in the hands of his staff and out of his control. But this situation was all his and he sure as hell was going to put out the fire standing before him.

JD took off his suit jacket and tie, and then unbuttoned the top two buttons on his shirt. He walked over to the microwave and pulled out the plate of food Tracy had prepared for him. He then went to the refrigerator and pulled out a beer. He sat at the breakfast bar across from where Monique stood. He looked at her, "Would you like something to eat?"

"I don't want anything from you. You the man who put my daddy in jail," Monique snapped.

JD said grace and began to eat. "He broke the law, that's what happens," he said as if it was common sense. JD studied the girl who stood before him. She resembled Al in skin tone and temper only. He wondered if she was as intelligent. "You know if your dad was in this situation, he would take a step back, look at the entire picture, and then determine how he would best profit from it."

"Don't try to act like you know my daddy. You don't know nothing about my daddy. You walking around like you the king of somebody's world, you ain't shit and neither is that bitch wife of yours," Monique snapped with hands on hips.

JD looked up from his plate at Monique with an intensity that made the child quiver on the inside.

"There are three things I know at this moment. One is you will never refer to my wife as a bitch again; two you will not use that language in my house, and three if you ever raise your voice at me again I will whip your ass like I was your father and then tell your daddy I did it. Do we understand each other?" Monique did not say anything at first, but then JD raised his voice. "Do we understand each other?!"

Tracy walked into the room before Monique could answer. "Is everything alright in here?"

"Little girl, I am not in the habit of repeating myself, I'm waiting for an answer." JD said.

"I understand," Monique, answered with a lot less attitude, but still with a pinch of anger.

JD got up and moved his plate to the sink. "So, where are you going?" JD asked. Monique shrugged her shoulders. "I don't understand that language. You want to try to answer the question with words."

"I can call Bear," Monique said with more attitude.

JD laughed, "Bear is not going to come within a hundred feet of you. Tuck made sure of that."

Picking up the cell phone from the kitchen table where he'd placed it, he put it in front of her. "You are welcome to try. But if he doesn't answer, you are welcome to stay here tonight. We're going to bed." He took Tracy's hand and walked up the stairs.

Early, the next morning JD was sitting in his office going over reports of everyone's positions from the night before. Things seemed to be in place. He sat back and took a drink of his coffee just as he saw Monique tip toeing down the staircase. When she reached the kitchen, he stood in the doorway of his office, watched her put her shoes on, and pulled out her phone. While she was waiting for her call to be answered, she was looking around the house. JD watched as Monique wandered throughout the lower level of the house. She began telling the person on the telephone about the house and it's furnishing. As Monique walked into the sunroom, she noticed the wedding picture on the stand. The picture was of JD, Tracy, Lena, Valerie, and Ben. As she looked at the picture JD could see the play of emotions going across Monique's face. He wondered if the anger she was displaying towards him and Tracy had anything to do with the fact that her dad was not in that picture.

He walked into the kitchen and stood near the patio door. "Looking for anything in particular?" JD asked.

A startled Monique dropped the picture and the glass shattered. The action reminded JD of a day in his mother's kitchen when Tracy dropped a glass and it shattered on the floor. Unlike Tracy who expressed remorse immediately, Monique stood there as if someone else had broken the glass.

"You want to clean that up" JD asked with a facial expression that let Monique know, it really wasn't a question. It was more of an order.

"I ain't got no broom or sh..... stuff" she said as she remembered JD's words from last night.

"I don't have," JD said as he walked over to the closet near the garage door and pulled out the broom and a dust pan than gave them to Monique.

"What?" Monique replied with distain.

"It's, I don't have a broom, not, I ain't got" JD said as he put his hands in his pockets waiting for her to begin cleaning the broken glass.

Tracy came downstairs with Kaylen in tow. "Valerie and Ben are on their way," she said as she kissed her husband. When she saw the picture and broken glass on the floor she asked, "What happened?"

JD looked up at Tracy's hurt face. It was the only picture she had of her and her family together and he knew what the picture meant to her. He picked up the broken frame with the picture in it.

"I'll have it reframed Tracy," JD said with a weak smile. "It will be like new."

Tracy looked at Monique. She hesitated for a moment wondering if she wanted to reprimand the girl for breaking the picture. "Okay babe," Tracy said to Jeffrey while still eyeing Monique.

Monique made a sucking sound with her teeth, "Where the trash at?" she asked as she rolled her eyes at Tracy.

JD opened one of the bottom cabinets and pulled the trash can out. Monique walked and emptied the broken glass into the bin. JD pushed the trash can back in and closed the cabinet door. He then opened the broom closet for Monique to replace the items. She walked over and threw the broom and dust pan into the closet, then began to walk away. JD grabbed the back of her blouse and pulled her back. "The dust pan goes on this hanger and the broom goes on that rack," he said.

"I ain't know," Monique replied still with the attitude.

"I didn't know" JD said as he closed the closet.

"I ain't in English class. What, everything got to be said just right and everything got to go in place. Shit, I ain't staying in this house," Monique said as she grabbed her purse.

Kaylen looked from JD to Tracy. Who were both standing there trying to decide which one was going to speak. "Well, I like the house Nique; did you see the computer room upstairs?" Kaylen asked excited.

"Naw, I ain't see no damn computer room," Monique answered as if mocking the girl.

"I didn't see," JD said as if he was losing his patience.

Seeing a spark of interest from Monique when the computer was mentioned, "Why don't you girls go check out the computer in the sunroom?" Tracy said, "The one upstairs is off limits." Tracy then turned to Jeffrey, "I'll start breakfast."

"See Kaylen, rich people have sunrooms, poor people have back porches," Monique said as she sashayed out of the room.

JD looked at Tracy, "I'll help with breakfast."

"You're not going into the office?" Tracy asked a little surprised.

"And leave you here alone with gangster girl, I don't think so." There was no way he was going to tell her, their day was going to be altered.

Tracy laughed and looked over at the girls. "She is a little rough around the edges."

"Not really." JD said, "She's lashing out at whoever let's her get away with it. She needs her dad."

Tracy put some bacon on and biscuits in the oven, while Jeffrey cooked eggs and hash browns. Once breakfast was prepared, Tracy called the girls into the kitchen to eat. As the girls sat at the table, Monique frowned. "What's this?" She asked.

"It's called food," JD replied.

Kaylen laughed. Monique gave her the look of death.

"You ain't got no Fruity Pebbles or Coco Puffs?"

"Don't have any," JD said correcting the girl yet again.

"What, rich people like y'all can't afford cereal," Monique replied completely missing the correction.

"We do have cereal. But if you cannot ask for it correctly, you will not get any." JD replied.

Monique rolled her eyes and then asked, "Do you have any cereal?"

"Yes, we do," JD replied but did not say anything more.

Tracy motioned to get the cereal and JD stopped her with his hand.

Monique exhaled than asked. "May I have some cereal?" JD did not respond he continued to look at her. "Please," Monique added.

"No, eat what's in front of you or go hungry," he then bowed his head to say grace.

Tracy bowed her head and tried to hold in the laugh at the look on Monique's face, but it escaped. When JD finished grace he looked at Tracy and she could see the laughter in his eyes.

Brian walked in through the patio door. "Good morning, don't we have a full house," he said as he looked at the table of people.

"Hey B," JD said.

"It's Good Morning," Monique corrected him.

Tracy smiled, "Good Morning Brian, would you like some breakfast."

"Sure, seems like you are having an interesting morning." Brian replied while detecting the mood in the room.

Tracy got up to fix Brian a plate when JD grabbed the plate in front of Monique and said, "Here you go Brian." He took the plate then sat at the breakfast bar and began to eat.

Tracy looked at JD then Brian. "It has been a very interesting morning," she said. Then she walked over to the cabinet pulled out a box of cereal, a bowl and a spoon and placed the items in front of Monique. She looked at Tracy with rolled eyes, then began to say something but looked at JD instead. "Do you have any milk?" She asked as her neck rolled from left to right.

JD looked at her, "Yes. In the refrigerator, help yourself."

Monique looked around but all she saw were cabinets. "Where is the refrigerator?" she asked.

Brian looked at her for a moment then walked over to the refrigerator and opened the door. "Here you go; mouth," he smiled.

Monique looked at him as if throwing daggers. "How I'm supposed to know; it don't look like no refrigerator." She pulled the milk out and slouched back down into her seat at the table.

"Get anyone shot at in the last six hours," Brian joked as he continued to eat.

"Ain't you," Monique started then stopped; rolled her eyes and said, "Don't you have a home somewhere?"

JD smiled to himself.

"Don't you?" Brian replied.

Monique made a sucking sound with her mouth and gave Brian the raised 'sister girl' hand.
Brian snapped his fingers, "Oh, no you didn't," he laughed.

"Yes she did," Kaylen giggled.

JD could have sworn he saw a small sign of amusement come into Monique's eyes. She wanted to laugh at Brian, but of course, she couldn't; that would take away from her gangster image.

Brian ignored the look on Monique's face and turned to Tracy. "How are the babies and where is Mrs. Gordon?"

Tracy was enjoying the feel of a full house. "JC is still asleep and I fed Jasmine before I came down. Mrs. Gordon is upstairs staying clear of the holy terror." She looked over at Monique.

"You got a baby?" Monique asked.

Tracy looked at the child, "Two," she smiled.

"You ain't fat" Monique replied.

"Thank you," Tracy smiled grateful for the sideways compliment.

"I know about JC, how old is Jasmine?" Kaylen asked with a little excitement.

"Eight weeks now."

"You just had a baby? Shit, my girlfriend had her baby five months ago and she is still fat. That's why I ain't gonna ever get pregnant," Monique exclaimed.

"I'm not going to," JD said frustrated, then added, "Thank God."

Brian laughed, "Do you go to school?"

"Yeah, I go to school and got good grades. I ain't," she stopped, "I'm not stupid," she said.

JD smiled as he leaned across the breakfast bar, "What kind of grades do you get?" he asked.

"Nique always gets straight A's, but she don't tell anybody," Kaylen blurted out.

"Why you all up in my business," Monique said to Kaylen.

"What's wrong with A's," Tracy asked as she put her plate in the sink.

"Her gang members won't like it if they knew she got straight A's," Kaylen said.

Monique got up in Kaylen's face. "I done told you about gettin up in my business."

"Hey, sit down," JD shouted. Monique complied with a huff.

"What gang?" JD asked. Neither Kaylen nor Monique said anything. "What gang?" His voice raised to a point that not only startled the girls but Tracy as well.

"It ain't no gang," Monique replied.

JD stood there and looked at her sternly.

"It's not a gang," Monique corrected. "It's just a group of friends I hang out with."

"Yeah, but they steal stuff, and like to fight people," Kaylen said a little angry.

"I should have let them whip your uppity ass," Monique said.

Brian looked at JD, "Sounds like a gang to me."

The door bell rang. "Thank you," Tracy said looking up at the ceiling. When she opened the door, Valerie and her husband Ben walked through.

Tracy hugged Valerie and said hello to Ben. When they entered the kitchen, JD shook Ben's hand and said hello to Valerie. Ben acknowledged Brian and went straight to Kaylen. He hugged his daughter and examined her to make sure everything was in place. "Are you okay, baby?" He asked.

"Yes Daddy," Kaylen replied.

Ben looked at Monique, "You okay?" he asked with a no nonsense tone.

"Yes Uncle Ben." Monique replied.

"Good," Ben turned to Tracy. "You got a spare bedroom?" He asked as he pulled his belt off.
Tracy looked at Jeffrey with confusion in her eyes. JD looked at Ben, "Top of the steps to your right," he replied and fixed another cup of coffee.

Tracy looked at Valerie, who turned to her husband, "Ben can't this wait until we get home?"

"Hell no, it can't. Let's go Kaylen," Ben said.

"But Daddy," Kaylen cried.

"But Daddy my ass. I'm not going to say it again, let's go."

Kaylen obeyed her father and walked up the stairs. The room fell silent as Tracy looked from Valerie to Monique, then Jeffrey.

"You going to get it," Brian laughed as he continued to drink his coffee.

Tracy looked at her husband. "Jeffrey, are you going to do something here?"

JD looked at Tracy, "No," he replied.

"You're going to let that man beat his child?" Tracy asked astonished.

"You damn right; and that one too" JD replied, pointing to Monique.

"He ain't my daddy," she said rolling her eyes. JD cleared his throat. "He's not my daddy," she corrected.

"He's the closest you have to one," Valerie said. "You have any more of that?" she asked JD referring to the coffee.

"Sure do," JD replied as he pulled a cup from the cabinet and poured the coffee. "Cream and sugar?" he asked.

"Yes, thank you," Valerie replied as she placed her purse on the breakfast bar and took a seat.

Tracy jumped at the first sound of the belt. She looked at JD as if begging him to stop it.

Valerie saw JD's face soften at the sight of Tracy grief stricken face. As much as she hated it, she knew Ben was right. It was rough raising kids these days. You have to let them know when they've crossed the line, Valerie thought to herself. She looked at Tracy "How's the baby Tracy? You look great."

Tracy hesitated for a moment, and then she heard the sound of the belt again. Nervously she took a seat at the table and replied, "Jasmine is fine." She looked over at Monique with sad eyes.

Brian watched Tracy, "Don't feel sorry for her. From what I witnessed last night, her ass whipping seems to be long overdue," he said referring to Monique.

Valerie smirked, "Nique has experienced Ben's raft before, and she knows what's coming."

"Where's my momma?" Monique snapped.

"At home waiting for us to clean up your mess again," Valerie snapped back.

Ben came down the steps, looked at Monique, "Let's go," he said.

"Ain't going nowhere with you. I'm gonna call my momma if you hit me." Monique yelled back.

"Maybe we should call her mother," Tracy said still a little shaken by the events taking place.

"We can call her afterwards." Ben said to Tracy then turned back to Monique.

"I don't have a problem whipping your ass down here in front of people; that's your call. But your ass is going to get whipped this morning" Ben said without a bit of sympathy.

"Ben," Tracy said sweetly.

"Tracy," JD said sternly.

Monique looked at Tracy and for a moment, she thought Tracy might be her saving grace. "Aunt Tracy, I'm sorry. I didn't mean to cause no trouble."

Tracy looked at her brother's child and was about to say something when Valerie stepped in.

"You know, Tracy might fall for that fake ass apology, but I don't. That was my child you put in jeopardy last night. You are getting that ass whipping."

Monique stood up so quick the chair fell behind her. "All y'all so call family can kiss my ass." Ben grabbed Monique around the waist and carried her up the stairs kicking and howling "I'm gonna do more than kiss your ass," they heard him say as he disappeared.

Less than an hour later Ben and Valerie departed with Kaylen and Monique in tow, JD turned to Tracy with anger in his eyes. Brian immediately excused himself from the room. "What possessed you to go to the projects at night?" JD angrily addressed Tracy. "At any point in time did it ever occur to you what could have happened to you?" Tracy shuddered at the intensity of JD's voice. She attempted to respond but JD cut her off. "I don't go into the projects without Brian or someone with me. What were you thinking or did you think?" His voice was amplified with anger as the events of the night before played in his mind. "Do you realize you could have been injured or killed?"

"I was trying to help my sister," Tracy said in an attempt to defend her actions.

"Attempting to help her do what, collect your estate earlier than anticipated? Your family has managed to handle their business all this time without you being around, why do you feel they need you now," he yelled. JD instantly regretted the words as soon as he realized they were spoken out loud. He knew Tracy was trying to reconnect with her family after being estranged for most of her adult life. And to be honest, he wanted that for her too, but not at the expense of jeopardizing her life.

"Jeffrey, Valerie called and asked me to help. I tried to call you, but you did not answer your phone. Then I called Brian. But I could not leave the child there alone. If anything had happened to her, I would not have been able to forgive myself."

JD looked at the tears that were forming in his wife's eyes. He hated the thought of him causing her any distress. He inhaled and tried to calm the fear that he had felt when he received the call from Brian. Closing the space between them, he pulled her into his arms and held her against his chest. Tracy wrapped her arms around her husband who was very upset with her and cried. Truth be told the events had scared her. It brought back memories of the attack that had caused her to lose their first child. "Tracy," he whispered into her ear, "I'm so sorry I yelled. All I could think about last night was what could have happened if Tucker had not shown up. I can't fathom the idea of anything happening to you." He cupped her face that was drenched in tears into his hands. As he stared at her, JD literally saw his life within her eyes. "You are my life Tracy, my wife, and the mother of my children. I don't think rationally when it comes to you. I know you could not leave that child there. I would not have been able to do that either. But your first priority should be the welfare of our children. What you did last night put your life in jeopardy, please don't do that again."

Tracy kissed his lips "I'm sorry. It won't happen again."

"I know it won't." He stepped back from her. "You have the fundraising event today. Once you return home, you are not to leave this house without my approval. I don't give a damn who needs help or what is happening. You do not leave this house." He walked over to the stand, took his keys, and slammed the door behind him.

Magna and Ryan walked in the patio door, with a look of dread in their eyes. "We've been lectured and were given orders not to allow you out of our sight until further notice." Magna stated.

"I was told to follow you into the ladies room if necessary to make sure you stay put." Ryan said as she took a seat at the breakfast bar. "I can't speak for Magna, but I plan on following my orders to a tee. I've screwed up enough."

Tracy still stood in the middle of the floor stunned at Jeffrey's' demand. She looked at the two women that were there to protect her. "There is more to this than what happened last night. Has something happened with Jeffrey's case?"

"We are not at liberty to say," Magna replied.

Tracy exhaled, then walked out of the room.

"This is not going to be a happy place for a while," Ryan stated, "I got the upstairs."

"I'll take the perimeter," Magna replied and began securing the house.

Chapter 13

The private reception hall at the Jefferson Hotel in downtown Richmond was the location for the reception for Jeffrey Daniel Harrison. The elite society turned out in full force to be one of the first to have bragging rights on supporting the candidate they all believed would eventually become President of the United States. The whispers about this long anticipated event were echoing throughout the room as guest after guest continued to arrive. The original invitation count had been for fifty of the wealthiest members of the Richmond Metropolitan area, however, it was clear that the number in the room was far greater.

After leaving the house earlier in the day, JD had done everything he could to keep his mind on the case. If he stopped for one moment and thought about the way he left things, he knew he would give in and call Tracy to apologize. And that he could not do. It was his job, his duty, his mission to keep her safe. With all that was taking place in the City for the next twenty-four hours, all precautions had to be taken. He knew she did not understand the depths of what was happening around her, but he did. The stance he took was necessary to keep her safe. The day didn't necessarily get any better. The most distressing problem being Jonas Gary had given them the slip. Luckily, he had shown up on the surveillance cameras near Tucker's home. From there, they were able to place a tracking device on his vehicle and place a team on him. Absolute was on the weapons, but had to kill a gang member that had tried to steal one of the guns from the truck. They had to take time to dispose of the body. These were the types of mishaps they could not afford. JD took a moment and placed a conference call to all the leads on the case just to re-emphasizes the small window of opportunity they had to bring Munford down and maintain order.

Now, he had to convince his brother-in-law to make a deal with him, and until last night, he had no idea how he was going to do that. Sitting in the warden's conference room, JD was armed and ready to counter point Al until he gave in. Brian and Samuel stood on the outside of the room, positioned at each entrance to ensure no interruptions. The door opened and Al walked in.

He smiled at his brother-in-law and extended his hand. "I wasn't expecting to see you."

"How are you Al?"

"I'm good. You know, as well as can be expected. How are Tracy and the children?"

"They're good," JD smiled and gave him his phone to look at the pictures. He allowed a few minutes for Al to enjoy the pictures.

"The baby looks just like Tracy, especially her eyes." Al looked up and grinned, "Man, you better have your shotgun ready."

"I'm polishing it off now," the two laughed.

A moment later, Al handed the phone back to him. "Thank you man, I appreciate you sharing that with me."

"I brought something else with me Al." He pushed the folder he had across the table.

Al stopped it's progress with his hands and looked up perplexed. "What's this?"

"Take a look," he said as his phone chimed. "I need to take this call."

Al opened the file. The first page read, *The United States Government in conjunction with the Commonwealth of Virginia offers the following conditions of pardon for Albert H. Day.* He looked up at JD, but his back was to him. Al continued to read.

JD finished his call, relieved to know the children were secure at James complex and Tracy was on her way to the event. He reclaimed his seat, just as Al looked up again. Both men leaned back in their chairs, it was time to negotiate.

"Here's the short of it. Anything you can give us to solidify our case against Munford will fulfill the initial requirement of the pardon. The second condition is something you are already doing. We are taking your concept and putting it in place to work for us with you leading the way." JD sat up and placed his arms on the table. "Al, I'm tired of looking over my shoulder. I'm tired of telling my wife no, because the things she wants to do may jeopardize her life. I don't want my children to grow up in a protected bubble, unable to enjoy the very things children should. Three years ago I was shot in the court room, by thugs that were controlled by Munford. During that same time, my wife, your sister was brutally beaten within an inch of her life, by members of a gang controlled by Munford. Last week, my wife took our children to the park and a man from Munford's team approached her. Sat right on the bench next to her. Every night since that happened I've closed my eyes thinking what could have happened. Those are my reasons for making this offer. Everyone of them is incredibly selfish; I will be the first to admit that. I'm trying to take this man down by the book and I believe you have information that could help me. But, either way, legal or not, Munford is going to stop being a threat to my family."

Al stared intently at the man sitting before him. The man really had no idea just how much Munford had interfered in his life. For ten years, he had held the key to JD's future, wondering when the time was right to reveal all that he knew. He wondered when JD would be ready to hear the truth. For ten years, he had made sure the man and his family was watched over. Never, in his wildest imagination had he anticipated that the man would marry his baby sister or turn the tables by looking out for him. There was one more question he had to ask before he made his decision. "Why are you making me this offer? You have enough to take Munford down, or you wouldn't be going forward with the case. So, why the offer?"

JD sat back and exhaled. "Al you have been helping people since you were sixteen years old. It may not have been in the conventional way, but you've been looking out for others most of your life. You could have made your mark in the streets with the same mantra of every other thug, I got mine,—you get yours. But you didn't. You gave people the opportunity to get what they needed from the streets and go legit. I can't be mad at that. Your gang didn't have me pulling out body bags left and right. You kept it as clean as you could in the street. You looked out for people, now it's time for someone to look out for you."

Al chuckled to himself. "Not to mention if you pull this off you will get mad love from my sister for life."

"Well, yeah, there is that," JD smiled. "Al, even if Tracy was not in the scenario, I would still make the offer."

Al shook his head. "I don't know if I can work for the feds."

JD stood, "That's part of the deal. Now, this next card I'm going to play is dirty. I'll admit that up front." JD pulled a picture from his pocket and pushed it across the table at Al. "Your daughter is hurting and she needs you, just like Tracy did when she was her age. It's time for you to take care of her."

Al picked up the picture, closed his eyes, and shook his head. "What in the hell did she do to her hair?" He sat the picture on top of the folder and looked up at JD. "That was cold."

"By any means necessary—any means necessary. I have to go. My wife is waiting for me to make an appearance at a fundraiser. She is already pissed at me, because I banned her from going out."

"You're joking right," Al laughed.

"Hell no, I'm not joking. She went to the projects to get your daughter and your niece last night with nobody on her. Hell yeah I told her she could not leave the house." JD laughed. "Sounds funny when you say it out loud." He exhaled. "Al, Munford is dangerous and wants to harm my family. I need to put him away permanently." JD extended his hand. "Get in touch when you are ready."

"I don't snitch JD."

"I know, but you make things right. That's all I'm asking you to do here—make things right." With that, JD walked out the door.

Ashley sat at the table with her husband and in-laws, with Cynthia, who was forbidden to attend the function, although her agency was hosting, on the telephone hammering away for blow by blow details. "Has she entered yet?" Cynthia asked.

"For the third time, no, she has not," Ashley answered losing all patience with her friend. "Roz has done a wonderful job with the set-up Cynthia. You would be impressed."

"Damn, I wish I was there."

"Well, you're not, so stop complaining."

"There is no stage, right?"

"No, stage, just a ballroom filled with people with money. The double doors from the hallway opened and Tracy walked in. A hush came over the room and then suddenly exploded with applause. "Damn, she did it. She stunned them to silence," Ashley yelled over the noise.

"You are taping this aren't you?"

"Yes, yes, yes. Cynthia, she is stunning." Ashley said, then turned to her sister-in-law Nicole. "The dress is prefect on her. You are amazing when it comes to shopping, I'm keeping you."

Tracy entered the room in a cream silk halter form fitting gown with gold rope that tied at the neck. It flowed tightly around the bodice, and over the hips, then flared at her mid-thigh. The back was open down to the waist with the gold rope trimming the outside. She looked like a roman goddess, with her hair up, gold single strand earrings dangling and one thick gold bracelet. Tracy stepped up to the microphone that stood in the middle of the room. "Good evening ladies and gentlemen. Thank you for such a warm welcome. This evening we embark on a journey—a journey that will influence our futures and the futures of our children for years to come. Leading that journey is a man of integrity, a man of wisdom, a man of strength. That man has sent me here to empty your pockets." The crowd burst into laughter as Tracy stood center stage and smiled. "I'm so happy to know you are open to that concept." She looked around the room as laughter continued. "I have been granted the pleasure of getting to know each of you personally tonight. Once my husband arrives, it will be my honor to introduce him to you. Until then, my dance card is open. Let the music began." People surrounded Tracy before the first note was played.

"Cynthia, her entrance was flawless. She was confident, elegant, and so poised. My goodness I can't believe she pulled it off. I have to call you back." Ashley hung up the cell phone and turned to her husband. "May I have this dance?"

"By all means," James replied in his deep velvet voice. "I'm afraid this is the only dance you may get tonight. I have to work the room."

"Well, by the looks of things, Tracy gave you a good start."

"That she did," James replied as he twirled Ashley around. "She amazes the hell out of me every time she is given a challenge."

"Tracy is and always will be extraordinarily amazing."

Applause erupted as Gavin and Carolyn entered the room. The first couple moved about graciously greeting people as a few held their breath to see what would happen when Tracy and Carolyn came face to face. To Ashley's surprise, it was Carolyn that paved the way for the rest of the evening. In a style that only Carolyn could exhibit, she pulled a photographer with her and cleared the area to allow pictures of her and Tracy together to be taken. The two posed for picture after picture. They even took a few with Senator Roth. The moment quieted the naysayers. Carolyn then took Tracy by the hand and literally began introducing her to people in the crowd. When she felt the time was right, Carolyn stepped out of the limelight leaving Tracy to handle things from then on. Before JD arrived, James had collected close to five million dollars in campaign contributions and the evening had just started.

Pearl walked over and whispered in Tracy's ear. Tracy excused herself from the couple she was speaking with and returned to the microphone. "Hello everyone. I am so happy to see you are enjoying the evening and I do apologize for the interruption. However, I believe it is time for me to introduce you to the next Governor of the Commonwealth of Virginia. My husband, Jeffrey Daniel Harrison."

JD entered the room and was immediately met with applause and hands extended to greet him. The crowd was more than he'd expected as he made his way through to the center of the room. It took him a good ten minutes to reach the microphone and he found himself speechless. He looked at the crowd, then back to his wife. He stepped up to the microphone and smiled. The crowd applauded. "Thank you. Thank you all for coming out this evening to help us make this journey." He stopped and looked back at Tracy. "Excuse me for just one moment." He took his wife into his arms and thoroughly kissed her as applause exploded around them. When he ended the kiss, he whispered in her ear. "I'm so sorry." She opened her eyes and smiled up at him. His world was right again. He took her hand and they stood at the microphone together. "You have to forgive me, but I have a beautiful wife and whenever I get the opportunity I like to kiss her." The crowd went crazy. After his brief speech, JD had to leave and Tracy was left to complete the evening.

Tracy stood near the window overlooking the scenic James River with a glass of wine she had been nursing most of the evening. JD's departure left her to listen as one guest's wife attempted to discuss the latest fashion. Giving the appropriate nod and a smile here and there kept the woman talking. It had been a long day, not to mention the night before. But if this was the way she had to help her husband, she would suffer through.

"Tracy, you were wonderful tonight." Stanley Covington smiled and kissed her cheek.

Saved, at least temporarily, she eagerly replied. "Thank you Stanley. It's nice of you to say." He looked at the woman and smiled, "May I steal her away for a moment." He took her elbow and walked away from the women. "I have someone I want you to meet. Mattie," he called out.

The slim brunette turned and smiled. "Stanley," she took his hand and kissed his cheek. "You are as handsome as always."

He smiled back, "Charm will get you everywhere with me, Mattie Gresham."

"I know," She smiled, "Hello Tracy."

"You two have met. Good."

"Yes we have. You did well tonight Tracy."

"Well. Hell, she knocked it out of the box tonight Mattie. She had the folks eating out of her hand. Mattie, I want you to talk Tracy into doing more of these events." There was a flash of surprise that appeared in her eyes and just as quick, the smile returned. "It will be my pleasure."

"I'll leave you two to talk," Stanley said as he walked away.

Mattie watched as he walked away then turned back to Tracy, "Well, it appears I have my work cut out for me."

"If you would excuse me, I think I'll go anywhere but here."

"Actually, I have a question for you." Ignoring the fact that Tracy was about to say something, Mattie continued. "Before you become an issue, I want you to consider what is best for Jeffrey's future. He's destined for great things. Not just being a husband or father. Jeffrey is a highly intelligent, charming, and caring man. The way he makes people feel just by being in his presence is remarkable. He makes them believe that they can be

better, that this state can be better and this country can be
better. And he is the only person that can make it all
happen. Don't try to make him an ordinary man. He's
more and I think you recognize that. And that makes you
a little afraid of losing him. That's why you've created the
needy wife syndrome. But for a man as driven and
determined as Jeffrey, that will only push him further
away. He needs a wife that is self-sufficient and as
committed to his future as he is. Are you that wife Tracy
or are you here to deter him from doing what he was put
here to do?"

She was so stunned at the woman's audacity that it
took her a moment to respond. Taking a step closer to
the woman Tracy placed her drink on the table. "When
you speak to me, refer to me as Mrs. Harrison. When
you speak of my husband, refer to him as Mr. Attorney
General or Mr. Harrison. Don't you ever presume that
you have the authority or position in life to question me
on anything, much less my husband." Her voice began to
raise an octave or two without her realizing it. "In fact, it
would be best if you never have anything to say to me....."

"Ladies," the very concerned smiling Carolyn Roth-
Roberts said as she approached the two, "let's lower our
voices." She looked around the room at a few curious
faces and waved. "Madison you've done it again. You
have said something you had no business saying.
Whatever it was, I suggest you take your leave at this
moment. Her presence is needed. Yours is not."

Mattie glared at the two women. The truth of the
matter was Munford is after JD because of his wife. If it
weren't for her family connection, she would not be
working against a man that was the best person to run this
country. That's what she did not like about this woman,
she was bad for JD and bad for this country. She took a
calming breath. Too much was happening all at once and
her patience was short. Doors were closing in on her and

she needed an escape. Losing her temper was not the answer. She had to clear her mind if she was going to keep her brother out of jail. "Carolyn you should have stuck to your guns and stayed with JD. If that hurts your feelings Mrs. Harrison, I'm sorry. I'm on the outside looking in. My mind is not fogged with emotions. Like it or not, you are his weakness. I'm trying to be his strength. You were good tonight, but what happens when the opposition attacks. How are you going to stand up to them when you can't even stand up to me?" Mattie said her piece, turned and walked out of the room.

"Keep smiling Tracy," Carolyn said. "Do not let them see you crack." She turned and faced the woman she considered her nemesis. "Wherever you go to draw the strength to continuously beat me at this game, you need to bring it to the surface and keep it there. Mattie is right on some things, but very wrong on one. You are not JD's weakness. You are his strength."

Gavin walked over. "Is everything all right over here?"

Carolyn looked up at her husband and smiled. "I'm getting damn good at this big sister thing." Tracy laughed when she really wanted to cry.

James and Ashley joined them. "I think it's okay to call it a night," Ashley stated as she placed her hand through Tracy's bent arm.

Tracy smiled and scanned the few remaining people. "There's a few more people, I need to speak with."

Carolyn smiled, "I'll join you."

"So will I," Ashley added and the women went off.

James and Gavin stood together watching the women. "Is it my imagination, or do I see Tracy, Carolyn, and Ashley working together?" James asked. "A year ago I had to keep my Ashley from murdering Carolyn."

"Miracles happen every day." Gavin replied. "My wife talked about giving me babies today."

"Carolyn?" James asked surprised at the notion. Gavin nodded his head. "I wonder what JD's miracle will be?"

Gavin watched as Tracy received another check from a guest. She handed the check to Carolyn and continued to talk with the donor. He pointed towards the women, "I think we are seeing it develop before our eyes."

James watched and smiled. "The butterfly is emerging from her cocoon."

⊸♡⊶

JD sat in the conference room of his office listening to the progress of the night. Each of the suspects had been taken without incident and all, with the exception of Jonas Gary had agreed to testify. However, none of them had anything on Munford, their only contact was through Gary. "And Gary isn't talking," JD stated after the reports were completed.

"He has requested to speak directly with you," Rossie advised.

"I'm not sure that's a good idea JD," Calvin interjected. "I don't want this man to think he has us by the balls by giving in to his demands."

"He knows we have Al. We may not need his testimony to take Munford out." JD stated.

"Maybe he knows Al Day doesn't have what you need. He may know what Al knows and know it's not enough to take Munford out." Rossie added.

"That's a lot of unknowns," JD chuckled.

Rossie smiled, "But, here's something I do know. The man has something that will seal this case."

"Why do you say that?" JD asked.

Rossie sat up and exhaled. "Mr. H. you've interrogated people. You were one of the best. There is a certain instinct that you get when a suspect has what you need. I get it with Gary. But, I'm young. This is my first big case. I could be wrong. I say you sit with him. Give him five minutes. That's enough time for you to assess things." He sat back.

JD looked to Calvin, who shrugged his shoulders, "It can't hurt to check him out."

Turing to Rossie, JD nodded his head, "You're going to be good at this."

Rossie's smile widened. "Thanks Mr. H."

"Alright." JD stood. "Let's go have a conversation with Mr. Jonas Gary."

The door opened to the room where Gary was being held and JD walked in. "Mr. Gary welcome to our facility. I take it you are being treated well."

Jonas was seated at a table with two chairs. He had a cup of coffee and an unfinished danish in front of him. "This is a nice place you have here. Definitely an improvement from our place. I could work here you know." JD smiled as he stood towering over the man. "Ah, the famous JD Harrison smile. I bet you used that charm to get your wife. I met her you know. Beautiful woman with a smile that could light up a room."

The man was trying to get into his head and JD knew it. "That's why you are here Mr. Gary. You got a little to close too my wife. That made you a person of interest for me."

"I can understand that wives are sacred, aren't they."

JD put his hands into his pocket and continued to look down at the man. "My wife is."

"I'm glad you understand that." Jonas stated. "I haven't seen my wife in a few days and I need you to rectify that situation for me."

"Why would I do that?"

"I'm here because I have something you need and you have something I want."

"Mr. Gary we've had a very productive night. I have four officers ready to testify against you on a number of infractions. I know what you want from me. I can't imagine what I would need from you."

"I would think a taped conversation would rule out hearsay."

JD never flinched or showed any expression of interest although inside he knew Munford on tape would put a nail in the coffin. He smirked. "I have taped conversations of several people Mr. Gary." JD looked at his watch. "It seems your time is running short. See, I agreed to give you five minutes of my time tonight. But I'm afraid that's all I have and you have one minute left. I suggest you use it wisely."

"Short and sweet it is. I want my wife and immunity and I will give you Chief Wilbert T. Munford on a platter."

JD placed his hands on the table and leaned over close to Jonas. "I have Chief Wilbert T. Munford and I have you on a platter," he grinned. "Your problem is you don't have a wife. You have a young woman you kidnapped from her family and have held hostage for ten years." JD stood. "I'm afraid your time is up Mr. Gary."

He turned to open the door and Jonas spoke. "I think you have time to hear a conversation ordering a hit on your wife and children."

JD froze, but did not allow his heart pumping furiously to show. He turned back to Jonas and smirked. "Goodnight Mr. Gary."

As soon as JD was out of the room, Calvin and Rossie met him in the hallway. Calvin handed JD the phone. "I have Brian on the line."

"Brian, where are my wife and children?"

"Here with me. We are en route to the house."

"Don't let them out of your sight Brian."

"I would die before I let anything happen to your family."

"I would prefer that not happen."

"Me too. There are still a lot of ladies that haven't had a taste of your boy."

JD smiled, hung up the phone, and gave it back to Calvin. "Do you believe him?"

Calvin nodded, "He's too cocky not to have something."

"I'm not giving him the woman."

"Just make him think you are." Rossie suggested. "If nothing else it will buy us time."

JD motioned to the agents in the hallway. "No one in or out of that room and no calls."

JD pulled out his cell and called Brian back. "Have Tucker call me." He hung up the phone, "All right. Let's buy some time."

Mattie sat in her car wondering what direction to take. Should she play with the devil or trust the system. The revelation, at the staff meeting, was of a sting operation in progress that might take Munford down. If that happens where will that leave her, or her brother. "Damn him." She screamed. For a brief minute, she thought of using the information to bargain with Munford. Tell him about the take down in exchange for her brother's record. But if they took Munford out, she and her brother might be in the clear. Making the decision, Mattie started her car and drove off. A goodnight's sleep and things might look better in the morning.

Munford was at his desk when his secretary knocked. "I'm calling it a night, how about you?"

Glancing at the clock, he smiled. "It's after eight. Go on home Lily. I'll see you in the morning."

"Goodnight Chief."

"Night Lily."

Munford stood to stretch. He walked over to the window and looked out over the city. Night had fallen and the skyline lights streaked the City. He loved the City, from the South of the James River to the North and soon, very soon he would be in control as Mayor. Within the hour, payment from the deal should be deposited and his financial worries would be over.

"Evening Chief."

Munford swung around with his gun drawn, no one was there. Scanning the room, as he moved around the desk, he saw nothing that would have caused a sound. But he wasn't crazy, he heard someone call his name. Munford moved back to his desk. He pushed the button that would alert officers that something was wrong. Nothing happened. He pushed the button again.

"Oh, sorry, I cut that off."

Munford looked up to see a man standing, no, more like reclining against the armoire in his office. The man was at least six-five, dressed in a suit and tie with Italian leather shoes. He held his weapon on the man. "Who in the hell are you?"

"Me? I've been given the pleasure of escorting you to the Attorney General's office. In essence, I'm your babysitter. Would you really shoot me with that? I mean, we just met. I haven't pissed you off yet."

Before Munford could respond, the gun was kicked out of his hand and the door to his office swung open. Several men in black suits walked in. They immediately pulled their weapons and pointed at him. "Drop your weapon Sir." One man shouted.

"What the hell are you doing? This is my office. He is the intruder." Munford pointed to the man who was now sitting on the sofa near the door.

"Chief Munford, drop your weapon now." The man repeated the demand.

Munford secured his weapon. "You want to explain why in the hell you have entered my office."

"Chief Munford, you are being taken into custody. Would you come with us please?"

"Hell no. Not until someone tells me what this is all about."

"Okay, we tried it your way. I'm giving you the option of walking out with dignity or I will carry you out."

"Do you know who you are talking to?"

"A dead man if you don't shut up." The man took Munford's arm and began walking towards the door. Munford jerked his arm, but the man did not let go. "Do that again and I don't care what Harrison say's I will kill you."

"Harrison? What does he have to do with this?"

The man did not answer. He turned to the men in the office. "Secure all files and the office."

As they walked out of the building, there were a few officers on the night shift that stopped and watched as the Chief was escorted out of the building.

Ten minutes later Munford was escorted into the basement of the State Attorney's building and placed in an interrogation room. On his way, a door in the hallway was open and he could see Jonas Gary sitting at a table inside. The door was closed before an expression could be registered.

Once inside the room Munford continued with the same indignant behavior he'd demonstrated at his office.

"I want answers and I want them now. Heads are going to roll for this."

The man with the deadly eyes was losing his patience when the door opened. "Thank God you are here." He shook Samuel's hand. "I swear I was about to kill him."

"Thank you for the restraint lil brother." Samuel smiled.

Munford looked between the two men, "Lassiter. I'll have your ass for this if someone doesn't tell me what in the hell is going on."

"I'll be happy to Chief," JD said as he walked through the door.

"Harrison, what is the meaning of this?"

"Chief Wilbert T. Munford you are being indicted on several felony charges but my favorite is misconduct of office."

"Have you lost your damn mind Harrison? You don't have the authority to remove me from office. What proof do you have?" Munford took steps toward JD. Samuel and Joshua impeded his progress. "I have rights."

"Can I just shoot him and take him out of his misery?"

Samuel looked at his little brother and shook his head. "No."

"The yelling is getting on my nerves," Joshua stated as he leaned against the wall.

JD only shook his head and continued. "Chief Munford, your passport has been revoked, your bank accounts have all been frozen, and you are officially hereby relieved of duty. Against my better judgment when we finish here you will be released on your own recognizance until you are scheduled to appear in court. At this point I suggest you get a good attorney." The men turned to walk out of the door.

"Harrison, I don't know what you think you have, but you'd better know what you are doing."

JD turned and inhaled. "I know exactly what I'm doing Munford. I'm going to let you sit here for a while and think about all that I might be up to."

Samuel and JD walked out the door leaving Absolute in the room alone with Munford.

Chapter 14

The ringer on the telephone was turned down low, but it startled Tracy all the same. The clock showed four-fifteen and her husband was not home. "Hello."

"Hi babe."

"Jeffrey where are you?" Tracy asked as she reached over and turned on the lamp then sat up in bed.

"I'm still at the office. It's been a long night and I'm afraid it's not over."

"Are you okay?"

"Yes, I'm fine. They tell me you were a hit tonight. I'm sorry I had to leave you there alone."

A soft smile creased her lips. "Things went well. James said you received a lot of contributions tonight."

"That's good to know." He exhaled, "You were beautiful tonight. I couldn't keep my eyes off you. While I was talking to Mr. and Mrs. Goodman, I was so distracted looking at you that they took pity on me and suggested I go be with my wife. I tried to get to you but people wanted to talk and you were surrounded by a crowd."

"You looked pretty good too, but you always do."

"Tracy, things are going to be a little rough the next few days maybe weeks. There may be long nights just like now. I know we had some harsh words today..."

"Jeffrey don't worry about it. Take care of what you are doing and I'll take care of home." There was a voice in the background. "Jeffrey, is Mattie there with you?"

"Yes, we are preparing for an early morning press conference."

"Is Pearl there also?"

"Yeah, do you need to speak to her?"

"No, it can wait."

"Okay babe. I have to go. Give JC and Jazzy a kiss for me."

"I will."

"Love you."

"I love you too." Tracy held the telephone after JD hung up. A minute later there was a knock on the door. "Yes."

"Is everything okay Tracy?"

"Brian? Come in. What are you doing here?"

Opening the door and looking in, the first thought that came to mind was that had to be the sexiest woman in the world. "We are all on duty 24/7 until further notice. I saw the light under the door and I wanted to make sure were okay."

She smiled, "I'm good. Thanks for asking."

"Ryan said you kicked ass tonight," he smiled.

"Things went well until..."

"Until what?"

"Until Mattie Gresham decided to tell me what she thought of me."

"Who gives a damn what she thinks."

Tracy threw the covers back and stood, to put on her robe, "I'm afraid I do."

Brian closed his eyes to the sight of his friend's wife wearing a pair of hip hugging pj bottoms with a body fitting tee shirt that did not cover her navel. And damn if she didn't look good. He inhaled and slowly peeked through one half open eye. When she was covered, he opened both eyes. "You shouldn't care."

"The thing is, I think she was right. I need to be a strong woman for Jeffrey. You want some coffee?" she asked while walking by him out the door.

"There is some already made downstairs." He followed behind her.

"She's at the office with Jeffrey, you know."

"Who is?" he asked as they walked down the stairs.

"Mattie," Tracy said using the perky voice she'd heard the woman use.

"Please don't do that again," Brian laughed and Tracy joined in.

After several hours with internal affairs, union reps, and his attorney, Munford was tired and pissed. That arrogant ass Harrison had the nerve, the audacity to question him—for hours. According to his attorney, they had enough to indict, but not enough to convict. Only Day and Jonas could connect him to anything. He knew Jonas wouldn't talk, but Day was another story. Without those two, they didn't have anything. But the indictments were enough to jeopardize the mayoral seat. Those damn Harrisons' had been a thorn in his side for too long—first his father and now him. Pulling out one of his untraceable cell phones, he placed a call.

"I go down, your brother goes with me. Get Harrison to talk and get me the damn location on Day." He hung up the telephone without giving Mattie a chance to respond. Then he made another call. "Once I get the information, eliminate the family." He hung up, took a shower and went to bed smiling.

A solemn JD stood at the podium in the press room of his office with Captain Davis, Rossie Brown, Samantha Stevens, and Calvin Johnson. He looked at the media that had filled the room. This was going to be a major hit to the citizens of Richmond. The red light on the network camera was on and he began. "It saddens me to come before you today with news of a dismissal of a government official. However, I believe if we ask you to vote for us, we should, at the very least, uphold the integrity and morals of that office. As we speak, Chief Wilbert T. Munford of the Richmond City Police Department has been removed from his position. Captain Maurice Davis will be taking over as Acting Chief of Police until further notice. At this time, charges are pending against Ex-chief Munford, for among other things, abuse of office and conspiracy to commit murder. There will be no further comments into the investigation at this time. However, acting Chief Davis is available for questions concerning public safety."

"Attorney General Harrison, what impact will this removal have on the cases handled by Munford?" One reporter asked before JD left the microphone.

"It is clear there will be some cases that will be impacted by this action. However, those numbers will be few. This has been an ongoing investigation for over a year now. A careful review of arrests handled by Munford has commenced and we will inform you of the outcome."

"Are there other officers involved?" another reporter questioned.

"Unfortunately, yes. Several officers have been relieved of duty and questioned. Some will be charged and others reprimanded according to internal affairs protocol."

"Attorney General Harrison, it is common knowledge that you and Chief Munford had been at opposite sides of the table on several issues. Is it possible this may be a personal vendetta?"

"The results of the investigation were sent to the US Attorney General's Office. Upon review of the findings, the decision was made to remove Chief Munford from office. The indictments were issued and delivered to my office to execute."

For the next three days, the media blast from the investigation was a whirlwind. Accusations from Chief Munford against JD were hurled every time he was in front of a camera. Jeffrey was spending long hours at the office or at campaign headquarters, while Tracy was confined to the house under twenty-four hour guard. Every time she called Jeffrey, Mattie answered indicating he was in a meeting and she would give the message. They had talked only once since the night of the event and now she was beginning to worry. Taking the chance, she called again, but this time she called the office. "Attorney General's Office"

"Hello Mrs. Langston. I know Jeffrey is busy but I was wondering if I could speak with him for a moment."

"Of course Tracy. Let me get him on the line for you."

Tracy held the line and was relieved when JD answered. "Tracy is everything okay?"

"Yes. Everything is fine."

"Are the children okay?" JD asked.

"Yes, they're fine Jeffrey."

"How are you?"

"Busy babe. Things are a little crazy and not as clean as I want them to be."

"I heard Munford on TV this morning and I saw the pictures."

"I know it doesn't look good, babe. But there is nothing to those pictures—you know that."

Tracy exhaled, "When are you coming home?" Tracy asked without responding.

"I'm not sure babe. Hold on for a minute." She heard Mattie's voice in the background. "Babe, I have to go. I'll call you as soon as I can." The call ended.

Another night went by with JD missing from the dinner table and Tracy surround by security. The next night when JD came in it was one in the morning and Tracy was upstairs in her office. He walked over, kissed her on the cheek and sat on the sofa then closed his eyes. "You look tired."

"I am babe. I don't know which is going to kill me first, this case, the campaign, or Mattie."

"Mattie?" Tracy asked, "Why is she a concern?"

"No reason babe," he stood and ran his hand through her hair, then hugged her. "I'm going to kiss my children then take a shower," he said and walked out of the room.

Tracy watched as her husband walked away and wondered why she was so angry. The next morning she was in the kitchen talking with Mrs. Gordon when JD came downstairs. "Good morning," he said as he entered the kitchen.

"Good morning Mr. Harrison. How are you?"

"I'm rested. How have you been?"

"I'm doing fine son. You know I leave to see my grandbabies today."

JD was drinking a cup of coffee, when he looked up at her. "In Atlanta? No, I didn't know."

"I haven't had a chance to tell you," Tracy said from her seat at the table.

"How long will you be gone," he asked and took a seat next to his wife.

"Two weeks. I'm going to spoil my grandbabies then come back and finish spoiling yours," she laughed.

"We are going to miss you," he said and looked at Tracy. "Right babe?" he covered her hand with his.

"Yes we are," she said as she pulled her hand away then walked over and hugged the woman. "I wish I could take you to the airport."

"No child. You stay right in this house where you are safe." She turned to JD. "You make sure nothing happens to my babies while I'm gone."

"I'll do my best."

Brian walked through the patio door. "You have a visitor," he said just as the front door bell sounded. "Are you ready Mrs. Gordon?"

"You go ahead," Tracy kissed her goodbye, "I'll get the door."

JD stood and hugged her. "You have a safe trip Mrs. Gordon."

Tracy opened the front door and was surprised to see Mattie standing there. "Good Morning Mrs. Harrison," she said as she attempted to walk into the house.

Standing in the doorway, Tracy wasn't sure she wanted to let the woman inside. For the last week, she had been controlling her contact with Jeffrey. Now, she was on her turf and it was her chance to limit her. "How may I help you?"

"May I come in?"

"No."

Mattie starred at her as if she had lost her mind. "Tracy I need to see JD."

"You can see him at the office."

"Things are crazy at the office. I need to see him now."

"Mattie?" JD called from the foyer, "What are you doing here?"

"Good morning JD," she said as Tracy stepped aside. "I have the press release for your review."

Tracy closed the door and walked up the stairs. JD watched as he listened to Mattie. A few minutes later, JD walked into Jasmine's room where Tracy was in the rocker feeding her. He stood in the doorway and watched for a minute then walked in. "Everything all right babe?"

"I don't know Jeffrey. This is the first time I've seen you for more than thirty minutes at a time. Mattie shows up and your attention is immediately drawn to whatever petty little thing she has to tell you. So you tell me, is everything all right?"

"Tracy," JD began, but his cell phone rang. He closed his eyes and exhaled. Pulling out his phone he answered, "Harrison."

"I'll be right down," he sighed.

Tracy stood and placed Jasmine on her shoulder. "You're needed. You should go."

"A lot is going on. The office is crazy."

"So you and Mattie keep telling me. Neither seems to be able to do without you."

"What are you talking about Tracy?"

"I'm talking about the office and Mattie and you. I thought she worked for the campaign."

"She does."

"Then why is she at your side twenty-four seven?"

"Tracy, I don't have time for this. Mattie controls the political message for the campaign. In case you haven't notice, this case is politically charged. Everything connected to this case has political implications. That's why she is needed." He stopped and exhaled. "Babe, I don't want to spend the few minutes I have with you arguing about Mattie." His cell phone rang again.

"What?" he yelled into the phone and Jasmine whimpered. "I'm coming." He looked at her, "I'm sorry,

Samuel is here. I have to go." He kissed the top of her head and walked out of the door.

Calvin met JD at the elevator of the office when he arrived. "We have a problem. Jonas Gary has slipped us again. The agents we placed at his home were found inside their vehicle drugged." He continued as they walked to JD's office.

"Are they alright?" JD asked as he exhaled.

Calvin nodded, "They are both at the hospital and should be fine."

"Good. Contact their families. Make sure they are notified. How did this happen?"

"Rossie interviewed them and should be here shortly with their statements. There's another problem."

JD could only shake his head. He wanted to take a moment to call Tracy to smooth over the harsh words from the morning, but the case was snowballing out of control. For his own sanity, he had to solidify his case against Munford, get the campaign back to issues, and take time for his wife. "What?"

"Good news with the statements received thus far, we definitely have Munford on abuse of office. However, there is no jail time associated with that, just release from duty. This will kill his push to be the city's first mayor. Bad news, what Gary gave us after the phone call with his wife was not sufficient to charge Munford with anything. He insinuated there were several schemes associated with gang related murders. But without his testimony, we cannot convict." Calvin took a seat, "Any word from Al?"

"No," JD replied dejected. "He'll make contact when he is ready."

"JD, without Gary, Al is our only hope to put Munford away."

"Mr. Harrison, you have an urgent call on line one," Mrs. Langston said from the doorway.

"Thank you, Mrs. Langston." He looked at Calvin, "We'll give Al a little more time." JD picked up the telephone. "Harrison." He stood at the sound of his mother's calm, but anxious voice, "Are you all right mom?"

"No, I'm pissed as hell."

"Hold on mom," he put his hand over the mouthpiece, and looked at Calvin, "Get Samuel in here." He put the telephone on speaker. "Mom calm down and tell me exactly what happened." Samuel and Calvin were back in the room.

"An officer by the name of Jonas Gary came by the house. He said he was a part of your investigation and wanted to make sure things here at the house were fine. So I let him in and we talked. But he was asking me questions about your father and Chief Munford."

Samuel immediately pulled out his cell phone to call Brian. "We need to get JD's mother under protection. Jonas Gary just paid her a visit."

"What else did he say?"

"He had the audacity to try and insinuate that since your father was once Munford's partner, evidence may surface indicating your father was a dirty cop. That's when I put his ass out my house."

"Okay mommy, did he say anything else?" Samuel wrote something on a piece of paper and placed it on the desk in front of him. JD read it and continued to listen to his mother.

"No, he just gave me his card and said to tell you he came by."

"Mommy I want you to pack a bag. Brian is on his way there. Get the box with daddy's gun out of the front closet."

"I don't need a gun," Martha argued.

"Mommy please, just do as I say. Inside the box, there is a compartment under the gun. Lift it up, the bullets are there. Load the gun and keep it on you until Brian gets there. Go do it while I'm on the phone." He looked at Calvin, "Get James on the phone. Tell him to meet me at mommy's house."

"I have it son." Martha said through the telephone. "Why did this man come here and why am I being forced to leave my house?"

"Mommy I'll explain everything when I get there."

"Someone is calling on the other line," she said.

"That should be James. Stay on the line with him until I get to the house."

As soon as JD hung up the telephone, all three men rushed out of the office en route to his mother's house.

While Ashley settled their mother into the east wing of her home, James, JD, Brian and Samuel sat in the library. James prepared a drink for all of them. "Thank you for doing this James. I have no idea how long it's going to be." JD exhaled.

"If anything happened to your mother, my wife would be hell to live with. So you are saving me some heartache." He smiled. "Besides she is safe here. With the security we have, it would take a small army to get in."

"That's why I want her here." JD sighed and relaxed for a minute.

"You should be here too." JD shook his head. "Here me out." James said. "I'll be the first to be against family living together. Believe me, it's not all it's cracked up to be. I also know how you feel about continuing to live in the neighborhood. But man you have to see that living where you are is too open. You are putting yourself and your family in arms way. I know that's not what you want, but that's what you have done. Here you are in a secured neighborhood. Without a code to the gate, they will have to scale a ten foot fence, travel across the moat and get pass the security beams before they can get to the house. Your life is changing and you are going to have to change with it. Brian has put in a hell of a security system in an inner city neighborhood. That's commendable. The man you are trying to take down kills people. They could come for you and one of your neighbors gets a stray bullet. How would you feel?"

JD walked over to the fireplace and exhaled. "I left the DA's office because of this. How in the hell did I get back into this position? Not only am I endangering Tracy and the children, now my mother had to be uprooted from her home."

"This is what happens when the good guy tries to take down the bad guy," Samuel joked. "They are going to fight you with everything they can to protect their enterprise. They will kill whom-ever is in their way. And at the time my friend—that's you."

"Brian, what do you think?" JD asked.

"We can handle security at the house. But I agree with James. Sometime in the near, very near future you are going to have to move from the neighborhood."

JD looked around, "James, I can't afford something like this."

James frowned. "Your wife is a multi-millionaire, of course you can. I have two hundred and fifty acres of land behind this fence. You could build on the other side of the moat and we would need a car to get to you. Say the word and I'll have a surveyor out here in the morning to walk off ten acres." He walked over to JD and put his hand on his shoulder. "Take it as a gift from us to you and Tracy. I know you have a lot on your plate, but at some point soon, I want you to seriously consider my offer."

"I'll think about it. I'm going to go up and talk to Ashley and mom before I leave." JD sat his glass on the desk and left the room.

James turned to Brian, "You are going to have to talk to him about this move. As we get closer to our goal, security is going to be an issue."

"That's not going to be an easy sell. JD has been a neighborhood kid all his life. Let's get him out of this shit and I'll talk to him about it." He stood and laughed. "You know he has no idea how much money they have."

James laughed, "I almost laughed when he said he couldn't afford this."

"It's going to hit him one day," Brian laughed. He turned to Samuel. "I'm going back to the house. You stay on JD."

"JD decided to work the rest of the day from home. We'll be there after his meetings with the Governor."

Using an untraceable cell phone, Jonas Gary placed a telephone call to Munford's residence. He left the pre-arranged code and waited. Five minutes later, the cell phone rang. "Where in the hell are you?"

"Around."

"The inventory did not reach its destination. People are upset."

That didn't surprise Jonas. "Harrison probably intercepted them."

"How in the hell would he know about that?"

"I don't know and don't care. It's water under the bridge now."

"People are looking at me to make this right."

"I suggest you do that."

"That's your problem. Your focus has always been staying one step ahead of Harrison. The truth of the matter is the man, unbelievably, is out of your reach. This situation would not exist if you hadn't been so damn intent on getting at Harrison."

"Sounds like you're turning," Munford scowled.

"No, not my style. But game respects game. And Harrison's got game."

"He's not going to have it for long."

Jonas shook his head, the man just will never understand. It was time to cut his losses. "I need to cut this short. I'm disappearing tonight. Harrison doesn't have you without me. Interesting thought crossed my mind today. You were once Harrison's father's partner."

"Yeah, what of it."

"Well, he's dead, put the dirty stuff on him. Distract Harrison. Make him play defense. You are on your own from here on." The call ended.

Munford exhaled. "One last hurdle, he called the number he had for Mattie. "The caller you are attempting to reach has requested the services to be disconnected." Munford looked at the phone and threw it into the fireplace. Then he thought about what Gary said. Damn if it didn't make since. He picked up his house phone and made a call to his attorney.

It was a little after six in the evening when JD walked into the house with Samuel, Calvin and Rossie in tow. Tracy turned to see them and frowned. "Have you heard what this man is implicating about your father?"

"Daddy," JC, called out as he climbed down from the table and ran into his father's arms.

"Hello son," JD picked him up then walked over to the television monitor to listen to Munford's attorney who was holding an opportune press conference. Calvin, Rossie and Samuel gathered around also. "I have advised my client to present the information in a public forum the same as the Attorney General has done with him. But he refuses to publicly tarnish the reputation of his one-time partner's memory. The evidence will show this is a deliberate attempt by Attorney General Harrison to keep information regarding his father's past suppressed. I have no further comments." The man walked off as more questions from the press were whirled at him.

"We knew it was coming." JD said as he looked down at Tracy. "Calvin, would you take everyone into the office. I'll be there in a minute."

"Sure," the men all said their hellos and went into the office.

JD put JC back in his seat. "I want you to be a good boy and eat all your dinner."

"Okay daddy."

JD exhaled and walked Tracy into the foyer. "The officer that approached you went to mommy's house today."

"Is she alright?" Tracy fretted.

"Yes, we moved her in with James and Ashley until this is over."

"When will that be Jeffrey?"

"I don't know." He exhaled. "We are going to be meeting late into the night. Don't wait up for me."

"Alright." She said and began to walk off. Stopping she asked. "How much damage is this going to do to your case?"

JD smiled inwardly. Tracy never asked if what the man insinuated was true. "I'm not sure, but we're prepared for it." He walked into the office and closed the door. An hour later, James and Mattie appeared and just as quickly disappeared behind the closed doors. Tracy took the children upstairs and decided to wait for Jeffrey to come up to bed.

It was after three in the morning when the meeting ended. The team was confident the indictments on the suspects were strong and would be upheld, with the exception of Munford. With Jonas Gary's disappearance, he was still not within their grasp. Everyone had left, but Mattie remained behind. Time was running out and this might be her only chance to get the information she needed from JD. The house was quiet. This was not where she wanted to do this, but she had no choice. The outcome of her actions could give her leverage in one of two ways. She could get him high enough to tell her the location or she could actually go through with the act and use it to blackmail the information out of him. "JD we need to discuss how we will handle the impact of all of this on the campaign."

"Mattie, I don't give a damn about how this will affect the campaign."

Mattie walked over to the bar and poured JD a drink. "That's exactly why you need me, especially now." She reached in her pocket and dropped a small white pill into the glass. She talked while allowing the pill to dissolve. "It is my job to give a damn, when you don't. The public needs to see you are capable of handling this situation and more. You want them to elect you as their leader. Then they need to know you can lead through adversity." She took a seat on the edge of his desk and crossed her legs. "Here, drink this." He took the glass and sat it on the desk, "I need to keep a clear mind Mattie. This is not going to get resolved tonight"

Placing her hand on his shoulder, she leaned close to him. "I know it's late. The press will expect a statement at the morning briefing." She squeezed his bicep, "Drink this, and relax. Give me something to work with and I'm out of here."

"I suggest you take your hands off my husband. Get your ass off his desk and get the hell out of my house." Tracy said in the angriest voice JD had ever heard from her.

"Tracy!" he frowned.

"Now! Get out now," she stepped inside the office as Mattie stood.

JD stood between the two women, "Tracy, we are working."

"I can see her working you over time. Why can't you?" She walked around JD and stood face to face with Mattie. "You have access to him at his office and at campaign headquarters. Here, is my domain and you will not disrespect me in my home."

Mattie saw how angry the woman was and knew it was time to leave. She picked up her purse. "JD I better go."

"No, Tracy Mattie is my guest."

"Really, you leave with her when she goes."

"It's all right JD. I'll see you in the morning," Mattie said and ran out the door leaving it open.

JD turned to his wife angry. "I don't believe you did that. She works for me Tracy," he said and walked out the door behind Mattie.

Tracy watched as her husband walked out the door angry. She didn't care this time. The chime on the security door had indicated the people from the meeting had exited through the front door. With all that happened throughout the day, she wanted to hold her husband in her arms and tell him, things would get better. Coming down the stairs, in her tee-strap pajamas, she was somewhat surprised to still hear voices. She watched from the stairs as the woman sat on her husband's desk and crossed her legs. Hadn't she told that woman to keep her crotch out of her husband's face? She watched as Mattie gave him a drink and his refusal. Then she put her hand on his arm. At one time, she would have turned and walked back up the stairs, but this was her home, no-one was going to disrespect her here. Then she felt tears began to well up in her eyes. Jeffrey went after the woman, she was standing in his office alone. Hurt and dismayed she turned, trying to get some semblance of control, she saw the drink on the desk. Picking it up, she swallowed it in one gulp. Frowning at the bitter taste, she put the glass back on the desk. The tears began to drop and the last thing she wanted was for Jeffrey or Mattie to see her crying over this. Leaving the property with all the security was not an option. So she ran out the office and through the patio door.

Within minutes, the cool September air swept across her bare arms. Going back into the house was the last thing she wanted to do. Looking around, she decided to walk to the back of the yard into the pool house. By the time she reached the door, her tears were now close to an uncontrollable sob. She opened it and walked inside.

Brian was startled awake while resting on the bed in the panic room that was added on to the pool house. The computer had not indicated any of the perimeter areas had been penetrated. Shaking away the cobwebs of the semi-nap, he walked out into the room where the computer monitors were located to look. A sound came from the doorway. He turned to see a woman standing there. "Tracy?" he questioned, frowning. "What are you doing here?" Without saying a word, she walked over, placed her tear stained cheek against his bare chest, and wrapped her arms around his waist. "What's wrong Tracy? Are the children alright?"

He wrapped his arms around her and tried to console her as she cried uncontrollably in his arms. "Where's JD Tracy?" he asked still not getting any sensible response from her. He held her tighter, "Okay, shh, shh." He cupped her face in his hands, pushed her hair from her face, and looked into her eyes. "Tracy, stop crying. I need you to tell me what's wrong." His lips were a mere breath away from hers when he asked again. "What is it?" Before he knew what was happening Tracy kissed him with an urgency that was not that of just a friend. He parted his lips for a moment at the pressure from her lips, and then realized who this was. He pushed her back at arms length and looked at her. "Have you been drinking?" He asked as JD burst through the door.

"What in the hell are you doing?" JD yelled clearly angry.

"Trying to figure out what in the hell is wrong with your wife," he replied just as Tracy slumped to the floor. Both men reached out to catch her before she hit the floor.

"Tracy?" JD called out her name, and although her eyes were open, she did not respond. "Tracy," he called out again.

"Her pupils are dilated." Brian said, as he looked closer at her. "Did she take something?"

JD didn't answer. "JD did she take anything—was she drinking?"

"No," he yelled back as he tried to get his wife to respond.

Brian pulled out his cell and pushed a number. "Come on, come on. Pearl is your doc friend there?

"Brian?"

"Is he there Pearl?" he asked with little patience.

"Yes," she replied half-asleep.

"Bring him to JD's house now."

"What's going on Brian?"

"Now, Pearl, now," he said and hung up the telephone. "Let's get her in the house."

JD picked Tracy up. She wrapped her arms around his neck as he carried her into the house and up the stairs. Brian pulled his shirt from the other room then followed them into the house.

Thirty minutes later, JD walked down the stairs with Dr. Theodore Prentiss. "Thank you Doc. Are you sure she is okay?"

The young man with a close hair cut and mustache nodded. "Everything seems stable. I'll run test on the blood work and let you know my findings. I have to tell you, the symptoms look like she took some kind of drug."

Brian and Pearl stood as the men entered the foyer. JD extended his hand, "I would appreciate that as soon as possible."

Pearl joined Theo at the door. She affectionately rubbed his shoulders as they stood in the doorway. "Doc, we would appreciate it if you didn't mention this incident to anyone," Brian said from behind JD.

"It's not a problem. I'm off duty." He turned, placed his hand in the small of Pearl's back as they stepped outside.

"Good night JD and Brian," Pearl said. "Call me if you need anything."

"Thanks Pearl," JD said as he closed the door. He stood there for a long moment before he turned to face the man he considered a friend. The scene replayed in his mind over and over like a bad recording. He took a deep breath and still could not control the rage that was building inside. His Tracy, was kissing this man and from what he could see his friend was kissing her in return. Before the scene replayed, again JD punched Brian with so much force he fell back against the stair railing then onto the floor.

Brian quickly regained his footing and wiped the blood from his mouth. "What in the hell is wrong with you?"

JD took another step towards him. He pointed angrily at Brian. "You were supposed to be my friend—my protector and I walk in on you kissing my wife."

Brian put his hand up to stop the man's progress, "JD, listen to me. I know what you think you saw, but you are wrong. You are not thinking straight man. That's not what was happening."

JD's chest heaved up and down with anger. "Get the hell out of my house."

Brian stood, shocked looking at his friend. He shook his head. "You're wrong man. You're wrong on this." Brian knew the hell JD had been through since this case broke and he was willing to give him a pass on the punch. But he was not going to be accused of doing the unthinkable—touching his friend's wife. He turned to walk out the back through the patio door, but he stopped and looked at his friend. "You know, I know you are angry, and that anger is directed at me. But you should be angry with yourself. You are doing all you can to keep your wife safe, but what are you doing to keep her as your wife. I'm the person that's here day in and day out with her and the children while you do what you need to do. If she turned to another man and she hasn't, it would be your doing—not mine. You think about that."

Quietly JD began to regain some level of control, but what he saw as betrayal was something he could not take. In a low, almost lethal voice he spoke. "I trusted you. I trusted you with my life—with my wife." He hesitated. "I don't want you near my wife, my children, or my home."

JD's words cut deep. It was best to leave and Brian did so, quietly closing the door behind him.

Chapter 15

With no sleep at six, the next morning, JD sat in the chair next to the door and watched as his wife slept in the bed. She had not moved, not even to change position. He knew, for he had sat in the chair since coming upstairs after his altercation with Brian. What in the hell could he have been thinking. From the day Brian, met Tracy, JD knew he was attracted to her. That attraction had grown into something more over the years, but JD never thought Brian would act on it. Never in his wildest imagination did he ever consider Tracy would be attracted to anyone but him. Arrogant thinking, hell yeah, without question but that's what he'd thought. The day he walked into the office he had at his first condo to see his sister's shy college roommate lying on her stomach on the floor with headphones on her ears and feet swinging in the air, was the day other women had ceased to interest him. He tried—Lord knows he tried, every other woman that came across his path once she returned to school. None of them, not the models, the news anchors, the actresses, Carolyn Roth, none of them could keep his mind from wandering to Tracy. Finally, he stopped trying and surrendered to the power she had over him. Since then, regret had never crossed his mind. When he married Tracy, he was more than ready to spend the rest of his life with her.

The truth was he couldn't live without her, but he wondered now if she felt the same. Tracy was only nineteen years old when they met. She was as innocent as the first snowfall, pure, innocent, and naive. Had he taken advantage of that? Should he have given her the same opportunity to see other people—to be involved in relationships with other men? Did she regret never experiencing making love with another man? Was she curious? Was she truly attracted to Brian?

Brian. The man was as much a part of his life as Tracy was. They had been friends since high school. They met on the football field. Brian and Douglas were already staples when he and Calvin went out for the team. The older players would tackle them relentlessly, but JD and Calvin would keep getting up. He guessed Brian and Douglas must have liked something about them, for the two men decided to help them out, by blocking for them. He remembered Brian saying, "If you want to get to him, you've got to come through me." That's how their lives had been every since. Anyone that wanted a piece of JD Harrison had to go through Brian Thompson first. That wasn't an easy thing to do. Brian could put your ass on the floor, before you could bawl up a fist. At any time, Brian could have fought him back when they were downstairs, but he didn't. Now, JD wondered why? Was it because he was guilty of kissing his wife? Or was it because he'd vowed to protect him, even from himself if needed?

Samuel could see JD sitting in the chair near the door of the bedroom as he walked down the hallway. The man must not have heard him approach because he never looked over his shoulder. Something heavy must have gone down. He received a call from Brian to take over security detail for the family. Brian stated he would be working from the office until further notice. When he attempted to ask questions, the man he had come to know very well gave him a warning look. This was one of those times, you did not ask questions, and you just followed orders. "JD."

"Yes Samuel," he answered without turning.

"I have the team downstairs. Brian asked me to go over the changes with you. Do you have a moment?"

"I'll be right down after I take a shower and get dressed. Feel free to have some breakfast while you wait."

"Will do," Samuel replied, then went back to the kitchen.

Magna, Ryan, and Donnell were in the kitchen when he returned. "He'll be down shortly."

"Why are we changing assignments?" Donnell asked.

Samuel shrugged his shoulder. "I'm not sure. But this is what we do. The secondary crew is in place as we speak, but we don't know them. We don't know their capabilities and right now, I don't trust anyone."

"That's a good philosophy to have in life." JD stated as he entered the kitchen. "What do you have for me Samuel?"

Brian will be running things from the office. Magna will control the command post in the pool house--Ryan will take Tracy and the children—Donnell and I are on you."

"Why do I need two of you?"

"The boss indicated he wanted someone in front of you before you enter a room and a man looking behind you at all times. That's what we are going to do."

JD leaned against the kitchen counter and folded his arms across his chest. "I'd rather have the extra man on Tracy."

"Noted," Samuel, replied. "Donnell and I will be on you." The two men stared each other down until JD threw his hands up in the air. "Fine." He walked out of the kitchen "I'm working from home today," he said just before storming into his office and slamming the door.

Donnell was the first to stand, "I'm taking the outside of the house," he smirked at Samuel and walked out the garage door.

Magna stood, "I'll be in the pool house."

She walked out of the patio door leaving Samuel and Ryan in the kitchen. Ryan exhaled, "What could make a man as cool as JD Harrison that pissed?"

"Only two things," Samuel replied nonchalantly, "You messed with his children---or his wife." She looked up. "You want to make a guess at which one Brian touched?"

Ryan shook her head, "I don't buy that. Brian is devoted to both, JD and Tracy. I don't buy it. Something else went down."

Samuel knew what his sister Pearl told him earlier about the call she'd received in the wee hours of the morning, but he wasn't going to share that information with anyone. "Whatever took place is not our concern. Let's concentrate on keeping this family alive."

After a moment's hesitation, Ryan stood. "It's still dark out. I'm going to help Magna get settled into the pool house."

"Ryan,"

"Yeah," she looked back at him when she reached the door.

"I need you focused and on point."

"I got you covered," she stepped outside the door. Something did not feel right. Her job was to protect this family from harm. Well, in her estimation of things, some harm had been done. To do her job she needed to know what. Entering the pool house, she walked over to the monitors and took a seat. "Magna, you're a computer geek, give me a hand with this."

"What do you need?"

She inhaled then released the air out, "I'll let you know when I find it. How much do we record and where?"

"The recordings are around the clock in every room."

"Bedroom too?"

"Yes, but not once JD gets home."

"Okay. I didn't leave until nine last night. Mr. H had just arrived when I was walking out. Can you get me back to there?"

Magna pushed a few buttons, indicated the date and time required into the computer. "This monitor will show you the recording. The other monitors are live feed." She pulled up a chair. Ryan looked over at her. Magna raised an eyebrow at her. "I've known JD and Tracy before they were Mr. and Mrs. If something has gone wrong, I want to know."

"Here I thought you were Ms. 'by the book'," Ryan smiled then they both turned their attention to the monitor. Fast forwarding through the recording, they stopped where Calvin, Rossie, James, Samuel and Brian met in JD's office. "Okay, there's the boss and Samuel leaving the meeting out the patio door." Not long after that they saw Calvin and Rossie leaving the house, leaving James, Mattie and JD in the office. "Shit, this is not going to be good." Ryan said as she fast forwarded the recording until James left. "I was afraid of that?" She said when she saw only Mattie and JD remained in the office.

Magna shook her head, "It's not what you are thinking. JD would not mess around on Tracy, believe me I know."

Ryan looked over at her, "How do you know?"

"Been there with women all over him and he has never waivered."

Ryan turned back to the monitor, "There is a first time for everything."

"Put a "C" note on it."

"You're on." Ryan fast forwarded more, until she saw Tracy come down the stairs. "Do you see that look on her face? Something's going on in that office. Ain't nobody in there but Mr. H and Ms. Thing."

Magna shook her head, "Nope, not in their home. JD wouldn't do that." She reached over and switched the monitor to the recording for the office. She put in the time and date from the recording they had just reviewed. Then hit play. The recording picked up where JD and Mattie stood.

"Roll it back ten minutes," Ryan suggested and Magna complied. "Now, let's see what's going on."

The two watched as Mattie fixed the drink and sat on the desk. When she reached out and touched JD's arm, they both looked at each other. When their attention turned back to the screen Tracy had entered the room and the interaction between the three was very animated. There was no sound, but they had an idea of what was being said, as Mattie quickly grabbed her purse and left the room. What surprised them was that JD followed her. While the monitor was still on the office, Ryan saw when Tracy took the drink, frowned and ran out of the room. "Put it back on the foyer," Ryan eagerly requested. Magna did then they followed Tracy actions leading out the door. "Pull the back yard up."

"It's coming," Magna said as she keyed information into the computer. They watched as Tracy ran into the pool house. "We don't have footage in here."

"Okay, let's see what happens." They watched the screen, "There's Mr. H. coming out the back door. Why is he stopping?"

Ryan looked over near the door. "He's seeing something through the window, but what?"

Magna smirked, "Look at the expression on his face. What do you think he is seeing?"

Ryan turned to Magna surprised, "The boss, and Mrs. H? No." she repeated the word. "No, Mrs. H loves that man."

The recording was still going, "Hold up, look." They saw as JD carried Tracy in the house. "Something's wrong with her," Magna said as she adjusted the monitors again to the foyer of the house. They watched as JD carried Tracy up the steps then Brian coming into the house on his cell phone. They watched Brian pace back and forth, looking out of the front window as if he was expecting someone. They fast forwarded and saw Pearl and another man enter the house. Brian took the man upstairs. They continued to watch until the entire scene played out. "Whoa." Magna exclaimed as they watched JD knock Brian to the floor.

"Oh shit," Ryan muttered. The two sat stunned, neither speculating on what may have happened. "I almost wish I hadn't seen that."

Magna shook her head. "We're missing something."

Ryan's cell rang. She answered, "I'll be right there." She closed the phone. "That's Samuel. I have to go."

"Not a word of this to anyone," Magna ordered.

"Who in the hell am I going to tell?" Ryan said and walked out of the door.

Magna started at the monitor. "Something's not right." She sat there and began to run through the recordings again. This time she began with the office and watched it frame by frame.

Walking into the kitchen Ryan looked at the clock, it was after seven. She fully expected to see Tracy in the kitchen especially since Mrs. Gordon was away, but she wasn't there. Walking up the steps, she looked over to Tracy's office and she wasn't there. She walked down the hallway to Jasmine's room and found JD there, now dressed in suit slacks and a white shirt open at the collar, about to lay the baby back in her crib. "Sorry Mr. Harrison. I was looking for Tracy."

"She's still a sleep." He said as he pulled the blanket over the child.

Ryan's cell phone rang. JD gave her an evil look as she backed out of the room. "Ryan."

"Get the glass off the desk in the office," Magna order.

"Go into the office. Use gloves or a napkin. Bring me that glass."

"Alright!" Ryan replied then followed what she was told. She placed the glass in a plastic bag and ran it out the back door to Magna. "What did you need the glass for?"

"I'll let you know when I know."

Ryan shook her head, "This is going to be a long ass day with all the attitudes."

Around ten JD went up stairs to check on Tracy, she was still in the same position. She had not moved. His anger was dissipating to concern. The last time she slept this late was the day after the Eagles gang attacked her. He remembered that day just how afraid he was of losing her. He was just as afraid now, but for a different reason. He pulled the covers up around her shoulders then went to check on the children.

When he returned downstairs he saw he had missed two calls on his cell phone. One was from Mattie. He definitely was not in the mood to talk to her. The other was from the hospital. He listened to the message then returned the call to Dr. Prentiss.

"Dr. Prentiss, I received your message. You indicated it was urgent."

"Yes, it is Mr. Harrison. I received the toxicologist report back on your wife's blood work. As I expected there was a substantial amount of Flunitrazepam in her system. It's commonly known at Rohypnol, or..."

"Roofies," JD whispered.

"You know of it and what it is used for."

"Yes," JD's mind was wondering. "Tracy doesn't take drugs of any kind. She barely drinks."

"There was a small about of bourbon also found in her blood work. Mr. Harrison, I don't know you but I have to ask. Has your wife been depressed or withdrawn lately?"

"Not that I'm aware of. Why do you ask?"

The doctor hesitated. "In addition to a date rape drug, at times it is used for suicide attempts."

A stunned JD shook his head, not believing the turn of the conversation. "Dr. Prentice, my wife did not try to commit suicide. I'll be the first to admit we have a lot going on in our lives, but nothing to that ext..." JD stopped mid sentence. "Dr. Prentice, how long should she sleep?"

"It has different effects on different people. Some would be in an amnesia state for three to four hours, then some as long as twelve hours."

"Is there anyway of knowing when the drug was digested?"

"Not from the test we took. However, we could look further."

"Would you please and let me know. One more question Dr. you mention a state of amnesia. Will Tracy remember what happened?"

"Probably not."

JD nodded, his mind still wondering. "Thank you Doctor Prentice, for everything.'

"I'll be back in touch with the results."

"Thank you," JD replied absentmindedly as he hung up the telephone.

Turk had seen and heard enough. He placed a call to Tucker. "How is your guest?"

"Healing. As soon as this case is a done deal, I'm going to take her home."

Turk smiled. "Good decision. Here's another. Charlie should make a visit."

Tucker exhaled and smiled. "It's been a pleasure to work for you."

The morning was going by slow. This was not what he was used to. By this time of day, he would have talked to JD at least five times, Tracy three, and JC twenty. That little boy was like a son to him. There were times when he was so envious of JD, but never once did he resent or wish for anything less for his friend. JD had done things the right way. He studied hard when he was in school. Any and every charity that wanted or needed help, JD was there giving support or cash when he could. That was the thing about the Harrisons; they would give you the shirt off their backs if they thought you needed it. JD had done it for him so many times, when they were young, Brian had lost track. The vow he took to protect JD and his family was deep from the heart. Brian was an only child to a single mother. JD, Calvin, and Douglas were the closest thing to family that he had. As much of a dog as he was, Brian would never step to any of his friend's women. Brian stood at the window of his office in The Ashley Building, overlooking Broad Street in downtown

Richmond. In the distance, he could see the entrance to the mansion. He knew JD and Tracy would be living in that building soon. Tracy. He closed his eyes as he thought of her. How many times had he wondered what would have happened if he had met her before JD? What would it feel like to kiss her, to hold her in his arms as a man would hold a woman—not like a friend? Well, he got his answer last night. He lowered his head and sighed. What in the hell was he thinking? What was she thinking? Why did she kiss him like that? For the hundredth time he tried to figure out what happened and was still unclear on all the facts. But one thing was real; JD had every right to knock his ass down. For a minute, he did lose his mind and kissed his friend's wife. Damn if she wasn't as sweet as he'd imagined. But years ago, he'd resigned himself to the fact that that was all he could do—imagine.

Sitting back down behind his desk, he knew this was not and never would be his cup of tea. But for now, this is what he would do. He checked the coverage plan for the family to ensure everyone was covered. The telephone rang, "Thompson Agency," he answered.

"Boss, I'm sending something to your computer. You need to take a look at it right away."

"Go ahead Magna. What is it?"

"I'd rather not tell. You need to see it for yourself. Don't lose your cool, just handle business when you are finished."

Brian stared at the phone when Magna hung up. He opened the email and clicked on the video attachment. He viewed an edited version of the security recordings from JD's house. Less than five minutes later, he was walking into Mattie Gresham's office slamming the door behind him. "What in the hell did you put in JD's drink and why?"

Before she had a chance to answer the six-three fuming man, another six-four man entered her office. "What in the hell is going on?" James asked as he scowled at Brian.

"Give me five minutes and I'll let you know."

"James I can explain," Mattie cried out as she stood behind the desk a good distance from Brian.

"Explain what?" James asked looking between the frightened woman and a furious Brian. "What happened to your lip?" he asked noticing the swollen cut.

"You want to know what happened after you left JD's house last night." Brian walked towards her, reached across the desk, and grabbed her by the blouse.

James pulled Mattie from Brian's grasp and stood between the two. "Brian my office, now!" James' voice boomed throughout the room.

Brian had never put his hands on a woman before, but at the moment, he wanted to kill Mattie Gresham. He walked out of the room before he was tempted to fulfill that desire.

James turned to Mattie, "You want to tell me what this is about?"

"I'm sorry James. I'm so sorry," she sat in her chair and cried.

It was after noon when Tracy finally moved and JD was there when she finally opened her eyes. "Tracy?"

"Morning," she groggily reply as she turned over.

"Tracy, turn over and look at me." She turned over but was still dazed. "Tracy I need you to open your eyes." She did. "Can you see Tracy?" she nodded.

"Good. Tracy do you remember drinking or taking anything last night?"

"What?" was all she could manage.

JD exhaled, she wasn't able to answer him yet. But he needed answers from her. He needed to know if this drug could explain her actions. But even if it did, it did not explain Brian's.

"JD," Samuel called out, but did not walk into the room.

Not making any headway with Tracy, JD covered her back up to let her sleep a little longer. He stepped outside the room, "Yes Samuel."

"James is trying to reach you. He said it's important." Samuel handed him the telephone.

"Thank you." He took the telephone, "Hello James."

"There's something you need to hear."

"Can it wait?"

"No. Mattie has been working for Munford."

"Munford wants information on Al Day's location. He blackmailed Mattie into getting the information from you."

"Mattie isn't privy to that information."

"I know. Somehow Brian found out she spiked your drink last night to get you lose enough to talk. If that failed she planned to get you in a compromising position and used it against you."

JD looked over at Tracy still groggy in bed. Munford was at the root of his nightmare. The man had to go down. "Where is she now?" he angrily asked.

"Brian is questioning her to see if there is anything you can use on Munford."

"What did Munford have on her?"

"She has a younger brother at the university. He was pulled over holding. Munford has threatened to give him a larger charge. Could ruin the boy."

"Get his name. Have Brian pass it on to Calvin to review his case."

"What do you want me to do about Mattie?"

Looking over at Tracy, he could only shake his head. The drink was meant for him. She must have drunk it after he walked out of the room. "Fire her."

"Alright. Do you want to tell me why Brian is here with a busted lip and not with you?"

"No." He hung up the phone. He knew going into politics and having a decent personal life was an unlikely combination. But he was determined to make both work. At the moment the playing field wasn't even. Munford had been wreaking havoc on his life for too long. That threat had to be eliminated before he had a chance at making his life work. He prayed Al would come through for him. With Gary gone, it may be his only hope to getting his life on track. Walking back into the room, he noticed Tracy eyes were open. He smiled down at her, "Hi."

Tracy looked up at him, then closed her eyes trying to get her thoughts together. She had no idea what time of day it was or why her body felt so weird. The one thing she did know was that woman was in her house last night with her hands on Jeffrey. "I want you to fire Mattie Gresham. I don't like her around you. Call me naive, jealous, or insecure—I don't care. I want her gone."

"Done," he said standing over her. He put his hands in his pockets. "Do you remember anything else about last night?"

"Other than that woman's hands all over you, no. Is there anything else I need to know?"

The thought of telling her about the entire night frightened him. Knowing why things happened helped some, but it had brought out some of his insecurities. For the first time he could admit he was afraid of losing her. "Yes." He saw her eyebrow arch up. "You need to know there is nothing I would put before you. The things I do are because of you. There is no woman on this planet that will make me risk losing you."

Pushing the covers aside, she attempted to stand, but her body seemed heavy. Forcing herself to move, she finally stood. "I'm going to take a shower. Then I'll fix breakfast. Then I'm calling your mother over to stay with the children. I'm going down to campaign headquarters and if you haven't done it, I'm firing every female in the office." She walked over to the bathroom.

"Babe," Tracy turned supporting herself by holding on the doorframe, "It's one o'clock in the afternoon. We've had breakfast and lunch."

Tracy saw a smirk form on his face and frowned. "Then I'll cook dinner and fire everyone afterwards."

"Okay," he nodded. He watched as she turned and closed the door behind her.

Chapter 16

The answer JD had prayed for came the next day, and his life was changed forever. Tracy was in the kitchen with the children. JC was in his high chair and Jasmine was in her seat on the table. JD's blackberry buzzed. The caller ID showed it was Brian. Stopping in his tracks, he hesitated. The image of Brian and Tracy played in his mind. He knew Tracy's reason for her actions, but he wasn't ready to listen. The problem here was Brian was still the head of his security detail and it might be business. "Brian."

"Tucker wants a meeting today at noon, The Renaissance." The call ended.

Normally they would discuss the security and possible reason for the meeting. Now, it was all business. As Samuel walked through the patio door, Tracy smiled, "Good Morning Samuel. Where's Brian?"

Samuel looked to JD then back to Tracy. "Good Morning Tracy. Brian is working from the office today."

"Brian working inside an office," she laughed. "I'm sure he loves that. Would you like some breakfast?"

"Thank you, but I had breakfast at home."

"Cynthia cooked?"

"No babe, that's why he is still alive," JD kissed her on the cheek. "Let's go Samuel."

Entering his office, JD asked Mrs. Langston to have Calvin come to his office. As soon as he came in JD began to tell him of the events that took place the day before including the scene with Tracy and Brian.

Calvin exhaled and took a seat. "Let's take care of business first. The name Brian called in is still active. The arrest was made, however, no formal charges has been filed. The officer that made the collar was one of Munford's men and is on administrate leave until his case is reviewed. How do you want me to handle it?"

"Find out what the kid was really carrying and have the department handle it accordingly."

"What about Mattie? Are you going to pursue charges?"

JD stood before the window in his office with hands in his pockets. If he showed Mattie any preferential treatment, Tracy would be upset. "Let's come back to that one."

Calvin got up and closed the door, then retook his seat. "Why? Mattie purchased an illegal drug to use against you. She may have failed in that light, but the drug did cause harm—maybe irrevocable harm. Why would you not press charges?

"What law did she break? And what do you think the media take would be on this. Do you think Mattie would be the victim? I do. And it would be at Tracy's expense. If the media got a hold of my wife kissing my best friend, how do you think it would play out for her?"

"So, you just let Mattie go—free. No consequences for her actions."

JD stared at Calvin and knew his friend well enough to know he had something on his mind. Taking a seat, he gave his undivided attention. "Say what you need to say."

"Thank you, I will." He sighed, "This has been coming since the day Brian met Tracy and you know it. You have known for years that Brian had a thing for Tracy. You even took steps to make sure they were spending time together. I never understood why, until now. Man, I love you like a brother and so does Brian. He would never cross that line."

"But he did cross the line Calvin," JD angrily replied, "He crossed the line."

"Did he cross the line or did you push him across?"

"What?"

"Every time something happened with Tracy, you didn't take care of it, you sent Brian. Do you know Brian has dinner with Tracy just about every night, because you are not there? Did you know after Tracy changed her mind about starting the new business she cried for at least an hour? You know who was there to console her— Brian. Did you know that most of the ideas Brian passed on to you at our meetings came from Tracy? You don't ask her opinion on business, and I damn sure don't understand that. She has a brilliant business mind. Have you even checked your bank accounts lately? Do you know that thanks to Tracy's investment mind you're a very wealthy man? I want you to notice I said you are—I didn't say anything about Tracy. Your wife could be such an asset in your campaign, but you keep her distant from it. See at some point you have to put your words into action. You talk about how much you love Tracy, but your actions don't show it. Your actions say she is your possession. And Tracy is just as much at fault because she lets you get away with this bull. The only reason I can figure is that she is still insecure about you. Which is sad, because your ass ain't going anywhere." Calvin threw his hands up in the air frustrated.

"Isn't."

"What?"

"Isn't going anywhere."

"Excuse me, I'm imperfect. But so are you and so is Brian. He talks a good game about being free for the women, but he is alone, has been for a while. The thing with him and Pearl you tease him about ended, when Samuel came into the fold. He is a respectful brother and you know it. A drug caused the behavior in Tracy. Now, I just want to think back to the incident with Vanessa, when she went down on you. You told me yourself you hesitated for a moment at her touching you and that's when Tracy walked in. What's the difference? Brian hesitated—so what. So did you."

His mind was screaming, because she is my wife, but he didn't say it. "Tracy does not like campaigning. You know it and I know it."

"Do you know why? I bet you Brian does. I know he does, because he told me what Tracy shared with him. JD, Brian has been there for you in ways you would never imagine. Your family is his family. He would no more cross you than you would cross me. You need to find a way to let this thing go. It happened. Settle it between you and Brian then move on."

"Would it be that easy if it was your wife?"

Calvin thought, then shook his head, "No. I'd kill him and then move on. But I'm an insecure brother." He chuckled, then sat back down. "Can I ask you a question?"

"Nothing has stopped you in the last hour?"

"That's true. But seriously, have you kissed Tracy since you saw her kissing Brian?"

"Of course."

"On the lips?"

"I don't understand your question."

"JD part of your problem is your pride. Tracy came to you untouched. Now, you feel Brian has touched her. I suggest a simple cure. Are you listening?"

"You have a captive audience."

"You laugh, but I promise this will work. Go home, take your wife in your arms, and kiss her so thoroughly that the touch of another man is a distant memory for you."

"Thank you for coming over." Tracy said to Carolyn as she entered the house.

"I'm in a generous mood these days. So, what do you need help with?"

They took a seat in JD's office. "I want to learn how to be a good political wife."

Crossing her legs and smiling, Carolyn beamed. "Well you came to the right person. And it's about time you recognized my skills."

"Will you help me?"

Carolyn sighed, "What brought this on?"

"The Carolyns and Matties of the world."

"Now, see I could be offended by that, but I'm not. I'm damn good at what I do. For me it's been a lifestyle. I was raised in a political family. Everything was about power and that's what politics is—being in power. Having a husband who has a career in politics is like no other. Compare it to being married to a movie star or a major sports athlete. Their life is not their own. They belong to the people, the constituents. You have been going at this, as if it's just JD. It's not. It's a partnership between you and him. Just like your marriage, this partnership has to be impenetrable. A good marriage is only as strong as its foundation. You and JD have built that foundation based on pure unadulterated love. It's a wonderful start. Now, you have to add trust. His career is frightening to you and rightly so. See, politics breeds greed, corruption, and selfishness. A heart breeds love, commitment, and togetherness—complete opposites. If you two are not one, on both, his political career, and your marriage, you will not survive either. Keep this in mind. Just like a house, a heart divided cannot stand alone. His heart is divided between politics and you. To survive this game you need a joint venture. This is what I have been trying to tell you for years now. The woman in JD's life has to be just as committed to his success as he. You've tried to keep the two separate. It can't be done. Tracy you are smarter, wiser, and stronger than he has ever given you credit for. You have to stop letting him treat you like a woman that needs his protection and let him see you as his partner. I think the outcome would surprise you."

"Where do I start?"

"Start by spending time at campaign headquarters learning all you can about the political machine." Carolyn laughed at Tracy's expression.

Ryan stood in the doorway, "Mrs. H you have a phone call."

"Thank you. Carolyn I'll be right back."

"You laugh at my mommy?" JC asked from the doorway.

Carolyn looked over at the pint size JD and wasn't sure what to do or say. Children were not her forte'. So she smiled. "Yes I was laughing at your mother."

His little feet padded over to where she sat and she frowned in horror as the child crawled up in her lap. JC did not seem to notice the uncomfortable position he had placed Carolyn in, as he sat in her lap and smiled up at her expectantly. "What?" she asked not knowing what the child wanted? The child pointed to the drawer, then smiled up at her. "You want a pencil or something in here?" She pointed towards the drawer. JC clapped his hands and showed the dimples he no doubt inherited from his father. She reached for the drawer and the child began to bounce in anticipation. "Okay, okay, but you've got to stop with the bouncing." Opening the drawer she saw pen, pencils note pads and paper clips. "You want a pencil?" she handed the child the pencil. The child shook his head no and pointed to the container in the corner. Carolyn put the pencil back in the drawer and reached for the container. Inside was a collection of M&M's, plain and peanut. She pulled the container out and sat it on top of the desk with the top up. "Go ahead, get one."

JC reached in, popped an M&M in his mouth, then put his finger to his lips. "Shh."

Carolyn raised an eyebrow at the child. "Your daddy's been giving you candy behind your mother's back. Aww." JC turned and looked up at her. "You want another one?" The child's head bobbed up and down. "Go ahead." JC reached in, retrieved another, and ate it. After he finished, he reached up, placed his hands on her cheek, and kissed her right on the lips.

"Thank you," he said, then slipped from her lap and ran from the room.

Carolyn sat there for the longest time, dumfounded. It was taking her a moment to get a handle on her emotions. Children give unconditional love. The child did not know her from Adam, yet he showed her love. What a sweet thing to do.

"Are you all right Carolyn," Tracy asked as she re-entered the room

Still shocked from the child's action she wasn't sure how to answer. "Yes, I'm fine." She stood. "You know I think I'm going to go now. We should do this sisterly talk thing more. You know."

"Okay," a confused Tracy replied.

"We'll do lunch soon." Carolyn said and hurried out the door.

Ryan watched from the foyer as Tracy still stood in the office doorway. "She sure was in a hurry to get out of here. What happened?"

"I have no idea."

JD wasn't sure why he had been summoned to the Renaissance by Tucker but he knew not to ignore the request. There were times in the past when Tucker's warnings had saved Tracy's life and he might have news from Al. Unfortunately, it was Calvin words that were echoing through his mind. Had he been pushing Tracy and Brian together? "Mr. Attorney General, may I have a moment of your time?" JD looked up from the plate of food he was not eating to see a well dressed man standing before him. Nothing about the man seemed threatening, but Samuel was a man of caution, he checked the man for weapons before allowing him to take a seat in the booth with JD. Ironically, the man put up no argument to the action and calmly took a seat.

The man smiled proudly at JD. "Your father would be very proud of the man you have become."

Returning the warm smile JD put down his fork and extended his hand. "Thank you Sir," he replied while shaking the man's hand. "You knew my father?"

The man looked out of the window as the past crossed his mind. He turned back to JD. "Your farther tried for years to get me off the street." He chuckled thinking back. "I know I drove him crazy with my antics back then." He sighed and sobered. "On the day he died, I realized it was meant for me to be in that place at that time."

JD sat forward. The curiosity of what happened to his father had never diminished with the teen's sentencing. Knowing the boy was going away for a number of years helped, but he always wondered if his father died instantly? Did he suffer? Was he alone?

Before the questions could be asked, the man spoke. "I was there the night your father was killed." The man reached into his pocket and pulled out a velvet bag. "James gave this to me to deliver to your mother before he was murdered." The man waited to allow the impact of the statement to resonate in JD's mind.

The moment the crease formed on JD's face the man knew the facts had been realized. "What's your name?" JD asked not taking his eyes from the bag that sat on the table.

"Charles Arnold."

JD looked up into the man's face. "Charlie." A sad smile touched his lips. "He mentioned you often at the dinner table."

Charlie smiled, "I ate your mother's left-over's quite often. Does she still cook a mean meat loaf?"

JD nodded, "Yes she does." Staring into the man's eyes he knew his life was about to change. "What's in the bag, Charlie?"

Charlie pushed the bag across the table. JD stared at it for a moment, he inhaled. Picking up the bag, an intense feeling of loss came over him. Pulling the strings apart, he reached inside and pulled out a wedding band. Without reading the inscription, he knew instantly, it was his father's. He brought the ring up for a closer inspection and could feel his father's presence. The size of the ring reminded him of his father being a big man at six-four with large hands that had tapped his behind once or twice. He smiled as a tear escaped. Looking inside, he knew he would find the same inscription he'd put on Tracy's band, *Forever, For Always, For Love.* Reaching up he ran his hand down his face to clear away the tears. He had to think clearly. "Did my father give this to you?"

Charles eyes held his. "Yes," he replied and waited.

"Were you there when he died?"

Charlie sat forward placed his arms on the table and entwined his fingers. "Son," he sighed as if he was about to reveal the fate of the world. In a way, he was. "It's time you know the truth." He looked over JD's shoulder and motioned for Samuel. "Don't let him up until I finish my story."

Samuel looked at JD then back at the man. He pulled a chair to the table, turned it backwards, and then took a seat as requested. An uneasy feeling came over JD as his full attention turned to Charlie.

"The night James died I was in an abandoned building at the corner of Dock and 17th street near the river. It was my spot for a year or two. James would stop in during his rounds to say hello, give me a piece of change or food whenever he was on duty. You see, your father was old school all the way. He didn't sit in the patrol car and cruise the city. He would park the car at Broad and 18th and walk his patrols." Charlie smiled remembering his friend. "He would say, I can't touch the people if I'm not out here." He took a deep breath and exhaled. "That night I wish he had stayed in the car." Charlie shook his head and continued. "He was on edge about something, I could feel it. I even asked if I could call someone for him when he came over to talk to me. He said no. Then he gave me that and said I want you to take this to my wife and get out of here. See, your father knew if I stayed around the man that was after him would not want any witnesses to what was about to go down. He literally saved my life. When he walked away from the store front, I watched through the broken glass. A car came barreling around the corner with the windows down. James pulled his weapon and turned towards the sound but he didn't fire. He hesitated. I looked over to the car wondering why. That's when I noticed it was a kid. That's why James hesitated. The boy raised the gun and fired. James stumbled back. That's when I knew he was hit. He turned towards the car and fired back. But the kid had an automatic. James was hit several times before he fell." Charlie sat back and let the tears flow down his face. He wiped them away before he continued. "The car never stopped. I started to run towards James, but was pulled back into the building by a young man. He indicated to me to be quiet, but I was losing it. His friend pulled out a gun and held it to my head. The young man said, I'm not going to hurt you, just be quiet." Charles snickered, "it wasn't him I was concerned with,—it was his friend with the gun. When I settled down we watched out the window and that's when we saw your father's partner standing over him. I thought thank God—help was there." He hesitated then looked straight into JD's eyes. That's when we saw Munford take a gun from his ankle strap and shoot your father."

JD sat up, shocked at what Charlie had just revealed. "No man. My father was shot by a teen in a drive by."

"Yes. But the final shot was at the hands of Wilbert T Munford."

For a moment, JD stared at the man without speaking. So many questions were flowing through his mind. "You actually saw Munford shoot my father." Charles simply stared at him. "Why didn't you tell somebody and who were the other witnesses?" JD yelled.

Charlie held up his hand to keep JD calm. "I need to finish the story."

"You need to answer my questions!" JD demanded.

Samuel put a hand on JD's arm. "Hear the man out," he calmly suggested. JD jerked his arm away and glared at Charlie.

"The young man walked out the door towards Munford with his gun behind his back. He stopped a few steps away and asked, 'Was that supposed to impress me?' Munford said, 'No that was to show you I control what goes down in the City of Richmond. You want to do business in these streets—it comes through me.' The young man then told Munford, 'I control my fate and now I control yours. If you come anywhere near my people I suggest you turn the other way.' It was clear Munford did not like the young man's answer for in the next beat he pulled his weapon. Before he could get a shot off the young man shot him in the foot. By the time, Munford hit the ground he had three guns pointing at him. The young man walked over and stood over Munford the same way he stood over your father." Charles sat forward. "He told Munford, 'I will find that man's son and when the time is right, I'm going to make sure he knows who needlessly took his father's life. Until then stay away from me and my people.' Munford called the young man a punk as he walked away. The young man turned back and shot Munford in the leg, then asked, 'You got something else to say?' When the young man walked back into the building I was angry and distraught over seeing my friend being shot and asked him why he didn't kill Munford. He said, 'I don't kill anyone unless they are trying to kill me. Now come on old man, let's get you cleaned up.' For the last ten years, he has been there for me in every sense of the word and I've been there for him. He asked me to come here." Charlie closed his eyes to get pass the emotions of telling the story. He then looked sincerely at JD. "The truth is a powerful thing. It can make or break a man. Your father said something about you the day you entered law school. At the time, I thought this was a man that was very proud of his son and he was just boasting. However, after following your life over the last few years I know

now that James saw in you what others are only now recognizing."

With a voice filled with emotions, JD asked, "What did he say?"

Charlie smiled, "He said, my son is more by the book than I am. He's going to be hard on women, but good for this world. I may not live to see it, but he is going to be the leader of this country one day." Charlie let the words sink in. "Now, son, it's on you what you do with the information I just gave you. But, your father would expect you to do what's right."

The impact of what Charlie had revealed weighed heavily on JD's mind. Minutes passed and no one at the table said anything. Samuel waited for the explosion. He knew some of this story, but he had no idea Munford actually pulled the trigger. The way the story was revealed to him was that Munford was only the mastermind. Now, that he knew the truth he wanted to kill Munford himself. He could only imagine what JD was feeling.

"Who was the young man?" JD asked as if he did not already know.

"Al Day." JD nodded his head and released a short grunt. "When in the story did you know?"

"I don't kill anyone unless they are trying to kill me." JD sat up and exhaled. "He's said it to me and I know it's the truth. Why did Al send you to tell me this? There were many times over the years he could have told me."

"Would you have been strong enough to hear it? I know you are filled with anger and resentment for being kept in the dark on this. You don't have to answer that question for me—answer it for yourself."

JD took a deep breath then exhaled. "Does my wife know about this?"

"Tracy," Charlie smiled. "No. Turk did not share his life on the street with Tracy. In fact, he did everything within his power to keep her sheltered from his life.

Some of us feel a little too sheltered the same as you. Both of you need to give that girl some credit—she is tougher than either of you know. I believe she is the one that will make you the man you are destined to be. But I'm just an old drunk that found his way." Charlie stood to leave. "It has been a pleasure to meet the son of a man who changed my life. Make him proud." He turned and walked out the door.

JD sat in the same seat for another twenty minutes flipping the ring through his fingers. So many thoughts were going through his mind; he wasn't sure how to filter through. Nothing could ever make him disappoint his father, but at the moment, the thought most prevalent in his mind was to kill Munford. "An eye for an eye," he mumbled. He continued flipping the ring, and then mumbled, "Vengeances is mine, said the Lord." A frown formed on his face. The next thought was why did he keep this from me? "Call Brian, tell him to make arrangements for me to see Al." Suddenly, he grabbed the blue bag, placed the ring in it, and stood as if on a mission.

"Hold up," Samuel stopped him by grabbing his arm. "Where are you going?"

JD looked down at the hand on his arm, then up at Samuel who stood a good two feet over him. Samuel removed his hands and held them up, but he did not step aside. "I'm going to see Munford," JD replied as he took a step.

Samuel stepped in front of him, "No you're not."

"Lassiter get the hell out of my way." JD pushed him angrily in the chest, but Samuel did not budge. "I'm going to kill him, that's what I'm going to do."

"I can't let you do that boss." Samuel had to stop JD from leaving. He had the size, knowledge, and strength to do so. If he had to do it physically, he would. It was his job to protect this man and he would, even against himself. But Samuel also knew anger could fuel a man's strength. "Order me to kill him and I will. But you will not." The statement took a little of the fight out of him as he stared angrily at Samuel.

"Everything allright in here JD?" Douglas asked as he came through the door.

Samuel did not take his eyes off of JD as he said, "Bring us a bottle of cognac and two glasses."

Douglas did not move until JD looked up at him. The two had been friends since high school. He liked Samuel and knew the man could kill him in an instant, but he was not going to leave until he was certain JD was all right.

JD looked over Samuel's shoulder at Douglas. "Make that three glasses." Once the door closed behind Douglas, JD looked up at Samuel. There were only a hand full of men he looked up to, Samuel was slowly becoming one. "Would you really kill him if I asked?"

"Yes."

The two men assessed each other a while longer. JD had the distinct feeling Samuel was a man of his word. "I'll make a note never to ask."

Tracy had just put Jasmine to sleep and changed into her pajamas when she heard the telephone ringing. She glanced at the clock wondering who would be calling so late at night. Checking the caller ID, she saw the number she hadn't seen in days. "Brian? Where have you been? Why haven't you returned my phone calls?"

"Tracy listen, JD is going to need you tonight. Be there for him."

Her heart dropped, "What's wrong with Jeffrey? Where is he?"

"He's going through something Tracy and only you can help him. I know things are a little crazy between you two right now. But, for tonight put that aside and be there for him."

Confused, she asked again almost in tears, "What's happened Brian? Is he hurt? Where is he?"

"He's hurt Tracy, but not physically. Just be there." Brian hung up the telephone.

Tracy stared at the phone, puzzled by the call. She immediately hung up and was about to dial Jeffrey's cell phone number when she heard the beep from downstairs indicating someone coming in the door. She hung up the phone, closed the door to Jasmine's room, then went downstairs. As she came to the bottom of the staircase, she could see Jeffrey in his office, sitting with his back to the door and a glass in his hand. There was something about his posture that indicated to her that something was wrong. As she stepped closer, she could have sworn she heard him cry. Her heartbeat quickened. This was a first for her. She had never seen him cry. Whatever was happening was hurting him and all she wanted to do was take the hurt away. Barefoot, she walked quietly over and stood in front of him and as she suspected, tears stains were on his face. He looked up and she could see the hurt and sadness there. At that moment she could feel his anguish. She climbed into his lap, placed her arms around his neck, her head on his shoulders and held him tight. With everything that had happened between them, for a moment she wasn't sure if he would respond to her. But she didn't care, she needed to comfort him. He set the glass on the desk and he eased his arms around her waist. The hold was light at first, but as he allowed the tears to flow his hold tighten.

Since hearing the story of his father's death, he was numb. Holding his wife began to chip away at the anger. This woman was his salvation, his lifeline. When he felt her tears on his neck, he knew she was hurting for him without knowing why. She never asked why, she only knew he was hurting. He pulled her tighter as he buried his head in the crook of her shoulder and cried.

An hour later, with his shoulder drenched in his tears as well as hers, he began to tell her the story. She sat there holding him, listening. The story angered and amazed her all at once. She was angry with the police chief for taking a man's life without thought of the effect on his family, especially his son. But at the same time, she was amazed at the foresight of her brother to keep this information under wraps until Jeffrey was in a position to avenge his father's death. Now she understood why Turk put her under Jeffrey's protection. He knew who Jeffrey was, where he came from, and what he stood for. He placed her in the hands of the man that would protect her from his arch enemy. More importantly, she now understood that Jeffrey wasn't smothering her or trying to keep her from her business. He was protecting her from danger. He did not know until now who he was protecting her from. Minutes ticked away with no sound but the clock on the wall. Still sitting in his lap wrapped securely in his arms she spoke. "There's this theory called six degrees of separation." She spoke reverently. "If a person is one step away from another person they know and two steps away from each person they know, then everyone is at the most six steps away from any other person on Earth."

JD frowned, then pulled away from her shoulder and looked into her tear filled eyes and smiled. This was the reason he fell in love with her. His wife was so philosophical. "Do you remember the night at my old place when we talked about the propensity of violence?" She nodded. "You said to me that if someone harmed a person I loved, I would have the urge to commit violence. I told you I would not because I believed in the justice system. I was wrong. I want to kill Munford for taking my father's life."

The look in his eyes frightened her, but only for a moment. She reached up and wiped the tears from his face with the palm of her hand. "No you don't Jeffrey. You want him to pay for what he has done to you and your family. Turk, in all his wisdom, has waited until you were in a position to deal with this man through the legal system. It would give him a win if he brought you down to his level. Beat him at his own game your way, not his. Your father lost his life because he did things the right way. He would expect no less from you. So here's what you are going to do. Tomorrow you will take the steps necessary to get an indictment against Munford for the murder of your father and whatever else you have on him. Then you will go to your mother, return your father's ring and tell her what happened to her husband. But tonight, you are going to take your wife upstairs. We are going to take a shower. You are going to make love to me and then we will stay up the rest of the night and talk about our future."

JD smiled. Old Tracy was still there, but a stronger woman of understanding was emerging. "Do you think Turk knew I would fall in love with you when he asked me to protect you?"

"No. He would have killed you if he knew half of the things you were going to do to me."

They laughed together. It was a sound that had been missing in their home for a while. They both stared lovingly at each other. "I love you Tracy. I've loved you since that night in my old condo. Women will be around all the time. No one—not one, will ever replace you in my life."

The sincerity in his eyes made her heart melt, as tears streamed down her face. "I don't know what happened with Brian. For you to ban him from the house, I know something happened. I love him, but not the way I love you. He's my friend and your friend too. I'm so sorry about coming between you two. I miss you and him acting like you own the world."

This time he wiped the tears from her eyes. "I saw you kiss Brian, but I also saw him try to push you away. At the time, I was so angry and frustrated with all that happened before, I couldn't see straight. Now, I know he was acting like a friend. The thought of his or any man's lips on yours would make me angry. I over reacted to the situation and made it worse than it was. Please forgive me for being an ass." He kissed her.

They kissed with all the pent up frustration and passion of the past month. Releasing all the hurt and mistrust and restoring the love that would sustain them for a lifetime. "As the future President of the United States I proclaim the order of events for the night changed." He stood, took her hand in his, and walked out of the office. "I'm making love to my wife all night long. Then we will discuss our future."

Tracy raised an eyebrow at him as they walked up the stairs, "Well you are my Commander-in-Chief, but that makes me the First Lady. I run this house and I'm about to put a hurting on you."

JD stopped and looked down at his once passive wife and laughed. "Hurt me baby—hurt me," then ran the rest of the way up the stairs.

Chapter 17

The actions of the next day were intense. Everyone in the AG's office was working on the preparation of documents for a special session of the Grand Jury. The indictments against Munford were being changed and his attorney had been notified. The more the story of James Harrison's death unraveled, the more people within the Department came forward. Near the end of the day, the infractions by Munford were too great to number. The man would be lucky to see the light of day in his remaining lifetime.

The day was a busy one for JD, professionally, politically and personally. Because his father's death was now a part of the indictments against Munford, he had to turn everything over to Calvin and Rossie to handle. After bringing them completely up to speed on things, he had a press conference scheduled to announce the additional indictments. That was the easy part of the day. He now had to take his father's ring to his mother and tell her how and why her husband was taken away from her. Last on his agenda, was to go to Brian and apologize for his actions. If it took him all night, he was going to get his friend to forgive him.

It was after eight at night by the time JD was finished talking with his mother. He was on his way to find Brian when Samuel received a telephone call from his brother. Sitting in the back of the SUV, he glanced at JD, who sat next to him as he listened to the information.

"What's going on?" JD asked after Samuel hung up the telephone.

"There's been some activity around the weapons. Pull over Donnell," Samuel said as he turned in the seat. When Donnell parked, he turned to listen as well. "From the description, it may be members of the Eagles. Joshua is sending over pictures." The pictures appeared as they watched the blackberry screen.

"They're dead?" JD asked.

"You know his philosophy—shoot, ask questions later."

"No shit?" Donnell almost smiled.

JD's mind wondered. "Joshua?" he asked knowing how Samuel's brother liked to kill people. "We need to ask questions first. A weapons charge on Munford will seal the case."

Another picture appeared and Samuel smiled. "He kept one alive for you."

A relieved JD looked up at Donnell. "Get us over there. If we get the right answer, Munford will be behind bars by morning."

Donnell turned around laughing and pulled back into traffic. "I'm going to enjoy this."

"We don't have him yet, but damn if it's not beginning to smell like a victory." JD pulled out his cell and called Tracy. "Hey babe, it's going to be late by time I get home. Give JC and Jasmine a kiss for me."

"I will. Jasmine is running a little temperature."

"Anything serious?"

"I don't think so. But I'll keep her in bed with me until you get home."

"Okay babe, I'll see you soon."

"Everything okay," Samuel asked when he hung up the phone.

"Yeah. The baby has a temperature. You'll find out about those real soon."

"When is the baby due Samuel?" Donnell asked.

"Next month, if I can live through it."

JD laughed, "Nothing humbles a man like a woman giving birth to their child. You realize there are things in this world that you cannot control. Like labor pains, or the things the woman you love calls you during them."

The report from Samuel was good. With any luck, they would be able to breathe a sigh of relief by morning. Brian sat in his office making notes on the events of the day wishing he were at the site where the action was. He had made up his mind earlier that this bull was going to end tonight. As soon as JD wrapped things up, he was going to clear this shit up, even if he had to whip his ass to do it. They'd been boys since high school, and he'd be damned if he was going to let something like this come between them. So what, he kissed his wife, hell JD had kissed Caitlyn before. Brian stopped writing, "Where in the hell did that come from?" He put the pen down, turned in his chair, and stared out the window. Over the last few years, Caitlyn had crossed his mind more than once. Since she disappeared, he had wondered time and time again where she was, how she was doing, was she married, did she have children? Why in the hell did she leave campus and him? This was the point where he would get pissed off and banished her memory from his mind. But just like before, she would creep right back in. One day he would find her and get the answers he needed to move on with his life.

"Hey."

He turned in the chair to see Pearl walking into the office. "Hey yourself. Working late?"

"It doesn't make sense to go home. The media is chomping at the bits for this story."

"Let's hope it ends tonight."

"Yeah." She took a seat in front of his desk and crossed her legs.

"What would the good doctor say about you trying to entice me?"

"Get over yourself," she smiled. "I am not trying to entice you."

"What do you call sitting in front of me with those long legs I just happen to remember the feel of very well."

"I call it your loss and his gain." They smiled, "You and I was just something to past the time. Something to distract you from your friends' wife or Caitlyn." Brian sat back in the chair. "I never knew which one it truly was, but after the other night I'm sure you know it's not Tracy."

"Why you in my business? Doesn't the doc keep your mind occupied?"

"Leave Theo out of this. I'm here as your friend. I don't know all of what went down, but I do know you would never do anything to hurt JD or Tracy for that matter. One of you needs to man up, apologize, then move on."

"You finished with the lecture?"

"I guess so," she said as she stood to walk out.

Brian watched the sashay of her hips. "Hey," she stopped and turned. "Tell the doc he's a lucky man. And stop wearing those swing dresses around me." Pearl smiled, turned around in the middle of the floor allowing the sway of the dress to show off a good portion of her thighs. "Get out," he smiled as she was leaving. His cell phone chimed, "Thompson."

"Boss, we have a situation at the house. Ryan has gone silent in pursuit of a figure on the lawn of the neighbor to the right. I'm moving through the house to secure the perimeter."

"Location of Tracy and the children." He said as he stormed out of the office.

"The house is secure. The family is in the bedrooms. This could be nothing boss."

"Too much happening tonight to take that chance. I'm en route to your location. Meet me in the pool house in seven minutes." Brian placed a call to Samuel. "What's your status?"

Brian hung up his blackberry as he stood in the pool house. Something didn't seem right. Magna wasn't there and Ryan was not answering their cell phone. He parked one street over and walked through the neighbor's house Magna mentioned. Scanning the outskirts of the property things seemed a little too quiet. Walking around the back to the pool house, he checked every monitor, closely scrutinizing each as he watched the feed. He saw a motion on the screen as he scanned pass one. He quickly returned to it. The hedges on the far end of the neighbor's yard moved. It was a still night in September, there was no wind. His concentration stayed on that monitor. There it was again, a movement from the house next door. Brian flicked on the house monitors. He quickly scanned to the rooms to get a location on Tracy and the children. A movement from another monitor caught his attention. A male figure was dragging a body behind a bush. Another, male body emerged from the back end of the neighbor's house. Brian immediately jumped into action, pushing the panic button alerting the police department, then he grabbed the portable handheld to keep a track of the intruders.

Reaching the door of the pool house, he peeked around to make sure no one could see him. Staying low and close to the hedges, he walked along the back patio, through the basement door and up the back staircase. Knowing, Tracy and the baby were in the master bedroom, he went there first. He slowly opened the door and quietly closed it behind him. The lights were low as he walked over to the bed. Tracy and Jasmine were asleep and if he was lucky the baby would remain that way. He placed his hand over Tracy's mouth and she jerked awake startled and swinging. "Tracy. Tracy. It's me Brian." Her eyes roamed widely until they reached his. Then she bit his hand. "Ouch." He pulled his hand away shaking it from the sting of the bite.

"Why are you sneaking around the house scaring me half to death? And where have you been?"

"Shh," he put his finger up to his lips. "Grab the baby and come with me."

She did as she was told. "What's going on?" she whispered.

"Try to keep the baby quiet. Someone's on the premises and I don't think they are friendly." They walked into JD's closet to the back wall. Brian pushed the clothes aside and put his hand on the security pad. The light turned green and a panel of the wall slide up. He picked Tracy up with the baby in her arms and placed her in the opening that resembled a laundry chute. "When you reach the bottom, move to the far corner of the room and stay close to the wall."

"Okay," she said with fear in her eyes.

"I'll be right behind you." He reassured her. Not wasting another moment, he pushed her head down and watched as she and the baby traveled down the soundproof chute. He then climbed into the chute, hit the panel on the wall to close the slide down behind them. His feet hit the floor of the basement with a thump. Remaining motionless for a moment, he listened to see if there was any indication that someone heard him. Secure they were undetected; he looked at Tracy, "Let's go."

"We can't. JC is still upstairs."

"I'll come back and get him."

"No. Go get my baby and bring him now," she cried.

He grabbed her around the waist. "Tracy, I have to get you and Jasmine to the safe room. Then I'm coming right back to get JC. I don't have time to argue with you about this. Hold on to Jasmine." He clamped his hand over her mouth, picked her up, and carried her kicking and mouthing what he was sure were very choice words at him. He felt the tears drop on his hand, but knew this had to be done. They reached the pool house undetected. He sat Tracy down just as the baby began to whine. He put the code in the door for the panic room, then placed both of them inside.

"My baby is in there. Brian, you left my baby in the house. Don't let anything happen to JC Brian, please—go get my baby."

The tears streaming down her face couldn't be helped, no matter how much it tore at his heart. "I'm going right now. Stay here. I've alerted the police. Do not open the door unless you hear my voice. Do you understand?"

She nodded as he closed the door and heard the automatic lock click. Brian checked the monitors before moving back towards the house taking the same route. He looked back as soon as he entered the house. A figure walked by the opening, but if you did not know the door was there, you would have no reason to look that way. Now there was a bigger problem. The intruders were closer to entering the interior of the house. Time was of the essences. He took the back stairs two steps at a time and made his way to JC's room. Grabbing the child out of the bed he made his way across the hall to the master bedroom, walked into the closet and closed the door. JC opened his eyes to see his uncle Brian. "Hey lil man. We going to play a game okay."

"Kay," a sleepy JC nodded.

"I need you to be real quiet all the way to the pool house. Okay. Can you do that for me man?"

JC nodded, "Where's Mommy?"

"She's in the pool house with Jasmine."

"Jazz."

"Hmm hum," Brian replied as he tucked JC under him and climbed into the shoot. "Hold on lil man." He reached the panel, the wall closed and down the chute, they went. It would have been a fun ride if the situation wasn't so serious.

When they reached the bottom just JC began to giggle. "Do it again Uncle Brian—do it again."

"Shh. Remember we are playing the quiet game."

JC put his fingers to his lips just as Brian had. He couldn't help it, Brian smiled at the boy and for the first time in his life, he wanted one. "You look like your daddy—do you know that?" JC bobbed his head up and down. "Okay, let's go find mommy." Placing the boy tightly against his chest, he checked the exit to make sure the way was clear. He watched as a figure walked through the patio door with a semiautomatic weapon. Another man with a similar weapon followed from the opposite side of the house. If he were alone, he would take both out. But, he had JD's son and it was his job to protect him with his life if necessary. Squeezing the child to make sure he was securely in placed he opened and stepped out of the underground door. Taking the three small steps up, he stayed close to the hedges leading to the pool house. Just as he took the next step, the last man to walk into the house turned and looked directly at him. They both raised their weapons at the same time. Brian's shot rang out first taking the man down. The other man in the house ran to the door and raised his weapon. Brian let off another round as the man took cover. Hearing shots from the front of the house, Brian, took off towards the pool house; a round of gunfire rang out. The first shot hit his shoulder, he continued to run. The second shot hit his side, he continued to move, but at a much slower pace. The third shot hit him in the back. That shot sent him to the ground. His body fell on top of JC who cried out. "Shh, lil man. You have to be quiet." The pain surging through his body was becoming unbearable, but Brian had to stay focus. "Uncle Brian needs you to pull your feet up."

"Kay." JC did as he was asked. He tightens his hold around Brian's waist. "I can kiss your boo-boo--make it better."

Brian smiled as he tightened his hold on JC and pulled his weapon closer to his side ready to squeeze the trigger at the footsteps he heard approaching. He turned to pull the trigger and saw Ryan standing over him with two guns in her hands firing into the house. Brian lowered his arms and the gun fell to the ground. He heard loud voices and gun-fire. He smiled thinking *the cavalry is here.* The last thing he felt was JC's little fingers touching his face. "Kiss and make better Uncle Brian," he kissed the child's fingers as his eyes closed.

They had what was needed to close the case on Munford, permanently. After all that he had learned of his father's death in the last twenty-four hours, JD was close to jubilant. The man had changed his life ten years

ago and now, he was finally getting it back. With
Munford put away, he and Tracy could finally live in
peace. No more secrets, or security day and night. They
could live a somewhat normal existence. JD watched,
from behind the police tape, as investigators continued to
review the crime scene. Four body bags were on the
ground near the rental truck that housed the weapons.
Joshua had left the scene once the interrogation of the
lone survivor was over. A smile appeared on his face as a
thought suddenly hit him, next week was Tracy's
birthday, and he knew exactly what her gift would be.

"This is the way a evening should end." Samuel joined
JD at the SUV, "The bad guys in cuffs."

"Or body bags," JD grunted. "We have one more to
take in. And I want the pleasure of reading the charges to
his face." In the distance, JD heard one of the detective's
pager go off.

"You deserve it JD. That's for sure," Samuel said as
his cell phone rang.

Donnell was walking in their direction, smiling. "You
got to love this. I want to be the one to bring Munford
in," he said, then pulled out his cell phone that was
ringing.

The sounds of multiple pagers resonated in the area
and JD stood shell shocked for a moment. The scene
was eerily reminiscent of the time Tracy was beaten. He
turned to Samuel just as he looked over at him. JD
pulled out his cell and pushed a button. "Come on baby,
pick up."

Samuel jumped in the driver seat of the SUV and was
pulling off as JD and Donnell hoped in. "A silent signal
was received from your home, two minutes ago." Samuel
said. He wasn't sure if JD heard him. "Officers are en
route."

"Ryan is not picking up," Donnell added.

"Neither is Tracy," JD franticly pushed another button. "No answer from Brian."

Samuel frowned as he pushed another button. "Joshua, give me a location on Munford." He waited, "Good, stay on him."

"Munford don't do dirty work. That's what Jonas is for," Donnell grunted.

JD's heart lurched when they turned the corner to his house and a police curser appeared coming from the other direction. Neighbors were standing in their doorways as gun fire continued to ring out. JD was the first to run from the car towards the house, but was tackled from behind by Samuel. Donnell ordered all of the neighbors to go back into their homes to keep them safe. A barrage of gun fire rang out again from the back of the house. Samuel was struggling to contain JD. The sound of police cruisers screeching to a halt could be heard in the background. Donnell reached them, "I'll take the lead. On three." He counted off, when they reached three, Samuel, and JD got up and ran behind him towards the front door. They stood to the side, as Donnell kicked the door in. He quickly peeked in, it was clear. They entered quickly with guns drawn. The foyer was riddled with bullet holes. JD ran up stairs, "Tracy?" he franticly called out. When he reached the bed room, it was empty. He pulled the drawer to the night stand open and took out his weapon. He looked inside the closet and saw the escape pad was exposed. Running out the room, he checked the children's rooms, then took the back staircase to the kitchen. Samuel and Donnell had searched the lower level of the house and reached the kitchen the same time he did. There were two bodies one in the walkway between the foyer and the kitchen, and another near the patio door. Donnell went down to the basement, as JD and Samuel ran out the patio door. Another body was near the hedges. "The safe room," JD yelled and ran towards the pool house. The sight of Ryan kneeling next to a body stopped them in their tracks. She was moving another body that was on the ground. Samuel and JD ran over.

She looked up with a look of horror. JD bent down just as Donnell joined them. "Brian," JD cried out as he gently moved his body. "JC," his father cried out.

"Daddy," his son cried.

As gently as he could JD pulled at his son, but the boy was firmly in his friends grasp and Brian wasn't letting go. JD leaned over and took his friends hand. "Brian, it's okay. I got him now, you can let go." Seconds ticked before, JD felt the hand relax. He pulled his crying son from under Brian but continued to hold on to his friend's hand. "It's okay JC, daddy's here." He hugged his son. "Get an ambulance here now," he yelled. He took a moment and examined his son. "Do you hurt anywhere JC?"

The boy shook his head no. "Uncle Brian got a boo-boo," he cried.

"I know son." JD said as he yelled again for an ambulance. Samuel and Donnell kneeled on the other side of Brian and began checking out his injuries. "Where's mommy JC? Where's mommy?" JD franticly asked his son. Brian squeezed his hand as JC answered.

"Jazz and mommy."

JD held onto JC as he bent closer to Brian. "Hold on Brian. Hold on man."

Ryan walked away from the scene and continued on to the pool house. The light on the safe room was activated. She checked the monitors and saw Tracy in there pacing back and forth with the baby on her shoulder. The room was sound proof and she had to hit the speaker button to talk to Tracy. "Tracy, it's Ryan hit the button on the right of the door."

"Where's JC and Brian?"

"JC is with JD and Brian," she trailed off. "Hit the button to open the door."

Tracy hesitated. Brian told her not to open the door until he returned, but JC was out there. She pushed the button, the lock clicked and the door slid open. "Where's JC?"

Ryan finally breathed a sigh of relief. "He's with JD. Come on."

Tracy walked from the pool house following Ryan towards the small crowd that gathered in her back yard. She heard JC cry, ran pass Ryan, and burst through the crowd. "Jeffrey."

"Tracy," JD pulled away as they turned Brian over. He grabbed her in his arms and held her and his children close as she cried.

She looked around him. "Brian," she cried out. "Oh my God, Brian."

JD held her a moment longer. He put JC in Ryan's arms, "Secure them." He then went back to Brian's side. The paramedic's were franticly working on the man as more officers filled the yard. The medical chopper could be heard above. JD took Brian's hand and held it against his chest. "Man don't do this. Don't leave me now. I need you."

"We're losing him," a paramedic said as he pushed JD aside and began administering CPR. The other EMT, placed the defibrillator next on the ground, then place the paddles on Brian's chest, "Clear." The man giving CPR stopped as the electric shock was sent to Brian's heart.

"Come on B." JD cried out.

"We got a pulse," the EMT said and continued to work franticly. "We need to get him in."

The EMT carefully positioned Brian face down on a backboard. Several men including JD and Samuel carried him while the EMT's ran along the side with tubes that were keeping Brian alive. The chopper landed on the street that was cleared by officers. They placed Brian on the chopper. JD and Samuel climbed in just as the chopper lifted off.

It was two o'clock in the morning by the time Tracy joined JD at the emergency room. The security at the hospital was tight. She entered the room filled with police personnel, FBI agents, and people from JD's office. Magna sat near the door in a hospital gown and a pole holding a bag beside her. "Are you all right?" Tracy asked.

"A bullet in the shoulder. I'll be fine."

Tracy nodded, "Thank you," she squeezed her hand and moved forward with Ryan still in tow. She finally reached Calvin and his wife Jackie, Douglas, James and Ashley, Samuel and Cynthia, but she still did not see JD. Hugging each of them, she held a distraught Cynthia a little longer. "You shouldn't be here."

With tears in her eyes, Cynthia just shook her head. "I can't believe this happened to Brian. He was supposed to be invincible."

"I know," Tracy whimpered as another tear ran down her cheek. She looked up at Samuel, "Where's JD?"

He pointed around the corner. JD was leaning against the wall with his head hung down. "He hasn't said a word. I thought it was best to give him some distance."

Tracy nodded, "Thank you," she said and walked around the corner. The look on her husband's face told the story. He was about to lose his best friend. She wiped the tears from her face, walked over, and put her arms around his waist. His arms comforted her and hers comforted him. "He put me and Jasmine in the safe room then went back for JC. He saved our lives. God is not going to take him."

JD held her a little tighter and sighed, "I love him and I don't think I ever told him that."

"He knows."

Three doctors walked out of the surgical unit towards them. "Who's the next of kin?" one of them asked the crowd of people that gathered as they walked in.

"I am," JD replied.

The doctor directed his comments to him. "Mr. Thompson sustained three gunshot wounds. We were able to remove two of the bullets. One is still lodged close to his spine. He lost a substantial amount of blood. His body is very weak. The team has decided not to attempt to remove the last bullet until he is in stable condition. The diagnosis is not good. If there are no complications, he has a slight chance of making it. I'm sorry the news couldn't be better." He walked away from the stunned crowd.

No one said anything for what seemed like minutes. Tracy could feel the increase of pressure from JD's hand as it tightened around hers. He looked down at the blood on his shirt as if it was the first time he had seen it. His gaze turned to her and she could not read what was in his eyes. "Where did you park the car?"

"Ryan drove."

He looked around until he saw Ryan. "Where are the keys to the car?" she gave them to him. Looking down at Tracy, he kissed her forehead then turned to look at Douglas and Calvin. He walked over pulling Tracy with him and put her hand in Calvin's, then looked up at him. "Take care of my wife."

Tracy wouldn't let his hand go, "Jeffrey." she held on tight as he pulled her fingers away. He turned without looking back and walked angrily out of the hallway. That's when she noticed the gun tucked in the back of his pants. "Jeffrey," she called out, now screaming while James and Calvin held her back.

Douglas and Samuel ran out after him. They saw the car pull off as they reached the parking lot. "He's going to find Munford." Douglas said as they ran to his SUV.

Samuel called Joshua. "All hell has broken loose. JD is on his way to you. Stop him."

"If he is here to kill Munford, I'm not going to stop him," Joshua replied then ended the call.

"Shit. Get us there."

The local news had preempted all programs on each of the three major stations showing coverage of the shoot out at the home of JD Harrison. Scenes from the house where the shooting took place as well as from the hospital where still were being shown. Word from the hospital, according to the reporter, was Brian Thompson is reported to be in grave condition. Munford sat in his study alone, replaying the scene when JD is climbing into the chopper near tears. "You're playing with the big boys Harrison, the big boys." He chuckled as he got up to fix another drink. He was enjoying this. The call from his attorney saying Harrison was amending the indictment to include murder was the last straw. It was time for Harrison to feel his wraft. The petty indictment was nothing compared to the information he could give. The deal he planned to get would even swipe away the murder charge, once he talked to the FBI and agreed to give information on his weapons contacts. The only regret he had was that no one in Harrison's precious family was taken out. But he eagerly continued to watch the coverage, hoping the media was keeping something under wraps. They would do that when dignitaries were involved in violent situations.

With a fresh drink in his hand, in his pajamas and robe, Wilbert T. Munford was enjoying the local news coverage.

"You're up late Chief, or should I say early. It's three in the morning."

Munford jumped from the sound of the voice and spilled some of his drink. "How in the hell did you get in my house?"

"I have my ways. Unfortunately for you, I'm the least of your worries."

JD walked in the room with his gun in his hand. Joshua met him in the doorway. "Sammy said I can't let you shoot Munford."

"Where is he?"

"Right this way," Joshua said eagerly pointing to the room he had just walked out of.

Joshua walked into the room to find Munford standing near his desk with his weapon drawn. He positioned himself directly in front of JD blocking any chance of Munford shooting him. However, JD walked in and fired his weapon, hitting the picture directly above Munford's head. Joshua had the feeling the miss was deliberate. "You killed my father, attempted to take my life, had your goons to attack my wife, shot up my house with my children inside, and now because of you, my friend fighting for his life. Pull the trigger and give me a reason to end your sorry ass life."

Samuel ran in the room with Douglas in tow. "JD," he walked around until he was directly in front of JD's weapon, putting his back to Munford. Joshua looked at his brother as if he had lost his mind. "You don't put your back to a man with a gun." He stood between Munford and his brother.

"You can't do this. Think about Tracy and the children. Think about your father. He expects you to fulfill your destiny. Don't disappoint him." JD took his eyes off Munford and looked at Samuel. "Your father would expect you to do the right thing. This isn't it. Let me have the gun."

Munford had heard enough. "You are just like your father, with your self righteous ways. Two god-damn goodie two shoes. I offered your father a way in. Was willing to give him a sixty-forty split on the take. He spit in my face, talking about public trust and protecting the community. The same bullshit you be spreading. I knew that eventually he was going to spill his guts. That's why I took him out. Just like him, you don't have the balls to eliminate your enemy. I did." Munford snarled. "And I'm going to get away with it. Don't think the FBI won't give me a deal to get information on my contacts. You know how this works Harrison," he laughed. "I'm going to get a pass for killing your father and there's not a damn thing you can do about it." Now, holding the gun at his side in a cocky stance, "I don't need this. You won't shoot me, because it's against the law." He laughed.

"Munford, shut up," Samuel yelled. "JD, give me the gun." Samuel watched as JD's eyes hardened. They were the eyes of a man that had reached his limit.

Suddenly, the house went black. Gun fire erupted, a semiautomatic weapon from the sounds of it. There was the sound of glass shattering and bodies hitting the floor.

When the dust settled, Joshua called out, "Sammy?"

"I'm good."

"JD."

"I'm good."

"Douglas?"

"Good man."

Joshua pulled a light and began to scan the room. Samuel was on the floor with JD under him. Douglas was on the floor in the doorway. Joshua noticed a movement outside the window, and then the lights came back on.

The men looked around. Munford was slumped over his desk with several bullet holes in him. "Ah hell," Joshua turned and looked at JD.

"Is he dead?" JD asked.

He stood, walked over to the body, and felt for a pulse. "Yep, he's dead." Joshua looked at Samuel. "Get him the hell out of here. I'll take care of this."

"Let's go JD," Samuel said as he took the gun from his hand.

"I'll stay until the police get here."

"Like hell you will," Douglas said and grabbed him.

JD pulled away. "If I leave, it makes me no different than him."

"Come here JD," Joshua ordered. JD exhaled and walked over. He pointed to the body. "He has at least six bullets in him. You shot once, it hit the picture over his head. You didn't do this. These shots came through that window."

JD turned and looked at the window, then down at Munford. "I meant to kill him."

"I know," Joshua said. "But you didn't. Now, I need you to let me do my job and get the hell out of here."

Jonas Gary stood on the outskirts of the property as he watched the whole scene unfold. Now he could leave knowing Wilbert T. Munford would not be singing his song to anyone.

Epilogue

The events from two weeks ago were still front page news. The take down of the Richmond Syndicate, as it's being called, was making headlines across the state and several bordering states.

According to Attorney General JD Harrison, in a press conference held last night, the future for the City of Richmond looks bright. As does the candidate's future. A poll taken earlier this week shows, eighty-seven percent of the citizens of Virginia approve of Harrison's handling of the case and would cast their vote for him as Governor. This is Victoria Murello reporting."

James turned off the monitor and looked at the staff sitting around the table. "It's been a hell of a week. Some of you pulled twenty-four hour shifts. We appreciate that. The election is fourteen months away. Contrary to the reporter's thinking, this race is far from over. We're taking a forty-eight hour break. Upon our return, we're going to dig in, we'll knock on more doors, we're going to make more telephone calls, we're going to have more rallies than before. Get some rest, get your drink on, bone up while you can." The staff laughed. "When you return, all your energy will go towards getting JD Harrison elected as our next Governor. The room erupted in applause and cheers. People exited leaving the core group behind.

James, Calvin, Senator Roth, Douglas, and Pearl kept their seats in the conference room. The moods grew solemn. "Anything new?" James asked Pearl.

"The second surgery was a success." Pearl replied. "They were able to remove the last bullet without any major problems. Theo says, its' a wait and see."

"We're talking about Brian here," Calvin smiled as he turned to Douglas. "Do you remember when we got caught in Mrs. Tate basement with her two daughters and had to climb out of the little window?"

"Yeah," Doug laughed. "Everyone made it through except for Brian. We knew he was a goner."

"What happened?" James asked.

"Calvin, JD and I were standing on the corner arguing if we should go back and get him. JD won out and we marched back down to the house." He laughed, as did Calvin. "Man, I thought we were goners. JD knocks on the door and Mrs. Tate is standing there frowning. Well it's about time you boys came back to help your friend. The girls are going to need all the help they can get on the chemistry test. Needless to say, we had no idea what she was talking about. Then Brian comes up behind her, stuffing his mouth with cake and this shit eating grin on his face. Then goes, the twins, and me been waiting for y'all to show up. Want some cake?"

"He has a way of pulling out of tough situations." Calvin nodded, "He'll pull through this one."

James smiled at the friends reminiscing. "Well are we ready to go back to the house? It's time for a little celebration."

"I'll meet you at the house." Pearl said as she stood and gathered her things. "I want to check on Brian's office before I leave."

James nodded, "We'll see you there."

The Brooks estate was abuzz with activity. Valets' were parking cars, caterers were setting up on the back patio, and one single photographer was there to capture memories of this very private occasion. Tracy looked out over the veranda at the whirlwind of activity taking place on her behalf and wondered if she could make it through the day. It was her thirtieth birthday. While she would have been content to spend a quiet day with her husband and children, JD wouldn't hear of it. He wanted this to be a special day, her day. Closing her eyes, she couldn't help but think of Brian. How were they going to get through this day without his silly pranks or him hitting on every single female in the room?

Ashley glided into the room dressed elegantly in a lavender form fitting a-line dress that showed off her shapely five-eight frame and long legs. "It is time for you to get dressed."

"Wow, you look nice," Tracy said as her friend twirled in the middle of the floor. "James is going to jump all over you when he sees that."

"I do, don't I," she smiled brightly. "I figure I better wear this little number while I still can."

Tracy waved her off, "You have always been able to wear just about anything."

"Yeah, except when I'm pregnant," Ashley replied as she pulled Tracy's dress from the bed.

Tracy's solemn smile brightened, "You're not."

Ashley put her hands on her hips, "Damn if that man didn't knock me up again."

An   elated   Tracy   hugged   her   friend. "Congratulations."

"Congratulations my butt," Cynthia said as she walked through the door, still very pregnant, but wearing a sexy little dress that showed off her legs. "Wait until you are eight months and ready to explode."

"Don't pay her any mind," Roz said waving her friend off, "She loves every minute of being pregnant. Samuel is spoiling her worse than what she was."

"That's exactly what he is supposed to do," Ashley interjected. "We carry the load for nine months, the least they can do is wait on us hand and foot."

"I'm with you on that one," Cynthia laughed.

The three women looked at Tracy who was still down. "Look Tracy," Cynthia took her hand, "The last thing Brian would want is you walking around mopping on your birthday."

"He would be the first one to walk in the room, pop you, and 'go chin up girl'," Ashley joked.

"I know, it's just hard going through the motions knowing he's there because of me."

"No he's not," Cynthia sighed. "Brian is about doing the job, whatever it takes. He was going to go back in that house to get JC whether you asked him to or not. There was no way he would have left JD's son in that house. Samuel said he played the numbers. It would have been difficult to get all three out at the same time. Getting you and Jazzy out first, then going back for JC was the safest way to ensure he saved your lives."

"It may cost him his life." Tracy sat on the side of the bed.

"Look, Brian ain't going no-where. There are still too many lonely ladies out there that need him to warm their beds," Roz proclaimed.

Tracy smiled, "That sounded just like something he would say."

"Hell, it's his mantra." Cynthia laughed.

"Either way, he wouldn't want this. Get your ass up and get dressed." Ashley pulled Tracy from the bed.

"Okay," a reluctant but cooperative Tracy sighed. "Is Jeffrey back yet?"

"No," Ashley replied as they continued to dress Tracy. "He went by the site of your new house this morning."

"Have they begun clearing the land?" Tracy asked.

Ashley, Cynthia, and Roz glared at her and began laughing. "You haven't been over there?" Ashley asked surprised.

"No. Why?"

"Girl, JD, and James had a crew on the land a week ago. The trees have been cleared, and the markings placed for where the house is going to be built. The architect handed the plans over to the CNN construction company and JD gave them sixty days to complete the project, he didn't care what it would cost."

"What. He didn't mention that to me."

"Guess what else he did?" Ashley asked a little excited.

"What?" Tracy asked, her curiosity raised.

Ashley went over and closed the door as she began laughing. "For whatever reason, JD looked at all of his bank accounts. I wish you could have seen the look on his face when he walked into the kitchen. Mommy and I were sitting there talking and he walked in and froze at the entrance with this piece of paper in his hand. He started to say something, then stopped and walked back out of the room. Mommy and I just looked at each other, going what the hell, then he came back in and yelled at me. *Did you know this?* I had no idea what he was talking about, so I asked, know about what. Did you know about this money? I asked what money. He threw the paper on the desk and Mommy and I looked at it, but before I could answer he asked, did I put the money in his account. I said, no fool, I don't have that kind of money, James do, but I don't. So where did it come from. He asked. I had to look at him because I truly did not believe he didn't know. So I said to him, Tracy has been investing a portion of your salary for years. That's your money."

Tracy inhaled nervously, "Was he mad?"

"Hell yeah and it gets better." Tracy sat on the bed. She knew Jeffrey always had a problem about money and the fact that she makes a lot of it. "He went back and checked your joint accounts. He came back in the kitchen while Mommy and I were laughing and said, we are millionaires,—hell I'm a millionaire by myself."

Cynthia looked at Tracy. "JD doesn't know how much money you make?"

Tracy shook her head slowly, "Since we had the argument about the block party, we never talked about money."

"Damn," Roz laughed, "How could he not know, he has to do financial statements when you run for office."

"He always brings me the paper work to fill out, he signs them and gives them to James."

"Well, he knows now," Ashley smiled. "In fact that was the same day he changed the plans on the house."

"Ashley," Cynthia cautioned. "That was supposed to be a surprise."

"You know about the house plans?" Tracy asked.

"Of course, all of us do," Cynthia replied.

"All of us who?"

"The three of us. We designed your new house girl," Roz squealed and it was fun. The friends gave each other a high five.

"Now, remember you are supposed to be surprised when you see the plans," Ashley said as she stood back and examined their work. "You look good."

"Yes she does," Cynthia smiled looking Tracy up and down.

Roz exhaled, "We are good."

Tracy walked over and stood before the full length mirror. She ran her hands down the front of the dress and smiled. The women looking back at her appeared confident and ready to take her place in life. "I'm thirty years old, a mother of two, a multi-millionaire, and wife to the next Governor of Virginia. Damn if I don't look like it."

Surprised by the comment, the friends looked at each other. "Oh shit, get out of the way Carolyn Roth-Roberts. Here comes Tracy Washington-Harrison."

Standing in the foyer of his house, JD looked around at the repair work. The doors and windows had been replaced, the bullet holes filled and the walls painted. It looked like the same house that he and Tracy had called home for the last four years—but it wasn't. Walking through the kitchen, he stopped in the dining room and remembered the meals with Douglas, Calvin, James, Brian, Cynthia, Ashley, Roz and Tracy. Turning he looked at where he was sitting at the kitchen table when they told their friends about JC. He walked though the dining room into the living room and remembered Tracy coming down the stairs to greet him when he got home from work. He walked over and stood in the doorway of his office. He remembered the conversation he had with Brian as he vowed to protect his family. "Brian." He exhaled and walked to the sunroom and looked out over the patio. That was where James told Ashley she was going to marry him. JD smiled. He opened the door and walked out. Beyond the patio on the grass, area leading to the pool house was where the memory he wanted to forget took place. The blood was gone, but the memory of Brian laying there with JC protectively under him was still vivid. He walked over to the spot, put his hands in his pockets, and prayed. "Lord Brian saved my son's life. Please don't take his."

Looking up he saw Samuel coming from the pool house. "Is everything okay in there?"

"Everything is in order. I left the surveillance camera operational and disconnected everything else. I'm sure Brian will make arrangements to have the equipment moved to the new location once the house is complete."

JD smiled solemnly, "I'm sure he will." He looked around the yard one last time. "Let's go celebrate my wife's birthday." Walking back through the house, JD realized he was closing a chapter in his life. Locking the front door, he knew a new chapter was beginning and other than his friend fighting for his life, the future did indeed look bright.

The gathering for Tracy's birthday celebration was being held on the lower level of James and Ashley's home. Cynthia had supervised the decorating of the grand ball-room from a chair, but you could certainly see the touches of TNT Event Planers throughout. Roz, supervised the catering while her husband Marco prepared the main meal. Monica, the CEO for Tracy's company Next Level, handled the greeting of guests, checking to make certain every person on the list was comfortable and enjoying themselves.

The guest list consisted of family. Senator John Roth and Tracy's mother Lena Washington had arrived early. Tracy's sister Valarie, her husband Ben and their three children were there. JD's mother Martha, her brother-in-law Joe Harrison, his wife Lillian, and their daughter, Alexis was there. James and Ashley's family members including his parents, Avery and Gwendolyn Brooks, his twin brother and sister, Nicolas and Nicole, his brother Vernon and his daughter Taylor were there, but his wife, Constance was not.

The last guests to arrive were Gavin and Carolyn. It was nice to see things were back to normal. Carolyn made a grand entrance that only she could pull off. This time Ashley greeted her with open arms. "Carolyn, as always, you have made your presences known to all."

Carolyn smiled brightly, "Thank you Ashley, I do know how to make an entrance."

Gavin reached around his wife and shook James' hand, "Hello James. You've had a busy week."

"It has been interesting." James smiled, "I could stand a few less surprises. Would you like a drink?"

The couple looked at each other and began laughing. "We can't." Carolyn beamed, "We are expecting."

Ashley smiled brightly, "Isn't that something, so are we." She took the drink from James hand, then patted his cheek. "Close your mouth baby," she said, took Carolyn by the arm and walked off.

"Are you okay James," Gavin asked as he watched the color drain from the man's face.

A somewhat confused James looked at Gavin, "Excuse me for a minute. Ashley!"

The elevator door opened as James whizzed by. JD and Samuel joined the gathering.

"It's about time you got here," Cynthia smiled up at her husband and kissed him.

"Have you been overdoing it?" Samuel asked his wife. "No. Probably."

JD laughed at her pouty expression. "Cynthia, where's Tracy?"

"Upstairs, waiting for you."

He smiled brightly, "Good," then took off towards the stairs.

JD walked into the east wing bedroom suites of James' home. This had been and would continue be home for them until the house was completed. He couldn't begin to express the gratitude he had for his brother-in-law.

During the last weeks, he'd provided security for his mother and now a sanctuary for his family. "Hey," he smiled at his wife who was standing at the window looking out.

"Hey yourself," she returned his smile as he walked over to her.

"Be still my heart. I love red."

"I know," she teased, "I'm red all under too."

"Really," he pulled her into his arms. "What do you say; we remove this layer and go right to the next."

She put her arms round his neck pulling their bodies closer. "It works for me," she replied just before her lips touched his.

The one thing JD never needed was probing when it came to kissing his wife. He was always more than ready to comply. The moment their tongues met, the same need, longing, urgency touched his soul. It didn't matter that they'd made love only hours ago, his body responded immediately. Feeling himself growing, he knew this was not the time. There was a room filled with people downstairs waiting for them. In another minute, he was going to let go—really, he was. His hands did not receive the message from his brain. They traveled down until they reached the fullness of her behind. He squeezed and pulled her closer, enjoying the feel of her thigh against him. He groaned as he ended the kiss. He placed his head against her forehead and whispered, "You don't have no drawers on. You're going to kill me, woman."

Tracy smiled as she pulled away and stopped at the door. "The freedom you feel without them is intriguing, don't you think?"

JD looked at his teasing wife, "I got intriguing for you." She ran out the door and he followed.

Instead of taking the elevator, JD made their entrance from the spiral staircase leading down into the ball-room.

He stopped at the center of the stairway. "Ladies and gentleman, allow me the pleasure of announcing the arrival of our guest of honor, my wife, the mother of my children and the love of my life, Tracy." He held his hand out and she made her entrance down the stairs. The red diamond strapped sandals attached to the sexiest set of legs imaginable was the first thing to be seen as she descended the stairs. The red dress clamped at the neck by a diamond chocker, showed every curve in her body and damn if they were not in all the right places. Her hair was up in a French roll, with a few strands hanging strategically around her face. The little makeup she wore was flawless. And the smile—the smile was magnificent. The crowd of family and friends broke out in applause and cat whistles. "Wait JD," said with a huge smile. He turned her around showing the back of the dress scooped from her shoulders to the top of her behind. "Is that the sexiest back you ever seen or what?" The crowd clapped louder and laughed. "And she is all mine—mine-mine-mine."

Tracy laughed and fell into his arms. "I love you."

"Not as much as I love you," JD replied. They continued down the stairs as people rushed forward to wish Tracy a happy birthday.

"She has arrived," Carolyn said to her father. "It's a good thing she has your blood in her."

Lena, who stood next to her husband, looked over at her step-daughter and growled. "Ignore her," Gwendolyn Brooks said. "She will never change."

"Can I smack her, just once?" Lena whispered to her friend.

"No," her husband bent down and whispered in her ear. Lena smiled up at her husband. "You're lucky I love you and have grown. This time last year I would have whipped her ass by now."

Gwen looked up at the Senator and coughed to cover her laugh.

The festivities went on for about an hour then the birthday cake was brought out. "Make a wish Tracy," JD said.

She looked around the room and smiled at the crowd. Closed her eyes and made a wish. The chime signaled that the elevator was arriving. As Tracy opened her eyes, the elevator door opened. A hush came over the crowd as they parted, allowing a clear path for her to see. In the doorway with dreads that neatly rested on the shoulders of his grey Armani suit, stood six-two, two hundred ten pounds, caramel skin tone with light brown eyes, Al "Turk" Day.

"Hello Tracy."

Reactively, she reached back and grabbed JD's hand. Not believing what she was seeing, she turned to him. And that's when he saw what he needed to see. The light in her eyes shined brightly. "He's free and clear."

Tracy turned back to the elevator, slowly pulled away from her husband and ran full force into her brother's arms. The impact of the embrace was felt throughout the room. Some knew who the stranger was, others didn't. Who he was, wasn't important, all felt the emotions of the reunion. The two held on to each other for the longest time, until JD walked over. He reached out took Tracy's hand in his and shook his brother-in-laws hand then turned to the crowd. "Everyone, please welcome the man that kept Tracy safe, then put her in my hands, her big brother, Al Day."

Ashley was the first to walk over. She didn't shake his hand, she hugged him. "Thank you for giving up Tracy."

As people approached to introduce themselves, Tracy held Al's hand on one side and JD's on the other. Valarie made her way over, all she could do was stare at her little brother as tears flowed down her face. "Are you free, I mean are you home?"

"I'm home. I even have a job," He looked over at JD and frowned. Valarie hugged her brother. "I'm so glad you're home." She wiped the tears from her face. "Maybe you can get your daughter in line now." She and Tracy laughed nervously.

"I'll see what I can do," he smiled back. A second later his smile began to fade. Walking towards him was his mother, Lena. He looked over at JD and said, "That's what your wife is going to look like in twenty years. It ain't bad, is it?"

"There are some parts of her I can do without," JD replied as Tracy pinched him.

"Welcome home Al." Al released Tracy's hand. He stepped closer to the woman standing before him, pulled her into an embrace, and held her tight. "Hello mother."

With tears streaming down her face, Tracy held up a glass of champagne. "Please raise your glass. Life certainly is a journey is predetermined by a higher power. The road has been difficult and I'm sure there will be trying times ahead. But I have faith, that we all, even our love one whose life is in peril, will make it through. She turned to JD. "To my husband, my life was sheltered until I met you. Someone said a house divided cannot stand. Neither can a heart divided. Your unyielding love has healed my heart and for that, my heart will always be yours."

JD took his wife into his arms and thoroughly kissed her. Afterwards he smiled down into her shining eyes and whispered, "Forever, for always, for love."

A Lost Heart
Prologue

Boredom had set in sooner than expected. After five years with the Federal Bureau of Investigations and four years with Thompson Security Agency, his own company, the quietness was about to drive Brian Elliott Thompson crazy. He was literally about to lose his mind. It was the tenth day since his release from the hospital, after a month long stay. His friends believed he needed more rest, he however believed it was time to return to work. Not to the pile of paper-work staring back at him from his desk, but to his real job, protecting the Attorney General of Virginia and his childhood friend, J.D. Harrison. That's what he should be doing, not sitting around sifting through paperwork. He was so tempted to push the stacks of paper off the desk, but that would cause Jenny, his secretary more work.

Patiently waiting for a return call from JD, he stood and stared out of his office window. Below was the view of the very building he would be guarding once JD was elected to the Governor position, the Executive Mansion. A grin slowly appeared on his face as he remembered the day James Brooks, JD's campaign manager, stood at that window and declared, he was setting him up in business to protect JD and his family once they moved into the mansion. James knew then that JD was heading in that direction. He wanted Brian to be free from the bureaucracy of the bureau to conduct protection for JD and his family as he saw fit. It was an honor to be given such a detail, especially since the man he was protecting was one of his closest friends.

Shaking his head Brian thought of their friendship. There were very few people he considered a friend and JD Harrison was one. The fact that he'd put that friendship in jeopardy, to this day, caused him internal turmoil. Looking back on the situation, he had no one to blame but himself. Kissing a man's wife was wrong, and even worst if you called that man a friend.

As if on cue the bruises on his back began to ache, but he refused to take any of the medication the doctors prescribed for pain. It was two months ago that a gang had invaded JD's home while his wife and two children slept in the bedrooms upstairs. Brian was able to get Tracy, JD's wife and Jasmine, their six-week-old daughter out of the house. However, when he went back in to get JC, their three-year-old son, he was shot three times in the back. From what his friends and family told him, for weeks no one was sure he would be here today. After a month in the hospital and a few weeks on house recovery, the pain let him know, he was still alive. The pain of bullets he could stand, the pain of possibly losing his friend was unbearable. Although at the time of the shooting, he and JD were not on speaking terms, there was no way he would allow him or his family to be harmed. First of all, it was his profession and his pride would not allow him not to give one hundred and ten percent to the job every day. Secondly, JD's family was his family. He loved his friend's children as if they were his own. And as for his wife, Tracy, well he loved her a little too much.

The door opened and then slammed before Brian could turn towards the sound. Recognizing the angry face seething at him, he realized his reflexes were slow. That was not a good sign.

"What are you doing here?"

Brian sat in the chair behind the desk before Pearl, could see evidence of the pain surging through him at that moment. Pearl Lassiter had become his champion since the shooting and seemed determined to make his life miserable by making sure he healed properly according to her rules. "I own the place," he mockingly replied.

"Really, do you have a will?" Frowning he looked up at her. "I just want to make sure I get something out of caring about you one way or another."

"Thanks for the confidence in my recovery. Do you want something this early in the morning?"

"Imagine my surprise when I stopped by your place to make sure you had breakfast and had taken you meds before I came to work, only to find you gone."

"I'm sure you were, but as you can see I'm fine."

She sighed, "Have you had breakfast?"

"No."

She placed a McDonald bag in front of him, "Breakfast steak burrito. Have you taken your meds?"

Opening the bag and pulling out the contents he looked at her, "Thank you."

"I take that as a no. I did not find them at your place, so I am going to assume you were at least smart enough to bring them with you."

"Unlike other times your assumption is correct," he stated as he bit into the burrito.

She placed her arms across her breasts. "Would you take them now while I'm here?"

Sitting back in the chair he replied, "I'll take them when I need them."

Putting her hands to her face in frustration, "Brian, I don't have time for this today. JD has to fly out in an hour and I need to know you are okay before we leave."

"Where are you going," he asked eagerly. He may have something to do after all.

"We are campaigning in Northern Virginia. Avery and Gwendolyn Brooks are hosting a fund-raiser."

"I'll give JD a call see what time we are leaving."

"We? What are you going to do if you go? You can't take anyone down if something was to hop off." Seeing the look of denial in his eyes, she softened her words. "Look, I know you want to protect your friend. However, at the moment, you are physically unable to do that. Give your body the time it needs to heal and you will be back on the job in no time. You'll probably be better, if that's possible." She added that last statement to give him a compliment she felt he needed."

"Thanks for the moment of reality and the pep talk. It doesn't help my boredom, but I hear you. Go meet with the posse; I'll talk to you later."

Smiling with relief, "I'll go as soon as you take your meds."

He looked at her as he pulled open the desk drawer, took the pain pills, and swallowed them down with his coffee. "Satisfied?"

"Yes, I am." She opened the door to leave. "I'll call you later."

Sighing as the door closed, Brian checked the computer for security updates on his clients. Presently he had four VIP clients that had top government clearance. Each had different levels of coverage, but none as high as JD. It was a foregone conclusion that he would be the next Democratic candidate for President of the United States. Until that happened and Secret Services Units were assigned, it was his job to keep his friend and his family free of harm. Under normal circumstances, JD would not make a move without him by his side, but not now. Since he could not protect his friend, he made sure that his top man, Samuel Lassiter was heading up the detail. Anyone going after JD would have to go through Shipwreck, as Brian called him, and that would not be an easy task. Samuel was fully capable and just as dedicated to protecting JD as he was, but it did not ease the disappointment of not being next to his friend. Then there was Tracy and the children. Magna Rivera, whom he was fortunate to get from the District of Columbia Gang Task force, and Ryan Williams, whom he'd taken from the streets, were handling the detail on them. To get through those two women, you had better bring an army fully armed with heavy artillery.

Yes, he had good men and women working for him, but it wasn't him and that was the problem. Since high school, he'd been the protector of not only JD, but their other high school friends, Calvin Johnson and at times Douglas Hylton as well. It was hard being placed on the side lines. Like it or not, there wasn't a damn thing he could do about it, for now.

Jeffrey Daniel Harrison, who most people called, JD sat at the desk in his home office and watched out the window as his wife Tracy and their three-year-old son JC played tee-ball. As his son hit the plastic ball with the matching bat, he smiled as the child like giggles echoed into his office. The scene only fueled his anxiety over the situation at hand. Brian has a son that he doesn't know about. He is missing out on not just seeing his son grow up, but on his development as well. Promise or not, that was something JD could not be a party to. The only question was how he was going let Brian know about his son without straight out telling him. The day he ran into

Caitlyn replayed in his mind. He tried to remember what he'd actually promised.

He and Tracy were standing at the podium holding hands and waving to the crowd of over one thousand supporters that had showed up to hear him speak at their Founders Day celebration. More than pleased with the turnout he whispered to Tracy, "I didn't think Nickelsville had this many people living here and I'm more surprised to see a few of us here."

"At least you had heard of this town. Today when we stepped foot off the plane was the first time I had heard of this place. But according to the internet, a family named Nickels built this town. It seems one of the Nickels sons fell in love with, married a black woman, and was shunned from Tennessee. He moved his family to the far end of the property, which happened to be in Virginia. It's said that by marrying a black woman he cursed the family's name and for several generations no sons were born to carry on the name, only daughters. Of the two daughters, one married a Béchamel. The town manager is a direct descendant from that family. The other daughter married and settled across the street in what is now known as Nickelsville Tennessee. If we go cross the street on Main Street we will be in Tennessee."

He looked at his wife; she always amazed him with her knowledge. "I guess we better stay on this side of the street then."

As they walked through the crowd shaking hands a young boy approached him. Pulling on his pants leg the boy called out, "Mister, Mister" and looked up at JD with the most excited eyes. JD looked down at the boy who appeared to be ten or eleven and smiled. He bent his six-two frame down to the boy to speak. "Hello," he shook the young boys' hand. "What's your name?"

"Elliott, what's your name?"

The boy's speech seemed young for his size. But JD dismissed the thought a moment latter after realizing there was a possibility that the education system in this part of the state may be lacking. "My name is JD."

"That's not your real name. My mom says a name can say a lot about the man you are going to become."

JD smiled, liking the boy immediately, "You're right, my name is Jeffrey Daniel Harrison."

Proud of himself the boy continued. "My mom say's you are going to be our new governor and then president."

"Your mom said that?" The boy nodded his head. "Where is your mom?" JD asked standing.

"Over behind the tree."

JD stood and took the boy's hand, "Let's go find your mom so I can thank her for the kind words."

Tracy smiled at her husband, "Looks like you have a new friend."

"Yeah," JD laughed, "He looks familiar to me for some strange reason. We're going to find his mom."

"Come on," the young boy said. "I'll show you where she is."

JD and Tracy followed the boy through the crowd shaking hands along the way. As they reached the area, the boy indicated his mother would be, a woman stopped the young boy. She was a very slender woman with blonde hair, beautiful blue smiling eyes, and a welcoming smile. "Elliott are you brothering Mr. Harrison?"

"No ma'am. I'm taking him to meet my mom."

"Mr. Harrison, I can take him to his mom."

"It's no bother at all. I would like to meet her. She has a wonderful son."

"Well, if you are sure it's no problem, she is passing out buttons at the third tree over yonder.

"Thank you," JD replied with a smile as they continued on the short journey.

As they walked closer to the tree, Elliott called out to his mother, "Hey mommy look who I have."

The woman turned to JD just as he was looking up from the boy and shock was a mild response to the look that appeared on his face. He looked down at Elliott who was smiling proudly at his mother and then his gaze returned to the woman.

"Caitlyn?"

The woman's expression was a less intense match to JD's as she stammered, "Hello JD." If Caitlyn could have crawled under the tree stump she was standing next to she would have. For the entire day, she had volunteered to work on the outskirts of the event just to keep this from happening. Now she had to face her past. She extended her hand to Tracy who was watching the event wondering what was wrong with her husband. "Hello, I'm Caitlyn, Elliott's mother."

"It's nice to meet you," Tracy smiled then looked up at her husband.

"Caitlyn, what—"the words did not seem to form.

Sensing Jeffrey and this woman needed a moment Tracy took Elliott's hand, "How about you show me where I can get some ice cream," she said bending down.

"Okay, come on. Y'all coming Mr. Harrison and mommy?"

"No Elliott, I'm going to stay and talk to your mom for a minute." Waiting for the boy and Tracy to leave the area, his glaze fell on Caitlyn again. "How old is Elliott, Caitlyn?" He asked trying not to show how angry he was.

She stepped closer to him so they would not be overheard, "He is about to turn ten and to answer your next question, no, Brian does not know he has a son. JD you can't tell him."

"Mr. Harrison. Mr. Harrison."

At the sound of his housekeeper's voice, JD's attention returned to the present. "I'm sorry Mrs. Gordon, what did you say?"

"Mr. Thompson is on the line for you."

"Thank you," he sighed. Talk about timing. "Hey Brian, what's up?"

"I hear you are on your way out of town. Why are you leaving a brother behind man?"

"The four walls getting to you?" He smiled hearing his friend's irritation.

"Man, you know I'm not used to staying still. If I don't get some action soon I swear I'm going to go crazy."

JD thought for a moment. "You know," he sat forward as the plan formed in his mind. "I could use your help on something."

"Name it man, I'm game for damn near anything."

"Well, it's not a big deal, and there will be no action it, but it would help me out."

"Talk to me man."

"I need an advance security check done on a location I plan to revisit. It's a small town in southwest Virginia. I promised this kid I would come back through for a visit with his family. The town is nice enough, but there may be some security issues. It would be great if you could go there, be the advance man on this visit."

"JD, I tell you I'm bored and you want to send me to Hicksville, Virginia?"

Laughing at his friends question JD pressed on. "It's not that bad man. Tracy and I were there and it was nice."

"If you were just there why are you going back?"

"I got a little attached to this kid and I gave my word to him that I would come back to see him. I want to take Tracy and the kids when I return and it is imperative that everything is in place. Look, I know this is not what you normally do, but I figure it will keep you out of trouble for at least a week."

"A week? Doesn't Calvin normally do this kind of stuff?"

"Yeah, but he is wrapping up the Munford case and can't get away. B, look, normally I wouldn't ask you to do something like this, but I'm planning on taking my children with me I need to know they will be safe."

"Alright man, but you are going to pay for this big time. Transportation, hotel, meals and if there are any decent women around, you're paying for them too."

"You know I can't pay for any women, man. I'm a politician."

"I'll put it down as food for my soul. What's the name of this place--Hicksville?"

"Nickelsville, Virginia." JD laughed as he gave Brian all the pertinent information for the assignment. He was certain once Brian hit the town; there was no way he would not run into Caitlyn or Elliott. Looking up he said a silent prayer, asking the Lord to forgive his little indiscretion, but he had his friend's best interests at heart.

Brian cursed when he hung up the telephone after arranging for the trip. First, there was no hotel in the town JD was sending him too, just Martha's Bed and Breakfast. Then there was no airport near the place, which meant he would have to drive the 323 miles to Nickelsville. If he wasn't bored senseless he would have called JD back and told him a thing or two. But the more he thought about it, the more he warmed to the idea. A drive in the country could do him some good. "What the hell." Brian locked up his office and began a journey that would change his life forever.

CPSIA information can be obtained at www.ICGtesting.com
Printed in the USA
LVOW082243120812

294033LV00002B/33/P